Praise for
Bringing Maggie Home

"*Bringing Maggie Home* is beautiful, deep, and engaging! Don't miss out on this powerful and emotive story."
—CINDY WOODSMALL, *New York Times* best-selling author

"In *Bringing Maggie Home,* Kim Vogel Sawyer has once again woven a story so rich and unforgettable that it leaves her readers both satisfied and hungering for more. Her storytelling ability invites her readers into each scene. We laugh and cry, squirm and ache with the characters as if they were family members...even the absent ones."
—CYNTHIA RUCHTI, author of twenty-one books,
including *A Fragile Hope* and *As My Parents Age*

"*Bringing Maggie Home* by Kim Vogel Sawyer is one of those books you can't put down until you've gulped the last page. The multilayered novel merges themes of restoration with a compelling search for a long-missing sister. I highly recommend this satisfying and richly imagined novel!"
—COLLEEN COBLE, *USA Today* best-selling author
of *Beneath Copper Falls* and the Sunset Cove series

"High praise for Kim Vogel Sawyer's *Bringing Maggie Home*! Kim intricately weaves the lives of three generations of women, each one affected by the tragedy of Hazel's losing a sister long ago. The depth of the characters and God's perfect timing are illustrated throughout their journeys. Already an award winner and a best seller, Kim takes her wonderful story to an extraordinary new level of writing."
—DIANNE BURNETT, *Publishers Weekly* reviewer and former
fiction editor for Christianbook.com

BRINGING MAGGIE
MAGGIE
Home

BOOKS BY KIM VOGEL SAWYER

Echoes of Mercy

Grace and the Preacher

Just As I Am

The Grace That Leads Us Home

Guide Me Home

Room for Hope

Through the Deep Waters

What Once Was Lost

When Grace Sings

When Love Returns

When Mercy Rains

BRINGING MAGGIE
Home

Kim Vogel Sawyer

A NOVEL

WATERBROOK

BRINGING MAGGIE HOME

Scripture quotations and paraphrases are taken from the following versions: The King James Version. The Holy Bible, New International Version®, NIV®. Copyright © 1973, 1978, 1984, 2011 by Biblica Inc.® Used by permission. All rights reserved worldwide.

The characters and events in this book are fictional, and any resemblance to actual persons or events is coincidental.

Trade Paperback ISBN 978-0-7352-9003-7
eBook ISBN 978-0-7352-9004-4

Copyright © 2017 by Kim Vogel Sawyer

Cover design by Kelly L. Howard; photography by @Yolande de Kort

Published in the United States by WaterBrook, an imprint of the Crown Publishing Group, a division of Penguin Random House LLC, New York.

WATERBROOK® and its deer colophon are registered trademarks of Penguin Random House LLC.

Library of Congress Cataloging-in-Publication Data
Names: Sawyer, Kim Vogel, author.
Title: Bringing Maggie home : a novel / Kim Vogel Sawyer.
Description: First edition. | Colorado Springs, Colorado : WaterBrook, 2017.
Identifiers: LCCN 2017013720 | ISBN 9780735290037 (softcover) | ISBN 9780735290044 (electronic)
Subjects: LCSH: Women detectives—Fiction. | Cold cases (Criminal investigation)—Fiction. | Missing persons—Investigation—Fiction. | BISAC: FICTION / Christian / General. | FICTION / Contemporary Women. | FICTION / Family Life. | GSAFD: Christian fiction. | Mystery fiction.
Classification: LCC PS3619.A97 B75 2017 | DDC 813/.6—dc23
LC record available at https://lccn.loc.gov/2017013720

Printed in the United States of America
2017—First Edition

10 9 8 7 6 5 4 3 2 1

For my girls—*Kristian, Kaitlyn, and Kamryn.*
I know I didn't do everything right,
but I hope you know I always loved you.

Hope deferred maketh the heart sick:
but when the desire cometh, it is a tree of life.

—Proverbs 13:12, KJV

Mama never let her waste real sugar and cream for her tea parties. She used the spoon to stir the air in Maggie's cup. "There you are."

Maggie's apple cheeks dimpled with her smile. "Fank you." She picked up the cup between her fingers and carried it to her rosy lips.

"I hope it isn't too hot."

Maggie made noisy drinking sounds. Her blue eyes rounded and she pursed her lips. "Ooooh, it is hot! I bu'n my tongue!"

Hazel stifled a chuckle. Playing make-believe with her doll had never been this fun. Maybe she should have let Maggie use her special tea set before. But she'd waited until her sister passed her third birthday, the same age Hazel had been when she received the set for Christmas from Memaw and Pappaw Blackwell. She hadn't trusted Maggie's baby fingers not to break one of the fragile cups or plates.

She picked up her own cup and held it close to her mouth. "Blow on it." She puffed breaths into her cup, smiling when Maggie imitated her.

With the sun warming their heads, they sipped and smiled at each other and helped their dollies eat pretend cookies from the serving plate centered on the crate. Hazel's imagination painted their surroundings from a dusty yard to the fancy city restaurant she'd seen in a magazine. With linen-draped tables instead of a handkerchief-covered crate. With ladies wearing silk instead of homespun. So easy to see in her imagination. She even pretended her hair was shiny yellow curls trailing down her back instead of wind-tossed, dirt-brown, pin-straight locks lopped at shoulder level.

She picked up the plate and offered it to Maggie. "Would you like the last cookie?"

Maggie reached out her pudgy hand.

The screen door squeaked open and Mama stepped onto the porch. "Hazel Mae? Maggie?"

Maggie rolled sideways to push herself to her feet, and her bottom bumped the crate. The teacups and serving pieces wobbled. Gasping, Hazel dropped

Mid-July 1943
Cumpton, Arkansas
Hazel Mae Blackwell

*H*azel set a porcelain cup and saucer on the overturned apple cra[t] front of her little sister. "Madam, would you like cream and sug[ar] your tea?"

Maggie nodded, making her Shirley Temple curls bounce. Her ha[ir] what Daddy called flaxen—shimmered under the noonday sun, almost a[s] low as the roses painted on the cup.

Jealousy sparked in Hazel's heart. Why couldn't she have inherited ma's sunshiny-yellow hair and sky-blue eyes the way Maggie had inste[ad] Daddy's dirt-brown hair and eyes?

"What do you say?" Hazel asked the question as tartly as Mama.

"Yes, pwease."

"*Pluh*-ease," Hazel said.

"*Pwuh*-ease."

Hazel sighed. Maggie was just-turned-three, as Daddy often rem[inded] Hazel when she got impatient with her sister. Sometimes she wished [they] hadn't waited so long after Hazel to have another baby. Wouldn't it be [nice if] almost seven years didn't stretch between them? Mama and Daddy w[ere al]ways telling her she was lucky to have a sister, and Hazel loved Magg[ie, of] course she did. But sometimes . . .

"Pwease, Hayzoo Mae?"

She lifted the lid on the doll-sized sugar bowl and spooned out p[retend] sugar. Then she pretended to pour cream. No matter how much Hazel [loved] the plate to steady the table, and the plate landed on the sugar bowl. Both the plate and the lid to the sugar bowl snapped in two.

The lovely daydream shattered. "Oh, Maggie, look what you did!" Hazel snatched up the halves of the once-pretty plate with its circle of painted yellow roses and green leaves and hugged them. Surely her heart was broken in half, too. "Why can't you be careful? I should never have let you touch it."

Tears swam in Maggie's blue eyes, and her lower lip quivered. Mama hurried across the yard, her bare feet stirring dust. Maggie buried her face in Mama's apron skirt.

Mama scowled at Hazel. "For shame, yelling at your sister. It was an accident."

Hazel stared at Mama's hand on Maggie's head, the fingers petting, sweet and soothing. Why didn't Mama soothe Hazel? She'd suffered the loss. "But she broke the serving plate. And the sugar bowl lid."

"You dropped the plate, Hazel Mae. You broke the pieces."

But she wouldn't have dropped the plate if she hadn't been trying to keep the crate from falling over. She said so, too, even though Daddy would probably say she was talking back.

Mama's scowl deepened. "Arguing won't fix things." Then a hint of sympathy crept into her eyes. She set Maggie aside and held out her hands. "Give it to me. If there's a clean break, I can glue it together."

Hazel swallowed the words hovering on her lips—*It won't be the same*—and reluctantly transferred the halves to Mama's keeping. She gave her the pieces of the sugar bowl lid, too.

Mama slipped all the pieces into her apron pockets. "Put your toys away and then come to the kitchen. I have a job for you to do." She returned to the house.

Her jaw clenched so tight her teeth ached, Hazel transferred the fragile tea set to the brittle grass. She turned the crate right-side up, settled her doll with its stuffed cloth body in the bottom, then began arranging the teapot, cups, saucers, and plates around the doll. Maggie bent over and reached for a cup.

Hazel pushed her sister's hand aside. "Don't."

"I hewp?"

"No. Let me do it."

"'Kay." Maggie picked up her doll, the one Daddy ordered from the Montgomery Ward catalog for her last birthday, and wrapped her arms around it. She rocked side to side, making her pink muslin skirt sway. "We pway again tomorrow, Hayzoo Mae?"

Not with the tea set. Not ever with the tea set. "We'll see."

She lifted the crate and carried it inside, Maggie trailing her. She ordered her sister to the kitchen, then trotted upstairs and tucked the crate in her closet, way back in the dark corner where Maggie was afraid to go. With the tea set safe, she clattered down the enclosed staircase to the kitchen.

Mama was waiting with the egg basket. She smiled as she gave it to Hazel. "Go to the blackberry thicket and pick as many ripe berries as the basket will hold. Don't dally now. I want to bake a cobbler for our supper."

Hazel's mouth watered. A cobbler used lots of sugar. It was a treat. Especially blackberry cobbler since Mama usually turned the dark berries into jam. "Is company comin'?" She hoped not. If they had to share the cobbler, they'd get only one small portion each.

Mama's eyebrows rose. "Don't you remember? It's Daddy's birthday."

She ducked her head. She had forgotten. She'd need to hurry so there'd be time to draw Daddy a card to give him at suppertime. She looped the basket over her arm and headed for the door.

"Take your sister with you."

Hazel spun around. "Oh, Mama, please don't make me. She'll slow me down."

Mama's lips set in a stern frown. "I have things to do, too, and I need her out from underfoot. Take her." She pushed both girls out the back door. "Hurry now."

How could she hurry with Maggie along? Her sister's short legs would wear out halfway to the patch. But arguing would waste time, and she could almost taste that blackberry cobbler already. So she ordered Maggie to tuck the ever-present doll under one arm, grabbed her sister's free hand, and took off at a brisk pace, giving little jerks now and then to keep Maggie going.

A wagon rattled up the road from the west, and a big shiny touring car came from the east. The girls clambered onto the rough edge where the ground sloped sharply upward. Hazel kept her arm around Maggie, tapping her toe impatiently at the delay. The wagon went on by, but the car slowed to a stop, and Mrs. Burton, the lady who ran the orphans' home on the west side of town, stuck her head out the open window.

"Good morning, girls." She pinned her warm smile on Maggie. The little girl always earned a smile from folks—she was so little, as pretty as a china doll, so likable. And Hazel couldn't decide if that made her proud or jealous.

"'Morning," Hazel said.

"'Mo'ning," Maggie echoed.

"Where are you two off to with that basket?"

Hazel wished she'd hurry on. They needed to get to the thicket. "Gonna pick blackberries. Mama's makin' a cobbler."

The woman sighed. "I'm sorry I can't give you a ride. Thicket's in the wrong direction for me. But you two have fun. Don't stick your fingers, you hear?" She gave a little wave and then the car growled on.

Hazel led Maggie to the center of the road again, where wheels had carved two smooth ruts. She squinted ahead, thinking. About a half mile up the road, a path carved by deer led directly to the blackberry brambles, but there was a shorter route. It was rougher and harder to get through, but the quicker she picked the berries, the quicker she could go home and get started on her card for Daddy. She wanted to spend lots of time on it and make it extra nice so he wouldn't know she'd forgotten his special day.

"C'mon, Maggie. This way."

Her little sister beamed up at her, her face all sweaty and curls drooping.

She looked so cute, Hazel caught herself smiling back. They left the dirt road and climbed a slight rise, ducking beneath low-hanging tree branches and pushing between bushes. Maggie panted, her little face red, but she didn't complain, even when branches pulled her hair ribbon askew.

"We're almost there." Hazel lifted a snarl of branches and gestured Maggie through the opening. Hugging her doll against her chest, Maggie squeezed past Hazel. Hazel moved behind her and let the branches slap back into place. Without warning, Maggie stopped.

Hazel sidestepped to keep from trampling her sister. "What're you doing?"

Maggie pointed silently to a chunk of displaced earth. Her face puckered with questions.

Even though they needed to hurry, Hazel couldn't resist crouching down and lifting the piece of ground held together by grass roots. Underneath, in a smooth hollowed spot, four little bunnies curled together in a ball. She lowered her voice to a whisper. "Lookee, Maggie—baby rabbits."

Maggie's face lit, and Hazel sensed a squeal coming on.

"Shhh." She touched a finger to her own lips and shook her head. "Don't scare 'em. Let 'em sleep."

Wonder in her blue eyes, Maggie knelt next to Hazel. "I pet 'em?"

"Nope."

"I wanna pet 'em, Hayzoo Mae."

Hazel gave Maggie the explanation Daddy had given her the first time she found a bunny burrow. "If you touch 'em, the mama won't come back. They'll die without their mama. You don't want the bunnies to die, do you?"

Her little sister shook her head so hard her sweaty curls bounced.

"Then we gotta leave 'em alone." She lowered the chunk of earth over the baby bunnies and rose. "C'mon." She grabbed Maggie's hand and moved on.

Maggie trotted alongside, stumbling now and then because she kept her face angled toward the spot where the rabbits slept. At the blackberry thicket, Hazel settled Maggie in a patch of shade with her doll and shook her finger at her. "You stay put." While her sister played with her doll, contentedly jabbering, Hazel picked berries as fast as she could. Her fingertips turned purple and she got stuck more times than she could count, but she ignored the pricks and kept picking, glancing into the basket now and then to judge her progress.

The basket was a little over half full when Maggie's happy chatter changed to a shriek. Hazel jerked, the basket rocking on her arm. She sucked in a breath and turned to scold, but the words died on her lips when she spotted a black snake, nearly five feet long, slithering through the grass only a few feet from where Maggie was sitting.

Hazel dropped the basket and leaped in front of her sister. The snake changed course, but now it headed in the direction of the rabbit burrow. She couldn't let that awful snake eat the bunnies for lunch! She pushed Maggie closer to the bushes where blackberries from the basket dotted the thick grass. "Start puttin' the berries back in the basket. I'll be right back." She snatched up a dead tree branch and darted after the snake, whacking the ground as she went.

The snake eased one way and then another, but it persisted in moving toward the burrow. Hazel skirted slightly ahead of it and waved the branch. It paused for a moment, its tongue flicking in and out and its bright eyes seeming to stare directly at her. She smacked the grass hard. "Get outta here, you dumb snake! You go on!"

The snake lowered its head and slithered away from her. She chased after it, yelling and swatting, until she was certain she'd frightened it into the woods. She swiped her brow and blew out a breath of relief. The bunnies were safe. She tossed the stick aside and hurried back to the thicket. Triumphant, she burst through the bushes.

"I did it, Maggie! I scared it off!" She stopped short. Maggie's doll lay in the grass near the overturned basket, but her sister wasn't there. She sent a frowning look right and left. "Maggie?"

Hazel inched forward, searching the area with her gaze. Squashed berries littered the area, proof that her sister had trampled through them. Had Maggie decided to play hide-and-seek? She singsonged, "Ma-a-aggie, where a-a-are you?" She listened for a telltale giggle. Only the whisper of wind replied. She didn't have time for games. She balled her hands on her hips. "Margaret Rose Blackwell, I'm not playin'. You better come out right now if you know what's good for you!"

A pair of bluebirds swooped from a scraggly oak, but Maggie didn't step out from the bushes. A chill wiggled down Hazel's spine despite the heat making her flesh sticky. "C'mon, Maggie, this isn't funny." She turned a slow circle, repeatedly calling her sister's name. Maggie still didn't answer. The stillness unnerved her. No squirrels chattering, no birds singing, not even a rabbit nibbling at the tender grass under the trees.

Worry churning in her gut, she searched the thicket. Then the surrounding area. Her heart gave a leap when she found Maggie's limp hair ribbon caught on a shoulder-high tree branch. She jerked it free and stared at it. Maggie had gone at least a hundred feet from the thicket. How had she wandered so far in such a short time?

Hazel shoved the ribbon into her pocket and cupped her hands around her mouth. "Maggie, wherever you are, you better stop right now an' let me catch up or you're gonna be in big trouble!" She waited several seconds, waiting, listening. More silence.

She hugged herself, battling tears. Why didn't Maggie answer? Maybe she'd curled up somewhere, like a bunny, and fallen asleep. She began hunting again, moving slow, peeking into bushes and under the thick branches of pine trees.

Minutes slipped by with no sign of her sister, and Hazel's fear grew so intense a bitter taste flooded her mouth. She broke into a run. She zigzagged through the woods, forming a rough circle around the blackberry bramble, always calling. Sometimes she cajoled, sometimes she threatened. Sometimes she choked back sobs and other times angry growls. She searched and called until her throat was too dry to make a sound and her leg muscles quivered.

She stopped, leaning forward and resting her hands on her knees. Her breath heaved. Her chest ached. Sweat dribbled down her face and mixed with her tears. Daddy and Mama would be so disappointed in her for losing Maggie in the woods, but she'd have to face them. She needed help. Sucking in a big breath, she gathered her bearings and then took off toward home.

Two

Seventy Years Later
Las Vegas, Nevada
Meghan D'Ann DeFord

"*L*et me get that for you, miss."
Meghan shuffled a few inches forward and allowed the cowboy whose knees had consistently bumped the back of her seat on the flight from Little Rock to Las Vegas to remove her carry-on from the overhead bin. She enjoyed the strain of his plaid snap-up shirt across his chest as he reached for the duffle. One thing about having to use these blasted crutches—she'd discovered gentlemen still existed. And some of them, like this one decked out in Western attire, from Stetson to Tony Lamas, weren't too bad on the eyes, either.

"How're you gonna carry this?" He eyed her from beneath the curved brim of his cream-colored hat. Clearly he was one of the good guys.

"If you'll hold my crutch for a minute, I'll strap the duffle on my back."

"Huh-uh." He flung the duffle over his shoulder.

"But I—"

"I'll carry it for you." He grinned at her, his tan cheeks sporting a pair of adorable dimples. "It'll keep us from holdin' up the line."

A glance behind him confirmed a crunch of impatient faces. He was kind to say *us* instead of *you*. "Thanks. I appreciate it."

She limped her way up the aisle, slowed partly by the crutches and her cast but mostly by the narrow space. Maybe she should have stayed in her seat until everyone else cleared the plane. Most of the chatter on the flight had been about slots and blackjack and poker. These folks were eager to throw their money away at the casinos, and she was delaying them. But she was eager, too. She hadn't seen her grandmother for three years.

As much as she rued the accident that had forced her to take a company-enforced six-week leave of absence, she wasn't unhappy about getting to spend the time with Grandma. Neither Grandma nor Mom was getting any younger, although Mom would spew some strong words if Meghan mentioned her age. Her partner from the detective unit, Sean Eagle, called her unexpected vacation a God-kiss. Some of the guys in the office found Sean's religious murmurings overbearing, but she wouldn't deny the hidden blessing in this trip.

They exited the plane, and a perky young airline worker bustled over to Meghan, her long brown braid swinging. "Over here, ma'am."

Meghan glanced around. "Me?"

"Yes, ma'am."

Meghan frowned. Since when were unmarried late-twenties women called "ma'am"?

"I've got a wheelchair waiting."

"I didn't order a wheelchair."

The woman sent a confused gaze up and down the crutches. "But . . ."

A genuine smile formed. "Really, I don't mind walking." If she spent six weeks sitting in a wheelchair, she wouldn't be able to wear her business suits afterward. She eased to the side so the other travelers could pass by and turned her smile on the cowboy. "I'll take that bag now. Thanks for carrying it off the plane for me."

His brows pinched. He glanced up the Jetway leading to the airport. "You sure you don't want me to carry it to baggage claim? I don't mind."

She couldn't wait to tell her mother that true gentlemen still existed in the world. At the unit, none of her male counterparts made allowances for her. In a way the cowboy's attentiveness embarrassed her, but mostly it pleased her. She discovered she liked being treated like a lady.

Of course, Mom would say the solicitous treatment was because of the crutches. Always so cynical . . .

She coughed a short laugh. "No, really, I can do it. It's just a matter of getting it strapped on."

He shrugged and passed the duffle to the uniformed woman standing near. "All right, then. Enjoy your time in Vegas, miss." He tipped his hat and sauntered off, blending in with the milling stream.

The helpful airline worker looped the strap across Meghan's chest over the top of the slim strap from her cross-body purse and situated the duffle on her back. The thick strap bit into her neck, but not enough to draw complaints. She might never again complain about nitpicky things like biting straps after walking away from the three-car pileup that stole two other people's lives.

Why'd she been so lucky when others weren't?

Meghan pushed aside a prickle of guilt and thanked the woman. Then she fell in at the rear of the line, the *thump* of her crutches echoing against the metal floor. She moved from the stuffy Jetway into a blast of air-conditioned air. And a mass of humanity. Slot machines were centered down the wide walkways, nearly every seat filled and observers forming small crowds around the players. The raucous tunes, *clang*s, and *ding*s of the machines combined with the chatter of voices made her want to plug her ears.

She followed the signs to baggage claim, forgoing the moving sidewalk and staying as far to the right of the hallway as possible to avoid being trampled by those with two good legs. Two different times, cart drivers stopped and offered her a ride, and she declined both opportunities. After sitting for so long, it felt good to be up and moving.

Mom would probably scold her for her stubborn refusal—"*Sometimes you are too independent for your own good, Meghan D'Ann*"—but Mom wasn't a good one to talk. Sometimes Meghan wondered if her mother had served as president for the entire generation of women's libbers. She even did her own plumbing.

A row of sober-faced limousine drivers waited near baggage claim, all holding signs. Curious, she glanced across the black letters printed on white squares of cardboard. Maybe a performer from one of the many shows available in the tourist town had flown in. She wouldn't mind sneaking a peek at Bette Midler or one of the Osmonds.

Terrence Blake. Huston Family. Dexter Inc. Meghan DeFord . . . She jolted to a halt. Meghan DeFord? That couldn't be meant for her. There must be another Meghan DeFord. Then again, it would be like Grandma to do something special to surprise her. Mom often complained about Grandma's penchant for extravagant gifting, and Meghan never understood why her mother found the trait annoying. But then, lots of things about Mom and Grandma's relationship puzzled her. Maybe during this long vacation with Grandma all to herself, Meghan would be able to sort things out.

She rolled her shoulder to adjust the duffle strap and then stumped up close to the driver who held the sign bearing her name. "Excuse me, I'm Meghan DeFord. From Little Rock, Arkansas. You . . ." She chuckled, glancing around self-consciously. "You're not here for me, are you?" If he said no, she'd melt of embarrassment.

He whipped the sign into the closest trash bin and stuck out his gloved hand. "Yes, ma'am, sent by Mrs. Hazel Blackwell-DeFord."

Just as she'd suspected. She smiled, memories flooding her. "What a treat."

He slipped the duffle from her back, and she allowed a sigh of relief to escape. He kept a grip on the duffle. "Do you have more luggage?"

She swallowed a snort. Did she ever! When Sean had dropped her off at the airport early that morning, he'd teasingly accused her of moving lock, stock, and barrel to Nevada. "I do."

"Let's go get it, then."

With the duffle dangling from his hand, he escorted her to the luggage carousel. It took some doing to work their way through the crowd, but they moved in close enough for her to see the bags passing on the black rubber conveyor belt. The flow of bags was almost mesmerizing after her long day of travel, but she shook off her sleepiness when she spotted her luggage.

"There's mine, those two red ones."

If he held any scorn about her battered luggage, he hid it better than the pair of teenage girls standing a few feet away. They pointed, laughed, and made faces at each other.

Meghan rolled her eyes. She didn't need them to tell her the suitcases looked awful. Mom constantly fussed about her still using them—*"Good heavens, you earn a decent salary. Buy some decent luggage!"* But they were a gift from Grandma for her high school graduation nine years ago. Even if they fell apart, Meghan wouldn't give them up.

The driver pulled the pair of scarred, duct-taped rolling suitcases from the carousel, flopped the duffle on top of the biggest one, and then shot her a nod. "This way, please." He rolled the cases in tandem away from the carousel.

She followed, stumping double time to keep up with him. She couldn't blame him for wanting to hurry. She'd dated a taxi driver once, and when she'd goaded him about speeding, he'd explained that the more riders he transported, the better his pay. The limo driver probably wanted to drop her off as quickly as possible and then move on to his next fare.

He led her to a sleek, silver limousine and opened the door. She considered asking him to snap a picture of her in front of the vehicle before she got in, but it would delay their leave taking. And who would want to see it? Her mother? The guys at the office? She could imagine their responses. Besides, even though awnings shaded the area, the heat radiated off the sidewalk through the sole of her slip-on sneaker. People said Nevada had a dry heat, but even with zero humidity, 110 degrees was still hot.

She handed the driver her crutches and climbed clumsily into the back. Cool air blasted her face and enticed the strands of hair that had escaped her ponytail into a wild dance. She flopped into the middle of the long leather sofa with a sigh. The vehicle bounced twice, the weight of her suitcases hitting the floor of the trunk. A resounding *thud* signaled the trunk lid closing, and then the driver slipped behind the wheel.

He sent a quick peek into the back. "All set?"

"Yes, sir."

He closed the window separating them, and the limo eased into the flow of traffic with a few accompanying *honk*s.

Meghan didn't bother gawking out the tinted windows during the ride from the airport to Grandma's house in Kendrickson. She'd seen Vegas before and, frankly, it wasn't her cup of tea. Give her a small town any day of the week and twice on Sunday. But she did enjoy the cushy seat, the floral-scented chilled air tousling her hair, and the bottled Dr Pepper from the built-in ice bucket. There was even a box of Junior Mints inside the wood-paneled bucket. It didn't have her name on it, but she knew it was meant for her. She and Grandma always shared a box when they watched television movies on one of the family-friendly channels.

Grandma . . . Funny how thinking her name raised so many memories. When she was a kid, Meghan's favorite part of the whole year was the summer month she spent at Grandma's house. Mom always tried to talk her out of going—tempted her with swimming or tennis lessons, trips to amusement parks, a new puppy. But nothing compared to those weeks with Grandma. Meghan loved her mom and she knew her mom loved her, but Grandma had a way of showering affection, of listening, of paying attention so intensely it seemed no one else in the world mattered. To Meghan, Grandma was the definition of unselfish love. And it'd been far too long between visits.

The limo turned a slow corner, and Meghan sat up to glance outside. A little tremor of excitement wiggled up her spine. They'd reached Grandma's cul-de-sac. She tossed the empty bottle in the trash and slipped the half-full box of candy into her pocket. She'd share the rest with Grandma.

She waited inside the air-conditioned interior, fidgeting, while the limo driver retrieved her luggage from the trunk and stacked it at the end of the driveway. Then he opened the door for her and helped her out. Sweat immediately broke out over her body. She hoped Grandma's AC was on high.

He handed her the crutches. "Here you are. Enjoy your visit now."

Meghan unzipped her purse. "Hang on. I need to—"

"The tip's covered. Thank you." He bustled off.

She shook her head, chuckling. Grandma had thought of everything.

She made her way up the curved driveway and through splashes of shade cast by a trio of dwarf palm trees. A chorus of barking dogs, their *yips* muffled by solid walls, serenaded her. She cringed at the intrusive sound. The neighbors must have a whole pack of hounds. How did Grandma handle it? She'd never had a pet. Not even a goldfish. Mom had a whole zoo—dogs, cats, a saltwater aquarium, and half a dozen guinea pigs. If Mom didn't resemble Grandma so strongly, Meghan would suspect they weren't related. Opposites in every way.

She crossed the rock-paved patch that served as a porch and paused at the double doors. She frowned, puzzled. The barking was louder. Sharp. Insistent. Were the dogs in Grandma's house? No way . . . Maybe Grandma moved and somehow Meghan hadn't gotten the message. She wouldn't put it past Mom to keep something like that from her. But Grandma hadn't mentioned a new address when Meghan called to ask if she could visit. This had to be her house.

Even so, apprehension nibbled at her as she rang the doorbell.

The barking rose in volume and shrillness. Someone called, laughter tingeing her voice, "All right, all right, settle down." The door swung open and Meghan's jaw dropped.

"Mom? What are you doing here?"

Three

Mid-July 1943
Cumpton, Arkansas
Hazel Mae

W hy, Hazel Mae Blackwell, what're you doin' racin' up the road like the devil's on your tail? You're gonna give yourself heatstroke."

Hazel caught hold of the edge of Miss Minnie Achard's wagon. Her chest heaved so hard she could hardly talk. "Gotta . . . get home . . . quick."

"How come?"

"My little sister . . . she's lost."

"Where?"

"The blackberry thicket."

The old lady's rheumy eyes went wide. "In them thick woods? Oooh, girl . . ." She scooted over. "Climb in. Me an' my mule'll getcha to your daddy."

Miss Minnie meant well, but her old mule was slower than a turtle. Hazel shook her head. "No, ma'am. Th-thank you, but I'll run. Can . . . can you tell any folks you see along the way we . . . we're gonna need help lookin' for her?"

Miss Minnie nodded, the brim of her floppy straw hat bobbing. "I'll surely do that, but you slow yourself down or—"

Hazel took off. Dust flew as her feet pounded the ground. Her lungs screamed for relief, but she pushed herself up the hill, legs quivering, arms pumping, sweat stinging her eyes, propelled by worry and guilt. Daddy'd take the strap to her for sure, and she'd accept every lick. A prayer begged in the back of her heart, never ceasing.

Let her be all right. Let us find her. I won't never lose sight of anything again if You'll let us find her. Please, God, please.

She rounded the final bend and scrambled across the backyard. Her rubbery legs collapsed as she mounted the first porch riser, but she forced herself upright and slammed through the screened door into the kitchen. "Mama!"

Her mother turned from the worktable, a frown pinching her face. "What took you so long? This cobbler crust's been ready for—"

Hazel stumbled forward. "Mama ... Mama ..." Nothing else would come out.

Mama's frown lines deepened into worry lines. She caught Hazel by the shoulders and gave her a shake. "Talk to me, girl. What's wrong?" She lifted her gaze to the backyard. Fear burst across her features. Her fingers bit into Hazel's shoulders. "Where's Maggie?" She leaned down and glared fiercely into Hazel's face. "Where is your sister?"

A sob wrenched from her throat. "I—I lost her."

Present Day
Kendrickson, Nevada
Margaret Diane DeFord

"Well, I'm not lost, if that's what you're thinking." Diane used her foot to shoo the quartet of barking dachshunds away from the threshold. "Will you all hush? You know Meghan." She laughed as they jumped and barked louder. She smiled at her daughter. "They're happy to see you."

Meghan didn't move. "Why are you here? Did something happen to Grandma?"

The worry in her daughter's eyes brought a rush of protectiveness along with a shaft of envy. How could Meghan so dearly love the person who irritated her more than anyone else in the world? "She's fine. I—"

"Margaret Diane, get her in and close the door. You're letting all the cold air out," Mother called from her wingback chair in the corner of the living room. "And for goodness' sake, get those beasts of yours under control. They could wake the dead."

Diane rolled her eyes and sent a scowl in her mother's direction. "She's on crutches. She can't exactly hurry."

Mother pushed out of her chair and crossed to the middle of the room. "It isn't the crutches slowing her down, it's the dogs." She clapped her hands at them. "You there, move! Move! Go away!"

Ginger, the oldest member of the group, tucked her tail between her legs and darted for the kitchen. Duchess, Miney, and Molly chased after her, still yipping.

"Now, bring her in here."

Diane stepped aside and swept her hand in a broad gesture. "The queen has spoken. Come on in."

Meghan cleared the threshold. With a huge smile, she thumped directly to Mother. "Grandma!" The pair embraced, Mother bending down slightly to match Meghan's more petite height. Mother's bobbed snow-white hair painted a stark contrast to Meghan's rich brown ponytail falling to her shoulder blades. They pulled apart, smiled into each other's faces, then hugged again, laughing. If Diane wasn't mistaken, tears glittered in their matching brown eyes. She gritted her teeth against the sting of jealousy.

Meghan shifted slightly, putting her weight on the crutches again. "Thanks for the limo ride. Sure didn't expect that! It was almost like being a celebrity. Loved finding the box of mints, too. I didn't eat them all—we'll share the rest tonight if there's a good movie on TV."

Mother chuckled. "We don't have to depend on television programming anymore. Most everything on there is junk these days. I bought one of those DVD players, and I picked up a stack of movies from the Hallmark store in the mall. I'll let you take your pick."

"Great!" Meghan peered at Diane over her shoulder. "Hey, Mom, could you get my luggage? There's no handsome cowboy close by to help right now." She giggled and turned her attention to Mother again. "You should've seen the guy who sat behind me on the airplane, Grandma—straight out of a spaghetti Western. At least six foot two and—"

Diane cleared her throat. "Will someone watch the door and open it for me when I come up with the suitcases?"

Mother frowned. "Margaret Diane, I'm certain I taught you it's impolite to interrupt when someone is speaking."

Her mother had taught her lots of things, including not to interrupt, but she was forty-seven years old now. Definitely too old to be scolded. Especially in front of her own adult child. She headed out the door with her lips pressed tight to hold back a retort that would no doubt be interpreted as disrespectful—something else Mother had taught her was wrong.

Heat waves shimmered on the pavement and made the soles of her feet, protected only by thin leather sandals, burn. She quickstepped to the suitcases and took hold of the handle on the biggest one. Hot! She swallowed a curse and jerked her hand back. Why hadn't she thought to bring hot pads out with her? Living in Nevada was like living in an oven. She wrapped the tail of her fuchsia tunic around the handle and tried again. Not great, but better.

She left the suitcase on the porch and hurried after the other pieces of luggage, grumbling as she went. Two suitcases and a duffle? Meghan must have brought her entire wardrobe. Had she forgotten how to operate a washing machine? And why was she still using these ratty-looking things? The neighbors probably thought Mother put them at the curb as a freebie for the homeless or needy.

Mother held the door open and Diane brought everything inside. She pushed her heavy bangs from her forehead, grimacing when her hand came away moist from sweat. "Honestly, Meghan, do you not understand the concept of traveling light?" She held her hands toward the stack of luggage. "This is ridiculous. I managed to get here just fine with only one suitcase."

Mother shook her head and looped arms with Meghan, forming a united front. She tipped her temple to Meghan's crown. "Ignore her. She's done nothing but fuss since she got here midmorning. And she just fibbed. She carried in five different pieces of luggage if you count the pet carriers." Mother pursed her lips. "She knows how I feel about animals in the house and she brought that menagerie of hounds anyway."

"Now who's fussing?" Diane crossed to the sofa and flopped onto the center cushion. She patted her legs, and the dachshunds all came running, tongues lolling and tails wagging. They leaped up and settled around her, two on her lap and one on either side.

Mother closed her eyes for a moment and blew out a breath. Then she stepped away from Meghan, the wide legs of her capri-length palazzo pants swaying around her tan calves. "You have a seat, honey. I've got a pitcher of sweet tea in the fridge. Let me bring you a glass."

"I can do it."

"No, no, you sit. I haven't had the chance to spoil you in more than a coon's age." Mother gave Meghan a little nudge toward the sofa. "I'll be right back with the tea and a little snack. I hope you still like oatmeal cookies."

"With butterscotch chips instead of raisins?"

"Of course."

Meghan laughed. "I'll take half a dozen."

Mother smiled and headed to the kitchen. As soon as she disappeared around the corner, Meghan leaned toward Diane and lowered her voice to a near whisper. "Why didn't you tell me you'd be here? And why'd you bring the dogs? You usually board them when you travel."

Diane stroked Ginger's silky ears. "Are you picking sides already?" Her voice held more resentment than she'd intended to divulge.

Meghan sighed. "Why do you create sides? She's your mother. Can't you get along?"

Diane turned her face toward the wide doorway leading to the eat-in kitchen. The sounds of ice bouncing inside glasses and of drawers opening and closing carried to the living room. Cheerful sounds. Welcome-home sounds. They hadn't started until Meghan arrived. "It takes two to tango."

"But only one to lead." Meghan reached out with one crutch and tapped Diane's knee with its tip. "You could lead her into something other than arguments if you really wanted to."

Molly nosed the rubber heel of the crutch. Diane pulled the dog more snugly against her side. "Put that thing down unless you want it to become a chew toy. And don't blame me for my mother's eccentricities. She's always been—"

Mother came around the corner with a tray in her hands. "Here we are. Sweet tea for Meghan and me, unsweetened tea for Margaret Diane, and enough cookies that we all—including the dogs—could have some. Not that I intend to share with those fleabags, nor do I expect my daughter to indulge." She waggled her still-dark eyebrows at Meghan. "She's always too worried about her figure to let empty calories cross her lips."

Diane gave Meghan a look she hoped communicated, *"See? She picks at me, too."*

Meghan smiled, although it looked strained. "You have to admit, though, Mom looks fantastic—better than a lot of women half her age. I can't tell you how many times we've been asked if we were sisters."

Diane wanted to sock the air—Meghan had defended her!—but she'd scare her little companions. So she only smiled smugly.

Mother lowered the tray to the coffee table and picked up a glass of tea. "My Margaret Diane has always been a beauty. Even as a child." She offered the glass, her brown-eyed gaze locking on Diane's with intensity. "A beautiful child is a blessing." Pain creased her features. "And a burden."

Mid-July 1943
Cumpton, Arkansas
Hazel Mae

Hazel sat on the grass near the blackberry bushes with Maggie's doll in her arms. The woods echoed with dozens of voices calling Maggie's name.

"Bet it was the Gypsies that took her. It's happened before—two different times in this very county, remember? That baby boy three years ago over by Beaty and another girl from Gravette about the same age as Maggie Blackwell. They always take the comely ones." The ominous comment drifted from the other side of the blackberry bramble, where a cluster of ladies who'd come out to offer Mama support sat together. Hazel shivered even though the early evening air was still hot and humid.

"Hush that, Nora. You want the little girl's mama to hear you?" Mrs. Crudgington, one of their closest neighbors, spoke sharply to the director of the orphans' home.

Mrs. Burton snorted. "The preacher and his wife took her to their wagon over by the road. She can't hear us from there."

Another of the women spoke. "Even so, there's no proof Gypsies had anything to do with those two children disappearing. Lots of bad things can happen in these heavy woods."

Hazel blinked back tears. So many bad things could happen . . . like a snake going after baby bunnies and persuading a big sister to leave her little sister all alone.

"But didn't Simon Krunk say he chased away a wagonload of Gypsies from town just two days ago? What's to say they didn't set up camp deep in the trees?" Mrs. Burton's voice held a know-it-all tone. "They could've been watching those girls come up the road and waited for their chance to grab the littlest one. They're wily, you know. The older girl would never have known if they was hiding in the bushes."

"If Gypsies had done it, they would've taken both girls." Mrs. Crudgington didn't sound too sure of herself.

"They wouldn't have wanted Hazel Mae since she's mostly grown, but that little Maggie . . ."

Hazel didn't want to hear any more. She jumped up and moved away from the bushes, away from the ladies' talk. She wanted Mama. But halfway to the road she stopped. The preacher'd taken Mama aside for praying. She shouldn't interrupt. She dropped to her knees there in the grass and bowed her head.

She told God again how she was sorry for leaving Maggie. She begged Him again to let the men find her. They'd found one of her shoes on the bank of Purcell's Creek, and Hazel carried her hair ribbon in her dress pocket. She jolted, remembering the ribbon caught on a tree branch as high as Hazel's shoulder. If Maggie was only walking, there wasn't any way that branch could've snatched the ribbon. Somebody had to have been carrying her.

Mrs. Burton must be right. The Gypsies had taken her beautiful flaxen-haired, blue-eyed little sister. She'd never see Maggie again. Hazel buried her face in the doll's curls and held the doll as tightly as she wished she could hold her sister.

Present Day
Kendrickson, Nevada
Diane

Diane took the glass decorated with a wedge of lemon from her mother. Condensation left the glass slick, and she gripped it between her palms. "How can a beautiful child be a burden?"

Mother turned and gave a glass of tea to Meghan. "You'd be surprised."

"I suppose you're talking about the time you dragged me out of the junior high football stadium because a high school freshman stopped to flirt with me."

Diane had wanted to die of embarrassment back then. Even all these years later, the humiliation stung. She turned to Meghan. "All the way home she lectured me about the dangers of talking to strangers." She took a sip of the tea, letting the liquid cool her aggravation. "Mother had a tendency to overreact."

Meghan took a cookie from the plate and bit into it.

Mother sat in her chair and balanced the glass of tea on her knee. "I don't think it's overreacting to want to protect your child from a potentially dangerous situation."

"Potentially dangerous? Seriously?" Diane laughed. She couldn't help it. Gracious sakes, she'd been a thirteen-year-old girl enjoying a little attention from a nice-looking kid, and they were only talking at the edge of the bleachers in full sight of everyone.

She pushed Ginger and Miney off her lap and plopped the glass back on the tray. "When Meghan was thirteen I let her walk to school by herself and allowed her to go to the movies with her friends . . . without an adult escort. Did you ever feel endangered, Meghan?"

Her daughter took another bite of her cookie, her gaze flicking between Diane and Mother.

Diane shook her head. "Fine. Don't say anything. But I'm telling you, Mother, I raised an independent, self-sufficient child who's become a well-adjusted, responsible adult. And I did it without hovering over her like a . . . a rescue helicopter."

An odd smile tipped up one corner of her mother's mouth.

Diane frowned. "What's that for?"

"What?"

"That smile."

"I'm not smiling."

Diane huffed. "Yes, you are."

Mother took a sip of her tea. "All right, I am. I'm not trying to goad you, Margaret Diane, but I find your last statement amusing."

"Amusing?" Her ire rose, and apparently the dogs sensed it. They began milling, poking their long noses in her face. She delivered reassuring pats while scowling at her mother. "How so?"

Mother set aside her tea glass and placed her hands on the armrests, as regal as a queen on her throne. "You're hovering right now like a rescue helicopter, swooping in to put a barrier between Meghan and me." Sadness tinged her features. "I assume that was your intention when you came unannounced and unexpectedly at the same time Meghan planned to visit. Am I right?"

Four

Hazel

 hen she had opened the door that morning and found her daughter on the porch, Hazel's heart leaped with joy. She opened her arms for a hug, but Margaret Diane stepped past her to plunk a pet carrier on the carpet. Beady eyes above a long snout peered from behind the wire door, and Hazel shuddered. Instead of welcoming words leaving her throat, Hazel blurted, "You brought a dog?"

"No, I brought dogs."

Indeed she had. Four in all. When she knew Hazel couldn't abide animals. Not in the house or in the yard. But Margaret Diane had always been a rebel despite Hazel's best efforts to tame her. Another of her failures.

Now Hazel met her daughter's stony glare and spoke gently. Kindly. Tiredly. "Be honest with me, please. Did you come to prevent me from enjoying uninterrupted time with Meghan?"

"I've always been an interruption in your life, haven't I, Mother?"

The sharp words stung, partly due to their caustic delivery, partly because they held an element of truth. Hazel sighed. "I've always loved you, no matter what you think."

Margaret Diane huffed—such an unladylike sound.

"And you haven't answered my question."

"I'm sorry." She examined the cranberry polish on her almond-shaped fingernails. "What was the question?"

The impertinence chased away the last of Hazel's patience. She slapped the armrest, the contact sending a shock all the way to her elbow. "Margaret Diane, there are times I—"

Meghan dropped the last bit of her cookie on the plate and flung her arms like an umpire calling a runner safe. "Stop it. I haven't been here for half an hour and already I feel like the rope tied to two horses running in opposite directions."

Hazel hung her head. How could she have allowed herself to get drawn into a childish exchange of tit for tat? It would accomplish nothing more than furthering the gap between herself and her only child. *Lord, forgive me.* Maybe she should ask the same of Margaret Diane. But pride—and fear of rejection— held the request inside.

She touched Meghan's knee. "I'm sorry, dear one. You're right. This bickering needs to stop."

"I wouldn't call it bickering." Meghan flicked a frown from her grandmother to her mother. "It's more like a war. A war that only has losers. Including me."

For the first time, a hint of regret showed in Margaret Diane's brown eyes. She looked down and petted the dogs with slow, steady strokes.

Meghan flopped against the sofa cushions as if too weary to remain upright. "I mean, really, Mom, would it hurt to tell Grandma why you're here? I sure wasn't expecting you. When I called you the day before yesterday so you'd have my flight information, you said you were on the road, but you didn't mention you were heading for Nevada. Why didn't you tell me?"

Margaret Diane shifted her gaze to Meghan. "Is it so unbelievable that I might want to share this lengthy time off from work with you? I hardly see you since you transferred to the investigations unit."

Hazel frowned. Her daughter hadn't told a bald-faced lie, but something didn't sound quite true, either. Meghan and Margaret Diane both lived in Little Rock. Granted, Meghan's job kept her occupied, but her granddaughter's weekly e-mails included snippets about her and her mother meeting for dinner or spending a day shopping together. Although Hazel frequently invited Meghan to visit, her vacations and holidays for the past three years had been monopolized by Margaret Diane.

"So why not just say so?" Meghan's tone held a thread of disbelief. "Why show up and, like Grandma said, sabotage our time together?"

Hazel spluttered. "I never used the word *sabotage*."

Meghan grinned. "Okay, I inserted that. Because that's kind of how it feels to me." She angled a weary look in her mother's direction. "Surprises are nice, Mom, but this visit doesn't feel like a surprise. It feels like a sneak attack."

Hazel clamped her lips tight and resisted adding anything to Meghan's statement. Her granddaughter had never been a timid child, but she'd always been respectful and sensitive to other people's feelings. Hazel had never heard her utter an unkind word to or about anyone. Her boldness in addressing her mother took Hazel by surprise. Hazel couldn't imagine having been so straightforward when she was as young as Meghan. She wasn't that straightforward even now, and no one would call her young.

Meghan gestured to the suitcases still standing sentry beside the front door. "You asked why I needed so much luggage. One of those suitcases doesn't have a stitch of clothing in it. It's all . . . memorabilia."

Margaret Diane frowned, but she remained silent.

Hazel couldn't. "What do you mean?"

Meghan's dark eyes lit. "Do you remember when I came out the first summer you moved to Nevada? You lived in Carson City then."

Memories swept over her of the adorable child with missing front teeth, crooked ponytails, and scraped knees. "I remember."

"You gave me your old camera—the one that took the picture, then spit out the film so we could watch it develop."

Hazel laughed. "Oh, yes. You had so much fun with that Polaroid. You said the camera was sticking out its tongue every time the picture emerged. I believe I snapped a photo of you imitating the camera. We must have used ten boxes of film."

"Thirteen." Meghan giggled. "I saved every last picture in a shoe box. I kept the photos from our other summers together, too. I brought them all with me." She propped the foot sporting the cast on the edge of the coffee table, then leaned forward, resting her elbows on her knees. "I also brought empty scrap-books and stickers, stubs from movie theaters and museums, and T-shirts from Disneyland, and—"

Hazel waved her hands, laughing. "Gracious, Meghan, what are you plan-ning to do with all that?"

Meghan's grin turned impish, rolling back the clock to her preteen years. "Reminisce. Fill up the scrapbook pages. Make a pictorial map of our years together." Tears glistened in her eyes, and her bright smile faded. "I can't believe your eightieth birthday is next month. I've been thinking and thinking what I could do to make it special, and then when I found out I'd be here for the big event, I thought, why not make a scrapbook of memories?"

She sat up, excitement erasing the glimmer of moisture. "I brought things from our summers together, but we don't have to limit it to you and me. Since Mom's here, she can help, too, and make pages representing her years with you. I know you've got photographs from her childhood, and you've got to have some from when you were a girl on the farm with your parents. We can even include those. Make it . . . a timeline of your entire life."

Her entire life? Then that would include— Cold chills attacked. Hazel rose, her joints popping with the effort, and crossed to the coat closet next to the front door. She took out a light sweater and draped it over her shoulders, then remained with her back to her daughter and granddaughter, staring into the shadowy space and attempting to rein in her galloping emotions.

"A timeline of your entire life." She couldn't do it. Not without sharing things she hadn't shared in seven decades. But how could she tell Meghan no?

She turned and pinned her gaze on Margaret Diane, her rebellious child. Her potential rescuer. "What do you think of this idea? Of course, we're pre-suming you intend to stay for the entire length of Meghan's visit. Perhaps we're mistaken."

The preparatory school where Margaret Diane taught American and world history and political science didn't open again until early September. She had no reason to return to Little Rock before then, so she had the freedom to stay. Not since Margaret Diane lived under her roof had they been together for such an extended period of time. What kind of mending might they be able to accomplish if they had six weeks together with Meghan as their mediator? But if Margaret Diane stayed, and if Meghan talked her into this timeline-of-life scrapbook, Hazel's deepest shame would be laid bare in front of the two people she most feared disappointing.

Her heart alternately begged *Stay, stay* and *Go, go* . . .

"I wouldn't have brought the dogs if I only intended to stay for a short time. I couldn't board them for more than a month."

Meghan arched one brow. "Does that mean you're staying the whole time?"

"That was my intention."

Hazel nodded, torn between relief and regret.

"Unless"—Margaret Diane shot a glare across the room, as piercing as an arrow from a crossbow—"you don't want me here."

Hazel slowly shook her head, her chest aching. "You're my daughter, Margaret Diane. Do you really think I'd order you to leave?"

"You did it once before."

Yes, she had, but Margaret Diane had conveniently neglected to share what precipitated the command. And Hazel had no desire to dredge it up again. Not with Meghan sitting there with bruises from head to toe and a cast on her foot. They needed to set aside their differences and allow the girl they both loved to fully heal.

Hazel returned to her chair and took a long, slow draw of her sweet tea. The ice had mostly melted, watering down the strong flavor she preferred, but she drank it anyway. When she nearly drained the glass, she set it aside and aimed a smile at Meghan. "So it'll be the three of us, then."

One of the dogs—the one with long, wavy hair on its ears, haunches, and tail—sat up and released a little *yip*.

Hazel cringed. "Or, more accurately, the seven of us. I doubt the dogs will be much help in putting together a scrapbook, but surely we three with human hands can manage it." She sighed, leaning back and letting her gaze drift to the vaulted ceiling and the fan blades slowly circling. "You know what they say about a three-strand cord—it's not easily broken."

Meghan

Why did it seem Grandma was talking about something other than putting together a scrapbook? The sudden melancholy in her voice and her expression raised Meghan's sympathy. And concern. She glanced at Mom, who also frowned at Grandma, but Meghan couldn't discern if Mom was concerned or just puzzled.

Meghan cleared her throat. "If you don't want to build the scrapbook, Grandma, we don't have to do it."

Grandma jerked, the way people did when waking from a bad dream. She met Meghan's gaze. The faraway look faded away, and the familiar glow of love and affection in her eyes returned. "You brought everything for that purpose. Of course we'll do it. But for now . . ." She pushed herself from the chair, more slowly than previous times, as if she'd suddenly remembered her age. "Let's take your suitcases to your room and get you settled. Margaret Diane's things are already in there, but if we can talk her into putting the dog carriers in the utility room or on the patio in the back—"

"I'm not putting the dogs out on the patio in this heat, Mother!"

"—there'll be plenty of space for both of you."

How would she last for six weeks playing buffer between Mom and Grandma? Tiredness struck hard. Meghan lowered her cast to the floor and reached for her crutches. "The bedroom in my apartment is half the size of your guest room, so even with the dogs and Mom in there, I'm sure I won't feel smooshed." She turned to her mother. "Would you take the biggest suitcase and my duffle to the room? The other one we can leave in here since we'll prob-ably do all the sorting and so forth on the floor."

Without a word Mom shifted the dogs aside and stood. She grabbed the two pieces of luggage Meghan had indicated and carted them around the cor-ner. The four dachshunds bounced along behind her with their ears flapping and tails wagging. When Mom was out of sight, Meghan sighed and aimed an apologetic grimace at her grandmother.

"I'll try to talk her into keeping the dogs locked in the bedroom. I know you don't like them running all over the house."

Grandma shook her head. "No, honey, don't bother. No need to stir con-flict. I'm just glad she didn't bring the fish, the cats, and the ferrets, too."

"She doesn't have the ferrets anymore."

"No?"

"She traded them for guinea pigs. Six of them."

"Oh, my soul . . ."

They both laughed, and to Meghan's relief some of the tension dissolved. They began ambling up the hallway to the guest suite at the back half of the house.

"You know something, Grandma? I'm really looking forward to putting the scrapbook together. I realized when I was packing the pictures and stuff that I really don't know much about you. I mean, beyond you as a grand-mother." Meghan pinched her brows together, sending her thoughts backward. "Especially since I've never had any contact with my father's family, I'd really like to know as much as possible about Mom's. I think it gives a person a sense of security—and stability—to know where she came from, what kind of peo-ple are in her gene pool, you know?"

Grandma chuckled, but it sounded raspy. Forced. "It might scare you a little bit. Did you ever consider that?"

Affection flooded her. She paused and released one crutch to give Grandma a one-armed hug. "If your parents were half as wonderful as you, I come from good stock. I'm not worried at all."

The furrow in Grandma's brow spoke of her worry, though. Another gravelly chuckle eased the deep lines. "Well, dear granddaughter, we shall see how much this old brain of mine recalls. Sometimes the good Lord, in His wisdom, allows some things to slip too far into the recesses of memory to be recovered. If that's the case, I hope"—tears winked in her eyes, turning her brown irises a tawny russet—"you'll forgive me."

Five

Late July 1943
Cumpton, Arkansas
Hazel Mae

*H*azel sat up in her bed and listened to the sounds creeping through the plaster wall separating her room from Mama and Daddy's. Ten nights in a row she'd heard Mama crying. Heartbroken wails. Noises that made Hazel's chest hurt so bad she could barely breathe. She'd also heard Daddy's voice, soft and low, as soothing as he was when Hazel or Maggie got scared from a bad dream or fell down and hurt themselves. But tonight . . .

Mama's sobs came same as the nights before, but Daddy didn't answer soft and soothing. Angry words—harsher than he'd ever spoken to anybody, even to Hazel when she confessed she'd lost Maggie—exploded.

"Mae, she's gone, an' no carryin' on is gonna bring her back. If you don't get ahold of yourself, you're gonna make yourself sick an' drive me back to the bottle!"

Mama's mutters came next, but no matter how hard Hazel strained, she couldn't make out the words. Daddy talked loud enough for their miles-away neighbors to hear.

"I ain't stayin' one more minute in this bed if you don't stop your cryin'. I mean it, Mae, stop it or I'm headin' out the door."

Silence fell. Hazel held her breath, her heart beating like the bass drum in a parade band. She lowered her head to her pillow, her breath easing out on a long, slow sigh. She closed her eyes, eager to let sleep carry her away.

Then a sob—just one, but one that made Hazel think somebody was being choked—erupted. And wails followed it, the loudest and most keening yet.

Hazel pulled the covers over her head. A door slammed so hard the walls shook. Thundering footsteps pounded past her door and down the stairs, Daddy's mutters and curses blasting out. She cowered under the covers for long minutes, anguish for Mama and worry about Daddy tearing her in two. What should she do? What could she do? Would anything help?

She lay still, staring wide eyed into the nighttime shadows for what seemed like hours, until Mama's wails softened into hiccups and finally died out. She waited for Daddy's feet to come up the hall, but all she heard was a hoot owl from the tree outside and the wind's whisper. Maybe Daddy'd gone out to the barn. If he was inside the barn, up in the hayloft or huddled down in the corner of a stall like he used to do before Maggie came along, he wouldn't know Mama'd stopped crying. Someone should tell him so he'd come back in.

Hazel slipped out of bed and crept to her door. The hinges squeaked when she eased it open, and she cringed at the creepy sound. Would Mama wake up? She stood still as a scarecrow on the threshold and listened, but no sound came from Mama's room. Sucking in a breath, she hurried on tiptoes to the stairs, down the risers, and out the back door.

Slivers of moonlight flowed between the tree branches and spotted the dirt path worn smooth by years of trekking back and forth to the barn. The ground felt as cool as clay against her bare feet—a comforting touch. At the other end of the path the old barn's doors lolled wide like a pair of open arms, inviting her in. She scampered toward the barn, her cotton gown flapping in the light breeze and her feet pat-patting a steady rhythm, and entered the dark space rich with the scent of animals, hay, and old wood. Daddy smelled just like it when he came in from milking. She'd always loved the smell.

She pulled in a deep breath, flaring her nostrils to absorb the barn's perfume. Another aroma sneaked in, a sickly sweet one she didn't love. Not at all. She rubbed her nose hard to erase it. She took a step deeper into the barn, her pulse stuttering. She couldn't see him, but she knew he was here. The flowers-soaked-in-sugar smell gave him away.

"Daddy?"

Rustling noises came from the last stall on the left. Gathering her courage, she scuffed across the floor in that direction. A square window above the stall let in enough moonlight for her to see Daddy slouched against the barn wall. An open bottle was tucked next to his hip. She hugged the stall post and stared at the bottle. Where'd he gotten it? Far as she knew, he hadn't had a drop since Mama's belly was all swollen with Maggie.

"What you doin' out here, girl?" Daddy's slurred words let her know he'd helped himself to more than just a few sips of the whiskey.

"Lookin' for you." She let go of the post and crept closer. Close enough to see Daddy's chin quivering. She swallowed. "Mama stopped cryin'."

His face scrunched into a horrible scowl. "Cryin' an' cryin'. The mournfulness of it. I couldn't listen to it anymore."

"She's done." Hazel spoke soft, hardly a whisper. As she recalled, the drink made his ears mighty sensitive. "All quiet now. So you can come back in."

He hung his head, hanks of his thick, dark hair falling across his forehead. He covered his eyes with his hand. "No. I can't."

She moved a few more inches, close enough to touch his upraised knee. "Do . . . do you need help walkin'?" It had been a long time, but she still remembered the days when Daddy sometimes couldn't stay on his feet and Mama had to hold him up. "I can help you. I'm big enough."

"Ain't that." He slid his head down until his forehead collided with the inside of his elbow. He curled his hand over his hair. His whole body jerked. Little shuddering jerks. Then funny sounds—squeaks and short coughs and hiccups—came out. It took a minute for her to understand, and when she did her mouth dropped open.

Crying . . . Her daddy was crying.

She hadn't known big, strong daddies cried. Her chest tried to turn itself inside out. She wrung her hands, so scared and uncertain and helpless, and her legs went rubbery. As rubbery as Daddy's had ever been when he'd taken to a bottle.

She dropped to her knees at his side. She touched his convulsing shoulder with her fingertips, afraid to touch him but also afraid not to. "I'm sorry, Daddy. I'm so sorry."

His arms snaked out and snatched her against him. His face pressed into the curve of her neck, and the awful sounds continued. She burrowed as close as she could even though the smell of the liquor made her want to heave. She held him as tight as her puny strength allowed and bit down on her lower lip to hold back her own tears. She'd done such an awful thing. No wonder Daddy hid his face from her. Would he or Mama ever look at her again without remembering how she'd lost their baby girl?

The preacher at church said when you'd wronged somebody, you should ask for forgiveness, but she didn't know of anybody doing something as bad as what she'd done. If she asked, would Mama and Daddy forgive her? She swallowed hard and prayed for the courage to ask.

"Daddy . . . Daddy, will . . . Can . . ."

"Please forgive me, Hazel Mae. Please, please forgive me."

Hazel went as stiff as a mouse under a rattlesnake's glare. "W-what?"

Daddy caught hold of her shoulders. He pushed her away but kept his grip, holding her at arm's length. His brown eyes, all watery and red rimmed, stared hard into her face while his fingers pressed so tight she knew they'd leave bruises behind. "If it hadn't been for me, you girls wouldn't've gone to the thicket. She wouldn't've wandered off. I'm so sorry for hintin' to your mama for that cobbler. Please forgive me."

Tears rolled down Hazel's cheeks, warm and salty. They touched her lips and burned where she must've bit down too hard. "I . . . I . . ."

Daddy shook her. Not a hurtful shake. A needful one. "Forgive me, Hazel Mae. Will you forgive me?"

Hazel nodded hard. "I forgive you, Daddy."

His face crumpled. He pulled her close again and buried his moist face in her hair. "Thank you, girl. Thank you."

She coiled her arms around Daddy's neck and closed her eyes. When the drink wore off he probably wouldn't remember asking the question. Wouldn't remember her answer. He might even ask her again, and if he did, she'd tell him the same thing to ease his mind. She'd even forgive him for tipping up that bottle and getting himself pickled after promising to never touch another drop of whiskey.

But she'd never forgive herself for doing what she did to drive him to it.

Present Day
Kendrickson, Nevada
Diane

Diane sat on the edge of the turned-down bed and smeared face cream on her neck and chest. In the adjoining bathroom—what Mother called the en suite—Meghan bathed with her cast propped on the edge of the tub. Diane wanted to crawl under the covers. The two long days on the road with four dogs, each with its own bladder schedule, had worn her out. Not to mention the tension of being in her mother's house.

She'd sleep tonight, though. The over-the-counter sleeping pill she'd taken an hour after dinner was kicking in. Fuzziness clouded her brain. But she didn't dare lie down until she'd helped her daughter. Good thing she'd come. How would Mother lift Meghan from that slippery tub?

She had to admit, Mother looked good for almost eighty. Her snow-white hair was cut in a stylish bob, and the always-present touch of blush and slash of pale pink lipstick gave her a youthful glow. Still slender, always dressed impeccably. Thanks to Daddy's settlement with the railroad—

getting hit by a passenger train that wasn't supposed to be on the track netted more than most people could earn in a dozen lifetimes—they'd never had to scrimp. Every top name brand available filled the hangers in their closets. Her friends always envied her and her voguish mother. But they didn't envy the way Mother hovered, always watching, worse than a stalker from a late-night television movie.

"Mom? I'm done."

Diane gave a start. She pushed herself upright and held her hands to the dogs, who rolled from their prone positions at the foot of the bed into pounce mode. "Stay." She waited until they flopped back into a furry heap. Then she crossed to the bathroom.

Meghan was standing, one foot in and one out of the tub with a towel wrapped around her from armpit to midthigh. Diane couldn't hold back a laugh.

"You remind me of the junior high PE girls who were always worried about someone seeing their naked tushies."

Meghan snickered. "I covered up 'cause the AC was a little much after my warm bath." She held out one arm. "Just let me lean on you so I don't put weight on my broken ankle. Don't try to lift me."

Diane slipped her arm around her daughter's slender waist and planted herself on the rectangular throw rug while Meghan swung her other leg out of the bathtub. "I don't know why Mother requested tubs when she had this house built. A shower with a chair is safer than trying to climb in and out of these things. That's all they offer in retirement homes." At least the ones she'd explored online offered only showers.

"But you can't take a bubble bath in a shower." Meghan leaned against the counter and grabbed a second towel. She began rubbing her long hair. "I'll have to ask if she still keeps bubbles around like she did when I was little."

Diane yawned and stretched. "Knowing her, she does. She's always done every little thing she could to spoil you and win your favor."

Meghan frowned. "Mom . . ."

"Admit it. She always spoiled you rotten." Which is probably why Meghan had begged to spend weeks every summer with her grandmother even though Diane had the entire season free from her classroom. "Why else would you decide to spend your whole medical leave with her instead of in your own comfortable apartment, where I was close by to help you?"

Meghan shot her a puzzled look. "Maybe because I haven't seen her in forever."

"I know. That's what you said when you called to tell me you'd booked a flight. I seem to recall you also said"—she gritted her teeth to hold back another yawn—"you hoped this would be the start of a new routine of spending all of your vacations in Nevada with your grandmother." The jealousy still roiled in Diane's stomach. That's when she'd decided to go to Kendrickson, too. She wasn't about to surrender Meghan to her mother without a fight.

"You have to admit, Las Vegas is a great vacation spot." Meghan flopped the towel over the rack and reached for her hairbrush. "Besides, how many more years will Grandma be around? I need to spend as much time with her as I can while she's still here."

All the more reason to get Mother situated in a room at a retirement home. If she didn't have a house available, Meghan would be less likely to make lengthy yearly treks. Diane toyed with the frayed edge of the toilet paper roll. "I'm surprised she can still keep up with the responsibility of this house, considering her age."

Meghan, working the brush through her wet hair, glanced at Diane in the mirror. "She's actually pretty spry. Funny, I don't think she's changed a bit since the last time I saw her. Still so stately and beautiful. Kinda lets us know what we'll look like when we reach eighty. We'll still be hotties." She grinned and waggled her eyebrows.

"Please . . ." Diane yawned again, not bothering to hide this one. "I don't want to think about being eighty."

"It beats the alternative."

Diane shook her head. "What alternative?"

"Dying young." Meghan gripped a handful of hair and battled a snarl. "Grandma's kind of beaten the odds in her family, hasn't she? Both of her parents died when they were, what, in their sixties?"

Diane shrugged. "I can't remember how old they were. I know her dad was gone before I was born—drank himself to death. And her mother died when I was two or three."

Meghan's lips formed a sympathetic pout. "Sad. They couldn't have been old at all. And then your dad died at forty-seven."

Pain stabbed even though the loss was more than three decades old. "He died in an accident. That hardly counts. He might've lived to be eighty if he wasn't out working his tail off so Mother could stay home and smother me."

Meghan drew back. Her hand holding the hairbrush went still. "Wow. Where'd that come from?"

Diane flung her arms wide. "From the depth of my soul." The pill was making her loopy. She should go to bed.

Meghan's jaw dropped. "You don't really blame Grandma for your dad's death, do you? She didn't send that train on the track."

"Of course she didn't. She never did anything wrong." Diane pressed the heels of her hands against her eyes. Color exploded behind her closed eyelids, a private display of fireworks. Why did all these emotions well up every time she came in proximity to her mother? She'd think all was well—that she'd put the past to rest—and then she'd look into her mother's face, and the resentment and irritation and bitterness would fill up and spill out. If observation wasn't necessary to prove her mother was at an age not to be trusted living alone, she'd return to Arkansas first thing in the morning.

She dropped her hands and took a step toward the bedroom. "I'm sorry. I'm just very, very tired."

Meghan caught her arm and held tight. "Mom, help me understand something that's bothered me for as long as I can remember. It's obvious you don't want to be around Grandma. You've always made every excuse to stay away on holidays and only came when I begged or cried. What did she do that was so bad? Did she beat you?"

Diane shook her head.

"Batter you emotionally?"

"No."

"Neglect you?"

"No!"

"Then what? Why do you dislike her so much?"

There were things she could've said, things she wanted to say, but she couldn't think straight. The pill . . . it was stealing her ability to form a coherent sentence. "I need to go to bed." She wriggled her arm.

Meghan held tight. "No, tell me. What did she do?"

Diane broke loose with such force she lost her balance. She stumbled sideways, slammed her elbow on the doorjamb, then grabbed hold of the stained trim with both hands. The dogs leaped off the bed and surrounded her, whining and jumping on her legs. She bounced her foot, sending them scuttling for the bedroom again.

"Mom?"

Diane huffed. "She ruined my childhood, all right? I couldn't have a normal childhood at all because of her and her . . . domineering, controlling, overly protective to the point of paranoia ways. She suffocated me with her presence."

Meghan stared at her as if she'd lost her mind.

Diane grimaced and ran her hand through her hair. "You wouldn't understand. But when I get around her, I remember all the nos and the don'ts and the stay-heres and be-carefuls. I remember how I couldn't breathe. I remember, and it affects me." She barked out a harsh, humorless laugh. "I guess you never really get over the hurts of your childhood."

"Some people do. And some people don't." Meghan's expression turned pensive. Wise beyond her years. "I guess it's a choice we make."

Her head was beginning to throb. "Do you need my help anymore?"

"No, I'm fine, thanks."

"All right, then. Good night." She turned and walked stiffly into the bedroom, flopped onto the bed, and pulled the sheet to her chin.

Meghan

om was already snoring by the time Meghan got the snarls out of her hair and wrestled herself into pajamas. The dogs lay in a row at Mom's feet, two on their sides, two on their stomachs with their chins resting on their paws. All four watched Meghan with round eyes but didn't get up as she moved quietly around the bedroom. Well, as quietly as she could on the clunky crutches, which wasn't terribly quiet. Mom must have been too pooped to notice.

She started to crawl into the opposite side of the queen-sized bed but then paused and stifled a groan. She'd promised to call Sean when she got settled in so he'd know she made it all right. Even though he was her work partner—and the unit didn't encourage partners to get too attached—she and Sean had formed a fast friendship. She wondered how they couldn't, given their close working conditions and their reliance on each other.

She'd never forget his stricken face when the paramedics lifted her from her mangled Toyota onto the wheeled gurney or the way he grabbed her hand. When she came out from under the anesthesia after surgery, he was there with Mom, waiting. A lump filled her throat. He cared about her—more than any man in her life, ever—so she shouldn't worry him.

She pulled her cell phone from its charger on the dresser and limped to the living room, where she wouldn't disturb Mom, the dogs, or Grandma. Grandma's wingback chair offered a welcoming embrace when she sank onto the floral cushions. She propped her cast on the matching island-sized ottoman, held the phone to her mouth, and pushed the voice recognition button.

"Sean."

The phone buzzed his number. Less than thirty seconds later his bright voice came through the receiver.

"Hey, Meghan. I'd about given up on you." His rumbling chuckle rolled and she smiled. Sean was one of the most innately cheerful people she knew. "How'd the flight go?"

"Great. No complications at all. People were really helpful, the way you said they'd be."

"Figured so." No smugness at all colored his tone, just a matter-of-fact confidence she'd always found endearing. "Kinda hard for real men to ignore a damsel in distress."

She laughed. "I'm hardly in distress." A broken ankle was nothing compared to what others in the accident suffered. Then again, their deaths distressed her. For the first time in her life she'd attended funerals for complete strangers. She'd needed the closure. Not that it helped much.

"Grandma had a limo waiting, and she'd furnished it with Dr Pepper and Junior Mints. So the spoiling has begun."

"Well, bless her heart. You deserve it after what you've been through. Tell her thank you for me."

"I will." She should hang up, go to bed, and get some sleep, but somehow it was nice to sit there in the peaceful, cloaked-with-shadows room with nothing but the gentle *ticktock* of the grandfather clock and Sean's resonant voice keeping her company. "How's my replacement detective working out? Are you two getting along okay?"

A soft laugh carried to her ear. "We get along fine, as long as I don't expect too much. He's not even a real rookie—still hasn't graduated—and nervous as a squirrel trying to store nuts on the peak of a steep roof in a windy county."

Her imagination conjured the image, and she stifled a blast of laughter. "What a thing to say!"

"You haven't met him, so don't judge."

"Okay. I'll take your word for it. But, really, if he's that green, he's landed in good hands. You'll be patient with him." More than any of the other detectives. The newbie didn't know how lucky he was.

"Yeah, well, I remember what it's like to be the new guy on board. But hey, enough about me. How's your grandma? I know it's been a while and you were kind of concerned about how you'd find her."

Meghan spent a few minutes telling him about Grandma having tea and her favorite cookies ready, how beautiful she looked, and the graceful way she still moved even though arthritis showed in her bulging knuckles and twisted fingers. As Meghan talked, love and admiration filled her, and she found herself battling the sting of tears. "I should've gotten out here before now. I mean, how much longer will she be around? I'm not crazy about the reason that brought me here this time, but I'm sure glad I came."

"I'll pray your whole time with her turns out to be a blessing for both of you."

Meghan smiled, touched by his sincerity. "Thanks. But if you really wanna pray about something—" She gave a jolt. Since when did she ask for prayer?

"What is it?"

She should've stayed quiet. What would he think about the rift between Mom and Grandma? Men weren't emotional like women. "Um . . ."

"C'mon, Meghan. What's up?"

Grandma had always told her God cared about her and her concerns. Sean believed it, too. Even if she wondered if God was real and really cared, she trusted Sean to care. "It might sound kind of trivial, but Mom showed up out of the blue."

"You mean without telling anyone she was coming?"

"Uh-huh, and she plans to stay the whole time."

"Really? Wow . . ."

She nodded, releasing a little huff. "Yeah. I'm still not one hundred percent sure why she bothered, other than to make sure Grandma and I don't bond too much over the next several weeks. Grandma isn't Mom's most favorite person in the world." Funny how much it hurt to say that. Maybe Meghan hadn't completely lost the hurt, confused little girl inside of her.

"That's too bad."

She swallowed and hugged the phone closer to her cheek. "They've already been squabbling. Mostly Mom's doing—her attitude stinks. And it really bothers Grandma. Her eightieth is coming up and I wanted this time to be special, but with Mom . . ." How childish this all sounded. As if Sean—or God—would care about such petty grievances. She scrubbed the air with one hand, wishing she could erase her words. "Never mind. Forget I said anything."

"No, obviously this is bothering you. You love both of them. If they're at odds and you're all under the same roof for several weeks, of course it's going to affect you. There's nothing wrong with wanting peace."

How well he understood. She blinked back unexpected tears. "That's exactly what I want—peace between Mom and Grandma. I love both of them, and it's like I've been caught between them my whole life. Grandma's not going to be around forever. They don't have years to waste. I really want them to find what you said . . . peace."

"Then let's pray about it."

She pulled the phone away from her head and stared at the screen. Her pulse stampeded. She scrambled for words the way the squirrel on the rooftop would scramble for his escaping winter storehouse. She placed the phone to her ear again and rasped, "Now?"

"Sure, now." He sounded as certain as she was hesitant. "God doesn't sleep. He's listening. So let's talk to Him."

When she was a kid, during the summer weeks with Grandma, Meghan had recited bedtime and mealtime prayers Grandma taught her, but she'd never said a prayer of her own. She had no idea what to say.

"Dear heavenly Father . . ."

She closed her eyes and bowed her head, the way Grandma had taught her.

"Your Son told His followers, 'My peace I give you. I do not give to you as the world gives. Do not let your hearts be troubled.' Peace is a gift directly from You, and right now Meghan needs it."

A lump filled her throat. She tried to swallow it, but it wouldn't go down. She curled both hands around the phone and held tight.

"Be with her, her mom, and her grandmother. Be the calming presence in their midst. Bind them together in love and caring, and stifle any temptation to stir conflict. Let their time together meld them into the close family Meghan's always longed for."

Her eyes popped open. She'd said very little. How could Sean know how deeply she wanted—needed—unity between Mom and Grandma?

"And, God, remind Meghan that You are her Father. Let her lean on You and trust You—not her mother or even her beloved grandmother—to be her deepest source of peace."

Now he was creeping her out. Of course he knew she'd been raised without a father—everyone in the cold-case unit knew. But she'd never told him or anyone else how much she'd always pined for a father's influence in her life. Why else would she have attached herself to the drug-abuse prevention officer who visited her fifth-grade class once a week the whole year? She'd chosen to go into a form of police work because of Officer Alan.

Her entire body quivered, but she wasn't sure if apprehension or longing created the reaction.

"When full healing comes, to You will be given all praise and glory. I thank You now for the work You will complete in Meghan, Diane, and . . . and . . ."

"Hazel," Meghan supplied.

"Hazel's"—she distinctly heard a smile in his voice, and she couldn't resist smiling, too—"relationship. Amen."

"Amen." She didn't know why, but it was natural and felt really good— warm and comforting—to release the word. She slumped into the chair, as weary as if she'd run a marathon, yet also strangely revived. She licked her lips. "Thank you, Sean."

"You're welcome. I'll pray for you every day, okay?"

"Thanks. I'd appreciate that." Her voice sounded croaky. Probably because of the knot of emotion still lodged in her throat.

"No problem. And you know something? I don't think your mom showing up is a bad thing. Even though it might be awkward at first, I think she needs to be there. Give me a call every now and then and let me know how things are going so I can pray specifically, all right?"

"I'll do that."

"Good. But now, do you mind if we call it quits? The time difference . . . it's way past midnight and—"

She gasped. She should've called much earlier. "I forgot! I'm so sorry."

"It's all right. I'm glad we had a chance to talk. And pray together." His tone changed, a bit of his usual confidence melting and something else, maybe shyness, creeping in. "I'm really glad you let me pray for you, Meghan. That means a lot to me."

She wasn't sure why it mattered so much, and now wasn't the time to ask. He needed to sleep. "I'll give you a holler tomorrow. Or maybe Sunday afternoon, okay? Sleep now. And thanks again, Sean."

She pushed the disconnect button and dropped the phone into her lap. She stared across the dark room, replaying Sean's prayer. He'd sounded so sure that Someone was listening, that Someone would answer. A lonely ache built in the center of her chest. Mom had always called religion a bunch of hogwash, a crutch for weaklings and imbeciles, or a club for hypocrites, but Sean's life didn't match those descriptions.

". . . *You are her Father. Let her lean on You and trust You—not her mother or even her beloved grandmother—to be her deepest source of peace.*"

She raised her gaze to the ceiling, imagining the black sky studded with stars on the other side. "If You're there, God, would You do what Sean asked? Would You bring us . . . me . . . peace?"

Late August 1943
Cumpton, Arkansas
Hazel Mae

Hazel sneaked out the back door of the house and scuffed across the backyard, kicking up clumps of dirt and tufts of uncut grass as she went. She closed herself inside the chicken coop, but it didn't help. Mama's and Daddy's angry voices reached her even there.

She sat cross-legged on the straw-covered floor. One of the laying hens came close and pecked at her bare toes. She gave the hen a little push, and it scuttled off, clucking. Her head low, she toyed with a piece of straw. At least Mama and Daddy were talking. That was better than sitting at the table and not saying anything to each other. The latest silence had lasted three days. Hazel had hardly been able to eat a bite during those long, stony days. Her neck muscles still ached from gritting her teeth so tight to keep from screaming.

But did they have to yell? She hated it when they yelled at each other. She wished they'd yell at her instead. She didn't know why it was easier on her heart. She just knew it hurt worse when they fought with each other.

She rested her chin in her hands and blinked back tears. Sweat dribbled down her temples. The dirty windows blocked most of the sun. The musty smell of the coop—it hadn't been cleaned in a good long while—made her nose twitch. Maybe she should get the rake, scrape out the soiled straw, and replace it with fresh. The chickens would appreciate it. Daddy might even thank her.

She didn't move. She didn't care about the chickens pecking around in poop-speckled straw. Didn't even care she was getting her dress yucky by sitting on it. The striped green muslin was already dirty from three days' wearing. Mama hadn't even noticed. And Hazel didn't care if she never wore another clean dress. She didn't care about anything. Not anymore.

Why hadn't she realized Maggie was the one who brought the joy to their house? Maybe she should've figured it out. After all, Daddy had agreed to stop drinking when Mama was expecting Maggie. When Maggie was there, Daddy was at the supper table every night, smiling, laughing, talking. Mama hummed when she worked, and sometimes she talked to Hazel like they were friends instead of mother and daughter. Not always, but sometimes.

Now Daddy stayed in the barn until late at night. Sometimes all night. Mama never hummed. When she talked to Hazel, she either snapped or talked so syrupy sweet it didn't feel natural. Nobody tucked her in at night. Nobody said bedtime prayers with her. Nobody prayed at all. Well, except for Hazel. She still prayed. Every night she prayed the same thing.

She whispered the prayer again, there in the smelly, dim, lonely chicken coop. "Let us find Maggie, God. Please bring her home."

The preacher'd told their family Maggie was most likely already home with God and Jesus. Her shoe on the creek bank—the creek that was moving fast and hard because of all the rain the month before—meant she'd probably fallen in, got swept far away. He even thought they should have a funeral, but Mama said no. Hazel was glad of that. How could people have a funeral when there wasn't a body to bury?

Hazel had gotten brave and told the preacher what Mrs. Burton said, hoping he'd send the sheriff after the Gypsy wagon, but he didn't believe the Gypsies took her. Said stories about Gypsies stealing little children was all superstitious nonsense. He'd told Hazel, *"I know it's hard, honey, but you have to accept that your little sister is gone."*

The preacher was a smart man and he knew lots of things, but Hazel wanted him to be wrong about the Gypsies. Because if the Gypsies had Maggie, that meant she was alive. And maybe she'd come back.

She had to come back.

Hazel slipped to her knees. The straw cut into her skin, but she didn't care. The preacher said when people prayed, they should do it on their knees as a sign of humility before God. She'd messed up with that last prayer, letting it slip out while she was sitting on her bottom. But surely He'd listen better if she knelt.

She clasped her hands beneath her chin and closed her eyes tight. "Dear God, let Maggie come home again. Please? We—Mama an' Daddy an' me— we'll never have peace until she does."

Seven

*H*azel rolled onto her side and pushed the button on her alarm clock. The *buzz* ended abruptly, but her ears continued to ring for a few seconds. She snapped on the bedside lamp and lay curled like a question mark, blinking, letting her eyes adjust. The morning sky would already be changing from pink to yellow at six thirty, but the thick shades and room-darkening curtains blocked even a blush of sunlight. Without the lamp, her room was as dark as the interior of a cave. And she liked it that way when she slept. But now was time to wake.

She tugged the light covers aside and swung her feet over the edge of the bed. For a moment she sat, hands braced on her knees, and stared at her old, wrinkled, scrawny feet sticking out from her pajama pant legs. Even with the nails painted shell pink, her feet weren't so pretty. But then, they weren't meant for beauty. They were meant for holding a body upright, and for that they served their purpose well despite the many decades of use.

With a soft, self-deprecating chuckle, she rose and moved in short, choppy steps to her en suite. By the time she finished her morning routine, her old bones had loosened enough to allow a longer stride. She stepped into her walk-in closet and bounced her hand along the neatly spaced outfits, looking first at those in shades of yellow, then blue, then green, and finally red. She chose a bright-red silk tank with a white paisley design embroidered on the front, a pair of navy-blue culottes, and a lightweight white sweater shot through with nubby threads of red, yellow, and blue.

She dressed in the closet, then examined herself in her full-length mirror to ascertain the sweater hung straight and no stray threads dangled from the culottes. She'd worn the ensemble for the Fourth of July celebration at church less than two weeks ago. Several people had complimented her on its patriotic colors and the paisley design dotted with pearl sequins that emulated a burst of fireworks. Independence Day had passed, but the outfit seemed fitting for today, when she would most likely do battle with her independent, headstrong, always-determined-to-challenge-authority daughter. Not that Hazel was much of an authority over Margaret Diane anymore. Goodness, the girl was closer to fifty than forty. Truth be known, Hazel had lost all authority more than thirty years ago. Which was how Margaret Diane wound up with a daughter and no husband.

Hazel grimaced at her reflection. Ah, what a poor job she'd done in raising Margaret Diane. Would the sting of failure ever completely leave? Not that she didn't love her granddaughter. The child was a gift. How could she regret Meghan's presence?

But Hazel's generation viewed the marriage license as a precursor to intimacy. In her generation, most babies were born to wedded couples, and those who weren't were adopted by wedded couples. Even the orphans' home back in Cumpton during the Depression years hadn't allowed single people to adopt a child. Deliberately single, unwed mothers? Unheard of.

And, oh, how Margaret Diane had struggled financially and emotionally to be both mother and father from the beginning with her little girl. Hazel wouldn't cast stones—God knew she herself was a sinner saved by grace—yet her heart ached for the hard pathway her child had taken.

She pointed at herself in the full-length mirror. "And when she starts getting snippy and you're tempted to scold, you remember she's not had an easy life between losing her daddy and raising Meghan all by herself. Give her grace." She offered a stern scowl at her reflection and received its scowl in return. Then she shook her head, chuckling. "Here you stand talking to yourself like an old fool. Go make breakfast and see if the aroma of blueberry pancakes will coax a smile from that daughter of yours."

Blueberry pancakes had been their Sunday morning tradition all through Margaret Diane's growing-up years. Today was Saturday, not Sunday, but maybe the scent—and its reminder of frilly dresses, walking hand in hand up the sidewalk, and sitting with open Bibles in their laps—would stir pleasant memories, soften her daughter's belligerence a bit, and give them a good start to the day.

Dear Lord, please?

Half a dozen browned, blueberry-studded pancakes waited on a plate on the corner of the stove and another four were sizzling on the griddle when the soft *thump-thump* of footsteps sounded in the hallway. Hazel smiled and turned to offer a good-morning.

Instead of Margaret Diane, Meghan entered the kitchen. Still attired in a skinny-strapped snug-fitting top and baggy pants made of T-shirt material, with her dark hair disheveled, she looked at least a decade younger than her twenty-seven years. She sniffed the air like a bloodhound and grinned. "Mmm, smells great in here." She stuck her nose over the drip coffeepot. "Flavored coffee?"

"Hazelnut."

Meghan giggled. "Grandma Hazel made hazelnut."

Hazel couldn't resist a light laugh. The girl could be so impish. "Yes, well, it's my favorite. Especially with the addition of cream. None of that skim milk for me."

Meghan grimaced. "Yuck. For me, either." She stumped close to the stove. "Whatcha makin'?"

"Blueberry pancakes. This is the last batch." The bubbles around the edges of the cakes had lost their sheen. Time to turn them. Hazel slipped the spatula under a cake and flipped it. She sighed in satisfaction at the height of the cake, the crisp edges, and its light-brown center. Perfection. "As soon as these are done, I'll fix you a plate. Are you starving?"

"I'm hungry, mostly because this smells so good, but don't hurry." Meghan leaned against the counter and watched her turn the remaining cakes. "We're gonna be stuffed if we eat all of these in one sitting."

Hazel gave her granddaughter a teasing bump with her elbow. "Ten pancakes divided by three breakfast eaters isn't too many."

"Two."

"Two what?"

"Two breakfast eaters."

Hazel frowned. "Where is Margaret Diane?" Had she packed her bag and sneaked off without a word, the way she'd done half a dozen times between the ages of sixteen and eighteen?

"She's still in bed."

"The aroma will get her up." Hazel held to hope.

"Probably. It did for me. But she won't eat those. She's vegan."

A scorched smell reached Hazel's nose. With a little grunt, she transferred the remaining pancakes to the plate. A dark circle on the bottom of each marred their perfect appearance. Why couldn't she do anything right? She blinked several times to hold back tears and then turned to Meghan. "What on earth are you talking about? Vegan . . . what does that mean?" Had her daughter joined some sort of crazy cult? As much as it pained her to admit it, it wouldn't surprise her.

Meghan shrugged. She broke off a small piece of one of the pancakes and popped it in her mouth. She released a low groan, eyes closed. "Just as I thought—homemade with milk and eggs, right?"

Was there any other way to make pancakes? "Of course."

"Mom switched to a vegan diet about a year and a half ago. She only eats plant-based foods. Since you put milk and eggs in the batter, she won't eat the pancakes."

Hazel's jaw dropped. "Is that why she only ate the steamed broccoli and cauliflower for supper last night?" She'd presumed the pork chops were too well done and the brown rice too bland for her daughter's taste, and she'd berated herself for fixing such a dismal supper.

Meghan nodded. "You seasoned the veggies with salt and pepper, which was fine, but you put butter on the rice. And of course pork chops are from an animal, so . . ."

"And she didn't say a word."

Meghan shrugged again, a silent apology creasing her face.

"Of all the harebrained—" Hazel bit down on the tip of her tongue. Hadn't she just prayed for a good start to the day? *God, not to be irreverent, but sometimes I wonder if You listen to me at all.*

She pulled in a deep breath and blew it out. She held her hands toward the ingredients on the counter. "Then what will she eat?"

"The blueberries. The flour." Meghan tapped her chin. "There's actually a vegan pancake you can make with soy or nut milk."

Hazel wrinkled her nose.

Meghan laughed. "I'm with ya, but she did a lot of research, and she swears she's healthier now that she's off animal products."

Hazel balled one hand on her hip and gave a mock scowl. "Well, I ate eggs and bacon and ham and fresh-churned butter every day when I was a child, and here I still am eighty years later. So what does that tell you?"

Margaret Diane, surrounded by her doggy entourage, scuffed into the kitchen. The lines of irritation etched on her forehead let Hazel know she'd heard every word of the conversation with Meghan. "It tells us you have a strong constitution, Mother. Congratulations. But my cholesterol has dropped almost a hundred points since I started yoga and went vegan, and my lean muscle mass has improved. So no bacon, eggs, or butter for me, thanks." She opened the sliding door and shooed the dogs into the small backyard.

Hazel started to remind her to go out and pick up the dogs' mess when they'd finished their business. Yesterday's deposits were still out in the corner near her pond. But she caught herself and swallowed the comment instead. Maybe God had listened to her morning prayers after all. "Well, later we'll visit the grocery store and get some things that will suit your diet."

"It isn't a diet. It's a lifestyle."

Hazel held back a sharp retort. *Thank You.* "In the meantime, I need to find you something . . ." She snapped her fingers. "I picked up a box of granola the last time I went to the store. I like to sprinkle granola over my yogurt—gives it a little crunch. When I got home and was putting it away, I realized it was gluten free. Maybe you can have some of that with yogurt and blueberries." She aimed a hopeful look at Margaret Diane.

"Yogurt is milk based, and milk comes from a cow. I never touch the stuff." Her daughter lifted one shoulder in a flippant half shrug. "But I'll check the ingredients on the granola. Sometimes even if it's gluten free it has animal by-products. You don't find gluten in fat, you know."

Hazel hadn't known, and an unwelcome rush of embarrassment claimed her. She opened the cabinet, withdrew the box, and set it on the counter. "If you can't eat it, you might as well throw it away. I didn't care for its texture." She gestured to the small round table in front of the bay window. "Have a seat, Meghan, and I'll serve these pancakes before they're cold and dried out. Butter and maple syrup?"

"Sounds great, Grandma."

At least Meghan was easily satisfied.

Hazel had already set the table with three place settings, but she still needed to get the juice and butter from the refrigerator. She opened the refrigerator door, and Margaret Diane let in the dogs. The menagerie trotted straight to Hazel, their nails clicking on the tile floor, and surrounded her feet.

Panic set in so quickly it stole her ability to breathe for a few seconds. She waved her hand at them. "Here now, you go on!"

Margaret Diane hustled over, frowning. "You don't need to holler at them. They're just used to having a treat every morning." She reached past Hazel and removed a package of string cheese from the shelf. "Come here, darlings. Mommy will give you your yummy."

How could she speak so sweetly to the dogs while glaring at Hazel?

Margaret Diane plopped into one of the kitchen chairs and began peeling the wrapper from a stick of cheese. The dogs leaped and yipped, their shrill barks like nails pounding into Hazel's temples.

Hazel pressed her hand to her forehead. "Would you not feed them at the table, please? I'd rather they didn't presume the humans' eating spot is also for them."

Margaret Diane jerked to her feet and stomped out of the kitchen. The dogs followed her, jumping over each other in their eagerness. With their departure, Hazel's limbs went weak. She braced her palms on the edge of the counter and hung her head. Her heart continued to thrum, her pulse pounding in her temple, and her entire body quivered. She pulled in long, slow breaths, willing her pulse to calm and the fluttery feeling under her skin to cease.

A hand descended on her shoulder and she jumped.

"I'm sorry, I didn't mean to startle you." Meghan eased beside her, her hand still cupped comfortingly over Hazel's shoulder. "I'm going to talk to Mom about the dogs. It isn't fair for you to be scared in your own house."

So Meghan had recognized her weakness. She scrunched her eyes closed. Images of baby bunnies and a black snake swooped in behind her closed lids. She popped them open and focused on her granddaughter's face. The concern she saw there pierced her even more than the memories.

"No, honey, it's all right." Hazel straightened. A few strands of hair had fallen across Meghan's forehead. She smoothed them into place with her fingers and tried to smile. Her lips quivered too much. She swallowed. "I love Margaret Diane, and she loves those dogs. So for my daughter's sake, I'll learn to share the house with them."

Meghan rubbed her hand up and down Hazel's arm the way a mother would soothe a crying baby. "Mom told me she didn't have pets when she was growing up because you hated animals. But I don't think it's hate as much as fear. Did a dog attack you or something when you were little?"

"No. I was never attacked by a dog."

"Then why—"

Hazel stepped away from Meghan's tender touch. "Those pancakes are fixing to be as hard and inedible as hockey pucks. Go, sit. I'll get the juice and syrup, and we'll"—she drew in another shuddering breath and raised her chin—"eat."

Eight

Meghan

I'll drive, Mother, and you can tell me where to go."

Meghan choked back a chortle. Mom wouldn't appreciate the humor, but if Grandma were less of a lady, she might really do what Mom suggested.

Grandma paused at the door with her bright-red pocketbook, which matched her sequined ballet flats, tucked under her arm. "Meghan, are you sure you don't want to go, too?"

For a moment Meghan considered hobbling along behind the two of them through the grocery store aisles. But an hour or so to herself, not having to play peacemaker, appealed to her. Besides, maybe they'd get a few things talked out on the drive to and from the store. She shook her head. "Thanks, but I'm going to start sorting photos and decide which ones I want to put in the scrapbook, so go ahead."

Grandma nodded. "All right. If you want to gather up a few more pictures, the albums from your mother's childhood are on the shelf here in the living room. And there's a box of loose photos in the bottom drawer of the built-in dresser in my closet. Help yourself."

"The morning's half gone already, Mother. Let's go before it gets any hotter outside." Mom opened the front door and gestured Grandma out. "I honestly don't know how you live with this—"

The door closed on Mom's complaint, leaving Meghan in silence except for the comforting beats of the antique clock and the occasional whimper coming from the bedroom, where Mom had shut the dogs in their pet taxis so Meghan could spread pictures across the floor without worrying about one of them getting carried off or chewed on. She stood for a few seconds in the middle of the living room, eyes closed, enjoying the reprieve. So peaceful . . .

She gave a start and glanced at the clock. Nine forty-five, which meant it was eleven forty-five back in Arkansas. What was Sean doing by now? He always started his day with Bible reading and prayer, a practice most of the detectives deemed unmanly. Why'd the guys have to pick at Sean so much? It wasn't like his Bible reading hurt anybody. Sometimes people were plain stupid. Even though it was Saturday, when lots of people slept in, Meghan hoped he'd still gotten up early and prayed for her and Mom and Grandma. They needed the peace he promised to request.

The suitcase with photographs waited on the Italian tile that served as a foyer. Meghan left one crutch beside the ottoman and half hopped, half walked the few feet to the suitcase. She took hold of the telescoping handle and, again hopping on one foot, pulled the suitcase to the ottoman. With a few grunts and a couple of the milder words uttered by some of the guys in the office, she managed to pull the suitcase onto it. She flopped into Grandma's chair and unzipped the case.

For nearly a half hour she entertained herself by looking at the pictures and enjoying the memories they raised. Strange how the fuzzy photographs brought such sharp images to her mind. She could not attach one unpleasant memory to Grandma. And apparently Mom couldn't find a pleasant one. Why? The question tormented her. She couldn't balance the Grandma she loved with the woman Mom perceived her to be.

Maybe Grandma's photographs would help.

She was familiar with the albums on the shelf. Every year, she and Grandma had spent time looking through the pages during her visits. So she grabbed her crutches, pushed herself to her feet, and stumped around the corner and up the short hallway to Grandma's suite. She stopped right inside the door and smiled. As a little girl, she'd loved sneaking into Grandma's bedroom early in the morning and crawling into bed with her. Mom grunted and fussed if Meghan disturbed her sleep, but Grandma murmured and pulled her close.

The warmth of security flooded Meghan's frame as she let her gaze drift around the tidy room. An unfamiliar quilt covered the bed, but little else had changed over the years. The pieces of the same sturdy maple bedroom set Grandma and Grandpa purchased after their wedding in 1963 sat in the same locations. The same silver comb, brush, and hand mirror—Grandma's high school graduation present from her parents—rested on a doily in the center of the dresser. A collage of framed family portraits, the first with Mom as a baby and ending when she was upper grade school, decorated the same wall. And the photo of Meghan as a toothless, pigtailed six-year-old remained prominently on the corner of the nightstand, seeming to guard Grandma's Bible.

As usual, not a speck of dust marred any surface, and the dark-blue curtains were drawn so they fell in alignment with the inside lines of the window casing. Meghan couldn't recall a time when her childhood apartment had been this clean—not even when Mom expected company. Another way Mom and Grandma were very, very different.

She entered the closet and moved past the rods of clothes to the built-in chest centered on the back wall. She leaned the crutches against the shoe shelf and went down on one knee, careful to keep her good foot underneath her so she'd be able to get up again. Then she slid the bottom drawer open. As Grandma had said, a rectangular box made out of thick gray cardboard with its fitted top bolstered by strips of yellowed Scotch tape waited in the drawer. She'd seen similar boxes holding department-store sweaters when she watched old episodes of *I Love Lucy* reruns with Grandma. Another pleasant memory.

A few lines written in pencil filled the upper-right-hand corner of the lid. She squinted to make out the message—*Mama and Daddy, these are my secret treshures. Please do not peak. Love, Hazel Mae*

Meghan scrunched her brow, touching her grandmother's signature. If this box contained treasures, why weren't they being displayed in the curio cabinet that held Depression-era glass, figurines, and Grandma's collection of little porcelain boxes painted with flowers and butterflies? Maybe she'd used the box for something else when she was younger and the childish treasures were long gone. She'd ask Grandma when she returned, but for now curiosity compelled her to lift the box from the drawer, handling it as carefully as she would a fine-china plate.

Meghan balanced the box on her bent knee and slipped the lid free. She gave an involuntary jolt of surprise at the jumbled mess of black-and-white photographs. This couldn't belong to Grandma. The box slipped from her knee and landed on the carpeted floor. Photos scattered, and she grunted in aggravation. She shifted to her bottom, then began gathering the brittle images, turning them right-side up as she did so.

One picture leaped out at her, and she froze in place with the photo staring up at her. A little girl, perhaps six or seven, with dark hair held back from her forehead by a lopsided bow sat on the bottom steps of a farmhouse porch. One arm was draped around the neck of a collie-type dog, and the other held an unhappy-looking cat in her lap. Even though the photo was black and white and from long ago, she was certain she glimpsed Grandma in the child's smile.

She turned it over and a handwritten note—*Hazel Mae with Boots and Farley, Sept. 1940*—confirmed what she suspected. The little girl was her grandmother. And there she sat, smiling, not a hint of apprehension on her face, with the family pets in her arms. So at one time she hadn't been afraid of animals. When had her feelings toward pets changed? Generally, children who loved animals grew to be adults who loved animals—like Mom, who had more pets than everybody else in the neighborhood combined and who volunteered at the animal shelter twice a month.

Her detective instincts kicked up a notch. Questions about Mom's attitude toward Grandma, a tearful comment Grandma had made about the Lord sometimes letting memories slip away when speaking about the scrapbook, her obvious discomfort around Mom's dogs when at one time she hadn't been afraid at all, even the scrawling words *secret treshures* on the box combined to form a whirlwind of curiosity.

Something in Grandma's past had colored her. Changed her. Something sinister? Something horrific? Something deeply painful? Meghan didn't know, but a part of her wanted to uncover it. And a part of her dreaded discovering the truth.

Diane

Diane untangled the reusable-grocery-bag handles from her wrists and set the bags on the kitchen counter. "Leave these—I'll put things away after I let the dogs out."

"You carried everything in." Mother began removing items from the closest bag. "I'll put things away."

Diane rolled her eyes. Mother could be so stubborn. But who'd won the battle about paying for the groceries? Diane had, and she was tempted to push for the win on this one, too, but the dachshunds were yipping for attention. Besides, Mother knew where she had space in her cupboards. "All right, suit yourself."

She rounded the corner to the hallway. As she passed the living room doorway, she glanced in. Meghan's ugly red suitcase lay open on the ottoman, a few photographs strewn across the arms of the wingback chair. But Meghan wasn't there. She paused. "Meghan? Where are you?"

"Back here—in Grandma's closet."

The *yips* from the guest room increased in volume, but Diane headed for her mother's bedroom instead. The closet door stood open, light painting a path across the carpet. Diane trotted the final few feet, expecting to find her daughter helplessly sprawled on the floor.

Meghan sat with one leg bent, the other stretched out in front of her as if she'd landed a cheerleading maneuver. She looked up and smiled. "You're back. Did you find lots of things you can eat?"

Diane blew out a breath of half relief, half aggravation. She glanced around the space, pursing her lips. Clothes arranged by color, sweaters folded to the same width and stacked so they resembled a solid unit. Not one sock lay on the floor. Not even a piece of lint. Why did Mother have to be so well ordered in every aspect of her life, even behind closet doors?

She shook her head and then looked at Meghan. "When you said you were in the closet, I thought you'd be like one of those 'I've fallen and I can't get up' ladies in the commercials."

Meghan laughed. "I didn't fall—I chose to sit. But you're right that I'm stuck. Help?" She held out her hands.

Diane took hold and pulled her to her feet. "What were you doing in here?"

Meghan grabbed the crutches and positioned them under her arms. Then she bobbed her chin at the floor. "Looking at Grandma's photos. Would you put them back in the box? I started sorting them by the dates on the backs, but not all of them are marked, so Grandma will have to help."

Diane arched one eyebrow. "They weren't already sorted?"

Meghan shook her head. "Nope. They were left in one big mess."

So there was one place where Mother's perfection hadn't reached. She crouched and transferred the photograph stacks to the box. She rose, lifting the box with her. She frowned at the photographs. "These are really old. I've never seen them before."

"Never?" Meghan maneuvered herself out of the closet and flicked off the light as she went.

Diane followed her and closed the door. "No. Our family albums start with pictures of me as a baby. Other than a wedding picture, I don't think there are any of my parents by themselves."

As a small child, she'd thought her mother's and dad's lives began as full-grown adults when she arrived on the scene. When she got older and wiser, she still felt her mother's real life hadn't begun until Diane's birth. Her obsessive mothering swallowed everything else. So these photographs of Mother as a child left her disjointed and uneasy.

She placed the box inside Meghan's suitcase and then hurried to the bedroom to open the dogs' crates. She knelt down and began unlatching them.

"All right, Ginger, stop jumping. You're going to hurt yourself. Miney, Duchess, that's enough now—I'm here. Yes, yes, Molly, I haven't forgotten you. Here you go, now, come on out."

The quartet, all free, pranced around her, licking, yipping, their noses wrinkling and teeth gleaming with their unique doggy grins. Diane couldn't help laughing. She needed to herd them outside—Mother would have a fit if one of them accidentally widdled on the carpet—but she took the time to give them scratches on the neck, strokes on their silky ears, and tummy rubs when they rolled on their backs.

She heard a chuckle, and she glanced over her shoulder to find Meghan in the doorway. Self-consciousness struck hard. She jerked upright and spun to face her daughter. "What?" The word barked out on a defensive note.

Meghan's smile didn't dim. "You're so sweet to those mutts. Is that the way you talked to me when I was a baby?"

Pressure built in Diane's chest. She'd always loved her daughter, never neglected her, but she hadn't coddled her. She wanted Meghan to see herself as capable. Capable of self-soothing as an infant, of entertaining herself as a toddler, of meeting her own basic needs as a child. She thought she'd done it right because Meghan was a strong, self-assured, independent young woman. But the expression on her daughter's face—the hopeful expectation that at one time Diane had lavished her with affection the way she did Ginger, Duchess, Miney, and Molly—made her wonder if she'd made a big mistake. She didn't know how to answer.

Meghan shrugged. "Never mind. Dumb question. Of course you wouldn't talk to me like I was a stupid dog."

"The dogs aren't—"

"Stupid. I know. Just an expression." Meghan shifted, grimacing slightly, the way someone whose sleeping limbs were waking up might react. "Grandma wants to know if the organic salad dressing needs to go in the fridge."

"Only after opening."

Meghan nodded and started to turn.

"Meghan . . ."

She angled a questioning look at Diane.

"I never babied you. Not the way I do . . ." Diane flapped her hand toward the dogs, who still writhed in delight around her ankles. "Because they need to depend on me. You don't. Do you understand?"

Meghan gazed at her for long seconds, eyebrows pinched inward, lips set in an unsmiling line. Then she gave a brusque nod. "Yeah, I understand. You wanted me to stand on my own two feet." She glanced at the cast wrapped in pink tape and bearing half a dozen signatures scribbled in black Sharpie. "Of course, now that I'm down to one good foot, I hope you won't mind if I lean on you a little bit."

"You can lean a lot if you want to." Diane pushed the statement past an unwelcome knot of regret.

A funny, crooked smile graced Meghan's face. "Thanks, Mom." She turned and hobbled off.

Nine

Hazel

*H*azel placed the last of the canned lentils and black beans on the pantry shelf. She turned one of the black-bean cans so the label was centered and then flipped off the light and stepped into the kitchen. She'd folded each of the reusable bags as she'd emptied them and they waited in a neat stack at the end of the counter. She transferred the stack to the bottom drawer next to the refrigerator, stood up straight, and gave the kitchen a quick perusal. Nothing out of place. With a satisfied nod, she entered the living room.

All four of Margaret Diane's dachshunds lounged on the sofa, filling two-thirds of the space. Meghan occupied the remaining cushion. Margaret Diane sat on the floor near Meghan's feet, and the two of them were examining black-and-white photographs. They painted such a tender picture, a smile tugged at the corners of Hazel's mouth.

Meghan glanced up and caught Hazel watching them. Her face lit. "There you are, Grandma. Come here and help me—some of these photos don't have anything written on the back."

Hazel took two forward steps, her gaze drifting across the old photographs. Her body went cold, as if someone had dumped a vat of ice water over her head. She planted one hand on her chest. "Where did you get these?"

"From the bottom drawer in your closet."

Hazel's pulse thrummed in erratic double beats. "What were you doing in my closet?"

Confusion marred her granddaughter's face. "I, um . . ."

Margaret Diane flapped her hand at the black-and-white images. "You told her she could help herself to the older photographs in your built-in bureau. Don't you remember?"

"Don't snap at me, Margaret Diane. Of course I remember. I'm old, but I'm not senile." Hazel grasped a handful of the fabric resting over her heart. Sequins pricked her fingers as memories pricked her mind. "I told you to look in the box in the top drawer."

Meghan offered an apologetic grimace. "I'm sorry, Grandma. I thought you said bottom."

"She did say bottom drawer." Margaret Diane folded her arms over her chest. "I distinctly heard her say 'bottom drawer.'"

Maybe she was growing senile. How else could she have made such a foolish mistake? Hazel's feet didn't want to cooperate, but she forced them to carry her to the circle of photographs. She bent over and collected them with jerky, almost uncontrolled motions. Her muscles had gone stiff and her fingers clumsy. A pulse beat in her left temple like a tom-tom. "Didn't you see the note on the top of the box? These weren't meant to be seen by anyone but me." Tears threatened and her voice took on a tremor.

Meghan slid the photos into one pile. "I'm really sorry. I thought the note was meant for your parents when you were still a girl. If I'd realized—"

"No, no . . ." Her granddaughter's genuine remorse pierced Hazel. She dropped the stack of photographs into the box and straightened, hugging the box to her heart. She aimed an apologetic smile at Meghan. "It was my mistake. As my daughter is fond of pointing out, I'm getting old. Sometimes I get things confused. I'll put these away now and get the right box."

Meghan cringed. "Um . . . Grandma, I already used a couple of them."

Prickles raced across her flesh like wind-driven raindrops down a windowpane. "What do you mean you used them?"

She pointed to a square piece of paper that resembled vintage wallpaper. Two photographs formed a pair of stair steps on the page. "Since the album is your birthday present, I scoped out what looked like birthday pictures."

Hazel stared at the top image. "That . . . That's not . . ."

Margaret Diane arched her brow. "It must be a birthday picture. It can't be Christmas because there's no snow and you're wearing a summery dress. Plus, you're holding what is obviously a new doll." She tapped the picture. "I can even see the tag hanging from the doll's wrist." She nudged Meghan. "Too bad we can't make out the price written on it. I bet it's a lot less than what I paid for the dolls I bought you for birthday presents."

Meghan flashed a grin at her mother and turned to Hazel. "If it isn't a birthday picture, when was it taken?"

Hazel's mouth was too dry to form an answer. Her pulse still pounded. Her head felt light and empty yet somehow heavy and full at the same time. Stars began to dance in front of her eyes. Her muscles went weak and the box dropped from her hands. She made one feeble grab for the box, and her body lurched. Meghan cried out, and Hazel's world went black.

Meghan

"Grandma? Grandma?" Meghan stroked her grandmother's soft, pale cheek. She'd gone over so fast there hadn't been time to catch her.

Grandma murmured, but she didn't open her eyes.

Mom knelt on the other side of Grandma, hands braced on her knees, her face almost as white as Grandma's. "What's she saying?"

Meghan frowned. "I'm not sure, but I think it's 'I won't forget.'" Worry ate a hole in her stomach. She reached for her cell phone, which lay on the floor next to the ottoman. "I'm calling for an ambulance."

Grandma's eyelids fluttered. She lifted one hand a few inches. "No . . ."

Both Meghan and her mom leaned in. Mom touched Grandma's shoulder. "Mother?"

Grandma's bleary gaze fixed on Mom's face. "No ambulance. Help me up."

Mom flicked a look at Meghan. The uncertainty in her eyes made Meghan feel as if she were the mother and Mom the child. She offered Mom a reassuring smile and put her hand on Grandma's snow-white hair. "Lie still a little longer, Grandma, okay? Just to make sure the woozies are gone."

Grandma emitted a weak snort. "I've never had the woozies."

Meghan and Mom exchanged a grin. Meghan patted Grandma's arm. "Then lie still until my woozies are gone." She swallowed tears. "You scared me."

Grandma closed her eyes. A grimace twisted her face. "I'm sorry. I . . . I don't know what came over me. Must have been the heat. As Margaret Diane said in the parking lot at the grocery store, it's hot enough to bake cookies on the sidewalk."

Then why hadn't she collapsed in the parking lot or in the front yard instead of in the air-conditioned living room? She'd been fine until the saw the pictures. But Meghan wouldn't argue, mostly because she was relieved Grandma recalled something so specific from an hour ago. If something serious, like a stroke, had caused her to faint, she probably wouldn't remember details of her morning.

Meghan tapped Mom's hand. "Get a wet cloth to put on her forehead. It'll help cool her down." It would also get Mom out of the room long enough for Meghan to ask a question she didn't want Mom overhearing.

Mom trotted around the corner, and the quartet of dachshunds followed her. Meghan bent low and spoke into her grandmother's ear. "Grandma, you kept saying, 'I won't forget, I won't forget.' What were you remembering?"

Pink crept into Grandma's cheeks, making her look more alive, but she kept her eyes closed. Her lips trembled, her chin wobbling. "Why did you bring out that box?"

Regret nearly collapsed Meghan's chest. Why hadn't she been satisfied to look at the photographs in the albums on the shelf? If she'd known the agony it would create, she never would have gone into Grandma's closet. "I'm sorry. I thought it was the one you wanted me to use."

"It wasn't—" Grandma shifted her head from side to side as if writhing in pain. "I tried to—"

Meghan stroked her grandmother's hair. Slow, gentle strokes, meant to soothe. "It's okay. If you don't want to talk about it, you don't have to."

Her eyes popped open. Her brown irises were nearly swallowed by her pupils. She reached for Meghan's hand. Her lips parted.

Mom bustled into the room. "I'm sorry it took so long. I put the dogs in their crates in case we needed to call 911. They'd be in the way of the paramedics. Here." She handed Meghan a cool, moist, folded cloth, then slipped to her knees. "Is she coming around?"

Meghan laid the cloth across Grandma's forehead. "Yes, she—"

Grandma yanked the cloth from her head and pushed it into Meghan's hands. "As I've already told you repeatedly, I possess full use of my faculties. Don't talk about me as if I'm not in the room."

Mom smirked. "I'd say she's coming around."

"Yes, I am." She held out both arms. "Help me up, please. My hips are throbbing. I want to sit."

Mom drew back. "Are you sure? You hit the floor pretty hard."

"My floor is covered with carpet. Quality carpet, with a good pad under it. I'm not in any pain other than my hips, and that always happens when I'm flat on my back. Please help me up."

Meghan slid her arm behind Grandma's shoulders, and Mom gripped her elbow. "All right, Grandma, but if you start feeling dizzy, you tell us to stop." Meghan pushed, Mom pulled, and together they shifted Grandma to a seated position.

Grandma pressed her temples with her fingertips and let her eyes slide closed again.

Meghan kept her arm across her grandmother's shoulders. "Are you all right? Do you want to lie down again? Maybe we should put the cloth on the back of your neck. Mom, why don't you—"

"Please stop fussing over me. I'm all right. I'm merely gathering my . . . bearings."

Meghan was certain Grandma had intended to say something else.

Grandma took slow, deep breaths and blew them out in long exhales. After the third expulsion of air, she opened her eyes and lowered her hands. "Well, the Lord and I just had a little chat—"

Mom sent a startled look past Grandma to Meghan.

"—and I've decided my telling you to look in the bottom drawer instead of the top one was more serendipitous than senseless. As Ralph Waldo Emerson said, 'Shallow men believe in luck or in circumstance. Strong men believe in cause and effect.'" Grandma turned her gaze on Meghan. Moisture made her dark eyes shine. "I'm nearly eighty. How many years do I have left?"

Pain stabbed straight through Meghan. She'd had the same thought, but hearing the words spoken aloud by the very person she worried about losing was much worse than saying them to herself. She took Grandma's hand. "You have lots of years, Grandma."

Grandma shook her head, wrinkling her brow. "There's no guarantee of that. There's no guarantee any of us will even have tomorrow."

Mom abruptly stood. "Now you're being maudlin."

Grandma sighed. "Not maudlin. Realistic. And that's why I have to speak now. I have to tell you about . . ." She searched the floor around her, her fingers skimming over the photographs that still lay scattered on the carpet. She released a tiny cry of elation and snatched up the scrapbook page Meghan had started. "About her."

Ten

Diane

Diane glanced at the page her mother held. She bit down on the end of her tongue. Her mother was speaking of herself. In third person. She'd wondered when Mother's aging mind would begin to slip, and apparently the time had arrived. But since she seemed fully capable of speech and the color had returned to her face, they should get her off the floor.

"It's fine, Mother, if you want to talk about *her*." She shot a wry look at Meghan. "But how about we put you in your chair? You'll be more comfortable there."

Mother stretched her hands to Diane. "If you'll help me up, I'll put myself in my chair. It's kind of you to be concerned, but that syrupy tone you're using is condescending. Save it for someone else."

Diane choked back a snort and took hold of her mother's elbows. With one smooth pull, she brought her to her feet. Mother wobbled for a moment, then seemed to regain her balance. She removed herself from Diane's grip and moved the short distance to her wingback chair.

"Now help Meghan from the floor. We might as well all be comfortable, hmm?"

Diane offered Meghan the same assistance, and Meghan perched on the edge of the ottoman next to her suitcase. Diane plopped onto the sofa, at the end closest to Mother's chair. "All right, we're listening."

Mother pinched the page between the fingers of both hands. She held it in front of her and stared at the top photograph with such intensity Diane suspected she'd drifted away to some unknown place in the far recesses of her mind. She glanced at Meghan and found her daughter as transfixed with Mother's face as Mother was with the photo.

Diane cleared her throat. "Mother?"

Her mother gave a start and her gaze lifted. "Pardon me. I was . . . thinking. Remembering. After so many years of pushing the memories aside, it's both a joy and a heartache to open the floodgates." She turned to Meghan and drew in a shuddering breath. "Maggie . . ."

Meghan put her hand on Mother's knee. "I'm Meghan, Grandma." Her tone held both confusion and deep concern, emotions Diane understood. Something seemed seriously wrong with Mother. Maybe they should call the paramedics after all. Carpet or not, she might have bumped her head harder than they'd realized when she hit the floor. And having a medical record would benefit Diane when petitioning the court to declare her mother incapable of independent living.

Mother sighed. "Not you. Her." She flipped the page around and tapped her finger on the picture of the little girl holding the doll. "This . . . is . . . Maggie."

Diane found herself leaning toward the photograph, drawn by the mingled pain and release in her mother's expression. "Who is Maggie?"

Mother's eyes slipped closed. The corners of her lips quivered—was she trying to smile or trying not to cry? "My little sister."

"You had a sister?" Diane and Meghan chorused the question.

Diane held up her hand to silence her daughter. "I thought you were an only child."

Mother shook her head slowly. A single tear escaped one of her closed eyelids and trailed down her cheek, leaving a path in her rouge. "No. I had a sister." She opened her eyes and looked at Diane. More tears washed the rouge from her cheeks, and a crooked smile formed. "Her name was Margaret Rose. My parents always called me by my full name—Hazel Mae. But she was Maggie. Always sweetly, simply Maggie."

Meghan stared at the photo, which Mother continued to hold aloft like a child showing off a perfect spelling test. "What happened to her?"

Mother sighed a sigh so deep and heavy Diane felt the anguish behind it. "She got lost in the woods shortly after her third birthday. We found her doll. We found one of her shoes. And her hair ribbon." She pointed to the box, to a rumpled, torn, faded pink ribbon at its bottom. "But we never found her."

"Oh, Grandma . . ." Meghan slid from the edge of the ottoman and knelt in front of her grandmother. She placed her hands on Mother's knees. "How awful."

"Yes. Yes, it was. When we lost Maggie, we lost . . ." Mother paused, her throat convulsing. "Everything."

Diane took the page from her mother's fingers and examined the photo. Although it was black and white and had faded over the years, upon closer examination she could tell the little girl in the picture had lighter hair than her mother's. Her face was chubbier, her eyes less deep set, yet her nose and mouth resembled Mother's. Margaret Rose . . . She'd been named for this child yet hadn't known she existed.

The same unsettling feeling she'd experienced when Meghan showed her the box of photos returned. "Why didn't you ever tell me about Maggie?"

Mother cringed. "My mother wouldn't allow it."

Diane shook her head. "Your mother's been gone for decades. She died when I was what—two, three? You could have said something before now." Was Mother conjuring some sort of story to gain Meghan's sympathy? If so, it was working. Tears winked in her daughter's eyes and sorrow was etched into her features. "It doesn't make sense that you wouldn't talk about her if she was important enough for you to name your only child after her."

Mother hung her head. "You're right. I should have told you about your namesake. But if I told you about her, I'd have to tell you what I did." She pinched the bridge of her nose, her shoulders shaking. "I didn't want you to know how . . . how careless and foolish and irresponsible I'd been. If you'd known, you'd have always been insecure with me. You'd have always been afraid."

Insecure and afraid wouldn't have been any worse than irritated and resentful. Diane pretended to ream out her ear. "I'm sorry, but you aren't making any sense. What exactly did you do?" A half laugh, half cough escaped her throat. "You didn't lose her in the forest, did you?"

Mother jerked her face toward the wall.

A chill wiggled down Diane's spine. "Mother, did you?"

Her mother's frame began to shake violently.

Diane watched her always-controlled, always-ladylike, always-perfect mother crumble before her eyes. As a teenager she'd wanted to witness her mother's tumble from the pedestal of perfection. Wanted to prove that her mother was human like everyone else. Hadn't she driven all the way to Nevada from Arkansas in the hopes of finding her mother incapable of caring for herself any longer so she could finally sell this big house, move Mother into a rest home, and be certain she'd never manipulate Meghan into caretaking for her?

But sitting there now while her mother hid her face and trembled with silent sobs, an unexpected sympathy washed through her. Instead of the desire to glory in her mother's frailty, she wanted to reassure her. But she had no idea how. So she sat silently, observing, her fists gripped so tightly her fingernails cut into her palms.

Meghan fired a frantic look at Diane and then turned to Mother again. "Grandma, it's all right. Whatever happened, it's all right. You can tell us."

Diane battled a stab of jealousy. She was the daughter. She should say something. She blurted, "Yes, Mother. Tell us. You'll feel better after you've told us."

Mother jolted, her spine straightening and her chin lifting. She wiped her hand down her face and turned. She pinned her gaze on Diane, her dark eyes still wet but also steely with determination. "Those tears weren't for me. They were for you." Her chin quivered for a moment, but she set her lips in a firm line and the quiver disappeared. "You didn't get to know your grandparents because they died young. You grew up without cousins. You were robbed of so many things." A weak, sad smile lifted the corners of her lips. "Maggie's loss . . . it took so much . . ."

Meghan glanced at Diane, as if expecting her to speak, but Diane had no idea what to say. She'd never had grandparents or cousins, so how could she miss them? Mother might as well have been talking in riddles.

"Grandma, what happened to Maggie?"

Mother leaned back in the chair, her gaze drifting to the ceiling. "I wish I knew for sure. The preacher convinced my mama and daddy that she drowned in the creek and her body was carried far, far away. One woman in town was convinced the Gypsies stole her. Others thought she was taken by a bear, others that she simply wandered deep into the woods and fell into a ravine or an old well. My parents went to their graves not knowing. And I suppose I will, too."

She sat up and turned a fierce—or was it desperate?—glare on Meghan. "But if I tell you about her, then someone will know she once lived. She'll no longer be forgotten. Someone like Maggie, someone who brought so much joy to her folks, should never be forgotten. You'll remember her, won't you, Meghan?"

Meghan

Meghan opened her mouth to reassure her grandmother, but before she spoke her cell phone played the theme song from *Rocky*. She cringed. "I'm sorry. That's my partner, Sean. If I don't take it, he'll worry."

Grandma waved her hand. "Take it. I've waited seventy years to talk about Maggie. I can wait a few minutes more."

Meghan punched the connect icon on her phone. "Give me just a minute, Sean." She slid the phone in her pocket, tucked the crutches under her arms, and moved as quickly as the crutches allowed to the hallway. But dog whimpers from the bedroom made her change course. She entered the hall bathroom and closed the door with her elbow. Sinking onto the toilet lid, she let the crutches fall to the floor. Then she lifted the phone again.

"Sorry about that. I needed to find a private spot to talk."

"Uh-oh. That bad, huh?"

"Not the way you think." She quickly filled him in on bringing out the box of photographs and Grandma's reaction to it, and then she repeated her grandmother's confession about the little sister neither Meghan nor Mom knew existed. "I've never seen anybody so overcome by emotion she lost consciousness. What a horrible burden Grandma's been carrying all these years. She really believes it's her fault Maggie died."

"How could it be her fault?"

"Apparently she and Maggie went to the woods together and Maggie got lost. Grandma said when she lost Maggie, her family lost everything." Awareness bloomed, and Meghan gave a slight gasp. "Mom told me years ago that her grandfather was an alcoholic who died of liver disease. That's why Mom has never touched booze and forbade me from drinking, too, just in case there's an alcoholic gene. I wonder if he started drinking after Maggie disappeared."

"That's incredible." She pictured him shaking his head in wonder. "It had to have felt good for her to finally spill the secret."

"It might be a while before she feels good. Right now I think she's pretty raw even if she's also relieved. She wants to tell me about Maggie so someone remembers her. I'm gonna let her talk as long as she wants to, and I'll make sure to write it all down so it isn't forgotten."

"You're a good granddaughter."

She smiled. "You're a good listener. Thanks for checking in on me."

"You're welcome." An odd *squeak* came through the line—probably him settling into the leather recliner that faced his big-screen television. "How's it going between your mom and grandma? Everything peaceful? I prayed for them this morning."

Affection flowed through her. How'd she get so lucky to land Sean as a partner? She couldn't imagine any of the other detectives caring about her personal life the way he did. "I appreciate that. And guess what? No battles today yet and it's almost noon! They went grocery shopping first thing, and Mom fussed about the heat, but she hasn't launched any complaints about Grandma. Of course, Grandma passing out in the middle of the living room kind of sent all conversation out the window."

Meghan paused, recalling Mom's face when Grandma fainted. "You know, it's funny. Mom usually has this look when she's around Grandma—this teenage sullen, rebellious look. But the minute Grandma's eyes rolled back and she collapsed, concern chased the 'look' away, and so far, even though Grandma confessed something that had to have shocked Mom, she hasn't painted it back on. That's a real . . ." Should she use the word? It sounded so religious—something she'd never claimed to be. Yet it fit. "Blessing."

"Well, Meghan, God works in mysterious ways. Maybe your grandma passing out was His means of softening your mom toward her."

Did God really care enough to be involved in the little details of their lives? A funny ache developed in the center of her chest. She'd have to give his suggestion some thought. "Maybe . . ."

"Do you need to get back to your grandmother? I can tell you're still worried."

She laughed. He was a good investigator if he could read her emotions from the distance of fourteen hundred miles. "If you don't mind, I would like to get back in there. I can hear Mom and her talking, and I don't want to miss anything important."

"All right, then, go. I'll keep praying for that peace you requested, and now that I know your grandma's been holding on to a secret, I'll pray especially hard for her to forgive herself."

She couldn't have asked for anything better. "Thanks, Sean. Bye now." She dropped the phone back in her pocket, retrieved her crutches, and hurried to the living room. "Sean was checking in on me."

Grandma nodded. She didn't quite smile, but she'd lost the tense expression she'd worn before Meghan had left the room. Whatever Grandma and Mom discussed during her phone call with Sean, it couldn't have been unpleasant. "He sounds like a very good man."

"He's a good friend."

Mom sent her a speculative look that she chose to ignore. She settled on the ottoman again. "Grandma, can I ask you a question?"

"Of course, honey."

Meghan blinked back tears at her grandmother's familiar, kind, inviting tone. "You said your mother didn't allow you to talk about Maggie."

"That's right. It hurt Mama too much to talk about her. So Daddy said we had to let her go." Pain flashed in Grandma's dark eyes, proving it still hurt her, but her voice reflected only the gentleness Meghan remembered from childhood.

She put her hand on Grandma's knee. "Then why did your mother let you keep pictures of her?"

Eleven

Mid-September 1943
Cumpton, Arkansas
Hazel Mae

Noises from Maggie's bedroom early on a Saturday morning brought Hazel out of bed like a lizard darting for shade. Nobody'd gone in Maggie's room in all the weeks since she disappeared. Had God answered her prayers and brought Maggie home? Hope beat like a bass drum in her chest.

She ran across the hallway on bare feet, her nightgown flapping, and burst through the doorway. But the hope plummeted the moment she found only Mama in the room. Then fear struck when she realized what Mama held. "What are you doing . . . with that?" Hazel was careful not to ask "with Maggie's doll." Mama either flew into a rage or broke down in tears whenever someone mentioned her youngest daughter's name.

"Packing it away." Mama placed the doll with its sausage curls and lacy dress in the bottom of a wooden crate. Then she reached into the bureau and pulled out the stack of Maggie's dresses. She dropped them over the doll.

Hazel's mouth fell open. How could Mama pack up Maggie's things? When Maggie came home, she'd expect to find her dresses and her new birthday doll waiting for her. She'd be so sad if they were missing. Mama wasn't thinking right.

Hazel darted forward. "Don't."

Mama gave her a sharp look. "What did you say to me, young lady?"

Hazel chewed her lower lip and wrung her hands. "I . . . I said 'don't.'" She swallowed. "Please?"

The stern lines on Mama's brow remained. "Go back to your own room, Hazel Mae, and leave me be."

"But, Mama—"

"Go!"

Hazel fled to Mama and Daddy's room. Daddy was slipping his suspenders over his shoulders. He frowned when Hazel barreled into the room.

"What're you doin' up, girl? Rooster ain't even crowed yet."

"Daddy, Mama's in Maggie's room. She's packing up Maggie's clothes and toys. You gotta—"

"Move, girl."

She shuffled out of his way.

Daddy strode past her to the bureau. He rubbed oil between his palms and ran his fingers through his dark, thick hair, forming shiny waves that flowed from his high forehead to his neckline.

Hazel pushed so close the spicy smell of his hair oil made her nose twitch. "Daddy, didn't you hear me? Mama's—"

"Never you mind. It's time."

"Time . . . for what?"

"To close up that room. Lookin' in there every day an' seein' her things is too hard on your mama's heart." He spoke with a flat tone. Hard. Chilling. "Gotta close it up. Gotta let her go."

Hazel drew back as if he'd slapped her. "But when she comes back—"

Daddy grabbed her shoulders and leaned down so his face was only inches from hers. "She ain't comin' back, Hazel Mae. Now instead of arguin' an' creatin' trouble, since you're up, go help your mama clean out that room. Take everything she wants gone down to the burn pile. I'll see to it this evenin' when I come in from the field."

Tears blurred her vision. "B-but, Daddy . . ."

He released her with a little shove. "Go on, now. Be a help instead of a hindrance." He turned his back on her.

Hazel scuffed out of the room, sniffling, wiping her eyes with the backs of her hands. She wanted to obey Daddy, but how could she do what he asked? She entered Maggie's room and stopped just over the threshold. The crate waited on the floor next to the bureau, overflowing with Maggie's dresses, slips, aprons, hair bows.

Mama sat on the edge of the bed with an open album in her lap, lifting out pictures and dropping them into a shoe box.

"Mama?"

Mama didn't look up, but her hands went still.

"Daddy says I'm—" Her chin quivered so bad it was hard to talk. She gulped. "I'm supposed to help you."

"Come over here, then."

She might have been wearing concrete blocks for shoes, it took so much effort to walk across the room.

Mama stood and dropped the album on the bed. "Take out any pictures of—" She gritted her teeth for a moment and closed her eyes. "Any pictures from June 1940 up 'til July 1943."

All of Maggie's short life. Hazel's chest ached.

"Put 'em in that box. Then put the album back on the shelf in the parlor."

Hazel looked into her mother's face, begging with her eyes instead of with words.

Mama wouldn't even glance at her. "Gonna go get your daddy's breakfast started." She left the room.

Hazel perched on the edge of the bed and looked at the page Mama'd already stripped. The little corners that held photographs in place were still there, but the page looked so sad and lonely with the images gone. She pulled the shoe box closer and peered inside. The ache in her chest made it hard for her to breathe. She started huffing, like she'd run a race, while she picked through the pictures Mama'd taken out of the album. Then she gasped.

She pulled a single picture from the box. Why wouldn't Mama keep this one? It wasn't of Maggie. Gripping it between her fingers, Hazel clattered down the stairs and into the kitchen.

Mama stood at the stove moving sizzling strips of bacon around in the skillet with a fork. "You done already?"

"No, ma'am, but you made a mistake." Hazel held up the picture so Mama could see it. "This is me, Mama. Me with the neighbor's dog an' our old barn cat, Boots."

Mama's eyes looked cold and distant. "Throw it out."

Hazel gazed at the picture. The dog, Farley, died a year or so ago. He used to come visit her a couple of times a week. Such a gentle dog. He never once chased the chickens or tried to snap at her. She still missed him. "But why?"

Mama rushed at her, her fists raised like a prizefighter. Hazel instinctively took a step backward and brought up her arms to defend herself even though Mama had never hit her in the face. Only on the bottom, and then only when she'd been very bad.

"I said throw it out!"

Hazel gaped at her, almost as frightened as she'd been when she couldn't find Maggie. Did Mama intend to get rid of her pictures, too, and pretend that she'd never had a daughter named Hazel Mae? "But . . . But . . ."

"You think I want to look at that picture with you holding on to animals like they're something special? Do you think I want to keep remembering how it was so important for you to save a burrow of bunnies—wild rabbits, for heaven's sake!—you had to leave your sister untended?" She grabbed the picture and waved it in the air. "I want it gone, Hazel Mae, do you hear me?"

Hazel nodded, too afraid to speak.

Mama shoved the picture back into her hands and stomped to the stove. "Go finish the job. And when you're done, none of us—not me, not your daddy, not you—will ever talk about her again." Mama covered her face with her hand and groaned. "I should've kept her home with me. I shouldn't have trusted—" She dropped her hand and noticed Hazel Mae standing there. Her face contorted. "Go!"

Hazel ran upstairs and slammed herself into Maggie's room. She leaned against the door panting, listening to be sure Mama hadn't followed. Mama had looked wild. Scary. If Mama came after her with that look on her face, Hazel would jump out Maggie's window and run into the woods. She'd be safer with the bobcats and bears than she felt with Mama right now.

Nobody came after her, so she crept to the bed and the album. Sniffling and blinking back tears, she meticulously removed every photograph of Maggie, every photograph of Hazel with Maggie, every photograph of Mama with Maggie, of Daddy with Maggie, of the four of them together as a family. And she came to the last photograph, taken on Maggie's third birthday.

Her fingers trembled as she slipped the picture of Maggie holding her birthday doll—the very doll in the bottom of the crate Daddy wanted her to carry to the trash pile. Her nose burned with the effort of not crying. She couldn't do it. But if she didn't, Daddy would know. He'd see that the box wasn't there, and he'd be mad at her. As mad as Mama was. She couldn't have both of them so angry and scary.

But Daddy hadn't said anything about the photographs. Mama wanted her to take them out of the album, but she never said to burn them. So Hazel wouldn't be disobeying if she hid them instead.

She hurried into her room and flung the closet door open. On the shelf, her treasure box sat underneath a stack of her favorite picture books—the ones she kept up high so Maggie couldn't tear the pages. She pulled down the box and the books and went back to the hallway. She peeked out to make sure neither Mama nor Daddy were around. Then she darted into Maggie's room and closed the door again.

Heart pounding, she dropped to her knees beside the bed and opened her treasure box. She took out the pretty leaves she'd collected, a few school papers with praises from the teacher written on them, a handkerchief her best friend embroidered for her, and a 1918 Mercury head dime she'd found when Daddy had dug a new well. When the box was empty, she transferred the photographs into the treasure box and slipped the lid into place.

As furtive as a cat stalking a mouse, she carried the cardboard box to her bedroom and returned it to its spot in her closet. Back in Maggie's room, she put her treasures into Mama's shoe box. She sat for several minutes gazing at her special things inside the box. But the pictures were more special. She had to save them. She slapped the lid on the shoe box and placed it, along with the picture books she'd never let her little sister use, on top of the crate. She took it all downstairs.

Mama glanced over when Hazel stopped in the doorway between the kitchen and dining room. Her gaze fell on the crate and lingered. "You got them all?"

Hazel nodded, inwardly praying Mama wouldn't ask to look inside the shoe box.

"Take it out, then."

Hazel scurried through the kitchen and out the back door as fast as her burden would allow. The sun still hid behind the trees. Mist hovered like a gathering of ghosts. The yard, cloaked in gray, looked as dismal as Hazel felt. She choked back a sob and moved onward. The dewy ground chilled her bare feet and she wished she'd put on shoes. But she wouldn't go back. She followed the winding path to the scorched patch where Daddy burned their trash every week. Old newspapers, a few tin cans, and a pair of worn-out gardening gloves already waited inside the short wire frame that kept the trash from blowing away until Daddy could light the fire.

She stood at the edge of the enclosure, her chest pounding, thinking about the things inside the crate and inside the box. She didn't want to let them go. Didn't want them turned to ashes. But Daddy would look for the crate and the box when he came out this evening. Sucking in big breaths of the morning air for fortification, she braced herself to throw the box and crate over the fence. But worry that the shoe box's lid would pop off—and her deception would be uncovered—stopped her.

Gripping the crate tight against her middle, she lifted one foot and pushed the honeycomb-shaped wire down. The sharp points pricked her sole, and she

grimaced as she stepped inside the enclosure. The fence sprang back, catching
the hem of her nightgown and scratching her calf. Little droplets of blood
welled up and trickled down her leg. She ignored the warm tickle and set the
crate and box in the middle of the burned patch as reverently as the preacher
laid his Bible on the pulpit at church.

She allowed herself another minute or two to gather her courage to leave
the things behind. Then she pushed the fence down and stepped out of the
circle. Thin lines of blood dribbled down her ankle and under her foot, leaving
little dots of red on the hard ground. She lifted her gown and examined the
scratches. They weren't deep. They'd heal without leaving a scar. But her heart
might always wear a scar at what she'd been forced to do.

As she headed for the house, dragging her heels, she said the words she'd
never say to her mother's face. "You might've made me throw her things away,
and you might not let me say her name ever again, but you can't make me
forget her. I won't ever forget."

Present Day
Kendrickson, Nevada

"That evening Daddy set everything in the burn pile on fire. Maggie's clothes,
her doll, they all went up in smoke, and Mama and Daddy never knew I kept
those photographs." Hazel tucked a strand of hair that had escaped Meghan's
ponytail behind her granddaughter's ear. "And not once in all the years since
have I opened the box and looked at them."

"Never?" Margaret Diane frowned at Hazel, disbelief evident in her
expression.

"No." Hazel met her daughter's gaze. "At first I was afraid that if I looked
at the pictures, I might accidentally talk about her. Looking at the pictures
would let her stay fresh in my mind. I had to be silent about Maggie to honor
my mother. Do you understand?"

Her daughter's doubtful look didn't fade, and Hazel couldn't blame her for the reaction. How ridiculous it sounded when spoken out loud. But it had made perfect sense to her as a ten-year-old, and the habit of leaving the lid on the box had prevailed through the rest of her childhood and even into adulthood.

She shifted her focus to Meghan, who gazed at her with a mix of remorse and affection. "If you hadn't taken out the box by mistake and opened it, Maggie would still reside in the bottom drawer of my closet bureau, buried in the corners of my memories." She cupped Meghan's face—her sweetly attentive face that suddenly hid behind the mist of tears. "Thank you, dear one, for letting her out. Oh, how I've missed her . . ."

Twelve

Diane

The antique grandfather clock in the corner sang its song and then chimed twelve times. Twelve tinny, echoing, irritating times. Diane gritted her teeth through the entire performance. She'd hated that thing when she was a kid—it woke her up hour after hour during the night—and the first thing she'd done after her arrival was unhook the chime and quarter-hour weights to silence the walnut clock.

She crossed to it and peered behind the rectangle of glass. Sure enough, the weights were back on their chains. Mother must have attached them when Diane wasn't looking. She opened the side door and reached inside.

"What're you fixing to do, Mom?"

Diane aimed a quick frown at Meghan. "Turn this thing off. Again."

"You did that?" The incredulity in her daughter's voice gave Diane pause. "I thought it was broken when it didn't chime during the night the way it used to. So I checked it out this morning and saw the empty chains. I thought the weights fell off somehow, so I hooked them on again." She smiled and sighed. "I love listening to that clock. It's so comforting, the way it counts the quarter hours. It reminds me how valuable every minute is."

Mother chuckled. "That's exactly how I've always felt about the old clock. When I got married, your great-grandmother offered to give me the clock for my new home. Your grandfather wasn't sure he wanted something so old and outdated taking up space in our tiny living room. But Albert grew to love it, and he especially liked the routine of raising the weights each Sunday morning before we left for church. He said it started the week off right."

Diane glowered at them. She'd experienced the odd tendency of women to pair off, leaving a third member of the party feeling like the fifth wheel. With her fellow teachers, she was most often part of the pair, but not with her mother and daughter. Never with her mother and daughter. They always made her the fifth wheel.

She flipped her hand toward the clock. "It doesn't keep you awake? It doesn't . . . set your teeth on edge? Great Scott, it's as old as the hills and sings about as well as a coyote with a toothache."

Both Meghan and Mother burst out laughing. If they were going to make fun of her, she'd rather be with the dogs. Diane snapped the door of the clock closed and headed for the bedroom.

"Mom, come back. I'm sorry if we hurt your feelings."

"Yes." Mother's voice warbled, proof she was still battling laughter. "We aren't laughing at you. We're laughing at your picturesque speech."

Diane rolled her eyes—not laughing at her . . . right—and kept going. She unlatched each dog crate and pointed to the doorway. "C'mon. Let's go out-side." When she passed the living room, she noted Mother and Meghan had returned to examining photographs. They seemed unaware of her presence. She opened the sliding door for the dogs and then began chopping vegetables for a salad. According to the obnoxious clock, it was noon. They should eat.

The dogs scratched at the glass and she let them in. "Stay out of my way—do you hear me? Sit." They sat in a row, grinning up at her. She shook her finger at them. "Stay put and I'll give you each a bite of cheese when I've finished the salad."

They swished the floor with their tails, Molly whimpering, but they all remained in their furry row while she chopped vegetables and shredded her favorite cheese substitute made from cashew milk.

Midway through the preparation, Meghan peeked around the corner, her eyes twinkling impishly. "Just checking. Are you making lunch for all of us, or are you too mad to feed Grandma and me?"

"I'm not mad."

"Then why are you pouting?"

Diane paused grating long enough to glare. "I am not pouting."

Meghan's lips twitched. "Are you sure?"

Oh, that girl had an ornery streak. It must have come from her father's side of the family. Diane slammed the door on thoughts of Meghan's father and slid the chunk of cheese slowly along the grater. "I'm forty-seven years old, Meghan, not five. I don't pout."

"Okay." The teasing glint disappeared, and she clumped near. The rubber caps on the crutches squeaked on the clean tile, raising a couple of whines from the patiently waiting dachshunds. "We said we were sorry. But if you could have seen your face when you mentioned the coyote with a toothache, you would've laughed, too."

Meghan's brows pinched together. "You know, I wish you'd stayed in the room. Grandma told me a couple of stories—stories I bet she's never shared with anyone before today."

Another unexpected wave of jealousy crashed over Diane. "Oh?"

"Yeah. They were so detailed, so full of emotion, as if she'd lived the experience just yesterday instead of decades ago. It's almost like these memories have been lying in wait for years to come out and now the floodgates have opened."

Diane lifted the cutting board and sprinkled the cheese over the salad. "Are you sure she isn't making things up to match the photographs?"

Meghan huffed, something she did only when very annoyed. "Why are you always so cynical?"

"Maybe because I know her better than you do." Diane carried the salad bowl to the table and returned to the kitchen for bowls and forks, talking as she went. "You spent a few weeks each summer with her and visited at various holidays—times when she was always on her best behavior. I lived under her roof for years. I've seen the worst, let me tell you."

"But if you'd seen her face, if you'd heard her voice, you wouldn't be able to deny the memories were real." Sadness colored Meghan's tone. She grabbed Diane's arm. "Mom, I know you had it rough, losing your dad when you were still a girl."

Diane froze with her hands cupped around the stack of bowls in the cupboard. The ache of loneliness built again at the mention of her father. "Yes. I did."

"I'm not trying to downplay your loss, but when I think about everything Grandma lost, I could cry. After Maggie died, her whole family fell apart. That's when her dad started drinking again. She said he blamed himself for the girls being in the woods because they were picking blackberries for his birthday cobbler."

Diane shot a sharp look at Meghan. "Blackberries?"

August 1972
Little Rock, Arkansas

"Margaret Diane, don't dawdle. Stay right here beside me."

Diane scurried to Mommy's side and curled her fingers over the wire edge of the squeaky shopping cart. She smiled up at Mommy, hoping for a word of praise for her obedience. But Mommy didn't smile back.

"I've told you and told you, you can't wander away from me. Keep your hand on the cart now."

Diane sighed. "Yes, ma'am." She walked next to the cart, skimming the colorful cans and boxes on the grocery store shelves with her gaze. She loved going to the store. When they finished shopping, she always got a little box of crackers with circus animals printed on it. The box had a string handle, like a purse. She liked the box even better than the crackers inside. And she loved reading the labels while they shopped.

Words jumped out at her. *Niblet Corn. Sweet Peas. Kitchen Cut Green Beans.* She wouldn't even start first grade for two weeks yet and she already knew how to read. Mommy and Daddy told her how smart she was and how proud they were of her. So why couldn't Mommy slow down and let her read all the words before turning a corner? If she'd let Diane walk slow instead of having to stay with the cart, she could read and read and read.

Diane shuffled along, the heels of her Mary Janes clumping on the tile floor, while Mommy added things to the cart—boxes of cereal, a canister of oatmeal, sugar, chocolate chips, cans of Daddy's favorite pork 'n' beans . . . The cart got fuller and fuller, and Diane's fingers started to go numb. But she didn't let go of the cart. Mommy got very upset when she let go.

They passed the low bins where damp, chilly air kept the vegetables cool. Diane read out loud the little signs taped to the front of the bins. "Cay-ruts, brocc-uh-li, po-tay-toes, to-may-toes."

"Good job, Margaret Diane."

Diane beamed.

Mommy picked up the vegetables she wanted, and then they turned toward displays of fruit. "All right, let's get some apples for Daddy's lunch box and some bananas to put on your breakfast cereal."

Diane already knew lots of the words for fruit, like *apples, bananas, grapes,* and *oranges*. But a new one caught her attention. A long word. As long as *strawberries* but with a different beginning. Purplish-black clusters that reminded her of itty-bitty grapes filled green plastic baskets. She stared first at the pretty fruit and then squinted at the word on the cardboard sign, thinking hard. She gasped with joy.

She let go of the cart and pointed to the baskets. "Look, Mommy! Black-berries! May I have some for my cereal?"

Mommy's face turned white. She grabbed Diane's hand and slapped it onto the edge of the cart. It stung, and Diane started to cry. Mommy shook her finger in Diane's face. "No, you may not have blackberries, and you won't get your box of animal crackers, either."

Diane's lower lip quavered. "But I learned a new—"

"I told you not to let go of the cart."

Mommy didn't care at all that Diane had figured out a brand-new, long word all by herself. Diane wailed louder.

"Stop crying."

Diane took several shuddering breaths. She didn't make any more noise, but she couldn't stop the tears from running down her cheeks while Mommy unloaded the cart at the cash register. Diane leaned against the cold wire cart and stared at the words on the bright-colored boxes on the shelf close by.

Animal Crackers . . . Animal Crackers . . .

She read the words over and over so she'd forget the word *blackberries*.

Present Day
Kendrickson, Nevada

Diane lowered the bowls to the counter. "Interesting." Mother had bypassed the thumb-sized blackberries in the organic foods section of the store that morning, claiming the seeds bothered her. They'd purchased blueberries instead. Maybe it wasn't only the seeds she found unpalatable.

Diane carried the bowls to the table. "The salad I tossed is large enough for all three of us, but you and Mother will probably want to add a sliced boiled egg, some bacon bits, or a few chunks of the fajita chicken she picked up from the deli. Do you want to call her to the table, or should I?"

"Go ahead. I'll get the chicken—it's in the fridge, right?"

"Right. And give each of the dogs one of those cheese cubes from the bag in the meat drawer, would you?"

"Sure."

Diane stepped into the wide doorway between the breakfast nook and the living room. "Mother, lunch is ready."

Mother's head was bowed over a photograph. Diane waited a few seconds, but she didn't move. Was she sleeping?

Diane cleared her throat and spoke a little louder. "Mother?"

She lifted her gaze quickly, confusion registering on her face. "What?"

Diane took a single step into the room. "Lunch—it's on the table."

"Oh . . ." But she didn't rise from the chair. She beckoned Diane with a flick of her finger. "Come here and look at this, please."

Diane's stomach growled. "Can we look after we eat?"

Mother held up a photograph as if Diane hadn't spoken. "See here? It's the only studio portrait we had done as a family. I remember Daddy driving us to Beaty to a little studio on Main Street. Mama made us all wear our Sunday clothes. My dress was simple muslin with a white-lace overlay Mama stitched from some old curtains, and she put a new ribbon in my hair. Yellow. As yellow as a buttercup." She touched the jaunty bow in the image and chuckled. "Although it hardly mattered, considering the photo was done in black and white. Even so, Mama wanted us all looking our best."

She angled the photograph toward the window, frowning, as if she found it difficult to focus. "Maggie was only a baby—a little over four months old—so she didn't have enough hair for a bow. But Mama tied a ribbon around the collar of her dress, see? And she fought with Maggie the entire session, trying to keep her from putting the ribbon in her mouth."

Despite her initial impatience, Diane found herself transfixed. It seemed years were fading away and the girl her mother had once been peeked from behind the wrinkled skin.

"Doesn't Daddy look dapper in his suit? When I was a girl, I begrudged inheriting his dark hair and eyes. Until I saw them on you."

Diane's heart gave a little jump.

"And my mama . . . We never had much money, but she was such an accomplished seamstress she could turn flour-sack material into the most glorious creations. She kept things simple for her everyday work dresses, but her Sunday-go-to-meeting dresses were as nice as anything a department store could offer. I wish I still had one of her dresses—maybe even this one, from the picture."

Diane leaned in and examined the dress. Trim-fitting, sewn from a tiny floral print, with a short stand-up ruffle around the neckline and cuffs, which appeared to be made from the same fabric. The dress didn't look homemade. She nodded. "It's very nice."

Mother beamed as brightly as if Diane had just offered her the crown jewels. "You can see by the way she holds her shoulders and by the angle of her chin, she was a proud woman. Always stately. Until . . ." Her bright expression faded. Her shoulders sagged. "Ah, well, sorrow will steal a lot of things from a person."

She straightened again. "But I can tell you this, my mama was always a lady. Everyone in Cumpton said so—Mae Clymer Blackwell was a lady." She gazed intently into Diane's face, almost challenging her to refute her words. After a few seconds Mother gave a start. "You came to tell me lunch was ready. You must be hungry. Let's go eat." She set the photograph gently into the box and pushed herself to her feet.

Diane shifted the ottoman aside to create a wider pathway for her mother.

As Mother stepped past the ottoman, she lowered her gaze to the box and paused. "Margaret Diane, do you suppose we could take this photograph somewhere and have it enlarged? Maybe colorized the way they do with old movies these days? I'd like a nice eight-by-ten to display in a frame."

Diane shrugged. "As long as there isn't a studio stamp on it. Most places are pretty picky about honoring copyrights."

Her mother's eyes widened. "Even on a picture taken so long ago? I'm sure the studio in Beaty is closed and the photographer long dead."

"Even then."

Mother huffed, something Diane had never heard her do. Then she shook her head, a rueful smile curving her lips. "I suppose I shouldn't complain if they're trying to be honorable. But I would like to investigate it one day next week, if you wouldn't mind."

"Sure. We'll hit up a photo-copier kiosk somewhere."

Mother's smile returned. "Thank you, Margaret Diane." She arched one brow. "Now, about that lunch. Is it one of your vegan concoctions, or is it something I will want to eat?"

Diane rolled her eyes. But she bit back a chuckle as she followed Mother to the kitchen.

Thirteen

Hazel

Sunday morning Hazel hurried to the kitchen early to start breakfast. Thanks to Meghan's exploring on her smartphone, she had a recipe for vegan pancakes, and she intended to use them to entice Margaret Diane out of bed and to church with her.

She paused as she removed bananas from the bowl on the counter. Would her actions be construed as manipulative? After taking a class on sociology in high school, her daughter had often accused her of passive-aggressive manipulation. Margaret Diane launched many accusations at her mother during her turbulent teen years, but it was the only one that Hazel feared might hold an element of truth.

Whether her motivations were selfish or selfless, she would make the pancakes and hope both her daughter and granddaughter would attend morning worship with her. She hadn't attended church with both of them since Meghan was barely out of the nursery, and she could think of no greater treat than to sit between the two most important people in her world while listening to the minister share from God's holy Word.

After mashing two bananas in the bottom of her large glass mixing bowl, she unearthed her food processor from the lowest shelf in the pantry. She measured in two cups of whole organic oats. Several *whirr*s of the blade—she cringed at the intrusion—turned the oats into flour. She combined the flour with soy milk, wrinkling her nose at the pungent scent, and then added the mashed bananas, baking soda, and a tablespoon of organic maple syrup. Hazel shook her head, chuckling. Where on earth did they get organic syrup—from organic trees? Soft chuckles continued to roll from her chest as she folded the ingredients together with a rubber spatula until the batter appeared smooth and well combined.

According to the directions, she would need to cook these pancakes on medium rather than medium-high heat and with a lid in place, so instead of her usual griddle she greased the bottom of the frying pan with coconut oil—organic, of course—and settled it over a lit burner. Just as she was spooning the first of the batter into the pan, the four dachshunds and Margaret Diane came around the corner.

Hazel placed the lid over the pan and aimed a smile at her daughter. "Pancakes will be ready soon. All vegan, I promise. Meghan found the recipe."

Margaret Diane didn't answer. She unlocked the sliding door and shooed the dogs outside. She turned with a yawn. "The dogs heard you thumping around in here and woke me up early. I'd rather be sleeping."

Hazel lifted the lid and peeked at the pancakes. The directions said to turn them when the surface was covered with little bubbles—waiting too long would burn them. She didn't want to serve scorched pancakes again. Only a few bubbles showed around the edges, so she put the lid in place and faced her daughter.

"I got up early because I usually go to the first service at church. It's the more traditional one. But I don't mind attending the contemporary service midmorning if that's what you and Meghan are accustomed to."

Margaret Diane made a face. She opened the door, and the four dogs pranced inside. "To be honest, Mother, I rarely attend church. I doubt Meghan goes, either."

Disappointment attacked Hazel. "But we always went to church. Even after Meghan was born you still came with me. When did you stop?"

Margaret Diane popped the lid off the plastic bucket of dog food and scooped brown nuggets into the row of dog dishes by the back door. "Shortly after you moved to Nevada, I guess. You weren't there to push it, so . . ."

Hazel set the lid aside and carefully turned the three pancakes. Her joy at the perfectly browned cakes was ruined by her daughter's statement. "I didn't realize I had pushed it. I assumed you went because you wanted to go."

Margaret Diane's arched brow spoke volumes.

Hazel turned her attention to the pancakes. If she didn't want them as hard as the kibble the dogs now crunched with apparent enjoyment, she needed to keep watch. Bitter words pressed for release. Even though Mama and Daddy's church attendance became more and more sporadic as Hazel grew older, she'd faithfully walked to the church or caught a ride with a neighbor every Sunday. She'd never forgotten the minister's solemn statement that it took only one generation of neglecting God to turn a faithful family into a faithless one. She'd decided early not to be that generation. But somehow her daughter had chosen to abandon faith.

Wasn't it enough that her beloved daddy had become, according to the town gossips, a backslider? She'd never quite forgiven herself for her father's descent into alcoholism. She'd tried so hard to be extra good, striving for perfection to make up for her grave error that cost so dearly. And somehow it wasn't enough. Margaret Diane, her only child, was following Daddy's rejection of God. She'd failed yet again.

She lifted the pancakes from the pan and stacked them on a plate. They formed an almost perfect cylinder. Almost. "Well, since you're up, eat these while they're hot. I set out blueberries, chopped walnuts, and the pure maple syrup you bought at the store. Help yourself."

Margaret Diane took the plate and crossed to the counter. She sighed as she sprinkled a handful of walnuts over the stack. "I've disappointed you again, haven't I? Everything I do disappoints you."

Early September 1951
Cumpton, Arkansas

"I'm sorry you're disappointed in me, Mama."

"I'm not disappointed." But Mama's pursed lips said otherwise. She pushed a lank strand of silver-streaked blond hair from her face and shook her head. "I just don't know how I'm going to cope all by myself with your daddy. He's getting more quarrelsome by the day."

Hazel couldn't argue. Back before their world changed, Daddy's drinking only made him lazy and slow. Now that he was older, the more he tipped the bottle, the uglier he got. She'd prayed for a chance to go far away to school so she wouldn't have to see his ugliness close at hand, and God answered by giving her a scholarship to Little Rock Junior College. With the money she set aside by clerking on Saturdays at the general store in Cumpton, she had enough for a bus ticket and to keep her going until she found a part-time job in the city. Everything was working out fine, and she even thought she'd battled past the guilt of leaving Mama alone with him. But at her mother's statement the guilt whooshed in again, stronger than before.

She knelt next to Mama's rocking chair and took her weathered, dry hands. "Then come with me to Little Rock. Daddy hasn't done any farming to speak of for the past two years. He can sit in the barn and drink his liquor without you being here. If he's not willing to give up the bottle for you, then maybe you ought to—"

"Leave your daddy?" Mama jerked her hands free and stood. She gawked at Hazel with as much shock as if Hazel had suggested she pick up a hatchet and chop Daddy to pieces. "I made a vow on our wedding day to be with him until death parted us, for better or worse, for richer or poorer, in sickness or in health . . ." She clamped her hand over her mouth, and a moan echoed behind it.

Hazel stood. She cupped Mama's elbows. She'd grown so tall she could look down at Mama now. Maggie had Mama's light hair and blue eyes. Would she be petite like Mama, too? Hazel shook her head. Why was she thinking of Maggie? She needed to focus on Mama.

"Listen." Hazel spoke softly, the same way she did when Daddy was full-on drunk. "He made a vow, too. A vow to cherish you and take care of you. He hasn't honored it for a long time, Mama." Her chest panged so hard an arrow might have pierced it. She loved Daddy so much, and she understood why he drank himself into a stupor every day. Sometimes it took every bit of self-control she possessed plus a dozen prayers to keep from sneaking away with one of his bottles and finding out how it felt to drink until she forgot what she'd done. "If you came with me, maybe he'd realize how much his drinking hurts you. Maybe he'd find the courage to give it up again. Maybe—"

Mama broke loose and turned away. "I can't leave him, Hazel Mae. He'd drink himself to death if both of us left him."

Hazel hung her head. Then again, maybe he'd stop drinking when she went away to college. Maybe looking at her, remembering how she'd taken away his little sunshine, was the deepest reason he drank.

"What're you gonna study at the college?"

Funny how Mama hadn't asked before now. She'd known about the scholarship for three months, known Hazel wanted to make use of it. The question came late, but Hazel was ready with an answer.

"Literature, Mama. I'm gonna study books—the way they're written and what the author meant to say by writing the story. When I'm done, I want to get a job in a library."

Mama stood silent for so long Hazel wondered if she'd fallen asleep on her feet. Then a little half snort, half laugh sounded. "You and your books. Always was one for gettin' lost in a story."

Hazel bit her lower lip. Daddy drank. Mama hid in the house away from folks. And Hazel had her means of escape, too.

Mama slowly turned and angled a curious look at Hazel. "Have you still got those storybooks in your treasure box? Those ones you read over an' over until you could recite them without looking at the pages?"

Hazel could still recite parts of them. She shook her head.

Mama frowned. "No?" She gazed outward, her brow still furrowed. "Wonder what happened to them. Funny how things can just . . . disappear."

Hazel knew Mama wasn't thinking about books. Longing to speak her sister's name again swelled up so strong her throat ached. Her breathing came hurried and shallow, and she gasped out, "Mama, I—"

Mama took off for the kitchen, arms swinging, feet moving fast. "You do what you have to do, Hazel Mae. Go ahead and go. I'll be fine. I'll be just fine."

Present Day
Kendrickson, Nevada

"That's not true." Hazel cringed, recognizing her untruth. Margaret Diane did disappoint her more often than not. Just as she'd disappointed her own mother. Perhaps she and her daughter were more alike than either of them cared to admit.

She added a tablespoon of coconut oil to the pan and poured batter for three more cakes. She glanced over her shoulder and realized Margaret Diane had taken her first bite of the pancakes. "Are . . . they all right?"

Margaret Diane chewed the bite and cut another wedge free. She swallowed and raised her fork, syrup dripping from the chunk of pancakes. "Yes, they're actually really good. Are you sure there's no animal by-products in here?"

Hazel swallowed a chortle. "I'm sure." She listed the ingredients. "I was surprised to see how they fluffed up. Usually you need an egg to get that kind of lift. But I suppose the baking soda helps."

"Probably." She took another bite. "I'll have to take this recipe home with me. These are better than the recipe I've been using. Mine doesn't call for bananas. Adding more potassium and fiber to my diet is always a good thing."

Hazel puffed up more than the pancakes. Praise from Margaret Diane was rare, and she wanted to savor it. "I'll write it all out for you after church."

Margaret Diane froze with the fork halfway to her mouth. She dropped the fork and turned a scowl on Hazel. "You just can't let it go, can you?"

Hazel blinked twice, trying to recall what she'd said. "What?"

"Church. I already told you I wasn't interested in going, but you had to bring it up again."

"But I—"

Margaret Diane rose and carried the plate to the trash can. She dumped the barely touched pancakes into the bin and then plopped the plate and fork in the sink. "I'll ask Meghan what she wants to do, but if she decides to sleep in or stay home this morning, I don't want you putting a guilt trip on her."

Hazel began to inform her daughter she hadn't meant to start an argument about church, but she glanced into the skillet. The entire tops of the pancakes were covered with little bubbles. They needed to be turned. She set the lid aside and reached for the spatula.

"And don't worry about writing out the recipe for me. I can look it up online when I get home." Margaret Diane departed, and the dachshund menagerie went with her.

Hazel flipped the pancakes, settled the lid in place, and then sank into the chair her daughter had vacated. How had they gone from enjoying a simple conversation to a full-blown war again? Was she destined to be ostracized from Margaret Diane forever? Hazel sighed and rested her forehead in her hand. Maybe she'd stay home from church today, too. Suddenly she felt very tired and very old.

Fourteen

Las Vegas, Nevada
Meghan

Meghan smiled and shook hands with yet another member of Grandma's church. If the greetings didn't stop, they might still be here for the next service. But she didn't mind. The people's friendliness reminded her of Sean, and they didn't seem fake at all, the way Mom often described Christians. Of course, Mom based her opinion on Grandma, so it wasn't exactly an unbiased comparison.

The canned music, piped through speakers positioned in all four corners of the large theater-like sanctuary, came to an end. Grandma gave a start. "Oh, goodness, that's the cue for the cleaning crew to come in. We'll be in their way. We'd better go."

The older couple who'd ambled over near the end of the song laughed. The man winked, his denim-colored eyes twinkling with humor. "The crew is so efficient they'll sweep us up with any leftover bulletins or gum wrappers." He gestured to the double doors at the end of the aisle. "Ladies first."

Meghan moved up the aisle with Grandma, careful not to catch the rubber tips of her crutches on the plush carpet. The couple followed them into the large foyer. Meghan winced against the sunshine flowing through the floor-to-ceiling windows. It seemed doubly bright after the subdued lighting in the sanctuary.

Grandma was blinking, too, and she dabbed her eyes with a Kleenex. "Punk, Rachel, let me introduce you to my granddaughter, Meg—"

"So this is Meghan!" Rachel stepped away from her husband, gripped Meghan's elbows, and looked her up and down. "I should have known when I saw the cast and crutches. Your grandma told our prayer group about your accident. We've been praying for your physical and emotional healing." The woman's face pinched with sympathy. "We're all very grateful your life was spared, but I'm sure you carry some heart wounds over those who weren't so fortunate."

Meghan gave a little jolt. Before coming to Nevada, she'd thought about the accident and battled waves of guilt several times day. But since arriving, she'd thought about it only a time or two. Were the prayers of these kind-hearted people being answered?

"You are as beautiful as Hazel told us."

Meghan's cheeks blazed with heat at the woman's final comment, and she choked out a self-conscious chuckle. "Well, Grandma's always been a little biased where I'm concerned, but if I'm good looking at all it's only because I look like my mom, who looks like Grandma."

Punk pinched his chin and grinned. "We've known Hazel three years now, but we hadn't known her for more than three minutes before we knew she had a granddaughter."

"Who works as a police officer." Rachel squeezed Meghan's elbow and then let go, returning to curl her fingers around Punk's arm.

"Actually, I'm an investigative detective." Meghan had never felt as if her life was threatened in the line of duty. "Police officers have it a lot harder than I do. I pretty much sit at a desk and do research or interview people—nothing too strenuous."

The elderly pair exchanged a smile. Punk nodded. "Well, I can tell you, Hazel talks incessantly about her granddaughter. She loves you very much."

Emotion flooded Meghan's frame. She aimed a watery smile at Grandma. "I love her, too."

Rachel shifted to face Grandma. "Will you be at book club on Tuesday?" The woman held her husband's elbow with her linked hands, and he gazed down at her with a fond smile as she spoke. Meghan couldn't stop a little swell of jealousy at the obvious devotion and affection the pair shared. What would it be like to be part of a relationship like theirs, one that had obviously lasted for decades?

Grandma dabbed her eyes again and pushed the tissue into her purse. "I'm not sure. I read the book, of course, and I enjoyed it. But since Margaret Diane and Meghan are visiting, I probably won't come."

"If you decide to skip the meeting, don't worry. I'll get next month's book for you and give it to you at church next Sunday morning." The woman turned her smile on Meghan. "It was very nice to meet you, young lady. Thank you for coming to Nevada for your recovery time. I know it's a real treat to Hazel to have you visit for so many weeks."

They said their goodbyes, and Meghan trailed Grandma through the foyer and out onto the sidewalk past the families arriving for the second service. Stepping from the AC of the large brick-and-glass building to the heat of mid-morning was like being captured in a wool blanket.

She blew out a breath that lifted her bangs. "Phew, it's hot out here. Let's hurry, huh?" She began a double-step pace that involved swinging herself as far as the crutches reached.

Grandma laughingly panted alongside her. "You're going to give me heat-stroke, Meghan. I can't move as adeptly as a monkey in the jungle's tree branches."

Meghan grinned and returned to her single step. "Sorry, Grandma. And hey, I'm sorry if Mom and I are keeping you from doing your regular stuff. It'll be okay if you still want to go to your book club and prayer group and whatever else while we're here."

"Oh, I enjoy Lit and Latte—"

Meghan aimed a questioning look at her grandmother.

Grandma laughed. "That's what we call our book club because we meet at a coffee shop to discuss the latest piece of literature. And of course I enjoy meet-ing with the other prayer warriors. But while you and Margaret Diane are here, I want to focus on the two of you. The other things will keep."

Grandma unlocked the car. Meghan dropped her crutches into the back seat and then slid into the passenger seat. The cream-colored leather had heated up during the service. Her skin went prickly and began to sweat, and she hissed through her teeth. She leaned forward and set the air-conditioner levers to high even before Grandma started the ignition.

Grandma didn't speak until they'd left the busy parking lot, aided by men waving sticks and wearing yellow vests, and merged onto the four-lane street. "What did you think of the service? Was it too tame for you?" She kept a two-hand grip on the steering wheel and sat up, alert and watchful.

Meghan chuckled. "Tame?"

"So many churches are moving from the old hymns to modern choruses, from suited pastors to leaders in jeans and untucked shirts." Not a hint of criticism colored Grandma's tone. "I like the early service at the interdenominational church because it still follows the more traditional pattern of worship, but I'm sure you noticed the attendees are mostly white-haired folks like me. The younger crowd comes to the second Sunday service or the one on Saturday evening, what they call contemporary services. Those have a band instead of the choir—something that might appeal to you. We can go to one of the contemporary services next week if you prefer."

Meghan considered Grandma's offer. Most of her friends would probably have considered the church service a little dry and unexciting, but she hadn't minded it. The peaceful atmosphere—with its low lighting, flowing music played on an organ or sung by a choir of at least fifty singers, and whisper of Bible pages being turned—had seeped into her center and invited her to relax more than she'd relaxed in . . . ages. Although the minister wore a suit and tie, what some might call stuffy and old fashioned, his open face and fervent words had given him an approachable, sincere appearance.

She shook her head. "Your service is fine, Grandma. Let's just stick with that."

Grandma's face lit. "So you want to go with me again next week?"

"Sure."

She reached across the console and gave Meghan's arm a squeeze, then gripped the steering wheel again. "Thank you. When you were still a little-bitty thing, you, your mother, and I went to church every Sunday together. It was my favorite part of the week because it was time set apart to worship the Lord and to be with my girls."

Meghan cringed. "I honestly don't remember going to church except during the summer when I came to see you. Well, I take that back. When I was younger, maybe grade-school age, Mom and I went at Christmas. And sometimes at Easter." At Christmas, she was given a brown bag filled with candy and fruit, and at Easter she received a chocolate egg. Beyond that, she couldn't recall much about the services. For some reason, the thought saddened her.

A half smile curved Grandma's lips. "I'm glad she took you for those special holidays."

"Probably because you always sent me a new dress for those holidays. I didn't have anyplace else to wear a dress when I was a kid." Not that she'd worn one this morning. She owned only one dress—a knee-length, tight-fitting, all-over-sequined number she pulled out every New Year's Eve for the department party. Not exactly a church dress.

Grandma's smile faded. She turned into the cul-de-sac and onto her driveway. "Why don't you hop out here. It'll be easier for you to get into the house through the front door than through the garage. It's so tight with your mom's car in there, too."

"All right." Meghan exited the car and waited until Grandma pulled into the garage before crossing the driveway to the front door. She stepped onto the porch and the door opened.

"There you are." Mom stood in the doorway, still wearing her sleep shorts and tank top, her dark hair balled in a messy bun on top of her head. She gestured Meghan over the threshold. "I thought the early service was over at ten fifteen. Mother said the church was less than a ten-minute drive away. I expected you back a half hour ago."

Meghan wiped the sweat from her forehead and glanced at the grandfather clock. The round face showed five past eleven. "We stayed after and visited with some of Grandma's friends. Lots of people came over to meet me, and they were all really nice. Like, genuinely nice." She hoped Mom got the hint.

Grandma came in from the kitchen, her hands at the back of her neck. "Margaret Diane, would you help me with this catch? It's stuck."

Sighing, Mom scuffed across the floor and moved behind Grandma. For the first time Meghan noticed Grandma wasn't as tall as Mom anymore. Age must have shrunk her an inch or so. Mom scowled, shaking her head. "Do you still wear that string of pearls to church? Great Scott, you'd think the world would end if you went one Sunday without them."

Grandma tucked her chin low and held her hair out of the way. "I suppose it's a silly habit, but your father gave me the pearls on our fifth anniversary. He always admired the way they looked with my church suits, and I wore them so often on Sundays it became a habit. Now I don't feel fully dressed for church unless they're around my neck."

Mom released the string and puddled them in her palm. "Before you wear them again, you might want to have a jeweler check the fastener. It looks all lopsided. That's why you couldn't get it undone."

Grandma took the string of matching creamy, pea-sized orbs and cradled them in her hands. "That's a good idea. It would break my heart if the clasp broke and I lost them. They're to be Meghan's someday, you know." She flicked a smile at Meghan, then turned to Mom again. "Maybe when we take the photograph to get it reprinted, we can visit a jeweler, too. Make a day of fixing things."

"Sure." Mom sauntered across the room and flopped onto the sofa in the middle of the dachshund quartet. Grandma headed to her bedroom, and Mom glared after her. "Well, isn't that nice."

Meghan frowned. "What?"

"The pearls. They're to be yours someday." Mom crossed her legs and bounced her foot, the movement jerky and impatient. "I guess she forgot she has a daughter."

Meghan sank onto the ottoman. All the comforting, good feelings she'd

built over the morning began to fade in the face of her mother's criticism. "Do
you really want them? You aren't exactly the pearl-wearing type, Mom."

Mom's scornful gaze roved across Meghan's white capris, yellow tank,
and matching short-sleeved lace cardigan. "And they'd do so much for your
outfit."

Meghan looked aside and bit the end of her tongue. Mom was right.
When did Meghan dress up? She wore business suits to work and T-shirts with
either shorts or sweatpants on the weekends. Even with her sequined dress, the
pearls would look ridiculous on her, not perfect the way they did paired with
Grandma's pale-pink linen suit and white blouse. But even if she didn't wear
the pearls, she would treasure them because they were a gift from her grandmother. Mom would probably sell them.

"So how'd church go . . . other than being swarmed by Mother's friends?"

If Mom was willing to set the subject of the pearls aside, Meghan could,
too. She put a smile on her face. "It was good. Quiet, low-key. Peaceful music.
Kind of like I remember from the Christmas Eve services we used to go to.
Except no candles. I told Grandma I'd go with her next week, too." She waggled her eyebrows, hoping Mom wouldn't take offense from what she intended
to say next. "You could come with us."

Mom flipped her wrist and shook her head.

Meghan rested her elbows on her knees. "Aw, come on, Mom. It's only an
hour, and it would mean so much to Grandma. She told me on the drive back
how her favorite time of the week when I was little was Sunday morning because she got to spend it with the two of us. What would it hurt to let her relive
those memories?"

Mom rose. Her eyes narrowed and her lips twisted into a grimace of half
scorn, half pain. "Maybe I don't care to relive mine."

Fifteen

Late September 1985
Little Rock, Arkansas
Diane

*A*re you going to take the baby to the nursery?" Mother lifted the edge of the soft flannel receiving blanket and peeked at Meghan's sleeping face.

Diane shook her head. "I'd rather keep her with me. She's so little yet." Not even two weeks old. Who'd have guessed love could grow so quickly? Especially considering how she felt about the man who got her in the family way. A swell of tenderness rose and nearly strangled her. Blinking tears, she gently lowered the flap of flannel over Meghan and held her a little more snugly.

The narrow foyer teemed with people, some handing out bulletins, others wrangling grade-schoolers, more standing in little groups and chatting. Mother slipped her hand through Diane's elbow and drew her through the crowd in the direction of the sanctuary doors.

"Excuse me," Mother said time and again, and each time people glanced over, smiled, and then seemed to notice the bundle in Diane's arms. The smiles turned to pursed lips, disapproving grimaces, or stiff poses of discomfort.

Diane wanted to escape. She tried to pull loose of Mother's grip, but she couldn't without jostling the baby. So she continued on with her baby sleeping innocently in her arms and with what seemed a hundred condemning glares boring holes through her.

Throughout her pregnancy, she'd suffered through judgmental glances and whispered mutters and cold shoulders. The reactions had irritated her or amused her, depending on her mood, but never had they decimated her. Until today. Because this time the people weren't condemning her. They were condemning her baby. Her precious, innocent baby. And that was wrong.

Mother led her to a back pew and they slid into the seat. People paraded past on the way to their seats, but no one stopped to ask to see Meghan. No one stopped to ask how Diane was faring. No one stopped. At all. Diane and Meghan might have been invisible for all the notice people took of them. And all the while, Mother sat there with a complacent smile on her face, oblivious, her fingers on Meghan's blanket.

Diane had been in church long enough to witness the celebrations when a new baby arrived. She'd watched eager people flock around a mother who brought her baby to church for the first time. Heard the congratulations and well wishes and happy laughter. Knowing what usually happened made her fully aware of how she was being snubbed. She knew why, too. Because she had only Mother sitting beside her instead of a husband.

Sure, she'd made a mistake. She gave something she couldn't take back with the expectation that it meant as much to him as it did to her, only to discover it didn't mean a thing. But hadn't Mother praised her for choosing to bring the baby into the world instead of snuffing out its life, the way her friends had encouraged? Why couldn't some of these holier-than-thou church people realize the sacrifice she'd made?

The final notes rang from the organ, and the minister stepped behind the pulpit. Under the blanket, Meghan released a little waking-up squeak. Diane's chest went tight, and she knew what would happen next if she didn't act fast. She rose, grabbing up the diaper bag at the same time, and hurried out of the sanctuary. She bustled toward the nursery, Meghan's squeaks changing to a whimpering wail as she went. She entered the nursery, zipped past the pair of smock-wearing workers who gawked at her as if they'd never

seen a new mother before, and plopped into the rocking chair situated behind a privacy screen.

"Shhh, shhh," she crooned to the baby while unbuttoning her blouse. She
lifted Meghan and pressed her wailing mouth against her breast. The baby's
cries stopped with a little grunt as she took hold, and relief flooded Diane.
Relief to have the throbbing pressure eased. Relief they'd made it before she wet
her blouse. Relief that she was safe behind this barrier, where no recriminating
glares could reach.

A tinkling lullaby sang from a tape player on the other side of the screen.
Diane hummed the notes and rocked while Meghan nursed. The baby's eager
slurps transitioned to weak, sporadic tugs, and finally she sagged against Diane's arm, her sweet mouth slack and her blue-veined eyes closed. Diane laid
her sleeping daughter in her lap and refastened her blouse. Then she cradled her
in the crook of her arm and left her hiding spot.

The pair of workers sat in chairs on opposite sides of a blanket spread on
the floor. Two babies—one on his back gumming a rattle and one on her
tummy batting at a clear plastic ball with ducks inside it—played on the blanket. Diane couldn't resist pausing to glance at the babies and try to imagine
Meghan a few months older and able to play. She lifted her gaze from the babies and discovered the younger of the workers looking at her.

Defensiveness struck without warning. Diane barked, "What?"

The woman's eyes widened. "Did you want to leave"—she pointed at
Meghan's blanket-wrapped form—"your baby?"

Diane rocked in place, an unexpected habit she'd developed. "No, she's
asleep now. I'll keep her with me."

The woman nodded.

The older one sat forward. "So you decided to keep her?"

For a moment Diane blinked in confusion. Hadn't she just said she intended to keep Meghan? Then it dawned on her what she meant. Her face
blazed hot. "Of course I did. She's mine."

"There are lots of couples who want to adopt because they can't have children of their own." The woman's eyes sparked with such indignation, Diane instinctively drew back. "Seems to me the unselfish thing would be to give your baby to one of those couples."

Diane peered into Meghan's sweet little face. The familiar swell of protectiveness, of a deeper love than she'd ever felt before, filled her. How could she give her baby to someone else?

"How do you intend to take care of her?"

"Georgina . . . hush." The younger woman's tone held mild reproof.

The older one swept her hand, as if slapping away the other's comment. "Don't hush me, Lynda. I'm only saying what everyone in church is thinking. She's hardly equipped to raise a child by herself. The baby deserves better."

Diane quivered from head to toe. Tears clouded her vision. She sucked back a sob and lifted her chin. "She deserves better than to be exposed to your prejudiced attitude, that's for sure. She won't ever be coming into this nursery." She charged out the door, up the hallway, and to the vestibule. She braced her hand on the door leading outside, ready to smack it open, but then she stopped.

Would she really leave? She'd ridden over with Mother, so she'd have to walk home. Less than a mile, but still a good distance while carrying a baby and a well-stocked diaper bag. More importantly, if she left, she'd give that woman and every other person who'd turned away in disapproval the satisfaction of running her off. Would she let them win?

She whirled and marched back into the foyer. Past the ushers to the sanctuary doors. Into the sanctuary, where a few people glanced over their shoulders and then zinged their attention to the front of the church. She settled in next to Mother, who leaned close and whispered, "Is she all right?"

Diane nodded. The baby was fine. The baby was more than fine. Meghan D'Ann DeFord was a precious, innocent, valuable life, and these sanctimonious busybodies would have to get used to her being in their self-righteous presence. Because Diane wasn't going to let them scare her away.

Present Day
Kendrickson, Nevada

Diane pointed at her daughter. "But don't think for one moment that because I don't choose to go to church means I'm afraid or ashamed or anything else. I decided I didn't want to spend time with a bunch of hypocrites, and that's all there is to it."

Meghan held her hands in the air as if she were at gunpoint and coughed a short laugh. "Okay, okay, sorry I asked."

Mother rounded the corner. She'd changed from her pink suit into a pair of grass-green ankle pants, a yellow, green, and white plaid blouse, and yellow flats—still plenty dressy but a huge step down from her formal suit. She came to a halt and gave Diane an up-and-down look that brought back another unpleasant rush of memories.

"How long will it take you to get dressed?"

Diane held her arms wide. "I am dressed. Quite comfortably, I might add."

"I meant in clothes appropriate for the public's eye."

Suspicious, Diane squinted at her. "Why?"

Mother beamed. "Because I want to take you and Meghan to a buffet lunch." She shrugged, her expression turning sheepish. "Well, they advertise it as a brunch, but it goes from nine in the morning until two in the afternoon, so that feels more like lunch than brunch to me."

Meghan shook her head, grinning. "Where is this buffet brunch-lunch?"

"In one of the older casinos built along the highway on the outer edge of Las Vegas."

Diane's jaw dropped. "You want to take us to a casino?"

Mother aimed a chastening look at Diane. "Did I say I was taking you there to gamble? Of course not. But you know as well as I do, some of the best restaurants in town are in the casinos. I've been to this buffet several times, and I remembered they have a whole vegan section, so you should be able to find plenty to eat." She put her hands on her hips. "Do you want to go or not?"

Meghan's shoulders were shaking and she was biting her lower lip, obviously holding back laughter. Diane understood why, too. She couldn't envision her pious, perfect, conservative mother stepping foot in a casino. What would the fine folks at church say? She cleared her throat to stave off a guffaw. "I guess we could check it out." She smirked. "Is that why you put on such a casual outfit—so nobody suspects you've been to church this morning?"

Mother pursed her lips. "As if I would engage in such clandestine behavior. Honestly, child . . ." She angled her head and raised her eyebrows. "Are you going or not?"

"Do I have time to shower?"

"I suppose. As I said, the buffet is open until two, but I'd like to eat before then. So please don't dally."

Diane gave a mock salute and trotted to the bedroom. All four dachshunds chased after her, so she closed them in their crates. Ginger, Duchess, and Miney settled down to nap, but Molly yipped and scratched at the wire door. "Hush that," Diane said, but Molly continued complaining the whole time Diane showered and dressed.

She sat on the end of the bed and twisted her damp hair into a bun. She frowned at the dog. "What's your problem, Molly? It doesn't hurt you a bit to be in that crate. Why can't you be easy like the other pooches?"

Her hands stilled midtask as her words seemed to ricochet back at her. Was that how Mother . . . and Meghan . . . felt about her? She shook her head slightly and snapped the rubber band into place. Her situation wasn't the same as the silly dog's. She had solid reasons for being resentful.

She rose and tapped the top of the crate. "Behave yourself. I'll be home soon enough and you'll be able to come out again." Once more a niggle of discomfort attacked her, but she pushed the feeling aside and strode into the living room. "I'm ready."

Mother pushed up from her chair and held her hand to Meghan, who was perched on the ottoman. That square of stuffed fabric had become her throne in the short time she'd been here. Meghan situated her crutches under her arms and flung a grin at Diane. "Mom, while we've got Grandma corralled in the car, we need to work on her."

Diane slipped her purse strap over her shoulder. "About what?"

Mother clicked her tongue on her teeth and headed for the kitchen. "She's got some idea about having a birthday party for my eightieth. I told her I'm too old for parties."

Diane trailed Meghan and her mother. The idea of organizing a party didn't appeal to her, but she wanted to side with Meghan anyway. "Nobody's too old for parties, Mother. Aren't you worried you'll make Meghan feel bad if you deny her?"

Meghan nodded. "Yeah. You don't want to make me feel bad, do you? And now that I've met some of your church friends, I'm sure there'd be plenty of people who'd come. We could invite your prayer group and your book club and maybe even—"

Mother turned and held up both hands. "Hold it right there. I haven't had a birthday party since I was nine years old, and I see no sense in having another one now." She slipped one arm around Meghan's waist and reached the other hand to Diane. "Having the two of you here for my birthday and putting together the scrapbook is party enough." A hint of something Diane couldn't recognize—panic? fear?—sparked in Mother's eyes. "Let's leave it at that, all right?"

Sixteen

Hazel

Meghan flashed a questioning look at her mother and then sighed. "All right, Grandma." Impishness danced on her face. "For now."

Hazel forced a laugh, willing away the rush of sadness that threatened to overwhelm her. "For good, young lady. I mean it. No party." Her words emerged more harshly than she intended, and she pasted on a smile she hoped would soften the command as she reached for the door handle. "Let's go enjoy our brunch, hmm?"

Meghan crawled into the back seat and Margaret Diane sat in the front passenger seat for the drive to the River's Edge Casino. Hazel chose the longer route so she could avoid merging onto and exiting the multilane highway. Even after all her years of living and driving in Las Vegas, being on the busy highway still raised her blood pressure. People drove as if they didn't have good sense, and more times than she cared to admit, she'd been the recipient of horn blasts or improper gestures, all because she honored the speed limit.

Margaret Diane and Meghan pointed out the window and discussed the changes to the city since their last visit. Housing areas and businesses had sprung up like mushrooms in the past several years, proof that the city had overcome the horrendous recession of the previous decade. The city was again sprawling onto the desert and growing more and more crowded. The signs of prosperity and progress contrasted starkly with the number of homeless folks camped at nearly every intersection. A bearded fellow in filthy dungarees held a different kind of sign, one that begged for a handout.

At a red light, Hazel lowered her window. Two scruffy-looking men trotted over, and she gave each of them one of the kits she'd constructed with her prayer group. They thanked her, and she said, "God bless you." One of them repeated the words to her. The light turned green, and she raised the window and pulled forward.

Meghan tapped Hazel on the shoulder. "What did you give them, Grandma?"

"Nothing extravagant. Necessities like soap, toothpaste, and deodorant, gift cards to fast-food restaurants, packets of nuts, crackers, and raisins, a pair of socks, a comb . . ." Hazel switched lanes—the turn to the casino always sneaked up on her. "Things that fit in the gallon Ziploc bag and can be used by someone who doesn't have a home. There's a Bible tract in there, too, and a booklet with the names of different organizations that could help get them back on their feet."

"That's really nice."

"Nice?" Margaret Diane glowered first at Meghan and then at Hazel. "Do you do that often?"

"Only when I'm stopped." Hazel sighed. "There are more needs than any one person can meet, but I hope the packets let them know somebody cares, bless their sad hearts."

Margaret Diane slapped her hand to her forehead. "Mother, for heaven's sake! Someday one of them is going to poke a gun in your face and demand your car. What will you do then?"

"I suppose I'll let them have it."

"Are you crazy?"

Hazel frowned. "Of course I'm not. A car isn't worth giving up my life for."

"But—"

"Mom, leave Grandma alone. She's doing good deeds."

Margaret Diane folded her arms over her chest and glared out the windshield.

Hazel hit her blinker and then eased right onto the access road that led to the casino. "If it makes you feel any better, I've been handing out those packs for more than four years now—"

Her daughter's mouth dropped open. "Four years?"

"—and no one's ever done anything worse than give one back because it didn't have money in it. I've never once felt threatened."

Margaret Diane barked a laugh. "You've got be kidding me. You open your window and hand a bag of toiletries and snacks to a complete stranger, but you never let me go trick-or-treating, not even in our own neighborhood, because somebody might try to hurt me. Does that make sense to you?"

Hazel pulled into the parking garage. The change from bright sunlight to shadowed interior made it hard for her to see, so she slowed to a crawl. She searched for an open parking stall on the lowest level so Meghan wouldn't have to traverse so far with her crutches.

"Mother, I asked you a question."

Hazel sighed. Goodness, her daughter could be snippy. "I heard you, but I'm trying to concentrate on driving. It's always a little hard for me to see in these parking garages. They're so dark."

Margaret Diane huffed and crossed her arms again. She searched both sides of the garage, her scowl fierce. Then she pointed. "There. On the left."

Hazel pulled into the spot and turned off the ignition. She squinted at the number and letter painted on the concrete wall. "Level A, slot 124. Can we remember that, or should I write it on something?"

Meghan chuckled. "Remembering A is easy. As for the 124, Grandma is the *one* who lives near Vegas, Mom and I are the *two* visiting, and the *four* dogs are the extra guests Grandma wasn't expecting—one, two, four. I got it."

Hazel laughed at Meghan's ingenuity, but Margaret Diane's sour expression didn't change. Hazel placed her hand on her daughter's arm. "If it upsets you that much, I won't hand out the bags anymore unless someone else is in the car with me."

"How often does that happen?"

"I frequently give friends a ride to Bible study, Lit and Latte, or the grocery store. I would say perhaps half of my excursions include a passenger or two."

She squeezed Margaret Diane's arm. "I appreciate your concern, honey. Thank you for worrying."

An odd look crossed her daughter's face, and then she huffed again. "Honestly, if your passengers are senior citizens like you, an extra one or two won't matter to a thief. Three little old ladies aren't any more of a threat than one."

"Then consider this." Hazel opened her purse and pointed to her Glock 9mm handgun.

Margaret Diane reared back as if Hazel had pointed the gun at her. "What— You—"

Meghan burst out laughing. "Whoa, Grandma, you're actually packing?"

Hazel frowned at both of them. "Margaret Diane, you're being needlessly fearful. It won't fire unless I pull the trigger. And, Meghan, owning a gun is serious business, so stifle your amusement." She waited until Meghan wiped the silly grin from her face and Margaret Diane closed her mouth. "Several of my single friends and I took the course to be approved to carry a concealed weapon. I keep it with me in case I need it."

Meghan held out her hand. "May I see it?"

"I suppose you're familiar enough with weapons that I don't need to fear you'll handle it carelessly." Hazel cautiously removed the gun and placed it, butt first, in Meghan's waiting hand. She turned her attention to her daughter. "I'm not unfamiliar with weapons. My daddy taught me to fire a rifle when I was eight, and your father and I frequently visited a shooting range before you were born. He was stringently opposed to having a gun in the house when you were little, and I honored his preference, but after his death I purchased a handgun—legally, I assure you—for our protection. So you can stop worrying that I'm a doddering old fool running scared."

Meghan dangled the gun barrel down and returned it to Hazel. "I'd never consider you a doddering old fool, Grandma. Living in a big city like this, I understand why you want to be armed, just in case."

Margaret Diane shook her head. "Well, I don't understand. You are one giant contradiction."

Hazel frowned. "What do you mean?"

She blasted a cynical laugh. "On one hand you loudly preached 'God is our protector,' but on the other hand you never let me out of your sight. And now . . . this." She held both hands toward the pistol lying on the console. "How does that thing figure into it?"

Hazel wasn't sure how to answer. Did she trust God . . . or didn't she? Her sister had slipped away. Her father lost himself in a bottle. Her husband died in an accident. Had God turned His head those days, or had He allowed the events to take place? The same confusion that had tormented her as a little girl and then as a heartbroken widow left to care for her daughter alone rose again.

She shook her head slowly. "I . . . don't know. I only know I feel a little more secure with it close at hand. In case I need it."

Meghan's warm hand curled over her shoulder. "You aren't doing anything illegal, Grandma, and if it makes you feel safer to have a gun, you should keep it. You obviously know how to be responsible with it. So don't let Mom's apprehension affect you, okay?"

Margaret Diane sent a glower in her daughter's direction. "It isn't apprehension as much as aggravation, Meghan. This woman can't seem to make up her mind what she believes. And then she wonders why I'm so messed up."

Hazel's vision clouded. *Dear Lord, she's right, isn't she? I have led her astray . . .*

February 1983
Little Rock, Arkansas

"Why can't I go by myself? None of my friends' moms are going. It's embarrassing!"

Hazel fluffed the ruffle circling the scooped neckline of Margaret Diane's electric-blue dress, then stepped back and swept a glance from the puffed sleeves to the twelve-inch flounce at the hem of the full skirt. The dress's snug-fitting bodice enhanced her daughter's slender form, and the bold blue color made her dark hair seem even more lustrous. She'd grown so tall and willowy in the past year, standing eye to eye now with her mother. She was such a beautiful girl.

Hazel swallowed a knot of part pride, part fear. "The school only asked for four adult chaperones. Maybe they already had all of them in place before your friends' mothers had a chance to volunteer."

Margaret Diane pranced to the opposite side of the room, out of Hazel's reach. "My friends' moms don't volunteer because they understand kids need to be away from their parents' prying eyes now and then. It's bad enough I can't go with my date. Nobody else is meeting up at the dance—the girls always get picked up by the guys. But not me. I have to show up with my mother. I might as well not even go."

Hazel's ire stirred. "Don't be ridiculous. Of course you're going." After Hazel had purchased her a dress, taken her to a salon to have her hair done up pretty in a braided crown decorated with sprigs of baby's breath, and even allowed her to get her very first manicure, Margaret Diane would go to that dance if Hazel had to hog-tie and drag her there.

Margaret Diane rolled her eyes. "If I don't go, Bobby will think I stood him up. I can't do that. But I wish you'd stay home. Just once, Mother, could you stay home and let me go someplace by myself? I'm not a baby. I'm sixteen already! I don't need you by my side."

The words stabbed like a knife. Margaret Diane did need her mother close by. If Hazel were there, she could protect her daughter from untoward advances by the young man who was serving as her escort. She could ascertain no one else bothered her—a teacher, another student, even another parent. Not all of them were trustworthy. There were stories in the newspaper every week about children being hurt, abducted, killed—some by people they knew and trusted. She couldn't risk such a thing happening to her beloved Margaret Diane.

"If I'm there, you'll—"

"—be safe. Mother, I know. You've told me over and over again that you're there to keep me safe. But if I need you to keep me safe, why do you keep dragging me to church?"

Hazel drew back, confused.

Margaret Diane nodded, her face set in a smug grin as if she'd won an important argument. "You make me sit in the pew every Sunday and listen to sermons about how God is love, and God is my Father, and God cares for His children. You claim you believe all that, but if you did you'd let me go to the dance with my date. You'd trust God to keep me safe instead of thinking you've got to be the one to do it. So what you're telling me is that you don't trust Him. Not at all."

Hazel closed her eyes for a moment and gathered her scattered thoughts. "I trust God. I do. But I don't trust people."

"Including me?"

Hazel hurried across the floor and took hold of her daughter's upper arms. "Yes, of course I trust you."

"Then let me go by myself. Prove that you trust me."

Hazel's hands tightened automatically.

Margaret Diane wrenched loose and scooted several feet away. But her scowl skewered Hazel even from that distance. "You're such a liar, Mother. You don't trust me. And I don't care what you say—you don't trust God, either."

Present Day
Las Vegas, Nevada

"You're right." Hazel hung her head. "Trust . . . doesn't come easily to me. I suppose I lost it the same day I lost my little sister." Awareness bloomed through her even as a weight descended on her chest. She pulled in a shaky breath and heaved it out. "All these years, where has she been? Was she washed away in the stream, the way our preacher said? Did she fall into an abandoned well? Is she in heaven? Or did the Gypsies take her after all? If so, is she alive? Is she safe and well? If only I knew, then maybe . . ."

She jerked her head up and found both Meghan and Margaret Diane staring at her. She released a self-conscious half laugh, half sob. "And here I sit blabbering like the doddering fool I said I wasn't." She forced her lips into a wobbly smile and reached for the door handle. "Let's go get our brunch-lunch, hmm?"

Meghan shifted forward and placed both hands on Hazel's shoulders, holding her in place. "Grandma, wait. Let me ask you something."

Hazel tensed, wariness tiptoeing across her scalp. "What?"

"You said you didn't want a party, that the scrapbook was enough of a present for your eightieth birthday. But I'm wondering if something else— Maybe I could—" She scrunched her face. "The only thing is, I can't promise it would happen."

Margaret Diane huffed. "Stop talking in circles and spit it out."

Meghan blew out a breath that whooshed past Hazel's ear, carrying the scent of her spearmint gum. "What if I tried to find out what happened to Maggie?"

Seventeen

Meghan

*G*randma turned so abruptly the bones in her neck, or maybe her back, popped. She stared at Meghan open mouthed and wide eyed. "You could do that?"

Now she'd gotten Grandma's hopes up. Meghan cringed. "I could try. I'm a cold-case detective, after all. And I've got these weeks off the clock when I could work on the mystery. But you'd have to understand it's a long shot." She kneaded Grandma's shoulders while she spoke, hoping to comfort while being brutally honest. "She's been gone seventy years. A lot of the people who were alive back then probably aren't anymore, and those who are might not remember anything useful. But I'm willing to try if you want me to."

Had she spoken too impulsively? Clearly Grandma's heart still ached over the loss of her sister. Would she survive the disappointment if Meghan failed?

Mom turned sideways in the seat and pinned a stern frown on Meghan. "How many seventy-year-old cold cases have you solved?"

Meghan wished Mom hadn't asked in front of Grandma. She hated answering, but Grandma deserved the truth. "Me personally? None. But forensic science is advancing every day. The guys in my unit have solved cases from thirty, forty, even fifty years ago."

"The ones where forensic science was used, I assume."

Meghan wanted to clamp her hand over her mother's mouth. Couldn't Mom let Grandma hold on to hope for just one day? She forced a reply through gritted teeth. "Yes."

Mom turned forward again.

Meghan focused on Grandma's lined face and watery eyes. "Like I said, I can't promise anything. It's been a long time. But if you want me to try, I'll investigate." She could get Sean involved. He loved a good challenge, and if the case was important to her, it would be important to him. Her heart swelled with the realization. She licked her lips. "What do you think, Grandma? Should I put out some feelers and try to figure out what happened to Maggie back in 1943?"

Grandma stared into Meghan's face for long, silent seconds. Meghan held her breath, waiting for her grandmother to make up her mind. Whatever she wanted, Meghan would do—even if it was to forget the whole thing. But curiosity writhed through her. She wanted to know what happened to Maggie all those years ago. She wanted it for Grandma, but also for Mom and for herself. Maybe, if Maggie was still alive, she'd have children and grandchildren— nieces and nephews for Grandma, cousins for Mom and her. They'd be more like a whole family. The thought made her insides churn with hopefulness.

Meghan's chest began to ache from the captured air in her lungs. She let it all out in a rush and held her hands outward. "Well? What do you think?"

Grandma's frame sagged slightly as though her spine had turned to rope. "I think we should go eat our brunch. And when we're done, we'll go home and write down everything I can remember about the day Maggie disappeared."

Kendrickson, Nevada

Meghan tapped the eraser end of the pencil down the list of names Grandma had recorded on a yellow notepad. Eight names. So few. She sent a disappointed look across the round breakfast table. "Is that it?"

Grandma chuckled. "Honey, I grew up in a very small town. Little Rock is a metropolis compared to Cumpton."

And now she lived in a suburb of Las Vegas, where more people attended her church than probably resided in the entire town of Cumpton. "Grandma, I forget—why'd you move to Nevada?"

"Because"—Mom called from the living room—"she panicked when the doctor said she had arthritis."

Grandma shook her head and then winked at Meghan. "She's half-right. The doctor diagnosed me with rheumatoid arthritis in 1990. He told me I could slow the progression of the disease if I moved to a dry, warm climate where the sun shone year-round. He listed a few options, and I chose Nevada because I wouldn't have to worry about hurricanes and because there are so many things for people to do when they visit."

"Have you had a lot of visitors here?"

Grandma smiled. A sad smile. "Not many. But his recommendation proved accurate. I have pain and stiffness in my joints, and my knuckles aren't as feminine as they used to be, but I've done very well. I can't complain." She reached across the table and pointed to the first name on the list. "You might as well cross her off. I wrote her down because I remember her so well, but Minnie Achard is likely long gone. She was old already when I was a child."

Meghan reluctantly crossed off the name. Now only seven remained. "Who do you think we should try to find first?"

"Maybe the Spanns' daughter, Beth. She was a year ahead of me at school, a real go-getter even then, always organizing the children for games at recess. I'm surprised she never ran for president. If she's still alive, she might remember something useful."

Meghan circled the Spanns. "Who else?"

"Definitely Nora Burton's daughter, Elaine. Of course, I'm assuming she's still living, too. She'd be . . ." Grandma scrunched her face and pinched her chin for a moment. "Oh, goodness, eighty-three or eighty-four. But her mother's the one who saw the Gypsy wagon a day or two before Maggie disappeared. I am very certain Maggie didn't walk away on her own. I found her hair ribbon caught on a tree branch almost as high as my head. Maggie would have been too short for the branch to snatch it from her hair."

Mom sauntered around the corner. "The wind might have blown it there."

Grandma glanced at her, her forehead pinching. "Yes. Yes, I suppose that's possible, but . . ." She turned to Meghan again, and earnestness replaced the uncertainty. "She was just a little thing, and I wasn't away from her that long. Either she fell into a hiding place so well concealed the men who searched for her couldn't spot it, or someone taller who could move much faster carried her. Nora Burton was adamant that the Gypsies had taken Maggie because twice before, children disappeared in our county around the same time the Gypsies were near."

"Two other kids?" Meghan's pulse gave an excited double step. "Are you sure?"

"Well, I don't know it for a fact, but I heard her say so. It's worth invigorating."

Mom shot Grandma a funny look. "Do you mean investigating?"

Grandma blinked twice. "Yes. Yes, worth investigating. Don't you think so, Meghan?"

"I sure do." Meghan reached into her pocket for her cell phone. "I'd like to call Sean. I don't have access to the office computers right now, but he does. There are databases with thousands of missing-persons files. He could search for the names of children who turned up missing from Benton County in the forties. Maybe the families of those children will recall something helpful. Do you mind involving Sean?"

Grandma shrugged. "If he can help, then call him. I don't mind."

Mom opened the refrigerator as Meghan pulled up Sean's number. "Are you sure you should bother him on a Sunday? You said something about him being real religious. He might be in church."

Meghan arched a brow. "At three in the afternoon?"

Mom grimaced. "Isn't Sunday a day of rest?"

Meghan hesitated with her finger poised above his contact number. Sean would be out of church by now—no church she knew of lasted until three in the afternoon—and she wouldn't be asking him to work today. He wouldn't be able to access the computer files until he went to the office tomorrow. Still, she wasn't sure.

She looked at Grandma. "You're a Christian. Would you mind receiving a phone call about something work related on a Sunday?"

Grandma chuckled. "It wouldn't bother me, but you know this Sean better than I do."

For reasons Meghan didn't understand, heat simmered in her face. She lowered her head slightly and pretended to adjust the phone's volume.

"If you think he'd rather not be disturbed today, then it can wait until tomorrow."

Meghan chewed her lip. If they waited until tomorrow, it would be evening before she could call. They'd lose a whole day—a potential day of digging for information. She shook her head. "I'm calling him. If he doesn't want to be disturbed, he'll let it go to voice mail. I can leave a message, and he'll take it from there."

Grandma smiled, warmth glimmering in her eyes. "You trust this man, don't you?"

The simmer became a smolder. "Yeah. I really do."

Mom carried a pitcher of tea and three glasses to the table and sat. "I'm glad you and Sean have such a good relationship—"

"Working relationship," Meghan blurted.

Mom's lips twitched. "Working relationship. But is it fair to dump this on him? He doesn't know Mother from Adam's house cat. Why should he have to spend his free time digging up information about a child who, in all probability, has been dead for decades?" She glanced at Grandma. "No offense intended, Mother."

Grandma's face paled and she brushed at nonexistent crumbs on the table's polished top. "You're likely correct, Margaret Diane. But"—she rested her elbows on the edge of the table—"what if she's alive? What if she's spent her entire life confused and uncertain about who she is? What if she has memories of her family and wonders why we never came to get her?"

Meghan gave a jolt. Grandma might have been describing some of her own feelings as a child—wondering who her father was, why he'd left her, whether he would show up on the doorstep someday. She wouldn't wish those feelings of confusion and longing on anyone.

Mom filled a glass, took a long draw, and swallowed. She shrugged—not a flippant shrug but an "I'm not sure" shrug. "That's a lot of what-ifs."

Grandma nodded. "I know. Believe me, I know the odds are against it. But in case it's true, don't I owe it to her to bring closure to those questions? After all, it was my carelessness that let her slip away." Twin tears appeared in the corners of her eyes.

Meghan jammed her fingers through her hair and blew out a breath. "First of all, Grandma, you were a little girl yourself. You weren't being careless—you were just being a kid. In my line of business, I've seen true, deliberate careless-ness. So I know the difference. And, Mom . . ." She aimed a stern look at her mother—the sternest she'd likely ever risked. "You're being a real party pooper and you need to knock it off."

Mom placed her hand against her chest as if shocked. "Me?"

"Yes, you. All your negative talk. Can't you be encouraging for once?"

Mom scowled. "I'm trying to be realistic, Meghan. Somebody needs to be, because the two of you have climbed into a fantasy boat and set sail on a sea of improbabilities. What both of you seem to forget is I spent my whole child-hood living under a cloud of fear because she"—Mom pointed her finger at Grandma—"lost one kid on her watch and didn't want to live with the guilt of losing another. Do you really think finding Maggie will fix all that?"

If Meghan found her father, would it fix her childhood insecurities?

Grandma rose, her bearing stiff and her movements as jerky as a rusty robot's. "I'm tired. I believe I'll go lie down for a nap." Her steps shuffling, she left the room.

Meghan heaved a sigh and glowered at her mother. "Happy now?"

Mom stared into the glass, her expression sullen.

"I don't get you at all. I know you and Grandma have your issues, but

I've never seen her be intentionally unkind to anyone. Even when they deserved it."

Mom flinched, proving Meghan's intentional barb hit home.

"Can't you look past your resentment and try to see everything Grandma's lost? So she became overprotective! Who could blame her? At least she didn't decide to dive into a barrel of self-pity or bitterness." Another barb—a sharp one she hoped pricked her mother in the center of the heart. "Maybe it was Grandma's fear of losing you that made her overprotective. But if she hadn't loved you so much, it wouldn't have mattered if she lost you. Why don't you consider that, Mom?"

Mom still didn't answer, so Meghan pushed herself from the chair, grabbed her crutches, and double-timed it out of the kitchen and to the hall bathroom, her private sanctuary. She sank onto the toilet seat and buried her face in her hands. She'd never been so disrespectful to her mother, and guilt nibbled at her. But at the same time, she had to stand up for Grandma. The way Grandma had always stood up for her.

June 1992

Meghan stepped inside the pink-and-white-striped inflated ring and pulled it up around her middle. She danced in place on the concrete. So hot on her bare soles! The sparkling water would cool her feet. And the rest of her, too. She scampered to the edge of the community pool and poised, ready to leap. But first she searched over her shoulder. "Grandma, Grandma, lookee at me!"

Grandma waved from her lounge chair and beamed a smile as bright as the sunshine straight overhead. "I'm looking, honey." Just like always.

Meghan grinned, bent her knees, and leaped. She gasped when her body met the cold water and then laughed at the droplets that splashed her face. She paddled with her hands and feet to the edge and grabbed hold. She called to Grandma, "Didja see that? I jumped in all by myself!"

"You sure did. Good job!" The mirrored lenses of Grandma's sunglasses reflected the pool's activity. Meghan even saw herself in there, and she couldn't resist waving at the pair of little pigtailed Meghans on Grandma's glasses.

Two boys with skin-colored pinchers on their noses swam up on either side of her. "Hey, kid, why don'tcha try jumping in without your floatie?"

"Yeah." The other one smirked at his buddy. "Only babies use floaties."

Meghan's stomach turned a somersault. Her chest felt tight. "I'm not a baby."

"Prove it," the smirking one said.

Before Meghan could answer, a shadow fell over them. She looked up. There was Grandma.

"Boys, you're too big to be at this end of the pool. This end is for younger children. Go swim in your own end and leave the little ones alone."

The boys snickered, but they pushed away from the edge and swam away.

Meghan blinked back tears. She'd been having fun, and those boys had ruined it. "Can I take off my floatie?"

"No, you may not."

"How come?"

"Because you can't swim yet. The floatie keeps you safe."

"I don't wanna wear it." She stuck out her lower lip. "They said I'm a baby."

Grandma crouched down and smoothed a strand of wet hair from Meghan's forehead. "Just because they said it doesn't make it true."

"But, Grandma—"

"Meghan, who knows you better—those boys, or you?"

She scrunched her face. She didn't even know their names. They didn't know her name, either. They'd called her *kid*. "I know me better."

"Are you a baby?"

Meghan stuck out her skinny chest. "No."

"You're absolutely right. You aren't a baby. You're a little girl who hasn't yet learned to swim. Taking off your floatie could be dangerous for you. That's why you need to leave it on, no matter what other people say."

Meghan scowled. "I don't like it when boys call me names."

"Nobody likes to be called names. But if you already know you aren't what they said, there's no reason to pay any attention to them." Grandma slipped her sunglasses to the top of her head and looked Meghan right in the eyes. "Sweetheart, there are going to be lots of times in life when people call you names or try to convince you you're something you're not. You have to be strong enough to ignore them and be true to yourself. That's called respecting yourself, and it's very important. People who respect themselves make wise decisions."

"Like using my floatie?"

Grandma smiled. "Like using your floatie. At least until you've learned to swim."

Meghan chewed the inside of her cheek and squinted at Grandma. Finally she sighed. "All right. I'll wear it."

"Good girl."

"But, Grandma, can I learn how to swim, please?"

"I'll see if I can sign you up for lessons."

"Thank you!"

"Until then, your floatie will keep you safe in the water. And I'll be right here watching. If those boys come back, I'll chase them off so they can't bother you, all right?"

"I can chase 'em off all by myself." Meghan flexed her puny muscles. "I'm strong."

Grandma smiled. "Yes, you are. You're the strongest Meghan I know."

Eighteen

Present Day
Diane

iane put the pitcher of tea back in the fridge and poured the contents of her glass into the sink. She patted her leg, and the dachshunds dashed from the living room and surrounded her. She sat in the middle of her mother's clean tile floor and let the dogs wash her fingers, her arms, her chin with their velvety tongues, hoping the warm affection would wash away the frustration and anger Meghan's words had raised. Minutes passed, and her seething didn't subside.

If she were at home, she'd put the dogs in the car and go for a drive. A long drive always helped clear her head. But she wasn't at home, and she wasn't familiar enough with Las Vegas to go gallivanting even with her GPS. The GPS wouldn't keep her out of unsafe parts of town.

Mother knew the area and could guide her, but Diane wouldn't ask her. Not because Mother would refuse. She'd agree. But she'd keep wearing the mask of hurt she put on before leaving the kitchen, her attempt to goad Diane into guilt. She'd subjected Diane to manipulative silences her entire life. Meghan had no idea what Diane had lived through, and she had no business passing judgment.

She stood and rounded the corner to the living room, to Mother's chair, where the box of photographs from the closet and the stack of family albums waited on the side table. Diane sank into the chair and settled the box on her lap. The scrapbook page with the photo of Maggie holding her doll lay on top of the now neatly stacked photographs. Diane set it aside and lifted out one stack. She went through them one by one, examining the faces. Mostly examining her mother's girlish face. As she searched the expressions captured in black and white, the pictures began to tell a story. A story that made her squirm.

The distinctive *thud-thump* of Meghan's crutches on the floor interrupted, and she looked up. Her daughter approached slowly, remorse glimmering in her brown eyes. Diane shook her head before Meghan could offer an apology.

"Don't say it. It's done, can't be taken back, and it's best to forge forward, all right?"

Meghan hung her head for a moment. Then she nodded. "All right." She inched closer. "What are you doing?"

"Looking. Here, sit down." Diane swung her feet from the ottoman and waited until Meghan seated herself on the padded square. "This is kind of interesting." She lined up six photographs along the arm of the chair. "This one is Mother with her parents. She looks maybe five or six years old, agreed?"

Meghan leaned in and seemed to peruse the picture. She nodded.

"Notice she isn't really smiling. Neither is her mother. And her father doesn't look all that thrilled, either. We probably wouldn't caption this one Sunshine and Happiness, yes?"

Again Meghan nodded.

"Now look at the next one—Mother with her mom. Clearly the mother is expecting. She's trying to camouflage the bulge behind an apron, but the way Mother's arms are wrapped around her mom's waist, you can see the baby bump. Look at their expressions here. Different from the first pic, don't you think?"

Meghan frowned at the photos, her gaze darting back and forth. "Yeah. So?"

Diane pursed her lips. "Stick with me." She tapped the third photograph— the one Mother wanted to have blown up for a frame. "See here? The baby's with them. Granted, it's a studio portrait so they're having to pay for it, which means being on their best behavior, but any fool could see those smiles are genuine, not strained. Here's your sunshine-and-happiness shot."

A slight smile tipped up the corners of Meghan's lips. "They do look happy together, don't they?"

"Yes. As they do in the next two pictures, even though they aren't all together as a family." Diane held them up one at a time as she mused aloud. "These must've been taken on Maggie's birthday, because she's wearing the same dress as the one with her doll, and Mother said it was her birthday doll. See here? Maggie's with Mother and my grandmother, all smiling and happy. And here she's with Mother and my grandfather, still all smiling and happy. But now look at this one."

She aimed the final photo she'd selected at Meghan. "It's Mother, probably twelve or so, with her parents. Look at their faces. Look at how thin my grandfather is. Look at how strained my grandmother is. Look at how sad Mother appears." Diane slapped it back on the armrest and swept her hand along the row. "What we're looking at is the timeline of my grandfather's alcoholism. Drinking—not drinking—drinking again. I'd bet my dachshunds on it."

Meghan's eyes widened and she gaped at Diane. "You mean you think the only time he didn't drink was when Maggie was with them?"

"That's what it looks like to me."

"Oh, Mom."

Diane understood the sadness behind her daughter's simple statement. If Maggie was the impetus that led Burl Blackwell to give up drinking and if Mother felt responsible for losing Maggie, then she no doubt also assumed responsibility for her father's descent into alcoholism afterward.

Meghan gathered the photographs and fanned them like a hand of poker. She sighed. "Poor Grandma. It's one thing to hear her talk about how Maggie's disappearance affected her. It's another to see the evidence in front of you."

Diane couldn't hold back a snort. "We've seen the evidence for years in the way she behaves—overly controlling and overly protective and paranoid. We just didn't know until now what caused it. It's all because of her." She picked up the page with Maggie holding her birthday doll. "Mother let one event shape her entire life."

Meghan stared at her silently for a few seconds, and then she started to laugh.

Diane frowned. "What's so funny?"

Meghan swiped her hand over her face, erasing the chortles. But a grin remained. "I'm sorry. You sounded so indignant. It tickled me, that's all."

"Of course I'm indignant. I've lived with the effects of her sister's disappearance my whole life."

"I have, too."

Diane huffed. "No, you haven't."

Meghan placed the photographs in the box and rested her elbows on her knees. All humor faded from her expression. "You lived with an overly protective mother. She became overly protective because she was afraid to lose someone else she loved. Then I lived with you being . . . I don't know how to phrase it. *Permissive* doesn't quite fit, but *uncaring* seems too harsh. Maybe I should say *underly protective*."

Had Meghan just insulted her? Diane frowned again.

"I'm not trying to hurt your feelings, Mom, but sometimes I wondered if I was in your way. I got more hugs and attention from Grandma during my summer weeks than I got from you the remainder of the year."

"That's not fair! I—"

Meghan held up her hand. "I know you love me. I know that now. But there were times, as a kid, when I wondered because you seemed so . . . emotionally distant. I wouldn't have phrased it that way when I was a little girl, but that's how I'd define it now."

Diane rose and paced to the opposite side of the room. The four dachshunds trotted after her, then sat in a circle, gazing up at her with expectant faces. She folded her arms over her chest and glowered at her daughter. "I'm not going to spend the next six weeks being criticized at every turn. I did the best I could with you, and everything I did was out of love."

Meghan met her gaze, and a slow smile curved her mouth. "Exactly. You did the best you could with me, out of love. And Grandma did the best she could with you, out of love. You did things differently, but your motivations were the same." The smile slipped away. "I don't resent you, Mom. I understand that you did your best with me. But I wish you'd realize Grandma did her best, too, and give up your resentment toward her."

Diane hugged herself harder. Ginger, always the most in tune with her owner's feelings, began to whine. Diane bent over and absently scratched the dog's silky ears. Head low, she muttered, "She didn't have to let things that happened in her childhood be such a big deal when she became an adult." Then she gave a mental jolt. Was she condemning her mother, or was she speaking of herself?

Meghan

Meghan and Mom gave up conversation and watched a movie until Grandma roused from her nap. The moment her grandmother rounded the corner from her bedroom, Meghan pulled out her cell phone and smiled.

"There you are. Are you game for talking with a cold-case detective from Little Rock, Arkansas?"

Grandma offered a sleepy grin. "Isn't that what I'm doing when I talk with you?"

"Nope, I'm only your lowly granddaughter. But Sean is the real deal." He had three more years of experience than Meghan, and she trusted that he would have more ideas on how to track down Maggie. "I texted him right after you went to nap, to make sure he didn't mind a business call on Sunday"— Mom rolled her eyes—"and he said to call whenever as long as it wasn't after eleven, his time." She glanced at the grandfather clock. "It's a little after six there now, so we should be safe."

"Unless he's eating supper."

Meghan sighed. "Mom . . ."

Mom raised her hands in mock surrender. "I'm just pointing out the obvious."

Meghan made a face at her and then turned to Grandma. "It's up to you. We can put it off until tomorrow evening, if you'd rather."

Grandma stood for a moment with her brow puckered and her lower lip pulled in. The expression of uncertainty pierced Meghan. *If You love her, God, help her do what's best for her.* She gave a start. Had she just prayed?

Grandma crossed to the sofa and sat next to Meghan. "Let's call him now. I thought of something as I was falling asleep, and if I don't tell him right away, I might forget it again."

Mom used the remote to turn off the television, and Meghan punched Sean's contact number, then touched the speaker button. She held the cell phone between her and Grandma.

After only one ring, Sean's deep, familiar voice came through. "Hello, Meghan! So you're going to introduce me to your grandmother, huh?"

Meghan snickered. "I've got you on speaker, so you've already introduced yourself."

His hearty laughter vibrated from the phone. "If I'd known, I would have been more formal. It's nice to meet you, Mrs. DeFord."

Grandma smiled as warmly as if the two of them were seated across a table from each other. "Hello, Detective Eagle. I appreciate your willingness to help solve my mystery."

"Anything for Meghan's grandma."

Tears winked in Grandma's eyes. "Thank you."

"You're welcome. I'm sure Meghan's already told you, we might not be successful. Your little sister's been missing a long time. But we'll do our best."

Grandma leaned in as if speaking into a microphone. "I understand. I won't hold a grudge if you aren't successful."

Meghan aimed the phone at her own mouth. "Sean, let me give you the quick rundown. Grandma and Maggie were at a blackberry thicket about a mile from their house. Grandma left Maggie for a few minutes, and when she came back, her sister was gone. She searched for an hour or so before getting help. They found one of Maggie's shoes on a creek bank, which led the authorities to believe she fell into the creek and got washed away."

Grandma took hold of Meghan's wrist and pulled the phone closer. "But I don't believe it."

"Tell me why not, Mrs. DeFord."

Grandma's fingers tightened. "There are three reasons. First, Maggie's short legs could only carry her so far, so fast. Second, I found the ribbon from Maggie's hair on a tree branch too high for her to reach on her own. Someone would have had to carry her for her head to reach it. And"—she locked gazes with Meghan, triumph glittering in her brown irises—"she left her doll behind. The third reason is the most important, to my way of thinking. If she'd gone wandering on her own, she would have taken it with her. It was her birthday doll, and from the moment Daddy gave it to her, she never let loose of it."

So that was what Grandma had remembered. Meghan nodded, excited. "That's a great deduction. What we call a solid clue."

Grandma smiled. She let go of Meghan's wrist and placed her hands in her lap again. Miney jumped up beside her and rested her chin on Grandma's knee.

"I presume if she had been swept away in a creek"—Sean's contemplative tone came through the phone—"someone would have found her, uh, remains eventually. I can investigate the discovery of any unidentified remains. It would be good to rule out that theory."

Grandma laid her hand on the dachshund's head. Across the room, Mom's eyes widened. Meghan shook her head at her mother and spoke into the phone. "Sean, Grandma told me that a lady in town suspected Gypsies were abducting children."

"Someone blamed Gypsies?"

Grandma nodded, her expression grim. "Yes. The widow who ran the Benton County Orphans' Home. She said a Gypsy wagon had been run out of

Cumpton a day or two before Maggie disappeared, and I distinctly remember her mentioning at least two other children from nearby communities who turned up missing at the same time a Gypsy wagon came through the area. To my knowledge, those children were never found, either."

"Do you know the names of the children?"

"Oh, heavens, no." Grandma ran her fingers through Miney's thick ruff and sent a worried look at Meghan. "But I believe she said one was a girl close to Maggie's age, the other a baby boy."

"Do you recall which towns they lived in?"

Grandma grimaced and leaned closer to the phone. "No. It was so long ago . . ."

The worry lines marching across Grandma's forehead stung Meghan's heart. She spoke briskly. "Check for missing children from Benton County, Arkansas, in the first half of 1940, Sean. That should be a good starting point."

"Will do."

Meghan touched Grandma's knee. "Is there anything else you can think of that might help Sean start the search?"

"No, but . . ." She took the phone from Meghan and held it close to her mouth. "Young man, may I ask you a question?"

"Sure."

"My granddaughter said you are a Christian. Is that true?"

"Yes, ma'am. I am saved by grace through Jesus Christ's sacrifice on the cross of Calvary."

The sureness in his voice raised a wave of both envy and longing in Meghan's soul. Unexpectedly, tears threatened, and she blinked fast to keep them from forming.

"Then can I trust you will pray about your search for Maggie?"

"Ma'am, I pray about every case that crosses my desk. I ask God to guide and direct the investigation. I ask Him to bring His perfect solution. And I ask Him to give peace to the ones who are affected by the case. Since this case affects somebody who means a lot to me—"

Meghan's pulse sped.

"—you can be sure I will be praying about it." A moment of silence fell. "Is there something specific you'd like me to pray for?"

Grandma closed her eyes and bowed her head, touching her forehead to the phone. "Yes. For God's will, certainly, and also that He would prepare Maggie's heart. I'm so eager to find her, so eager to hold her again, so eager to tell her I'm sorry." A tear slid down Grandma's cheek and plopped on Miney's head. "Will you pray her heart will be open to receiving me?"

"Mrs. DeFord . . ." The huskiness in his voice let Meghan know he'd been touched by Grandma's request, and her heart rolled over in gratitude for his innate tenderness and compassion. "How about we pray about it together right now?"

Nineteen

Hazel

Hazel pointed at Meghan's cell phone and gave a nod. "Now that is a nice young man."

"Yeah, he really is." Meghan stiffened her spine, and her eyes sparked. "He gets ribbed a lot at the office because he doesn't tell coarse jokes or go drinking after work with the guys. But it doesn't change him. And he never retaliates. I really admire Sean's firm stance on right and wrong. He's one of those people who does more than talk the talk—he walks the walk, if you know what I mean."

Hazel nodded. "I do know what you mean. I remember Atticus Finch telling his little daughter in *To Kill a Mockingbird,* 'Before I can live with other folks I've got to live with myself. The one thing that doesn't abide by majority rule is a person's conscience.' It sounds as if your Sean is a man of integrity."

"That's a good way to put it." Meghan frowned, absently transferring the cell phone from palm to palm. "Before becoming his partner, I battled the tendency to cave to other people's opinions rather than rock any boats—you know, trying to be everybody's friend. But he's inspired me to stand firm on what I believe. He's a good mentor for me. I got lucky when they partnered me with him."

Hazel gave Meghan's knee a pat. "Maybe it wasn't luck at all. Maybe it was a blessing."

Meghan grinned. "Maybe."

Something moist and warm brushed Hazel's arm. She jerked and looked down. She drew back in surprise. "Well, you little scamp. What are you doing sitting up here with me?" The dachshund blinked at her, her furry ears forming soft peaks. She pawed Hazel's leg, clearly begging for attention. Hazel shook her head. "You're pestering the wrong person, pooch. I won't pet you."

Margaret Diane burst out laughing. "Mother, she's been sitting beside you for more than five minutes. You were petting her while you were on the phone."

Hazel frowned. "I did no such thing."

"You did, Grandma." Meghan seemed more concerned than amused. "Don't you remember?"

"No." Hazel glared at the dog, who gazed up at her with round brown eyes and her mouth forming a doggie grin. Her old shepherd pal, Farley, used to smile that same way. Sadness rolled through her. "Which one is this?"

"Miney." Margaret Diane snickered. "You know, from the litter I jokingly named Eenie, Meenie, Miney, and Mo. By the time I decided to keep her, the name had stuck. Isn't that right, Miney?" The dog's ears perked even higher. But she didn't move.

Temptation to stroke the animal's head—this time with full use of her senses—tugged hard. *"You think I want to look at that picture with you holding on to animals like they're something special?"* Her mother's voice, harsh and condemning, roared through her memory. Hazel cupped her hands under Miney's stomach and gently urged her off the sofa. "Go to your mama. I don't want you." But even she recognized the lack of conviction in her tone.

Before either Meghan or Margaret Diane could question her, she aimed a tart look at her granddaughter. "Please tell me more about this partner of yours. Do you have a photo of him? I'd like to see a face to go with his voice."

"Maybe next time we'll do FaceTime. Then you can see him for yourself."

"And he would be able to see me?"

Meghan nodded.

Hazel wrinkled her nose. "I'd scare him to death. No, you just tell me." She wanted to see Sean through Meghan's eyes.

"Well . . ." Pink stole across Meghan's cheeks. She leaned into the cushions and aimed her gaze to the ceiling. "He's never said so, but I think he might have some Native American blood in him. For one thing, his last name is Eagle. Doesn't that sound Native American? For another, his complexion is always a shade darker than anyone else's. He has thick dark-brown hair he keeps cut short—almost like someone in the military." She angled her face toward Hazel and winked. "He's got the fighting-man bod, too. Downright hunky."

Hazel pursed her lips to keep from smiling. "Meghan . . ."

"Hey, I've got eyes. Pretty hard to miss a good-lookin' guy when he's sitting across a desk from you day after day."

Hazel chuckled. "If I didn't know better, I'd say you were smitten with your partner."

Margaret Diane sat up, too. "*Smitten* is an old-fashioned word. My generation would say Meghan has the hots for him."

"And neither of your generations needs to weigh in on that." Meghan bounced a firm look across both of them. "Sean's my partner and he's also my friend. I know I can count on him. But he's never hinted at anything more."

"Maybe you should hint."

Margaret Diane said what Hazel was thinking. What little she'd gleaned about Sean Eagle during their brief telephone exchange intrigued her. And Meghan's description, particularly of his character, impressed her. He seemed exactly the kind of man she'd prayed would come into Meghan's life. She prayed the same thing for Margaret Diane. Hazel's daughter was still a young woman. There was time for her to fall in love with a decent, caring man and enjoy years of happiness. If she was willing to give up her fierce independence.

"Color me narrow minded, but"—Meghan folded her arms over her chest and lifted her chin—"I think the man should be the one to make the first move. And Sean hasn't moved. I'm not going to mess up our good working relationship by resorting to flirtation."

Margaret Diane's lips twitched. "But you've been tempted?"

Meghan snorted. "Grandma would be tempted. He's that cute. But . . ." Her stiff stance relaxed. "He needs to date someone who goes to church, who believes like he does."

Her granddaughter's change in demeanor, from teasing to melancholy, pierced Hazel. She squeezed Meghan's knee. "I'm sorry if we've embarrassed you, honey. We won't talk about Sean anymore."

"Today," Margaret Diane interjected with a smirk.

Hazel frowned at her daughter. "Until Meghan decides she wants to talk about him. For now, should we do another page in the scrapbook? Or are you getting hungry? I thought I'd get out the little gas grill and cook some asparagus, zucchini, and corn on the cob for our supper."

"Why, Mother, that sounds fantastic!" Margaret Diane pressed her palms to her bodice, her eyebrows high. "You're becoming a regular vegan chef."

Her Margaret Diane had paid her a compliment. A genuine, heartfelt compliment. Hazel's chest swelled with happiness. "I'll get the grill ready."

Diane

Diane flopped onto the mattress on her side and propped up her head with her hand. She poked Meghan on the shoulder. "Okay, it's just the two of us now. So tell me, do you have the hots for Sean Eagle?"

Meghan rolled her eyes. "Mom, for Pete's sake, are we in junior high?"

Diane laughed. "Not even close. But I think it's been since you were in junior high that I saw you get all embarrassed and blushing when a boy's name was mentioned."

Meghan's face flamed. She reached for the bedside lamp.

"No, don't turn it off yet."

"I'm sleepy." Meghan yawned—an extraordinarily long, forced yawn. "And we've got a full day planned for tomorrow."

"I know, I know." Diane ticked off the activities with her fingers. "Get Mother's photograph enlarged, take her necklace to a jeweler, maybe meet some of her Books and Mocha—"

"Lit and Latte."

Diane huffed. "Reading group for lunch, browse the flea market." She frowned. "We've got almost six weeks. I don't know why she thinks she has to do everything in one day."

Meghan closed her eyes and linked her hands over her belly. "She probably wants to stay busy so she doesn't have to think. I imagine Maggie is dominating her thoughts right now. And even Sean said finding her will be a long shot."

"I didn't hear him say that."

"He said it to me when he called after dinner."

"Aha!" Diane poked Meghan again and grinned when her daughter opened her eyes and scowled. "Why'd he call back? He couldn't know anything about the case yet, so it had to be personal."

Meghan groaned. "We weren't going to talk about Sean."

"You brought him back into the conversation. Why'd he call?"

"He wanted me to remind Grandma that he'd do his best but that it was really up to God whether we find out what happened to Maggie or not. Because finding her will be such a long shot."

"Mmm-hmm." Diane rolled onto her back and stared at the rotating blades of the ceiling fan. "Too bad he's so religious. I think he'd be a pretty good catch for you if he could get off his God kick."

Meghan bolted up on one elbow. "Mom! That's a terrible thing to say."

Diane tipped her face toward Meghan. "No, it's an honest thing to say. There's nothing wrong with believing in God if that's what you want to do, but when you have to bring Him into every conversation . . . well, it's too much. I'm a teacher, but do I talk about teaching to every person I meet? Of course not. I'd bore them if I did. But religious people don't seem to get that. They think they've got to insert God-talk no matter the subject. That's probably why the other detectives at work dislike him."

The light from the lamp behind Meghan painted a halo around her dark hair. A thick shadow fell over her face, but it didn't hide her scowl. "I never said the guys at work didn't like him. It's really the opposite. Yeah, they rib him— call him Preacher and try to break him down into going to the bars with them.

But I think if he gave in and went, they'd lose respect for him." She lay down again and seemed to examine the ceiling. "When they're stuck on a case and need someone with a level head to get them going again, they all go to Sean. He's not the captain of our unit, but he's . . . our stabilizer." She sucked in her lips for a moment, her forehead puckering. "He's got something the rest of us don't, and I think it's because he's got God."

Diane fidgeted, uneasy but uncertain why. "I thought you didn't want to talk about Sean."

They lay in silence for several minutes. The dogs shifted in their crates. One of them—probably Molly—whined and scratched at the plastic side until Diane said, "Lie still." The noise stopped. Diane closed her eyes, ready to let sleep carry her away.

"Mom, since we're talking about guys . . ."

Something in her daughter's tone warned of trouble. Diane's eyes popped open. She licked her dry lips. "I thought you wanted to sleep."

"In a bit." The mattress bounced as Meghan rolled onto her side and rested her cheek on her bent arm. "When Sean prays, he calls God his Father."

Diane nodded slowly, but her pulse was racing faster than a car in the Indianapolis 500. Chills broke out across her frame. "I know. I heard him on the phone. So?"

"Grandma had her father. You had yours. But I've never—"

The chills changed to heat—an intense, searing, painful rush of shame-induced heat.

March 1, 1985
Little Rock, Arkansas

Diane awakened with her cheek on Kevin's bicep. He smelled like BO, stale popcorn, and beer. Like a frat boy. She screwed up her nose and rolled away from him.

He grunted and came awake. "You goin' back to your dorm?"

"Not yet."

His arms snaked out and pulled her snug against his frame. "Good." He brushed his lips on her temple, giving her a whiff of his sour breath.

Nausea attacked. "Kev, go brush your teeth, huh? I have something important to tell you."

In the slash of midmorning sunlight pouring through the uncovered window, his grin turned leering. "I don't much feel like talking, but I do feel like—"

She pushed on his chest with both hands. "No." The way her stomach felt, if he kissed her on the mouth she'd puke. "Go brush your teeth, okay?"

He muttered, but he pulled himself out of bed and padded into the bathroom. She lay on the rumpled sheets, her heart pounding and her stomach whirling. She had the most incredible thing to tell him. The most frightening thing to tell him. She hoped he'd be excited. She needed his excitement to chase away her fear.

He scuffed back to the bed and fell across it onto his belly.

"Kevin, guess what?"

"Can't guess." He cupped the back of her head and tried to pull her face to his.

"I'm pregnant."

He froze. "What?"

A nervous laugh escaped her throat. "I'm pregnant. Isn't it wonderful? We're gonna have a baby."

"What makes you think it's mine?"

The question stabbed as violently as a knife through her chest. When she had started going out with Kevin, her friends warned her he was a player, but she'd been certain he had changed. For her. The same way she'd changed for him.

She sat up and folded her arms over her chest. "I haven't been with anyone else." She gulped. "Ever."

He rolled over, sat up, and ran both hands through his thick honey-blond hair. Still holding his head, he muttered something she couldn't decipher, but she didn't need to hear the words to understand the tone. He wasn't happy.

She'd surprised him. That's why he was upset. Kevin didn't like surprises—he'd told her so the first time they went out. She should have planned a better way to tell him about the baby, but she couldn't wait. She needed his help. How could she do this alone?

She inched close and curled her hands over his taut shoulders. "I know it's a shock. It took me by surprise, too."

Kevin jerked, dislodging her hands. "How'd it happen? Aren't you smart enough to use birth control? Of all the—"

His accusatory words raised her anger. "I'm not the only one who could take precautions. You—"

"Don't you dare pin this on me." He jumped up and whirled on her. The fury in his face sent her scuttling to the opposite side of the bed. "You did it on purpose, didn't you? Thinking you'd get me to marry you. My family has money—is that what you're after?"

"No! I don't need your money. I thought . . . I thought . . ." She thought she loved him. Thought he loved her. What a stupid notion. Tears filled her eyes, and she held one hand toward him. "Kevin, please, we're gonna be parents. I need you to—"

He stepped back, shaking his head. "I'm not gonna be a parent. No way. Not now. Not with you."

His cold glare and harsh words stole her ability to breathe. She pressed her fist against her lips and choked on sobs.

He hung his head. The muscles in his square jaw bulged and released, and the veins in his forehead darkened and then faded. Diane waited for the explosion that was sure to come. But then he looked at her, and his expression was tender. She swallowed and clung to hope as he rounded the bed and sat next to her.

"Di, honey . . ." He brushed her cheek with his knuckles. "Do you love me?"

She nodded and fresh tears spilled down her face.

"Then you'd do anything for me, right?"

Hadn't she already proved that by sleeping with him? "Yes. Anything." Even marry him at the courthouse tomorrow and live in a rat-infested basement apartment if their parents disowned them.

"I want you to get rid of it."

Ice filled Diane's veins. "W-what?"

"Get rid of it." He stroked her hair, spoke sweetly, as gentle as he'd ever been. "We aren't ready to be parents. And you can't be far along, right?" His palm slipped to her flat belly. "It's not worth ruining our lives for, is it?"

She'd been so afraid since she missed her second period. So scared to tell her mother, to tell Kevin, to admit it was true. She'd wished a hundred times it wasn't true, that there was no baby growing inside her. But in that moment all she wanted to do was protect the little life.

She leaped away from him and shook her head. "No. I can't. I can't kill it."

His gaze narrowed. "People do it all the time. That's why abortion's legal—so you don't have to have a baby if you don't want to."

She clutched her stomach. The spot where right now his baby's heart beat safe inside her womb. "But I . . . I want to have it." She gulped and whispered, "With you."

He stood and stomped past her to the closet. He grabbed out clothes and dressed as if she wasn't in the room. When he'd tied the laces on his sneakers, he finally threw a snarling look in her direction. "If you have it, it'll be yours. Not mine. If you decide to get an abortion, I'll pay for it. Then we can keep going out. But if you have it, you're on your own. Don't expect anything from me."

Her throat convulsed with the effort of not throwing up. "I . . . I . . ."

"Make up your mind, Diane. Do you want a kid, or do you want me?"

Present Day
Kendrickson, Nevada

Diane tossed the covers aside and sat up on the edge of the bed. "That's a closed subject, Meghan."

"But—"

"No!" She pulled in a slow breath and released it in increments, the controlled expulsions calming her jangled nerves. She turned a steady gaze on her daughter. "Mother might be digging up her past, but I have no desire to do the same. Believe me, your so-called father isn't worth unearthing." She headed for the bathroom. Maybe another toothbrushing would remove the bitter taste from her mouth.

Twenty

Las Vegas, Nevada
Hazel

azel pointed to an empty spot in the old strip-mall parking lot. "That should work well—centrally located to all the shops."

Margaret Diane pulled her car into the slot and heaved a mighty sigh. "I'm glad this is our last stop of the day. My nerves are frazzled. I cannot believe the traffic in this town! And on a Monday, no less. I'd assume midday during the workweek would mean fewer vehicles on the streets." She pulled expanding window shades from the pocket on the driver's door and flopped them into place, covering the windshield.

Hazel slipped the strap of her hobo bag over her shoulder. "It is summer, which means lots of tourists. And many of the people who live in Vegas work nights, so they do their errands during the day."

Meghan piped up from the back seat, "I guess they call Las Vegas the City That Never Sleeps for a reason. Maybe you should let Grandma drive us home, Mom—give yourself a break from driving."

Margaret Diane shot a frown over her shoulder. "I can drive just fine, thank you."

Meghan shrugged and popped her door open. "Only a suggestion."

Hazel chuckled. "Do I need to take the two of you home and put you down for naps? You're starting to sound grumpy." The statement carried her backward in time to her daughter's toddler days and to Meghan's summer visits. The years had slipped by so fast. Melancholy tried to sneak in, but she deliberately pushed the sad feeling aside. "Maybe some ice cream will sweeten you up. It's been an hour since we had lunch." If nothing had changed from the last time she visited the row of flea market and specialty shops, there was an ice cream parlor near the east end of the strip. "How about a snack? My treat."

Margaret Diane rolled her eyes.

Too late Hazel remembered her daughter didn't partake of dairy products. "Or maybe a glass of iced tea. Or lemonade? I seem to recall the ice cream place has lemonade, and you can put different fruit in it." Lemonade was vegan, wasn't it?

"Lemonade sounds good to me," Meghan said.

Margaret Diane opened her door and grabbed the little cloth bag she carried as a purse. "How about we get something to drink on the way home? Most shops won't let you take food or drinks inside, and I'd rather finish our shopping." She paused, aiming a frown at Hazel. "What exactly are we looking for, by the way?"

Confusion gripped Hazel. She blinked. "Looking for?"

Margaret Diane pursed her lips. "In the antique store, Mother. We set out to run four errands. We printed your photograph, we dropped off your pearl necklace at the jeweler, we had a sandwich with a couple of your book friends, and now we're at the antique store. Why are we here?"

There must have been a reason she wanted to come to the old strip mall that now housed a flea market and specialty shops, but she couldn't remember why. "I . . ." Her mouth was too dry to form words. She needed something to drink.

Meghan reached over the seat and put her hand on Hazel's shoulder. "Grandma likes to browse the antique shops, Mom. We came to browse, right, Grandma?"

So she hadn't forgotten a specific task. Relief flooded Hazel. She nodded, her breath releasing on a sigh. "Yes. We came to browse."

Margaret Diane slipped from behind the steering wheel and closed her door without a word, leaving Hazel and Meghan inside. Meghan rubbed Hazel's shoulder. "Ready to go?"

The fog of confusion was lifting. Hazel forced a short laugh. "Yes, I suppose so, if I can get my creaky bones to move. Goodness, this heat. It must be frying my brain."

Meghan laughed, too, but a hint of worry glimmered in her brown eyes.

Hazel patted her granddaughter's hand and then opened her car door. "Come on. Your mother's waiting on the sidewalk, and she has less tolerance for the heat than I do. We'd better shake a leg."

At least four of the shops along the strip advertised antiques, and Margaret Diane led them to the one closest to the car. A cowbell clanged when they opened the door, the sound raising memories of Hazel's days working at the general store in Cumpton. A musty odor hung in the shop, the scent of items long unused. For reasons she couldn't explain, the aroma stirred sadness in the center of her soul.

Margaret Diane located a rocking chair near the front windows and slid into the seat. She waved her hand at Hazel and Meghan. "Explore to your heart's content. I'll sit here and relax." She sniffed. "Antiques aren't my thing."

Hazel gestured for Meghan to precede her up a narrow aisle between shelves holding all variety of glassware, plates, and bric-a-brac. The two moved at a slow pace, gazes roving back and forth, pausing now and then to more closely examine an item. Many so-called antique stores were overpriced garage sales these days, but Hazel found little of what she would deem junk on the shelves of this shop.

"Oh, Grandma, look. Don't you have a bowl like this in your curio cabinet?" Meghan touched the rim of a pale-pink glass serving bowl with a raised rose pattern decorating the sides.

Hazel cupped the bowl in her hands and lifted it from the shelf. She smiled. "I certainly do. It's a piece from Mama's set of Rose of Sharon dishes." She placed the bowl on the shelf again but continued to gaze at the translucent bowl. "Lots of people in Cumpton had the same dishes. My best friend's mother had them in green, and our preacher's wife had clear ones. I always liked the pink best, and so did Mama, although she said it was prideful to say such a thing out loud."

Meghan grinned. "I bet your mother liked the pink because she had daughters."

Hazel smiled. Daughters . . . How good it felt to acknowledge that her mother had more than one daughter. But then she gave a start. Daddy had started buying the dishes for Mama long before Maggie was born. Had Daddy chosen pink because of Hazel Mae? She swallowed a lump of emotion and traced a rose with her finger. "Daddy brought ours home one piece at a time from the gas station." She angled a grin at Meghan. "Can you imagine buying dishes at a gas station these days?"

Meghan snickered. "Nope."

"Lots of things have changed since back then."

Meghan turned over the little price tag dangling from the bowl and whistled through her teeth. "Whew, these things are expensive. Do you have the whole set? It'd be worth a small fortune."

Remorse twisted Hazel's heart. "No, those dishes were sold years ago when Mama passed away and the farmhouse and contents went up for auction. I took that one bowl because it had a nick on the rim and the auctioneer only wanted to sell undamaged merchandise. I couldn't bear for him to throw it away because of one little nick." She shook her head. "If God cast us aside over the nicks in our lives, none of us would make it to heaven."

Meghan giggled.

Hazel raised her eyebrows. "What's funny?"

"You reminded me of something Sean said one time—about God using cracked vessels. Another detective accused him of calling us all crackpots."

Hazel chuckled. "Well, that's a term we need to avoid. But Sean is right. There is no one so damaged that grace can't redeem him. That's one of the best things about God, I think. He never sees us as too far gone." Not Hazel, who'd so dismally failed in raising her daughter. And not Margaret Diane, who sought peace in vegetables and intellect. God could still reach her, and Hazel would never stop praying.

A soft smile lit Meghan's eyes. "I like hearing you talk about God. It makes me feel . . . warm and cozy inside." She touched Hazel's hand. "So don't stop, okay?"

Hazel understood the hidden message—*Don't let Mom's attitude about God silence you.* "Okay."

They continued up the aisle, and at the far end an open doorway waited. Above the door a small metal sign stamped Employees Only gave a warning to stay out, but at eye level a hand-printed sign stating Please Come In was tacked to the door's frame. Meghan glanced over her shoulder. "Wanna go in, Grandma?"

Hazel shrugged. "We might as well see everything."

Meghan grinned and swung her crutches forward. The moment she cleared the threshold, she gasped. Hazel hurried in behind her, then stopped and stared. Floor-to-ceiling shelves lined three walls of what had probably been a storage closet, and dolls cluttered every shelf. Big dolls, little dolls, dolls wearing frilly dresses, and others completely unclothed. Those with cloth bodies slumped on the shelves, and those with hard plastic bodies stood proudly over the others. Barbie dolls were tucked in every small space between larger dolls, and a stack of perhaps two dozen more lay in a lopsided pyramid on a bottom shelf.

Meghan burst out laughing. "Holy cow, this would have been my dream room when I was six! Look at 'em all." She turned a slow circle, eyes wide and mouth open in amazement. "How many do you think there are?"

Hazel did a quick estimation. "At least three hundred, I would think, not counting the Barbies." She inched her way around the room, scanning the faces with pink-painted cheeks, rosebud lips, and glass eyes. Most of the dolls seemed to be from Margaret Diane's era. She spotted Raggedy Ann, Chatty Cathy, and Baby Tender Love, and memories of Christmases past washed over her.

She tipped back her head to view those on the highest shelf, and she began to tremble. Her purse slipped from her shoulder and hit the floor. She covered her mouth with her fingers and whispered, "Oh, my . . ."

June 16, 1943
Cumpton, Arkansas

"Oh, Burl, what were you thinkin'?" Mama shook her head at Daddy. "She's too little for a doll like that. You should've saved it for Hazel Mae's birthday."

Hazel stared at the beautiful doll clutched in Maggie's chubby arms. Hazel's doll had a molded head and a cloth body. She'd longed for one with hair she could comb and style, one with jointed arms and legs so it could sit up on its own for tea parties. But Daddy'd given her dream doll to Maggie.

His grin never faded. He pointed at Maggie's doll. "That thing's the spittin' image of Maggie. Look at its golden curls an' blue eyes. When I saw it in the catalog, I knew it had to be hers." He chucked Hazel on the shoulder. "You've already got a doll, Hazel Mae. You don't need another one, do you?"

Hazel hung her head so Daddy wouldn't see the jealousy in her eyes. Envy was a sin.

Maggie held the doll aloft and announced, "Her Minnie."

Hazel snagged up the box the doll had come in. "This says her name is Cynthia." Cynthia . . . such a pretty name. Hazel's heart nearly twisted into a pretzel with longing to claim that doll as her own.

Maggie shook her head until her blond curls bounced. "Her Minnie. Not Sinfee-uh."

Hazel jabbed her finger on the box. "But—"

Mama snapped her fingers. "It's Maggie's doll, Hazel Mae. She can name it whatever she wants to."

Hazel shrunk back and clamped her lips shut. How could anybody choose the plain name Minnie over a beautiful one like Cynthia? If she ever got a doll so pretty and sweet, she'd name it Cynthia.

Present Day
Las Vegas, Nevada

Meghan hurried to her side, the tips of her crutches squeaking on the tile floor. "What's wrong?"

Hazel raised her arm and pointed to a doll half hidden between two slouching baby dolls. "It's her."

"Who?" Meghan stood so close her breath brushed Hazel's jaw.

"Minnie . . ." The name wheezed from Hazel's lips. Her legs trembled so badly she feared they would collapse. She planted both palms over her pounding heart. "I need to sit down."

Meghan bolted to the doorway in two swings on her crutches. "Mom! Bring Grandma a chair!" Her voice reverberated from the dropped tiles of the ceiling.

In less than a minute, Margaret Diane and another woman with streaky red and brown hair—probably a store worker—burst into the small room. The worker pushed a stool, similar in style to the one Daddy had used when milking their cows, behind Hazel. Hazel sank onto the round seat and hung her head.

Margaret Diane crouched next to her. "What's the matter? Are you sick?"

"I'll be all right. I'm just a little light headed." She pulled in several deep, slow breaths while Margaret Diane stared intently into her face. Slowly her pulse calmed, and the fuzzy feeling faded. She patted her daughter's hand. "You needn't hover, dear. I'm fine now."

Margaret Diane straightened, but she remained next to the stool, her brow forming deep lines of either concern or consternation. Hazel was never sure how to read her daughter's expressions.

She shifted her gaze to the store worker, who stood nearby wringing her hands and chewing on her lip. "Young woman, could you retrieve a doll from the top shelf for me? That one." She pointed at the doll with fuzzy sausage curls and blue glass eyes lined with thick lashes.

"I need to get a stepladder. I'll be right back." The woman hurried out of the room, her flip-flops slapping against her bare heels.

Meghan stumped around to Hazel's opposite side, her face aimed at the top shelf. "That's an old doll. Did you have one like it?" Her deliberately light tone didn't fool Hazel—the girl was worried.

Hazel took her hand. "I'm sorry if I frightened you, but I haven't seen Minnie in so long. The sight, the remembrance . . ." She released a low, rueful chuckle. "It overwhelmed me."

The worker returned with a folding ladder. She set it up and climbed the rungs. She put her hand on the doll's neck and glanced at Hazel. "This one?"

Hazel nodded.

The woman handed it to Margaret Diane, and Hazel held out her arms.

Margaret Diane hesitated. "This seems to be porcelain, Mother. And . . ." She frowned at the attached price tag. "If you break it, you'll have to buy it."

"I intend to buy it anyway, so please give it to me."

Twenty-One

Diane

The worker had descended the ladder, and she stood close and watched Diane place the doll in Mother's waiting hands.

"That's a Vogue doll," the woman said, "and it's composition rather than porcelain, but it's still fragile."

"In other words, we need to be careful with it." Diane slipped her hand under the doll's head. As shaky as Mother appeared, she may not have the strength to hang on to the doll.

The woman linked her fingers, her bold blue fingernail polish flashing in the fluorescent lights. "The box got ruined when a water pipe burst in the storage room, but I can tell you it's a Cynthia doll from 1940. You'll find her name stamped on the sole of her shoe."

Mother turned the doll upside down and peeked at the bottoms of the leather shoes. She nodded, smiling. "Yes. Cynthia."

"She has a mohair wig, and she's wearing her original dress, socks, and shoes. There are only spiderweb cracks in the composition on her legs and arms, something fairly common in dolls of that era, but there are no chips or curling. If it wasn't for the missing box, we could advertise this one as mint." She took another step closer, her gaze locked on the doll. "Cynthia was sold individually and also as part of a three-doll collection—the My Sister and Me set—with Linda and Toddles. Linda is a good-sized doll, twenty inches tall. Toddles, sometimes called Toodles, was the smallest at only eight inches tall, and Cynthia was in between."

Meghan shot a puzzled frown at the worker. "You know an awful lot about the merchandise in here."

The woman let out a soft laugh. "If you'd picked up something from any other booth in the shop, I'd be clueless, but this is my mom's booth. She collected dolls her whole life, and whether I wanted to or not, I learned about them."

Diane understood the "whether I wanted to or not" comment.

The worker gestured to the highest shelves. "When she consented to selling them, she insisted that we put the oldest, most valuable dolls up high so children can't get to them. She never even let me play with the oldest dolls, and she certainly didn't want strangers' children putting their hands on them."

Diane stifled a snort. Mother and the worker's mom had a few things in common. Did Mother still have the little flowered tea set Diane had never been allowed to touch? She glanced to see if her mother was listening, but Mother was smoothing the lace on the doll's faded yellow dress, a faraway look in her eyes. She probably hadn't heard a word. Diane turned to the woman. "Why'd your mother decide to part with her collection?"

The woman sighed. "Mom moved into assisted living last year after falling and breaking her hip. The facility is a lot more expensive than we thought it would be. She needed extra money, so I brought her dolls in to sell on consignment."

Diane caught the hint. There'd be no negotiating on price. She hoped Mother wouldn't be foolish enough to pay what they were asking. Eventually she'd be in a rest home, too, and squandering money now wouldn't help her then. She held out her hands for the doll. "Let's put it back, Mother."

Mother cradled the doll against her shoulder the way Diane used to hold Meghan to burp her. "I'm not putting her back. I had to burn Minnie even though I didn't want to. Now I'll have her back again, and I can give her to Maggie."

The worker gaped at Mother as if she'd lost her mind. Small wonder, considering the cryptic comments. Even Diane had a hard time following her, and she knew about Maggie's lost birthday doll.

She leaned down and spoke near Mother's ear. "They're asking over one hundred fifty dollars for this doll. You don't even know that we'll find Maggie. It would be foolish to spend that much money on a maybe."

Mother's eyes narrowed. Her dark irises sparked. "I am buying Maggie's Minnie." Still gripping the doll to her shoulder, she struggled to rise. Meghan took her elbow and helped. Mother wobbled for a few seconds and then seemed to find her balance. Her chin high, she thrust the doll at the worker. "Box her up, please."

Diane rolled her eyes. "Mother . . ."

"And that one, too." She pointed to a doll with its straight brown hair tied in pigtails and its cheeks dotted with freckles. She turned a sheepish look on Diane. "Your dad and I bought you a Chatty Cathy like this one for Christmas when you were four. Although warned to be gentle, you yanked the string so hard you broke the speech mechanism within a week, and your dad punished you by throwing the doll away. I've always felt bad about that. You were so young, and you could have still played with the doll even if it didn't talk." Her lips quivered into a hesitant smile. "So now you'll have another one."

The story was sweet, and deep inside herself Diane was touched by her mother's regret even though she couldn't remember having a doll like the one on the shelf. She pulled in a breath, intending to thank her, but other words tumbled out. "And by buying a doll for me, you can justify buying that other one."

Mother's face fell.

Meghan gasped. "Mom! That was a terrible thing to say!"

It was. Why had she said it? Maybe the talk about the cost of rest homes and Mother's frivolous spending had inspired the comment. She should apologize.

"I'll wrap both of these." The woman carried both dolls and inched toward the door. "They'll be at the register whenever you're done shopping." She hurried out.

Meghan put her hand on Mother's shoulder. "Do you want to browse the rest of the booths, Grandma?"

Mother shook her head. "No. I've spent my allowance. Let's go back to the house."

"But we'll get lemonade first, right?" Meghan, ever the peacemaker, bounced a hopeful look from Mother to Diane and back. "With strawberries in it?"

Diane answered before Mother could. "Yes. My treat." It was a small gesture, but maybe Mother would see it as the apology she wasn't able to say.

Kendrickson, Nevada
Meghan

Early Wednesday morning, Meghan's cell phone growled a short *Mah Nà Mah Nà* from the old Muppets program—her text-message notification. The dogs whined and shifted in their crates, and she instinctively intoned, "Shhh." No sense in waking Mom, who still slept soundly on the opposite side of the bed.

She rolled over and pawed at the nightstand until she located the phone and squinted at it, yawning. The time showed five till six. She grunted under her breath. Who would text her at such a ridiculous hour? She pulled up her text messages and glanced at the sender, then the message. Her heart fired into her throat. All sleepiness fled. She shot straight up.

The mattress springs popped, and Mom came awake. "Meghan? Good grief, lie still." She flopped over to her other side, bouncing the mattress worse than Meghan had, and burrowed into her pillow.

Meghan grimaced. "Sorry," she whispered. With the room cloaked in total darkness, she had a hard time locating her crutches, which she'd left leaning against the wall beside the nightstand. She managed to snag them, tucked them under her arms, and made her way around the bed and out the door. Grandma always left a lamp glowing in the living room, and she followed the thin ribbon of yellow to Grandma's chair.

She flopped into the soft cushions, laid her crutches across the ottoman, and read the message again.

Wanted you to know I found no reports of unidentified remains, but I located the names of missing children from Benton County. Eight in all between 1937 and 1946. Also found a report about one-year-old twins who disappeared from Delaware County in Oklahoma during the same time period. Seems suspicious. One other detail has me troubled, too. Would like to chat with you and Mrs. DeFord. Call me this evening, please.

Meghan shook her head. Eight children inexplicably missing in a single decade. Ten if the two from across the border in Oklahoma were woven into the mystery. When Grandma mentioned two others besides Maggie, the count had seemed high. But ten? Suspicious was an understatement. The number was unbelievable. What else could be troubling Sean besides the high count? Her finger twitched with eagerness to call Sean right away, but he'd be at the office already. She couldn't bother him during work hours.

Still, she tapped a quick reply.

Will tell Grandma what you discovered. Will call later today. Thanks.

She slapped the phone into her lap and stared across the dimly lit room. The house was quiet. The grandfather clock gently *ticktock*ed a soothing rhythm. She should go back to bed, but she doubted she could sleep. There were questions to answer, and she wanted to find the answers now. The most pressing question echoed through her mind. Disregarding the twins from Oklahoma, how could so many children from a rural county in Arkansas simply disappear?

Meghan chewed her lip. If it had happened more recently, she'd suspect a pedophilia ring. Sex trafficking was far too common in today's world. Not that pedophiles hadn't existed in the thirties and forties—of course they had—but people back then were less likely to act on those kinds of urges because of the social ramifications. In all likelihood a pedophile would build a relationship, albeit a sick one, with a single child and nurture it over time. Even if a pedophile had taken these children and killed them, authorities would have found skeletal remains at some point.

Grandma was convinced Gypsies had taken Maggie, but the group of nomads would stick out like the proverbial sore thumb. Would they dare to return to an area that many times? Curiosity writhed through her. Had one person or a group of people taken the children? For what purpose? Why had they never been recovered? A shiver rattled her frame. What kind of evil had haunted the idyllic community tucked into the Ozark Mountains?

At six thirty Grandma wandered into the living room, wearing robin's-egg-blue seersucker pajamas and a matching robe. She gave a start when she spotted Meghan. "What are you doing up so early?"

Meghan held up her phone, ready to share the text, but an internal voice cautioned her to wait. She shrugged. "Woke up and didn't want to bother Mom, so I came out here. Can I help you with breakfast?"

"You can keep me company while I make . . . make . . ." Her forehead pinched.

Meghan tipped her head. "Coffee?"

Grandma sighed. "Yes, coffee. Maybe I need some before I talk to anybody. Then I'll make more socks." She shook her head. "Sense!"

Meghan giggled and pushed herself to her feet. She positioned her crutches and followed Grandma to the kitchen. She leaned against the counter and observed Grandma moving around the neat room, opening cupboards and frowning into the spaces. An uneasy feeling crept across her scalp. "Grandma, are you okay?"

Her mouth slightly open, Grandma glanced at her. "What? Oh." She laughed. "Yes, I'm fine. Just groggy yet. Some days it's a little harder to wake up than others. Will you want cream and sugar?"

Meghan had taken cream and sugar every morning since her arrival five days ago. She started to say so but decided against it. She nodded. "Please."

Grandma closed the cupboard doors without removing the coffee canister and stepped past Meghan to the refrigerator. She rummaged inside and emerged with a little carton of cream. She scowled into the fridge. "Where did I leave the sugar?"

"Grandma . . ." Meghan gestured to the ceramic sugar bowl with its silver spoon sticking up. "It's right here."

Grandma turned and frowned at the bowl as if she'd never seen it before.

Meghan cupped her grandmother's arm and gently squeezed. "Did you not sleep well last night? It's okay if you want to go back to bed. There's no law that says you have to have coffee ready by six forty-five every morning."

Tears welled in Grandma's dark eyes. Her chin quivered. "I . . ." She licked her lips. A single tear rolled down her wrinkled cheek.

Concern made Meghan's chest go tight. "What's wrong?"

She pulled in a shuddering breath. "I'm very confused."

Fear chased away concern in the space of one heartbeat. Meghan forced herself to smile. She hoped it would give her grandmother some reassurance. "You're just tired. Mom and I have kept you hopping since we got here. You aren't used to so many people, not to mention animals, underfoot. How about I fix the coffee and you go back to bed for a while?"

Grandma sniffled and hung her head. "I'm a very poor hosiery."

Meghan quirked her brow. "You mean hostess?"

Grandma nodded.

Meghan slung her arm around Grandma's shoulders. "We're family. You don't have to play hostess for us. Come on, Grandma, you know Mom won't get up for at least another hour. I bet you'll feel more like yourself when you wake up."

Grandma continued to sniff, her pose so dejected Meghan wanted to cry. Finally she sighed. "All right. If you're sure you don't mind, I will go lie down. I am . . . tired."

Meghan delivered a kiss on her grandmother's soft cheek. "Then rest is the best thing for you. I'll make the coffee. And breakfast, too. You've been spoiling Mom and me. Let me spoil you back."

Grandma nodded. She scuffed around the corner, her steps stiff and shuffling, the way Tim Conway walked when he pretended to be the old man from Grandma's *Carol Burnett Show* videos.

Meghan held her breath and followed several feet behind her, stealthily so she wouldn't know she was being followed. Not until her grandmother closed herself in the bedroom did Meghan puff her cheeks and blow out the air. Thank goodness she hadn't mentioned Sean's text. Grandma wouldn't have been able to rest if she'd known what he discovered.

Meghan turned awkwardly in the narrow hall and returned to the kitchen. As she lifted down the coffee canister, a worry struck. What if a nap didn't clear Grandma's confusion? She'd acted so strangely. Could something be seriously wrong with her? And if there was, would she be able to help Sean continue the investigation?

Twenty-Two

Little Rock, Arkansas
Sean Eagle

*S*ean hung up the phone, leaned back in his chair, stretched, and mouthed "Thank You" at the ceiling. Mrs. Baldwin's grateful praises still rang in his ears. The Baldwin family could rest easier tonight knowing that the questions surrounding their daughter's suspicious death in 1982 were now answered and the man responsible was already behind bars. He'd worried that Mr. Baldwin, frail and suffering from emphysema, wouldn't live long enough to hear the answers. But God had guided the detectives in the right direction, and DNA testing, unavailable back in '82, proved their theory. Gratitude rang in his heart, along with a prayer.

Help me find the answers for Meghan's grandmother, Father, please.

Sean didn't know the woman, but he hadn't been able to stop thinking about her since he heard her voice last Sunday evening. She'd sounded so kind, so trusting, so hopeful. How she could still hold on to hope after so many years was a testament to her faith. He wanted to see her faith rewarded. And he wanted it to happen on this side of heaven.

None of the detectives in the department believed he'd solve this case. Two of them outright laughed at Sean for even trying, especially since he was investigating on his own time. But he had to try. He wanted it for Mrs. De-Ford. He wanted it for Meghan, too. But of course, most of all, he wanted God's will for both of them. If the search brought Meghan's mother and grandmother together again, that might be satisfaction enough. It might have to be satisfaction enough. No one in the department had ever solved a case that stretched back so many decades. But there was always a first time, and he felt deep down he was onto something bigger than one little girl lost in a blackberry bramble.

He read down the list of names he'd gathered from the missing-persons data files.

Amelia Arnold, age 2 years 4 months; Seba, Arkansas; February 3, 1937

Henry Leonard, age 2 years 3 months; Pactolus, Arkansas; August 21, 1938

Delia Holt, age 2 years 7 months; Mason Valley, Arkansas; March 4, 1940

Eugene Hastings Jr., age 9 months; Beaty, Arkansas; April 12, 1942

Matilda Beckett, age 3 years 2 months; Gravette, Arkansas; October 16, 1942

Margaret Blackwell, age 3 years 1 month; Cumpton, Arkansas; July 14, 1943

Francis Killian, age 1 year 11 months; Pea Ridge, Arkansas; June 15, 1944

Bertha Fair, age 1 year 8 months; Lime Kiln, Arkansas; January 1, 1946

James and Robert Phillips, age 1 year 1 month; Colcord, Oklahoma; May 6, 1946

A brief physical description of the child followed the date he or she was last seen, and even though Sean had already noted the similarities, he experienced another chill. Every child, from the toddler taken from Seba to the one-year-old twins in Oklahoma, had blue eyes and blond hair. Something meaningful hid in that bit of information. He hoped he and Meghan, with Mrs. DeFord's help, would uncover the significance.

"Hey, Beagle." Tom Farber always twisted Sean's unusual name, probably in the hopes of getting a rise out of him. So far, with the Holy Spirit's help, Sean had managed to disappoint the man.

Sean spun in his chair to face the detective and his partner, Greg Dane, who stood near the door leading to the elevators. "Yeah?"

"Dane and me are heading to Rosey's for a sandwich. Want something?"

Rosey's, a little bistro in the River Market area near the cold-case department's office building, had the best reuben and fries in town. Sean's mouth watered as he thought about chomping through a towering stack of corned beef on toasted rye bread. But he shook his head. He'd brought some microwave soup with him so he could work on Mrs. DeFord's case through lunch. "Thanks anyway."

Farber shifted his attention to Sean's temporary partner. "What about you, Sanderson? Wanna come with us?"

As usual, Miles Sanderson looked to Sean for guidance. Sean waved his hand at the younger man. "Go ahead. I recommend the reuben."

"Sounds good." His grin wide, Sanderson bounded out of his chair and strode across the floor to Farber and Dane.

Sean understood the younger man's elation—the others hadn't asked him to lunch or for an after-work drink until now. No doubt the green recruit thought he'd finally made the team. Sean just hoped Sanderson wouldn't let the older, rowdier men lead him astray. Miles was a good kid but a little too eager to please. The way Meghan had been when she first arrived in the department.

"Hey, Miles."

The man paused and shot a questioning look over his shoulder.

"Got a lot of work to get done this afternoon. Don't let those two hooligans talk you into extending the lunch hour."

Farber and Dane smirked at each other, but Sanderson nodded in all seriousness. "No, sir, I won't."

Dane gave a mock salute. "Bye, Preacher. Enjoy the quiet." The three headed out. Since the other two detectives, Tyler Roach and Anthony Johnson, had left a few minutes earlier, the office was now all Sean's own.

He took the cup of soup from his side drawer but placed it on the corner of his desk instead of heading to the break room's microwave. *Blue eyes, blond hair.* The simple descriptors all in a row haunted him. What did it mean?

Kendrickson, Nevada
Diane

Diane observed her mother loading their lunch dishes into the dishwasher. Glasses on the top rack, plates and pans on the bottom, silverware categorized by utensil. Meghan's worry about Mother's inability to function earlier that day had raised questions in the back of Diane's mind, but she witnessed no hint of confusion in Mother's actions now. Except—

"Mother, did you rinse those beforehand?" Mother had never let Diane put unrinsed dishes in the dishwasher. How well she remembered her mother's fastidious instructions. She remembered her own argument, too—why have the luxury of a dishwasher if you were going to wash the dishes before putting them into the machine?

Mother angled a smile in Diane's direction, serene and controlled—in other words, her usual self. "This is one of the models with a built-in garbage disposal. It will chew up any leftover bits of food. Isn't that convenient?"

Yes, Mother's faculties were in fine form now. Diane sent a look at Meghan she hoped communicated her doubt about the severity of the morning's confusion.

Meghan gave no indication she even noticed. She fiddled with the cloth napkin crumpled on the table. "The jeweler said your necklace would be ready this afternoon, Grandma. How about Mom and I go pick it up for you while you rest?"

A scowl crossed Mother's face. But for once it wasn't meant for Diane. "Young lady, will you please stop trying to send me back to bed? Granted, I'm no spring chicken, but I'm not ready to be put out to pasture, either."

Meghan pushed the napkin aside and rose. She grabbed her crutches and double-stepped to Mother. "I'm not trying to put you out to pasture. You usually lie down for an hour or so each afternoon. Now that lunch is over, it should be rest time."

Mother shook her head, her dark eyes glinting with a hint of orneriness. "For kindergartners, yes. Do I look like I'm in kindergarten?"

Meghan flashed a sheepish grin. "Well . . ."

Diane rose and joined them. "I think what Meghan is trying to tell you, without coming right out and saying so, is you're going to have an important phone call this evening with Detective Eagle. She wants you to be alert and able to answer questions."

Meghan sent a warning frown at Diane and then touched Mother's arm. "Sean will likely ask you lots of things about the day Maggie disappeared. Wouldn't it be wise to rest and refresh your memory before he calls?"

Mother gazed at Meghan for several seconds and then leaned against the counter and folded her arms. "I know what happened this morning alarmed you, and I'm very sorry. But you don't need to worry. I'm eighty. I'm bound to have moments when I have trouble gathering my thoughts. It's really not that unusual."

"It isn't?" Meghan skimmed a wide-eyed glance at Diane. "You mean you do that a lot?"

Mother chuckled—not quite her normal, carefree chuckle but close. "I wouldn't say a lot, but frequently enough to know it will pass when it happens."

"But you were so . . . mixed up. And emotional." Meghan bit the corner of her lip. "That doesn't seem like you at all."

Mother closed her eyes for a moment and sighed. She pinned her gaze on Meghan. "I'm sure my embarrassment heightened the reaction. I'm generally alone when I lose track of my thoughts. To appear incompetent before an audience is humiliating."

Ah, yes. Mother could never be imperfect.

Meghan's face pursed in sympathy.

Diane recalled something else. "What about fainting? Is that something you do frequently, too?"

Mother scowled. "No, of course not."

"But you get light headed? The way you were at the antique store on Monday?"

Mother balled her hands on her hips. "If the two of you are going to gang up on me, I might have to send one of you home."

Diane knew which of them would get the boot. She imitated Mother's pose. She could be stubborn, too. She'd learned from the best. "How often do you suffer light-headedness, Mother? And before you answer, remember that Meghan and I have been here for five days and we witnessed both light-headedness and fainting within the first three."

If Mother's scowl got any deeper, her eyebrows might disappear in a forehead furrow. "It was hot those days."

Diane rolled her eyes. "It's always hot in Nevada, Mother."

Meghan cleared her throat, obviously an unspoken message to Diane to knock it off. "Grandma, were you overly warm this morning when you couldn't remember the word for *coffee* or find the sugar bowl?"

"I wasn't warm—I was groggy. I wasn't awake yet." Mother's words snapped like a hatchet descending on a chunk of firewood. "You're making much too much out of a few issues of aging, and I won't listen to one more word about it. If it will make you feel better, I will lie down for an hour, but I want you both to know I'm doing it under duress." She pointed at Meghan. "And don't you and your mother go pick up my necklace! I want to examine it myself and be sure it is fixed correctly before I take it from the store. I won't be swindled."

Meghan held up both hands in surrender. "All right, we won't go. I promise."

At once, Mother's stern expression softened. She sighed and wrapped Meghan in a hug. "I know you're only concerned, sweetheart, and I appreciate it. But you don't need to worry about me. I'm fine. For eighty, I'm fine." She stepped free and moved toward the hallway. "The dishwasher is ready to be run. Will one of you start it, please?" She disappeared around the corner.

Meghan bent, reaching for the door of the dishwasher.

Diane moved into her pathway. "Let me get it before you knock yourself off your crutches." She started to close it, but something caught her attention. She paused, frowning at the empty detergent holder. Had their conversation stolen Mother's concentration and derailed her from her normal routine, or was this another example of her forgetting something?

She retrieved the gel detergent from under the sink and filled the little square. As she snapped the cover in place and closed the door, she made a promise to herself to observe Mother more closely. She'd gather the proof she needed—with Meghan as a witness—that Mother was reaching the age where living alone was no longer wise. From there it would be an easy reach to convince both her mother and her daughter that the responsible, sensible, most compassionate thing was to seek placement in an assisted-living facility. Not even Meghan would be able to argue about it if Mother was falling at her feet.

While Mother napped and Meghan worked on another scrapbook page, Diane would browse the Internet for local facilities.

Little Rock, Arkansas
Sean

Sean purchased his dinner at a drive-through and headed home. The scent of beef, onions, and grease rose from the bag on the passenger seat and invited him to dig in. Even though the food would be cold by the time he reached his house in southeast Little Rock, he'd wait. He'd fussed too many times about inattentive drivers to become one himself. And that burger with cheese, bacon, and grilled onions would be a mighty distraction in his hand. He needed his focus on the late-afternoon traffic.

Downtown Little Rock buzzed with activity all day, the *rattle* and *clang* of the streetcars competing with tourists and locals enjoying the River Market shops and restaurants, but five o'clock—closing time for many of the offices— doubled the number of cars on the streets. When the city set up the Arkansas Cold Case Investigations Department six years ago on the fourth floor of one of Little Rock's historical buildings at the heart of River Market downtown, he'd wondered if the police chief had made a good decision. Downtown? So far from the 12th Street station? But Sean had grown fond of the location.

He wouldn't have enjoyed the cramped, dark quarters of the single base- ment room the previous cold-case detectives—a handful of volunteer retired detectives who worked on unsolved rapes and murders that took place in the city—occupied even if it was part of the police station. The top floor of an old apartment building at the heart of River Market served the team well. One small office near the elevator gave the captain his personal space, and the large open-floor area gave all six detectives their needed elbow room. Lots of win- dows allowed in light and offered a view of the city as well as the Arkansas River and the sister city, North Little Rock. He often relied on the ideal setting to soothe him after uncovering particularly ugly truths about the last minutes of someone's life.

He eased onto Highway 30 and followed it south, picking up speed to match the flow of traffic. So many people, and all in a hurry. He glanced at other drivers—moms with kids in car seats, men with their faces set in tense scowls, all no doubt driving home to deal with homework and evening activi- ties or putting supper on the table. Family stuff.

An ache built in the center of his chest. He hadn't been part of a family circle since his folks' car accident his freshman year of college. He sure hadn't expected, then, to still be alone fourteen years later, but there wasn't a soul— not a wife, a child, or even a dog—waiting at the other end of this drive for him. Most of the time his caseload kept him too busy to think about what he was missing, but ever since Meghan came on the scene at work, he'd had mo- ments like this, especially when he was alone, when he longed for family. And Meghan's pretty face always inserted herself into those longings.

It was stupid, though. They were partners. Close because they had to be. Not once had she ever hinted that she saw him as anything more than her mentor and colleague. Which was probably best, considering she wasn't a believer. He knew the biblical passages about not being unequally yoked, and he'd never forget his mom's admonition about dating—*"Don't let yourself fall in love with a girl who doesn't love the Lord."* So he'd kept his feelings in check. Or so he thought.

The day he stood beside Meghan's crushed Toyota and watched the Jaws of Life cut back the hood, terrified about what he'd see when the interior was finally revealed, he realized how deeply he cared about her. More than a partner. More than a friend, even. But he wouldn't act on his feelings. He'd seen too many halves of a couple sitting in a church pew, incomplete and sorrowful, because their other halves wanted nothing to do with God. If he was meant to have a family someday, God would bring a faithful woman into his life.

Until then, he'd be Meghan's friend, and he'd keep praying for her salvation the same way he prayed for Dane, Farber, Roach, and Johnson.

While his tires hummed on the highway and the hamburger taunted his senses, Sean reviewed the questions he intended to ask Mrs. DeFord this evening. She might not have answers right away. She might not have answers at all. But hopefully she'd remember something that would guide him in the right direction. As he drove, his thoughts turned into a prayer, as they always seemed to do when he was burdened. By the time he reached his simple 1960s-style ranch house on Arapaho Trail, the peace he'd come to expect had settled his mind.

He glanced at the time. Five forty in Arkansas meant only three forty in Nevada. It'd probably be a couple hours, maybe three, before Meghan called. They'd all have a chance to eat their supper before chatting. He turned off the ignition, grabbed the bag holding his supper and his briefcase stuffed with printouts from his research, and bounded out of the car. Carrying the bag in his teeth, he trotted across the grass with his briefcase in one hand and house keys in the other. As he slipped his key into his front-door lock, his cell phone sang "Unchained Melody," Meghan's ringtone. His foolish heart flipped in his chest.

He propped the briefcase against the siding, snatched the bag out of his mouth, and fished for his phone. The music seemed to grow louder by the second, and he was sure she'd hang up before he got the call answered. Finally his fingers connected with the phone. He yanked it free, pushed the connect icon, and rasped out, "Hello?"

"Hello, Sean. Is this a good time to talk, or are you . . . busy?"

So she'd picked up on his breathlessness. He tucked the phone between his ear and shoulder and forced a laugh. "Yeah, yeah, this is fine." He turned the key in the lock and the door popped open. He tossed the food bag on the narrow console table next to the door, cleared the threshold, and gave the door a whack with his elbow. "So . . . you ready to chat?"

Twenty-Three

Kendrickson, Nevada
Hazel

*M*eghan bumped Hazel with her elbow and grimaced. She
pointed at the cell phone pressed against her ear and whispered, "I caught him in the middle of something. We might have to wait a
bit."

Hazel nodded, but she wanted—she needed—to get this conversation
over with. A strange sense of urgency had sizzled beneath her skin ever since
lunchtime, when Meghan told her how many children Mr. Eagle discovered
on the missing-persons list. So many other families with only a shadow where
a child should be. She wanted answers for all of them.

Meghan cleared her throat and spoke into the phone again. "I hope I'm
not bothering you too early, but Grandma and I have nearly been climbing the
walls. She wanted to be sure to finish our conversation before supper since she
has Bible study this evening. So I thought I'd take a chance and try to catch
you. If this isn't convenient—"

The mutter of a low-toned voice emerged from the phone, but Hazel
couldn't understand what he was saying. Meghan was nodding, though, a
smile on her face.

"Good!" She winked at Hazel. "I'll put you on speaker, then, so Grandma
can be in on the conversation, too." She lowered the phone and touched something on the screen. "Okay, Sean, we're both here."

"Good afternoon, Mrs. DeFord."

Hazel enjoyed the sound of the man's fluid, respectful voice. Whoever had raised him had done a fine job. "Hello, Mr. Eagle. I apologize if we've interrupted your routine. I suppose we were a little eager to talk to you."

"I completely understand." Rustling came from the phone, then the distinct sounds of chewing. "I'm eager to talk to you, too." His voice sounded muffled, evidence that he'd filled his mouth with something.

Seated in the wingback chair, Margaret Diane petted the row of dachshunds lounging on the ottoman. "You interrupted his dinner. Have him call you back."

"No, it's all right." The detective must have heard Margaret Diane even with her across the room. "If you don't mind me eating while we talk, I can do both."

Hazel exchanged an uncertain look with Meghan. "Are you sure? If you'd rather eat first and then call, we have time to wait." But did they? The gnawing unsettledness increased. Hazel gripped the bodice of her blouse. Why was her heart pounding so? Her left temple throbbed with her racing pulse.

"Please believe me when I say I've learned to eat and work at the same time." A throaty chuckle rumbled, and a bit of Hazel's unease lifted. "If you aren't offended by the sounds of me consuming a bacon cheeseburger and fries, I will eat while we talk."

If he didn't mind, she wouldn't be offended. "All right, Detective."

"Call me Sean, ma'am."

"Fine . . . Sean." She liked using his name. "What did you want to ask me?"

Her expression attentive, Margaret Diane leaned forward in the chair. Meghan tipped closer to Hazel, too, and Hazel automatically cupped her hand beneath Meghan's under the phone. The room seemed to buzz with compressed energy.

"You said a woman in town thought Gypsies were stealing children."

Hazel nodded. "That's right. Mrs. Nora Burton."

"I did quite a bit of research concerning child abduction and Gypsies, and the idea appears to be folklore born of prejudice. There's no real evidence that this ever took place."

"Oh." His matter-of-fact statements crushed the tiny bud of hope Hazel had held to all these years. She blinked hard, determined not to cry. "I see."

"There's something else I've discovered that makes me question the theory about the Gypsies stealing children. Every last child taken shares two common descriptors—blond hair and blue eyes." A slight pause accompanied by a gulp disrupted the flow of words. "The Romani ethnic group, commonly called Gypsies, are predominantly dark haired and dark eyed. If they took children with such a different appearance, they would have attracted a great deal of attention. Since they were often looked upon with disdain and tried to live separately from other ethnic communities, I can't imagine them wanting to call attention to themselves. So I think we can eliminate the idea that Gypsies stole your little sister."

Hazel drew a shuddering breath and forced herself to speak evenly. "So you think Maggie is dead."

"I'm not convinced of that, either."

Hazel collapsed against the sofa cushion. Her hand fell into her lap. A high-pitched ringing filled her ears, and she strained to hear Sean's voice over the intrusive sound.

"Not one report of skeletal remains matching any of these children has been found. That tells me they didn't wander off and die. I also find it unlikely that someone in Benton County would kill such a large number of children and hide their bodies so well they were never recovered. Of course, I have to explore whether someone who didn't live in the county but traveled through frequently might be responsible for taking the children. As much as we don't like to talk about such things, there are evil individuals who prey on a certain type. The commonalities in appearance compel me to consider the possibility."

Hazel hugged herself and asked God to erase the unpleasant images Sean's words had painted in her mind.

"I know this might be hard to recall, but do you remember anyone, whether someone local or a traveler, who paid extra attention to Maggie?"

Hazel closed her eyes. Images flooded her mind. Her lips tugged into a smile. "Maggie was such a pretty little girl. From the beginning, Daddy called her his sunshine and his doll-baby. She really was as pretty as any baby doll. Lots of people noticed her and commented on her curly yellow hair and bright-blue eyes." The jealous pangs she'd suffered as a child now seemed so petty. She opened her eyes and added staunchly, "Nearly everyone noticed Maggie. She was such a little darling."

"Do you remember, in retrospect, anyone who paid inappropriately excessive attention to her?"

She shivered. "N-no. I . . . don't recall."

Meghan scooted closer and put her arm around Hazel's shoulders. "You're creeping Grandma out, Sean."

"I'm really sorry. I know it's a tough topic, but we have to look at the situation from every conceivable angle and eradicate as many variables as we can in order to follow the correct pathway. If you'd rather be spared the details, I can do the investigation on my own and report the end result when I'm finished."

"No!" Hazel hadn't intended to shout, but the word exploded from her.

The oldest of the four dachshunds stood and whined, and like dominoes falling, the others rose in turn and added their nervous yelps and whimpers. Margaret Diane herded the quartet to the kitchen, scowling as she went.

Hazel jerked the phone from Meghan's hand and held it close. "Please forgive me for yelling at you. But I don't want to be left out of the search. I've wondered . . . I've waited . . . so very long. I want to be a part of every step of this journey, even if it means scuffing my knees over many false leads along the way."

Meghan squeezed Hazel's shoulders and retrieved the phone. "Keep us in the loop, Sean, okay? I think it'll be easier on Grandma than wondering what you're finding."

"All right. Just so you know, my next plan of action is to extend my search for unidentified human remains matching the ages of these children. I'll start with the states bordering Arkansas and then, if necessary, research the entire United States. It might take some time to compile a complete report, so please be patient with me, but I would like to either confirm or eliminate the possibility that any of these children are still living."

"*. . . any of these children are still living.*" Hazel clung to his words. Maggie had to be alive somewhere. She had to be. If Hazel could hug her sister one more time, could ask forgiveness for leaving her alone to go after that snake, then—and only then—could she go to her grave with peace.

Meghan

"We appreciate everything you're doing, Sean." Guilt taunted Meghan's heart. With her away, he was already carrying more than his fair share of their caseload and training a new detective. She should be the one investigating instead of leaving it all on Sean. "Please don't use all your spare time on this case, okay? No sense in wearing yourself out." She knew him well. His diligence wouldn't let him rest until he'd found answers.

"There's one more thing I wanted to tell you and your grandmother. Are you both still on?"

Grandma sat up and turned her pert gaze on the phone. "We are both here, young man."

"Good. After I put together that list of missing children from Benton County, I felt it needed to become priority. Nine families who lost children under suspicious circumstances in one decade? So I shared everything I collected with the captain. He agreed that this shouldn't be an on-my-own-time case. So he put it at the top of my stack."

Guilt struck again. Harder this time. A confusing mix of guilt that her grandmother's case had been placed above others' and guilt for feeling guilty about the case's prominence. More than ever, she wanted to be an active part of the investigation. She glared at her cast and inwardly cursed it.

Grandma's mouth dropped open and she reached for the phone again. "You will look for Maggie all day? Not just during breaks? She's your official case now?"

Another chuckle rolled from the phone, and Meghan envisioned him smiling and nodding. "That's right, Mrs. DeFord. Maggie and the other nine missing children make up my new official case. I've got a lot more exploring to do, but I've even been cleared to take a trip to Benton County for interviews if necessary. I hope it helps you to know we're all interested in finding out what happened to Maggie."

Tears flooded Grandma's eyes. Her chin quivered. She choked out, "She isn't forgotten anymore. I'm grateful. So very, very grateful."

Meghan's guilt was swept away in light of Grandma's joy. She leaned toward the phone Grandma held two handed in front of her. "Let us know how we can help, Sean. I'm sorry I'm not there, but I'm only a phone call away. So holler anytime, okay?"

"Will do, Meghan. I'll let you go now. But I'll be in touch if I have questions or if I uncover anything else of importance. Enjoy your Bible study, Mrs. DeFord. Bye."

The screen went black, and Meghan slipped the phone into her pocket. She smiled at Grandma. "Well, things are progressing, huh?"

Mom swept around the corner with her menagerie and sat on the ottoman. The dogs flopped onto their bellies around her. "So what did I miss? Anything important?"

"Our captain gave Sean clearance to make Maggie and the other children's disappearances an official investigation." Meghan glanced at Grandma, who sat with a satisfied smile curving her lips. "Sean might even travel to Benton County."

Mom's eyebrows rose. "What about his other cases? Did they all get set aside?"

Grandma's face pinched with concern. "I was so excited about the idea of bringing Maggie home I forgot that he has other people needing his help to solve their mysteries. Maybe we should tell him—"

Meghan shook her head. "It was the captain's decision, Grandma. And I agree with him. This has got to be the oldest case the unit has ever covered. Those children are all in their late sixties or seventies by now."

"If they're still alive."

Did Mom have to say everything that flitted through her mind? Some things were better left unsaid. Meghan frowned at her. "Sean hasn't found solid evidence that they aren't alive. They're on the book as 'missing,' which means we need to try to find them. But given the length of time that's passed since they disappeared, we don't have months to wait. The captain was smart to put Sean on it right away."

An odd smirk appeared on Mom's face.

Meghan squinted at her. "What?"

"You'd like to be working alongside him on this one." A statement, not a question.

Meghan's face went hot. She looked aside.

Mom laughed. "Maybe you should."

Meghan jerked her gaze toward her mother. "Maybe I should . . . what?"

"Be a part of the investigation."

"I already am."

Mom huffed. "I meant as something more than a telephone contact. If he's going to Benton County, maybe you should go, too."

Meghan pointed mutely at her cast.

Mom rolled her eyes. "You traveled all the way to Nevada with that thing. What would prevent you from traveling back with it? We could rent a wheelchair and push you around." She whirled on Grandma, who'd sat quietly with her lips pursed during their exchange. "What do you think, Mother? Would you like to return to Benton County?"

Grandma pushed off the sofa and stood. "Right now I need to fix us supper and then go to Bible study. You are both welcome to join me. It's a small group—less than three dozen people—and we're always glad to include visitors."

Mom examined her fingernails.

Meghan caught her grandmother's hand and gently swung it. "I'll go with you. I'd like to meet the people in your prayer group and thank them all for praying for me." A lump filled her throat. Their kindness, their compassion toward someone they didn't even know, touched her more deeply than she knew how to express.

"That sounds fine." Grandma moved stiffly in the direction of the kitchen. "I'll bake some potatoes. Then we can each top them with whatever we choose. Does that sound all right?"

"Sounds good, Grandma."

"That'll be fine, Mother."

When Grandma left the room, Meghan shifted to the front edge of the sofa cushion and leaned toward her mother. "Not one more word about the possibility of Maggie being dead, do you hear me?"

Mom drew back as if Meghan had impaled her. "What did I do?"

"'If they're still alive.'" Meghan imitated her mother's snide tone. She shook her head. "All Grandma has right now is hope. Don't take that away from her." She stood, jammed her crutches into place, and hobbled past her mother, refusing to acknowledge the irritation glittering in Mom's eyes.

Twenty-Four

Las Vegas, Nevada
Hazel

During Bible study, Hazel's mind continually wandered from the scriptures shared by the group leader. Her daughter's flippant question *"Would you like to return to Benton County?"* haunted her mind. It had been so long since she'd visited the town where she was born and raised, so long since she'd seen the farmhouse where she fed chickens and learned to ride a bike and played tea party with her doll in the yard. A desire to return to that place, to those times, twisted her heart and brought the sting of tears.

"Grandma?" Meghan leaned close and whispered, "Are you all right?"

She was worrying her granddaughter again. She must gain control of her emotions. She sniffed hard and forced her lips into a smile. "I'm fine, honey." She aimed her gaze at the man standing at the front of the room with an open Bible on his palm and tried once more to pay attention.

"We see these beautiful words in the thirty-first chapter of Deuteronomy, starting with verse seven." He slipped glasses onto his nose and began to read. "'Then Moses summoned Joshua and said to him in the presence of all Israel, "Be strong and courageous, for you must go with this people into the land that the LORD swore to their ancestors to give them, and you must divide it among them as their inheritance. The LORD himself goes before you and will be with you; he will never leave you nor forsake you. Do not be afraid; do not be discouraged."'"

The words—"beautiful words," the leader had aptly called them—raised a wave of remembrance.

Christmas 1965
Cumpton, Arkansas

Hazel waited on the turquoise-and-white vinyl seat of their brand-new Chevy Bel Air for Albert to open the door for her. He fussed if she tried to do it herself. Especially now.

He opened the door, allowing in a gusty, cold wind. Hazel tightened her scarf before stepping from the car. At once Albert scooped her into his arms. She squealed and looped her arms around his neck. "What are you doing?"

He laughed, his warm breath creating a cloud that kissed her face. "I don't want you sliding on the ice and falling. We can't risk bruising your precious cargo."

She shook her head. Ever the trucker. Must even their coming blessed event be described as a package to be toted? "You'll never make it up those warped porch steps if you can't see your feet. You'd better let me walk."

The curtain on the front window of the old farmhouse whisked aside and a pale, unsmiling face peered outward. Hazel wriggled. "Put me down, Albert. Mama's looking."

He laughed again and held her closer. "Let her look! We're married. What's wrong with showing her how much I love my wife?"

"Oh, Albert." She nestled her head in the curve of his shoulder, warmed by his snug arms around her and his bold words of affection. She loved him, too. More than she'd thought possible. He'd come into her life when she was past the age of fluttering eyelashes and whimsical daydreams of romance. He'd convinced her having a baby was a joyous, rather than frightening, prospect. He was better than any storybook hero.

She lifted her face and sighed. "But I don't want you to hurt yourself carrying me up the steps. So let me walk, okay?"

"Okay, okay." He teasingly growled the words, then gently set her on her feet. He gripped her mitten-covered hand. "But I'm still going to hold on to you."

She squeezed back, grateful for the contact. She hadn't been home for Christmas since Daddy died four years ago. She felt like a stranger. A shiver shook her frame.

"It'll be all right." How could he know she hadn't shivered from cold but from worry? He pulled her close and touched the tip of his cold nose to her forehead. "Remember what we read this morning in Deuteronomy? We're to be strong and courageous because the Lord goes before us. There's nothing on the other side of that farmhouse door that can hurt you."

He was wrong, of course. There were memories inside the house that could pummel her emotionally and leave her soul battered and bruised. But she would be brave for Albert and for the little one growing inside her. She smiled and blinked back hot tears. "I'm ready. Let's go in."

Present Day
Las Vegas, Nevada

"Are we ready to trust and move forward, powered by God's hand of strength?"

Hazel nodded with the others around her, her vision cloudy. She sniffed hard and whisked her fingers beneath her eyes. Meghan shot her a concerned frown, but Hazel offered a reassuring smile. Her granddaughter's expression relaxed and they both faced the leader again.

She recorded each of the prayer requests in a little spiral notebook she always carried in her purse. Her handwriting had gotten shaky in the past year, and she hoped she'd be able to read her notes later. But if she couldn't, God would know what was scribbled on the pad, and she would trust Him to make sense of it. Just as He'd had to make sense of some of her jumbled thoughts of late.

People broke into small groups to pray together, and Hazel crooked her finger at Meghan. Meghan leaned close and Hazel whispered, "Let's go to the car. I'm weary, and I want to drive home while I'm still awake enough to be alert."

Meghan nodded, and the two of them slipped out to the parking lot. Hazel had chosen a spot near the double doors to the smaller sanctuary used for group meetings, and with the sun creeping toward the horizon, a thick shadow embraced her vehicle. What would Albert think of her late-nineties Buick? He'd never let their vehicles go beyond fifty thousand miles before trading them for new, sportier models. Given the high number on the odometer, he would probably have traded off the Buick years ago. For some reason, the thought made her sad.

She unlocked the doors with the remote and then started around to the passenger side to help Meghan.

The stubborn girl shook her head. "I can do it."

She'd said as much to Albert only one time, on their very first date. She could still hear his firm voice. *"You're a lady, Hazel Blackwell, and I am a gentleman. Let's conduct ourselves that way, huh?"* Truck driver by trade and gentleman by design—that was her Albert.

She took hold of the door handle and gave a pull. "I know you're able, but it gives me pleasure to help you. So don't argue with me."

Meghan grinned and shook her head. "Now I know where Mom and I get our bullheadedness. It comes naturally."

Hazel laughed. She took Meghan's crutches and put them in the back seat, then moved around to the driver's side. As she started the car, she chuckled again. "'Bullheadedness,' as you put it, is passed to you through the Blackwells. My father had a stubborn streak more than a mile wide, and I was told he inherited it from his father. Your grandfather DeFord, on the other hand, was determined but also very logical and levelheaded. I would never use the term *bullheaded* to describe him." She pulled out of the parking lot and into the flow of traffic.

Meghan sighed. "Mom doesn't talk much about her dad. I think, in part, because I don't have one and she's afraid it'll make me wish for one even more. And probably in part because it bothers her to think about him being gone. Was she pretty much a daddy's girl?"

The longing in Meghan's tone stung Hazel. A daddy was so important. Meghan—and Margaret Diane—had been robbed. A lump filled her throat, and she swallowed before answering. "Albert adored Margaret Diane, and the feeling was mutual. I quit my job at the library when I found out I was expecting and stayed home all through her growing up. I think, in a way, my being there all the time strengthened the special bond she had with her father. His job took him away from home for days at a time, so when he returned, it was a grand reunion."

The evening traffic was thicker, more impatient, but Hazel set her cruise for the established speed limit when she reached the highway and chose to ignore the drivers who honked at her as they whizzed by.

Meghan shifted slightly to better face Hazel. "Why didn't you ever have another baby? Is it because you got started kind of late?"

Hazel couldn't resist a chuckle. "Thirty-two was late, I suppose, when you consider how many women in our church already had school-age children by the time they reached their midthirties. No, it was a personal decision to only have one child."

Regret stabbed her heart. She couldn't admit to her precious granddaughter that fear kept her from adding to their family. If she had two or more children, how could she keep watch over all of them? Only one sometimes proved challenging. Especially during Margaret Diane's rebellious teenage years.

She hit her blinker and eased onto the exit ramp. "When Albert died in the accident, I decided it was best I'd only had one child. It would have been much harder for me to go on, emotionally, if I'd needed to care for several children."

"I suppose that's true." Meghan sat quietly for a few seconds, then touched Hazel's elbow. "Thanks for telling me a little bit about your family. I like knowing about those who've gone before. Kind of helps me understand who I am today, you know? Especially since . . ." She bit the corner of her lip. "Grandma, did Mom ever tell you who got her pregnant?"

Oh, that awful day. Would she ever forget her daughter's bitter yet broken face, the tears, the sorrow? And the adamant refusal to name names no matter how many times Hazel asked. She hadn't even put a name on the birth certificate, despite the nurse's turned-up nose and pursed lips. Maybe it was best Margaret Diane hadn't told. Hazel would likely have made use of her pistol and ended up in a jail cell. "No, honey, she never did. I guess it hurt her too much to talk about it."

Meghan gave a slow nod, her brow puckering. "You don't think it's because she . . . didn't know?"

Hazel had never considered such a thing. The idea made her squirm inside. She gripped the steering wheel so tightly her knuckles ached. "Your mother was a rebel in many ways, Meghan, but I refuse to believe she was promiscuous. I raised her in the church. She knew right from wrong. And she told me at the time that she loved the boy and believed he intended to marry her."

"So she knows who he is, then."

Hazel nodded. She released the steering wheel long enough to give Meghan's knee a quick pat. "I don't blame you one bit for being curious. I'd be curious, too, if I were you. But you can't push a rope. If your mother doesn't want to talk about him, she won't." Another idea struck. "Maybe, when you're back in Arkansas again, you and Sean can do some investigating and uncover his name. If you really want to know."

"Yeah, maybe." Meghan leaned into the corner of her seat and sighed. "I'm kind of thirsty. Could we stop at a convenience store?"

"Con . . . convenience store?"

"Yes, please. I can get a big cup of Dr Pepper from the fountain machine. I like being able to add squirts of syrup to flavor up my drinks."

What on earth was Meghan referring to? A cold sweat formed on Hazel's frame. Her hands began to tremble. "I . . ."

"If you'd rather not stop, it's okay. I know you said you were tired. I'll drink some water or juice at the house instead."

Hazel wanted to grant her granddaughter's simple request. Especially since she'd been useless when answering the important question. But she couldn't make sense of where she wanted to find something to drink. "Maybe you and your mother can go out and get a soft drink . . . later."

Yes, that was a good compromise. It would give the two of them some time alone. Time for Meghan to talk to her mother about her parentage. Time for Hazel to recover her senses.

"That's fine, Grandma. Head home."

"Head home . . ." A wave of longing washed over Hazel, so intense it brought the desire to wail. She turned into her cul-de-sac, pulled into the driveway, and put the car in park with the engine still running. She turned to Meghan and blinked back tears.

"I want to do what you said. I want to . . . head home."

Meghan frowned. "What?"

"Margaret Diane asked if I wanted to go back to Arkansas. You told me to head home. That's what I want to do. I want to go to Cumpton. Let's go. You, Margaret Diane, and me. I'll take you to the farm where I grew up. We can visit the store where I worked after school and on Saturdays all through high school. I'll even try to find the blackberry bramble where I last saw my little sister." With each mention of a specific place, her desire to return grew stronger. She grabbed Meghan's hand. "Let's all go to Benton County, Meghan. Take me home."

Meghan chewed the bottom of her lip, her brows puckering. "Do you mean drive to Arkansas? Or fly?"

"Whichever is easiest for you with your cast."

"Flying's easiest for me, but Mom has her car here, and her dogs . . ." Meghan grimaced. "I'm not sure how this will all work, Grandma."

The tears Hazel had tried to hold back escaped. A sob wrenched from her throat. "Please, let's find a way. I . . . I want to go home."

Twenty-Five

Kendrickson, Nevada
Diane

Diane set her hairbrush aside and examined Meghan's reflection in the square dresser mirror. "She really said that? She wants to go to Cumpton?"

Meghan sat on the edge of the bed with her fingers gripping the rumpled sheets. "Yes. And she was all teary eyed when she said it. The way she was talking—so sad and almost desperate—kinda shook me up. I don't know if it's smart to let her travel that far, but if there's any way we can work it, I think we should try."

Diane turned and leaned against the dresser. She folded her arms over her chest. "Didn't your partner say he'd be going to Benton County to investigate?"

"If he needs to, yes."

"It might be good for her to be there when he goes. To answer questions and so forth. Maybe being in her old stomping grounds will help her remember some other things that could help him solve the mystery." Not that Diane believed they'd ever figure out what happened to those kids. She wouldn't deny it was a sad situation, but how would they find anything of worth after all these years?

"Even if Sean doesn't end up going to Cumpton, I think we should take her." Meghan set her jaw in a stubborn jut. "If it means that much to her to show us where she grew up, we should go."

Diane faced the mirror again and returned to brushing her hair. The dark-brown tresses, still thick and threaded with fewer than a dozen strands of silver, crackled under the boar-hair bristles. Thank goodness Meghan had inherited the Blackwell dark hair. If she resembled the man who'd callously tossed her aside, Diane wouldn't have been able to look at her day after day.

"Have you ever been to Cumpton?"

Diane glanced at her daughter in the mirror. A faraway look had entered her eyes, and she surmised the imaginative pictures filling her mind. "Yes. My parents and I went back for a couple of Christmases and my grandmother's funeral, but I don't remember it. I was too young."

"You don't remember anything?"

Diane slapped the brush onto the dresser and strode to the bed. "Not a thing." She slipped between the sheets and reached for the bedside lamp's switch.

"Aren't you curious at all?"

She aimed a sour look at Meghan. "Are you going to sit there all night, or are you going to sleep?"

Meghan sighed and flopped backward.

Diane turned the switch and rolled onto her side, facing her daughter. The soft glow from the light burning in the living room sneaked through the bedroom's open doorway and allowed a glimpse of Meghan's frowning profile. Clearly neither of them would be going to sleep anytime soon. Diane sighed. "What are you plotting?"

Meghan pointed her elbows at the ceiling and slid her linked hands behind her head. "Trying to work it out. To go to Arkansas, I mean." She peeked at Diane from the corners of her eyes. "Do you think we could make it happen?"

Diane shook her head. "Isn't that rather counterproductive, considering you came all the way out here for your recuperation?"

"I guess." Meghan puffed her cheeks and blew. "But it means so much to Grandma. She really wants us to see her childhood home. I'd be game. How about you?"

"Oh, Meghan . . ."

Meghan lowered her arms and shifted to her side. "It would be pretty expensive for us all to fly and then rent a car at the other end. If we took your Jeep, it'd be too crowded with all of us plus the dogs and our luggage. But if we rented an SUV, one of the bigger ones, we could fit in that pretty well, I think."

Clearly she'd been planning her strategy. "You want the three of us plus my dogs to drive from Nevada to Arkansas in a rented SUV."

"Or maybe an RV instead—then we wouldn't even need to stop at hotels." Meghan pressed her folded hands to the underside of her chin and pleaded with her eyes. "Why not? We'll call it a girls-only road trip."

What other kind could they have, given their single statuses?

"We could scope out touristy things along the way. I've always wanted to see the Grand Canyon."

Diane and her parents had gone to Grand Canyon National Park the summer before Daddy died.

"And I've never been to New Mexico. I bet that'd be a cool place to visit, too."

The Carlsbad Caverns were in New Mexico. Mother and Daddy promised to take her there for her eighth-grade graduation. But Daddy died, and she'd forgotten about it. Until now.

"We could travel through the Oklahoma Panhandle across the state to Benton County. I figure if we give it a week, we can stop frequently to let the dogs run and to visit any sites that appeal to us."

Diane shook her head, half amused, half irritated. "How are you so familiar with the geography between Nevada and Arkansas?"

Meghan grinned. "I mapped it on my phone. Just exploring, you know." She reached out and bopped Diane's shoulder. "Come on, Mom. Think of all the memories we'd carry away. When else will we get the chance to do something so fun and . . . and spontaneous, all of us together?" Her expression pleaded. "I want to do this. The way real families do."

Defensiveness descended like a stone on Diane's chest. "Has our family been that bad?"

Meghan sighed and closed her eyes for a moment. When she opened them, remorse glowed in her brown irises. "It's not been bad, Mom. Not even close to bad—really. But we've never done anything together. All of us. Together."

"But a long road trip, Meghan . . ." Could she survive being cooped up with her mother in a vehicle for a week? Two if they drove both ways. Here at the house, she could escape to the guest room when something her mother said or did aggravated her. There'd be no separation at all in an SUV or RV on the highway. "It'd cost a lot, too."

"Insurance is covering my expenses while I'm off work, so I don't have to worry about my bills. I've got some money stashed away in savings, and I can also cash in on my vacation pay. I have more than two weeks accumulated, so that would cover a lot. I bet Grandma would offer to pay for the whole trip, but I'd rather each of us contribute."

Diane would take out a loan before she let her mother fund her vacation. She almost laughed at the emphatic thought. When Diane was in college, she'd railed at her mother for being forced to get a part-time job and contribute toward her own education expenses. How things had changed. "I could cash one of my smaller CDs."

Meghan's face lit. "Then you're in? You want to do it?"

Diane wouldn't go so far as to say she wanted to go, but she was willing to accompany them. "Will you have time to finish your birthday scrapbook if we take a long trip?"

She flipped her hand in a dismissive gesture. "I'll get it done with no problem at all, and if we decide on the RV, there'll be room to work on it while we're traveling. Photos from the trip will make a great end to the scrapbook." She lunged forward and captured Diane in an awkward hug that felt more like being tackled. "Thanks, Mom!"

Diane wriggled out from beneath her daughter's weight. "Before you thank me, remember you've got to clear all this with your grandmother."

"Oh, she'll be game." Meghan settled on her own pillow again, still grinning.

"And it would probably be best for her to get clearance from her doctor before we stick her in a camper and transport her across five states."

Meghan immediately sobered. "Do you think there's something more wrong with Grandma than getting older?"

A snide comment about there having always been something wrong with her mother formed on her tongue, but she held it inside. "Like what?"

"I don't know. Like Alzheimer's or dementia or something. I know it's been a while since I visited her, but we talk on the phone a lot, and this forgetfulness and getting weepy so quick doesn't seem like her."

No, Mother had never been one to let emotions run amok. And forget something? Never. She hadn't been PTA president for six years running without good reason. "It's hard to say, but a doctor will know. So before we decide this trip is a go, we need to insist she get a physical. Now"—Diane arched one brow—"can we get some sleep, please?"

Meghan giggled. "All right. Good night, Mom." She punched her pillow a couple of times, burrowed into it, and closed her eyes.

For long minutes, Diane lay in the quiet room watching sleep overtake her daughter. Something she'd never done in all the years Meghan was under her roof. Because she'd been so determined not to be like her own mother. Even while gazing at Meghan, she could picture her mother's intent gaze from her spot at the end of Diane's bed.

Christmas Eve 1977
Little Rock, Arkansas

The pop of bedsprings woke Diane from a sound sleep. She opened her eyes and squinted through the shadows. She didn't jump when her bleary gaze zeroed in on her mother. "Mother, you woke me up." Her voice sounded growly, the way Daddy's did after he'd finished a cigar on the porch.

"I'm sorry." Mother spoke softly, soothingly, almost a whisper. She scooted closer and ran her hand over Diane's hair. "Close your eyes and go back to sleep."

Diane pulled the covers higher on her shoulder. "Why're you in here? Did I have a bad dream?" She couldn't remember a bad dream. She couldn't remember dreaming at all.

"No, sweetheart. I was just checking on you. To make sure you were all right."

"Oh." Diane yawned. She pawed under the covers for the teddy bear she always slept with and brought it up under her chin. "I'm fine." She closed her eyes. But the mattress didn't move. Which meant Mother hadn't moved. She opened her eyes again. "I'm fine. You can go." Then she remembered what day it was.

Diane sat straight up. "Are you making sure I don't sneak out and snoop under the tree?" She tipped her head, listening, but she didn't hear any rustling from the living room. Maybe Daddy'd already put the presents under their decorated tree and had gone on to bed. She hoped the bike she asked for—the purple glittery one with the gold banana seat—was out there waiting for her.

"Honey, I know you won't snoop. That would spoil the surprises."

Diane choked back a snigger. Mother didn't know her very well at all. She'd found half a dozen presents on the top shelf of the hall closet, where her parents didn't know she could climb. She couldn't wait to play with her tape recorder and wear the corduroy bell-bottoms.

"Lie back down."

Diane slowly lowered herself to the pillow and pulled her ratty teddy bear, the one Daddy had bought even before she was born, close.

"Close your eyes."

Diane squinted at her mother. "I will. Are you gonna go?"

"Soon."

"When?"

"When I've had my fill."

"Fill of what?"

"Of the sight of you."

Mother was so weird sometimes. And how could Diane sleep with somebody sitting there staring at her? She moaned, "Motherrrrr . . ."

"Close your eyes."

With a huge sigh, Diane closed her eyes.

Then Mother began to sing. A lullaby. Diane gritted her teeth. She was eleven already. Not a baby. Why wouldn't Mother go? She burrowed farther under the covers and made a promise to herself. If she became a mother someday, she would never torment her kids with stupid songs and weird things like watching them sleep. She'd be a totally cool mom instead of a whacko.

Present Day
Kendrickson, Nevada

Diane finally understood why Mother had sat on the bed and watched her sleep. Meghan looked so peaceful, so young, so sweet. Love swelled in Diane's breast—an intense, searing sweep of emotion that made her long to turn back time and gaze for hours on her daughter's baby face, her toddler face, even her pimply teenager face.

She reached slowly across the gap separating them and tucked a wispy strand of hair away from Meghan's cheek. Her daughter stirred and opened one eye.

"What're you doing?" Her sleep-thickened voice made Diane smile.

"Nothing. Just . . . getting my fill."

Meghan snorted softly and rubbed her nose. "You're so weird, Mom."

Why did it feel like she'd just been given the biggest compliment ever? She crooned, "Shhh, go to sleep." She wished she knew a lullaby. She'd prove her weirdness and sing it again and again to make up for all the times she hadn't sung her daughter to sleep.

Twenty-Six

Hazel

A road trip with the two of you?" Hazel took another sip of her coffee. Hot, flavored with hazelnut, thickened with cream. Such a marvelous way to start the day. But not as good as planning a vacation with her daughter and granddaughter. She'd never dreamed Margaret Diane would agree to such a venture. The idea made her giddy.

"It'll probably take a chunk of change to fund the journey." Meghan's face pinched into a brief grimace of remorse, then brightened. "But I think it'll be worth it. I've always wanted to go to Cumpton and see where you grew up, and I love the idea of having you as my tour guide."

"The dogs will go, too." Margaret Diane spooned sugar into the herbal tea she drank in place of coffee. The stuff smelled like burnt grass and looked like algae-infested water. "Is that a problem?"

Hazel wouldn't let it be a problem. Not for this trip, this chance of a lifetime. "I'm sure we'll get along as well in the car as we've managed in the house." She glanced at the row of dachshunds munching from their food bowls. "They'll be in their pet taxis, won't they?"

"They're happier that way in the car, but if we end up renting an RV— something Meghan is pushing for—I'll let them roam free." Margaret Diane picked up her cup and blew on the surface of the tea.

The aroma made Hazel want to gag. How on earth did the girl put something in her mouth that smelled so awful? She held her own cup beneath her chin and inhaled, clearing her nostrils of the tea scent. "Fine."

"But before we go"—Meghan exchanged a look with her mother that put

Hazel on alert—"Mom and I would like you to see a doctor and make sure it's all right to travel so far."

Hazel's ire rose so quickly it brought a pinprick stab in her temple. She thumped her cup on the table. "I don't need permission to take a trip."

Meghan took Hazel's hand. "Of course you don't. You're a grown woman who can make her own decisions. The doctor wouldn't be giving you permission, Grandma. He'd be letting us know there's no worry about you traveling over an extended period of time."

Margaret Diane rested her elbows on the table and held her cup between her palms. "It's mostly to ease our minds—"

Hazel sent her daughter a sharp look. She would expect Meghan's concern, but Margaret Diane was concerned, too?

"—since you've had those light-headed spells. Before we get in a car and take off, let's make sure the spells aren't anything to worry about."

Hazel examined their faces. She read sincere worry in both sets of brown eyes, and her aggravation diminished. "I suppose I should be grateful you want to be sure I'm healthy enough for the trip. But I can also tell you the worry is misplaced. I've hardly been sick a day in my life. My mother had a strong constitution, and she passed it on to me. I'm sure it's only because my body is aging. Things don't function as efficiently as they used to."

"And as soon as a doctor confirms your prognosis, we'll pack our bags and go." Margaret Diane finally began drinking the tea. She didn't even make a face. Such a brave girl.

Meghan slid a sheet of paper across the table. "I've got it all mapped out, Grandma. Our first stop will be at the Grand Canyon."

The Grand Canyon. She'd visited it once, many years ago, with Albert and Margaret Diane. Now she'd see it with Meghan. She nodded. "I like that idea."

Margaret Diane rolled her eyes. "Oh, yeah, it's a marvelous idea. One of you on crutches and one of you with dizzy spells, peeking over the edge of a mile-deep hole in the ground. You'll probably give me heart palpitations." Despite the sarcasm, something akin to eagerness glittered in her eyes.

Hazel winked at her.

Margaret Diane grinned and took another sip of her tea.

"After that"—Meghan continued as if her mother hadn't interrupted—"we'll find some places to visit in New Mexico and maybe even in Oklahoma. I'm not sure what, but a Google search ought to turn up something worthwhile. Oh, and speaking of Google searches, I need to locate a reputable company that rents out RVs. I really like the idea of having something we can spread out in and use as our home away from home on this trip. Do you have any suggestions, Grandma?"

Hazel smiled, smug. "I certainly do. But you won't need Google to find it. A gentleman at our church—a member of my Bible study group—has a small RV he loans out to people in our congregation. Several people have borrowed it to take on brief mission trips."

Margaret Diane's brows pinched together. "We aren't doing anything remotely close to a mission trip. Would he let us use it?"

"I don't know, but it wouldn't hurt to ask. Meghan said reputable, and John Wedman is as reputable as any man I know. Do you want me to call and ask him?"

Meghan looked at Margaret Diane, who looked at Meghan. They both turned to Hazel simultaneously and shrugged.

Hazel burst out laughing. "At least you're in agreement. I'll call him midmorning. Maybe we could drive over and take a look at it, make sure it's what you have in mind."

They finished their breakfast, and while Margaret Diane straightened the kitchen, Hazel and Meghan worked on a few scrapbook pages. The images stirred memories to life, and the accompanying emotions left Hazel feeling both weak and revived at the same time.

Meghan had decided to divide the book into four sections—Hazel's childhood in Cumpton, her relationship with Albert, her relationship with Margaret

Diane, and finally her relationship with Meghan. Strange how each stage of her life required a separate section. Shouldn't there be overlap? Hazel hoped their planned trip would give them a fifth section—one dedicated to togetherness.

Midway between nine and ten, Hazel called John, and as she'd suspected, he was more than willing to let them borrow his RV. "But I need to caution you. Even though it's a Class C, it's one of the smaller models. Sometimes Wanda and I felt like we were bumping into each other in there. With three of you—"

"We're also bringing four dachshunds."

His chuckle rolled. "—and four dachshunds, it will be even more crowded. So you come see it, go inside and get a feel for it. Then you decide."

They made arrangements for the women to come by before lunch, and then Hazel hung up. She smiled triumphantly at her daughter and granddaughter. "Things are falling into place. Isn't it ex . . . Ex . . ." She frowned. What word did she intend to use?

Meghan tipped her head. "Exciting?"

Hazel slumped with relief. "Yes. Exciting."

Margaret Diane and Meghan exchanged a look heavy with meaning.

Hazel rose and headed for her bedroom. "If we're going to drive over to the Wedman place, we might as well enjoy lunch at a café afterward. I want to change into something more appropriate for an excursion." Her navy-blue ankle pants and white blouse were fine for any of Kendrickson's restaurants, and John Wedman wouldn't care what she was wearing. But she would change anyway. To prove to herself that she still knew how to put an outfit together. After her struggle to recall a simple word, she needed the reassurance.

Diane

Cozy. That was the word Mr. Wedman used the most to describe his RV as he led the women along a sidewalk to the back edge of his two-acre patch of ground on the edge of Kendrickson. The older-model RV, which reminded Diane of an overgrown pickup truck and topper, lurked under an unpretentious carport on a slab of concrete. He chuckled every time *cozy* emerged, and Diane began to wonder if he was playing a joke on them.

"Yes, Wanda and me sure enjoyed our cozy little motor home. Lots of good memories stored up in it. Just couldn't make myself get rid of it after she passed." He cleared his throat and unlocked the door. He aimed a watery smile at them. "Go on in and take a peek at my cozy home-for-the-road."

Mother went in first, followed by Meghan, who needed a boost from Diane to mount the fold-down metal step. Then Diane entered. Apparently John had come out and readied the vehicle for their inspection, because she couldn't spot a speck of dust and it held the slight essence of lemons. Every window from front to back was open, allowing in the breeze. Even though the wind was anything but cool, the moving air kept the place from feeling overly stuffy.

Meghan had some trouble navigating the narrow walkway with her crutches, but her smile never dimmed. Her gaze bounced from the mounted fans in all corners of the main living space to the built-in cabinets to the three-burner stove and finally to the opening for the sleeping area. She plopped onto the corner of the bed that jutted at an angle into the kitchen area, and then she released a sigh.

Mr. Wedman remained outside, but he braced his hands on either side of the door frame and leaned in, beaming at them as they explored. "I keep the dining room table set up most times, but it does change into a bed. Then there's the bed in the back, and the one above the cab, so each of you could have your own place to sleep. 'Course, that bed in the back's classified as a queen, so if two of you wanted to share, you wouldn't have to take the table down every night."

Meghan smoothed her hand over the bare mattress. "That sounds good, especially since the table is the only place to sit other than the driver's seat and passenger seat." She aimed a teasing grin at Diane. "Grandma and I could share the queen and you could take the bunk, huh, Mom? Or are you too old to climb up there?"

Diane arched one brow in reply, and the gray-haired man laughed as raucously as if she'd spouted a torrent of defensive words. "When Wanda and me took the motor home out, we always had our cats, Cindy and Mittens, with us. They loved riding up in the bunk and looking out the window. Might still be a few fur balls up there. I am old enough that I'm not fond of climbing into the bunk. Hope you don't mind fur balls."

Meghan smirked. "Mom's partial to fur balls." She shifted her smile to Mother. "What do you think, Grandma? Are you ready to take to the highway?"

Mother turned a slow circle. "As John said, it's very compact, but it has everything we need. It's amazing to me that the makers managed to fit in both a bathroom and a kitchen."

"Wanda had me take out the factory cupboard with a little fridge below and pantry above and replace it with a bigger fridge." Mr. Wedman leaned farther in and gestured like a salesman peddling his wares at the state fair. "When we traveled, she always wanted to cook, so she needed the fridge space. Losing that pantry meant losing storage, so I put a drawer under the bed there where Meghan's feet are. You can tuck a lot of canned and boxed goods in that drawer."

Meghan leaned forward and shifted her feet. She laughed. "I didn't even notice the handle when I sat down. Ingenious."

The old man puffed up. "Oh, now, I wouldn't call it ingenious. Maybe practical. Or inventive. But not ingenious."

Diane eased sideways past Mother, who was examining the cooktop, to the pair of captain's chairs in the cab. She slid into the driver's seat and examined the instrument panel. It seemed similar to her Jeep. "Would I need any special training to learn how to drive it?"

The man stepped in, leaving the door open. "That's one of the nicest things about this particular model. It's six inches shy of twenty-four feet and only a foot wider than a standard diesel pickup truck, so if you're used to driving, say, a full-size SUV or double-cab pickup, you shouldn't have trouble adjusting to this."

"You'll probably be the one doing the driving, Mom," Meghan called from her perch on the corner of the bed. "Unless Grandma wants to take the wheel."

Mother waved both hands and made a sour face.

Meghan laughed. "Do you think you can handle it?"

Once again, Mr. Wedman released his deep, throaty chuckle. He dangled a set of keys like a toy in front of a cat. "Only one way to find out. Got your driver's license on you?"

Diane patted the little cross-body wallet resting on her hip.

"Buckle up, then, and let's take her for a spin."

rue eagerness quivered through Diane's frame as she climbed down from the driver's seat of Mr. Wedman's cozy RV. Although initially apprehensive about the trip, now she couldn't wait to pack, load up, and—as Meghan had put it—hit the road. Diane had left the engine idling, as he'd instructed her, and vibrations traveled from her soles to her scalp, adding to the pulse of energy coursing through her.

The man ambled around the front of the RV to Diane. His ever-present grin and twinkling blue eyes reminded her of her father's cheerful personality, and she couldn't help but smile in return. He slipped his hands into the pockets of his baggy knee-length shorts and waggled his eyebrows at her. "Well . . . what do you think?"

She could tell by his expression he already knew, but she answered anyway. "I can handle it."

"And it's fun, yes?"

She giggled—the most girlish giggle she'd released in years. "I was kind of nervous at first, but once you get used to it, you're right—it is fun." Sitting in the high seat, guiding the vehicle on the highway and along city streets was a nearly heady experience. She'd felt powerful, almost invincible behind the wheel. Is that how her trucker daddy had felt when he drove his semi?

Meghan and Mother came around the RV and joined them, and Mr. Wedman inched toward the driver's door. "Let me park this thing, and then I'll answer any questions you might have."

The three of them stood aside while he expertly drove the vehicle onto its pad. The engine stilled, and Diane keenly experienced a rush of loss. He climbed out, locked the door, and then rejoined them, a smile stretching across his face.

Mother held her hand to Mr. Wedman and he gave it a quick squeeze. "John, thank you so much for letting us take it out. I wrote down everything you said about recharging the generator, emptying the tank, and filling the water reservoir." She scowled at the notepad in her hand. "The only thing I don't know is how much you charge for rent."

He pinched his chin and aimed his gaze skyward, as if deeply thinking. Then he sighed and scuffed his toe on the ground, head low. "My rates might make you balk, but I have to be fair and charge everybody the same."

"I wouldn't expect anything less."

Diane swallowed a chortle at Mother's tart tone. She'd witnessed her mother bargaining with vendors at farmers' markets, but maybe when it came to fellow church members, she set her dickering skills aside.

He lifted his head and looked Mother square in the face. "You'll be expected to fill the gas tank while you travel, watch the oil level and add a quart as needed, make sure the reservoir doesn't run dry, and give the insides a scrubbing when you bring it back."

Mother frowned. "Yes, yes, you told us all that while Diane was test driving. I have it all written down." She tapped her notepad. "I'm still waiting to find out what we need to pay you for the privilege of using it."

"My standard rate is three dollars a day or three cents a mile, whichever is the least."

Diane's jaw dropped and Meghan squeaked, "Th-three dollars . . . or three cents? You've got to be kidding. That's less than a tenth of what rental places charge."

"I'm not a rental place."

Mother was spluttering, her face reflecting disbelief. "Rental place or not, you have to charge for the wear and tear on your motor home. John, be reasonable."

He shook his head, his expression serious. "That's my rate. The only reason I charge at all is it helps cover my insurance bill. If I let other people drive it, I have to keep better coverage than just liability." He flipped up the collar of his polo shirt and folded his arms over his barrel chest. "It's available if you want to take it. All I need is a signed waiver that I'm not responsible for any personal injuries you might suffer while you're using it." He grimaced. "That's to satisfy the insurance company, too. I can't imagine anybody suing me because they fell off the step or something."

Diane could imagine a lot of people who would sue for things even less petty than that, but she had no problem signing the waiver. "Thank you again, Mr. Wedman. When we get our travel plans set we'll give you a call and put the dates on the calendar. Is that all right?"

"Perfectly fine. Funny, it's usually off my property more than on during the summer, but this season's been slow." He shrugged. "Maybe God was keeping it here for you ladies to use."

His nonchalant yet introspective statement stabbed straight to the center of Diane's heart. But the poke wasn't as much painful as unsettling. She cupped Mother's elbow and turned her toward the house. "As I said, we'll call you when we're set." They still needed to arrange Mother's doctor visit, and that could take a few days.

He followed them to Mother's car, then stood in the shade of his roof and waved as they drove away. Meghan leaned forward over the console, propping her elbows on the backs of the front seats. "I wish I'd thought to bring a measuring tape so we'd know how much luggage the storage areas will hold. With three of us being gone for two weeks, we'll need a lot."

"Not necessarily." Mother gripped the steering wheel and kept her gaze forward as she spoke. "John recommended we stay at KOA campgrounds because they usually have laundry facilities. If we take his advice, we can do some loads of laundry when we recharge the generator and fill the reservoir."

Meghan bumped Diane's shoulder. "You seemed really comfortable driving it. Do you think you can handle it for so many miles?"

A sense of satisfaction filled Diane's chest. "Oh, yeah. No problem at all."

Mother shot a sideways look filled with understanding at Diane. "You are your father's daughter."

Warmth flooded Diane's frame, and she gave her mother a full-fledged, sincere smile of thanks.

Meghan fidgeted as if an electrical current ran through her seat. "When we get back to the house, I'll figure out the locations of KOAs along our route and see if they require reservations. Since it's summer, I hope they aren't all filled up."

"If God made the RV available, He probably has open lots at KOAs waiting for us, too." Diane jolted. Had she really said that out loud? And without a hint of sarcasm? Mother's smile and Meghan's astonished expression assured her she had. She cleared her throat. "Either way, we can always find a Laundromat, so we don't need to load the thing to the hilt with clothes. Or groceries, for that matter. Let's plan out our meals and buy what we need at grocery stores along the way for, I don't know, maybe three days at a time. That way our produce will stay fresh."

"Sounds like a plan." Meghan slumped into the back seat and released a big sigh. "I can't believe we're really doing this. Unbelievable. Someone remind me to call Sean this evening and find out if he's got a date set to be in Cumpton for the investigation. We need to plan this so our days coincide with his."

Diane bit down on the end of her tongue, but Mother voiced the thought trailing through her brain.

"If it's meant to be, our days in Cumpton will be the same as his."

Diane gazed out the window, gritting her teeth. Since when did the idea of God orchestrating events seem natural to her? Mother was rubbing off on her whether she liked it or not.

Little Rock, Arkansas
Sean

Shortly before quitting time, the double doors to the cold-case unit slapped open and the team's captain, Ken Ratzlaff, strode across the scuffed hardwood floor. Every detective's gaze followed his progress. As much as Sean respected Captain Ratzlaff for his knowledge and experience, he'd learned over his years as a detective that the man had a short fuse, and sometimes even perceived infractions inspired a verbal dressing down. So he tensed when the captain stopped on the opposite side of his desk and slapped a manila folder on top of his computer keyboard.

Sean picked up the envelope and fingered its sealed edge. "What's this?"

"Your traveling papers."

Sean raised his eyebrows. "For Cumpton?"

"Someplace else you need to be in the next few weeks?"

Sean shook his head. He used his pocketknife to slit the top flap and emptied the papers on his desk. "What's my departure date?"

"I wrote in the twenty-second, and you've got clearance for a full work-week in Cumpton if you need it."

"So the twenty-second through the twenty-sixth." Sean mused aloud, thinking of the preparations he'd need to make at home to be gone for five days. Summer was still in full swing, so the neighbor girl would probably come over and take in his mail, and the teen across the street could be convinced to mow his yard. He liked to keep his house and yard looking neat and inhabited—less chance of a burglar targeting his place. Still, it was amazingly easy to get away when no wife, children, or four-legged creatures required his presence. He pushed aside the thread of regret. "I don't see any problem with that." Sean searched the paperwork, frowning. "You're sending me by myself? No partner?"

Ratzlaff grimaced. "I could send Sanderson with you, but I'd rather he stayed here—kept working on solving that string of campus rapes in 1996. He ought to be able to go forward on that without you, and you won't be so far behind when you get back from Cumpton." He angled a wry look at Sean. "Does it bother you to travel alone?"

"No, sir. Not at all. We just usually investigate in pairs."

"I figured DeFord might show up at the other end since the case is so personal to her." Farber and Roach snickered, and the captain shot a glare in their direction. The two bent over their computers. He focused on Sean again. "If she does show, try to limit her involvement. She's supposed to be on leave. Besides, this is a one-man investigation. Given the number of years that've passed, I'm not holding my breath on it, but I can't in good conscience ignore it, based on what you've uncovered."

He might be gruff, but underneath, Ratzlaff had a good heart. Sean smiled. "Thanks, Cap. DeFord's expressed her appreciation that we're looking into her great-aunt's disappearance. If she's able to make it to Cumpton when I'm there, I'll do my best to make her rest."

"Do that. We want her back in full force at the end of her leave. Overdoing could extend her absence." He glanced at Sanderson, who was staring at his computer screen and biting his thumbnail. The captain shook his head slightly and turned to Sean again. "We want her back."

Sean nodded. Sanderson was okay no matter what the others thought, but Sean missed Meghan. More than he'd expected to. More than he'd ever admit. He wanted her back, too. "I'll give her a call this evening and let her know I've got clearance to travel."

The captain headed for the doors. "Call her now. It's an official case, and she's a contact. I won't dock your pay."

The moment the doors swung shut behind Ratzlaff, Anthony Johnson spun in his chair to face Sean. "You're heading to Cumpton? You know that's basically a jog in the road, don't you? Not even three hundred people live there anymore."

Sean had already surmised the population had declined since the time Hazel Blackwell-DeFord resided there. "Yeah, I know." His papers indicated the unit had arranged hotel accommodations in Bentonville, roughly a twenty-five-mile drive from Cumpton. He'd traveled farther distances for investigations before. "Excuse me, gonna give Meg"—he coughed into his hand, hoping the others hadn't heard his slip-up—"DeFord a call."

Johnson smirked, but he settled his attention on his own work without ribbing Sean.

Meghan's phone rang four times, and he was mentally preparing a message to leave on her voice mail when she answered. At the sound of her voice, he automatically smiled. "Good afternoon. It's Sean."

"Yes, I saw your ID come up. Sorry it took me so long to answer— Grandma and I are working on a scrapbook page and I had glue on my fingers. So what's up?"

Her perky tone let him know she was enjoying the day. His news would make the day even better. "I got my clearance this morning to spend a week in Cumpton."

"Really? That's great!" A muffled comment followed, and he envisioned her pressing the phone to her shoulder and sharing his words with her grandmother. "So when are you going?"

"The twenty-second through the twenty-sixth. I'll probably drive to Bentonville Sunday afternoon so I can head to Cumpton first thing Monday morning." With five sets of ears tuned in to his every word, he kept his tone clipped, professional, unlike the relaxed conversations the two of them had enjoyed in the evenings during her time away. It wasn't easy to remain detached.

"So soon?"

She had no reason to curb her tone, and he clearly heard her disappointment. He frowned, shifting slightly so his back was to the others in the room. "What's the problem?"

She explained their intention to borrow an RV and drive the distance between Kendrickson and Cumpton, stopping at various points along the way. "We can save our sightseeing for the trip back and drive straight to Cumpton, but we'd have to leave first thing tomorrow morning for us to be there by the twenty-second."

"Not enough notice, huh?"

"We can't leave until Grandma's seen her doctor. Her appointment's scheduled for next Tuesday."

Sean's concerns rose a notch. "Is she all right?"

"Oh, sure." Her overly bright response indicated subterfuge. "Mom and I want her to have a checkup before we go. You know, to be sure she's up to such a long road trip."

He'd text her later to get the details, but for now he needed to stay on track. "Obviously it would be beneficial for me if she was in Cumpton while I'm there. She'll know places and people and can offer guidance. But if it doesn't work, it's all right. I can investigate single-handedly, too."

"I know you can. You're a great investigator. But Grandma really wants to help. We'll see what we can get accomplished at this end to put us there for at least a few of the same days. I didn't imagine the paper pushers would get things organized so quickly."

Neither had he. "I think everyone's on edge with this one, considering the number of potential victims and the length of time that's passed. So things got expedited."

Her sigh carried to his ear. A weary sigh, and he hated that his news had dampened her spirits.

"Don't sweat it, DeFord." He used the offhand, casual tone he usually reserved for Farber or Dane. "One way or another, the case will be covered. I'll talk to you later, all right?"

At her dismal farewell, he disconnected the call and turned back to his desk. Farber, Dane, Johnson, and Roach were all grinning at him. Only Sanderson remained focused on his computer. Sean held his hands wide. "What?"

Farber glanced at the others. "Sounds like you won't have any company-paid rendezvous after all."

Sean clenched his jaw. He met Farber's teasing gaze with a firm glare. "Meghan's not that kind of girl."

A knowing glint entered the other agent's eyes. "Okay." His lips twitched, and he glanced at his partner before aiming a smirk at Sean. "When you talk to *Meghan* later, tell her hi from the rest of us."

Sometimes Sean felt like he was in a frat house rather than an investigations unit.

Twenty-Eight

Kendrickson, Nevada
Meghan

eghan laid her cell phone flat on the table and pulled up the calculator app. She began punching buttons, thinking out loud. "Fourteen hundred miles divided by sixty-five miles an hour for eight hours a day . . ."

"What are you doing?" Confusion colored Grandma's tone.

She didn't glance up. "Trying to figure out how we can be in Cumpton before Sean has to go back to Little Rock on the twenty-sixth."

"When is the twenty-sixth?"

"A week from tomorrow." She poked numbers, frowned at the result, then groaned. "I wish I'd paid more attention in math. This isn't making sense."

Mom set aside the pan of raw almonds she'd been preparing for roasting. "Let me do it."

Meghan leaned back and allowed her mother to take over the phone. "I didn't intend to be in any hurry to get there, but Sean's travel papers just threw a"—she borrowed one of Grandma's phrases—"clinker in my works. What's the earliest we can be in Cumpton if we go straight there, no stops along the way?"

Mom put on her thoughtful scowl, what Meghan always called her teacher face. "If we drive for eight hours a day, which I've already told you is my limit, at sixty-five miles per hour, which is the fastest speed Mr. Wedman recommended, we can cover five hundred twenty miles in a day's time." She handed the phone to Meghan. "Of course, that's barring road construction and presuming KOA campgrounds will be located at convenient intervals. Since the total distance is about fourteen hundred miles, then we're looking at three days of travel. So to have at least one day with Sean in Cumpton, we'd need to leave here early on the twenty-third."

Grandma's appointment with the doctor was set for three o'clock in the afternoon on the twenty-third. Meghan bit back another groan.

"Three days of travel . . ." Grandma tapped a photograph's edge on the table. "If we left first thing tomorrow, we could be in Cumpton and meet up with Sean the same day he plans to arrive."

"We can't leave tomorrow." Mom returned to the cookie sheet of oiled, salted almonds. She tucked the tray in the oven and set the timer.

Grandma lifted her chin in a stubborn jut. "Why, yes, we can. It's early yet. There are several hours left in the day for us to drive to John's for the RV and get it packed."

Mom turned a stern gaze on Grandma. "Given the distance and the time allowance, I concede that it is possible for us to be in Cumpton at the same time as Sean. But we agreed you'd get the okay from the doctor before we set off."

"The doctor appointment can wait." Grandma turned almost petulant. "This trip can't. Not if I'm to be there to help Sean with the investigation."

As much as Meghan had wanted her grandmother to have a thorough examination, she couldn't help siding with her. Especially in light of how much Grandma wanted to help Sean in person. "She's right, Mom. The timing's all off now with Sean leaving earlier than we expected. We have to be in Cumpton for at least one day while he's there. Maybe if we put Grandma on a cancellation list with the doctor, she'd get in before Tuesday. Should we try?"

Mom gazed at her with her teacher face intact for several seconds, but Meghan refused to squirm the way her students would likely shrink beneath that glare. Finally Mom sighed. "Call and see if it's possible to put her on the cancellation list."

Grandma aimed a triumphant grin at Meghan. "Hand me my phone, please."

Meghan slid it across the table to her.

Mom gestured to the mess on the table. "Then put that scrapbook stuff aside and start calling KOA campgrounds. If we don't have a place to park the RV, there's no sense in taking it out."

"You can park an RV anywhere, even in a Walmart parking lot." Grandma spoke staunchly as she scrolled through her saved numbers.

"But we can't fill the water tank in a Walmart parking lot," Mom shot back, "so we need campground locations." She flipped her hand at Meghan. "Start searching. While you two are doing that, I'll make a list of the things we need to pack." She rolled her eyes. "Good gravy, I can't believe I agreed to dive into this whirlwind with the two of you. I must not have any more sense than God gave a goose."

Meghan hunched her shoulders and giggled. She wouldn't touch a line like that.

While Meghan investigated KOA campground locations between Las Vegas and Cumpton, Mom and Grandma retrieved the RV from Mr. Wedman and went to the grocery store. By evening, they had their stops organized and the RV's cabinets packed with nonperishables. They kept Grandma's washer and dryer busy with sheets, towels, and travel clothes all afternoon and into the evening. If by some stretch of good luck or karma or answered prayer Grandma got an earlier appointment, they'd be ready to take off the moment they left the doctor's office. Assuming she received a good report, Mom reminded her. Meghan refused to consider any other alternative.

Friday after breakfast Meghan sent Sean a text to let him know they were trying to get to Cumpton as quickly as possible, and his reply made her heart roll over.

I'll pray it all falls into place. Looking forward to seeing you.

Even if he didn't mean anything personal by the second sentence, it touched her. And the first sentence echoed in her mind all morning. If Sean was praying, it would happen. She trusted everything would fall into place.

Shortly after lunch, she and Grandma settled in side by side on the couch to watch a movie. They hadn't gotten past the opening credits when Grandma's telephone rang. The caller ID showed the clinic's number. Meghan let out a whoop and snagged it up. She hit the talk button and shoved the phone at Grandma.

Frowning, Grandma put it to her ear. "Hello. Yes, this is Mrs. DeFord. Today at two forty-five?"

Meghan clapped both hands over her mouth and checked the grandfather clock. Already one ten. How far was it to the Las Vegas clinic?

"I might be a few minutes late, depending on traffic, but I'll do my best to be there . . . Yes, thank you. Goodbye."

Before Grandma finished the call, Meghan had struggled off the cushions and put her crutches in place. At Grandma's goodbye, she bellowed, "Mom! We've gotta get Grandma to her doctor's office in an hour and a half!"

Mom stayed behind to ready the dogs for travel, just in case, and Meghan rode shotgun while Grandma drove. She sent a text to Sean.

The doctor's office got Grandma in early. Might leave Kendrickson later today. Will keep you posted.

Within seconds her phone buzzed with his response.

PTL! Praying all goes well.

She smiled the rest of the way to the clinic.

Grandma found an open parking space near the center of the large out-door lot. The sun tried to blister Meghan's head while they walked what seemed like miles across the asphalt. She bit down on the tip of her tongue to keep from encouraging Grandma to hurry up. Would the receptionist cancel the appointment if they arrived late? To her relief, they entered the reception area of the clinic with two minutes to spare.

While Grandma checked in, Meghan crossed the tile floor, careful not to set the tips of her crutches on the toes of any of the half-dozen people already waiting, and sank onto the stiff cushion of a vinyl-covered, double-sized chair in the corner. She'd expected them to take Grandma straight back to a room, but instead Grandma joined her. The vinyl squeaked in protest when Grandma sat.

"Not ready for you yet?" She did her best to keep a light tone, but Grandma must have sensed her fretfulness because she patted Meghan's knee.

"It's not all about me, dear. Others need to see the doctor, too."

Meghan sighed. "I know, but . . ." She and Grandma had other important places to be. When would Sean's prayers kick in and speed up the process?

Grandma reached for the stack of magazines on a nearby table. "Even if we don't leave until tomorrow morning, we'll have the majority of the week in Cumpton. Remember what Rousseau said. 'Patience is bitter, but its fruit is sweet.'" Grandma picked up a copy of *House Beautiful* and browsed it, but Meghan stared at the round clock on the plain-painted wall and watched the second hand count the minutes.

At 3:18 a woman wearing bright-pink scrubs and a purple bandana around her frizzy red hair emerged from behind a swinging door near the reception desk. She seemed to search the area. "Hazel?"

Grandma lifted her head. "I'm Mrs. DeFord."

The woman smiled. "Please come with me, Hazel."

Grandma sighed.

Meghan started to rise, but Grandma plopped the magazine in her lap. "No, you stay here. I'm capable of taking care of myself."

Meghan watched the woman escort Grandma past the door. Then she pulled out her phone and sent Sean a quick text message.

Grandma's with the doctor now. Keeping my fingers crossed!

His reply came before she could count to ten.

Crossed fingers unnecessary. God's got this.

The certainty in his answer stole her ability to breathe for a few seconds. What would it be like to hold such fierce confidence in someone? She loved Mom. She loved Grandma. She would even say she trusted them to do their best for her. But she couldn't imagine stating "Mom's got this" or "Grandma's got this" and leaving it at that. Meghan would still worry, fret, and try to finagle things so they'd happen the way she wanted.

Her fingers itched to ask Sean how he could be so sure God had it, but he probably had paperwork to complete to finalize his travel plans. She shouldn't pester him. With reluctance she slipped her phone into her pocket and made herself read an article about safely stripping wallpaper from lath-and-plaster walls.

She read two more articles in the *House Beautiful* magazine and then picked up a tabloid-type publication plastered with photographs of movie stars. She'd never been much interested in following Hollywood's important people, but the magazine helped her pass the time. When she looked up from the second magazine, she was surprised to discover it was a few minutes after five o'clock. The waiting room was nearly empty, too. Where was Grandma?

She tossed the magazine back on the stack, situated her crutches, and hitched across the floor to the receptionist's desk. "Excuse me, my grandmother, Hazel DeFord, went to a room around three fifteen. Could you tell me when she might be finished?"

"DeFord?"

"That's right."

"Spelling, please?"

Meghan slowly spelled out Grandma's name, both last and first.

The young woman tapped a few words on the keyboard and squinted at the screen, her lips pooched out as if she'd just tasted a lemon. Suddenly she pushed away from the desk. Her chair's wheels carried her several feet backward to a long counter crowded with stacking trays and office equipment. She scooped a couple of pages from the printer tray and scowled at them. Then she pulled with her feet and rolled herself back to the computer.

She thrust the pages over the reception counter at Meghan. "Your grandmother was transported to the imaging center behind the clinic for a sonogram. You can pick her up there."

Meghan frowned at her. "What?"

The woman flapped the pages. "It's all in the paperwork."

They must be talking about someone else. Grandma wouldn't have needed a sonogram. "Are you sure this is about Hazel DeFord? She's not pregnant."

A half smile, more snide than soothing, tipped up the corners of the woman's lips. "Sonography is used for more than obstetrics. Please take these pages with you to the imaging center. Someone there will explain."

Twenty-Nine

Hazel

Hazel sat on the edge of the high table in the whitewashed room and bit on her lower lip. She was too old to dissolve into tears. But couldn't they have allowed her to put on her clothes before sharing the results of her sonogram? The gaping gown exposed her wrinkled back, and her bare feet dangled at least twelve inches above the floor, leaving her feeling vulnerable. And undignified. Being appropriately attired might not change the outcome of the test, but surely she'd be better equipped to accept the news.

"Are you absolutely sure my carotid artery is blocked? I haven't had anything remotely close to a stroke." Many of her friends had suffered strokes from blocked arteries whether in their hearts or their necks. She wasn't unfamiliar with the malady. Could anyone reach her age without being exposed to such? But somehow she'd never envisioned herself as one of the sufferers.

Dr. Nobbs rolled the wheeled stool closer and placed his hands on her knees. "Now that I've seen the sonogram, yes, I'm sure. I suspected as much when I listened to the arteries in your neck. I can let you use my stethoscope and listen, if you'd like. You'll be able to discern the difference between the blood flow in the right and that in the left."

"It's the left one that's blocked, isn't it?"

He nodded.

Which explained why, when she grew stressed or alarmed, she experienced a pounding in one temple but not the other. "Is the blockage responsible for my light-headedness and occasional confusion?"

"Yes."

She sighed. "I suppose I should be relieved it isn't only because I'm an old lady."

The doctor chuckled. "Confusion can happen with age as well, but this time I'm sure it isn't an upcoming birthday that's at fault. Based on the narrowing of the artery and what you've been experiencing over the past several months, I believe you've had a series of transient ischemic attacks, what we commonly call TIAs. Many people refer to them as ministrokes because the symptoms are similar to having a stroke."

Alarm bells rang in Hazel's mind, bringing the familiar pounding in her left temple. "Has my brain been damaged?"

He shook his head. "Absolutely not. TIAs cause temporary confusion or dizziness, but the symptoms last only a few seconds until blood carrying oxygen flows through again. So there's been no damage at all to your brain."

That, at least, was a relief.

"Our goal is, of course, to unblock that artery so the blood can flow freely. We want to prevent you from having an actual stroke." Dr. Nobbs stood and crossed to a counter stretching the length of the room. He scribbled on a sheet of paper. "I'm going to refer you to Dr. Bashad. He is one of the best vascular surgeons in the state. We're very lucky to have him here in Las Vegas. He works predominantly out of St. Mary's Hospital. Have you ever been to St. Mary's?"

"No. I haven't been to a hospital since 1966, when I gave birth to my daughter."

Dr. Nobbs shot a smile over his shoulder. "Obviously you've been in very good health, then. You're fortunate."

She wished she felt fortunate. She was too scared to feel fortunate.

"I am confident that Dr. Bashad will be completely successful in removing the blockage." He dropped the pen and turned with the paper in his hand. "We'll need to confirm with Dr. Bashad's nurse, but generally we don't delay these kinds of procedures. The risk of the blockage increasing and causing a stroke is too great, so as soon as you're dressed we'll go make the call together to schedule surgery. In all likelihood, it will be sometime early next week. In the meantime, it's imperative that you—"

Panic struck. "Early next week? I can't have surgery next week." If she'd been fully dressed, she would have leaped off the table and escaped. Maybe that's why they'd left her in this unladylike gown. "I'm taking a vacation with my daughter and granddaughter. We're driving a motor home to Cumpton, Arkansas, to look for my little sister."

The doctor frowned at her as if she'd lost control of her senses. And maybe she had, because she couldn't seem to stop talking.

"I've waited seventy years to find her, and now a detective is helping me. He'll be there next week. Margaret Diane and Meghan have made arrangements to take me to meet him, and I've even grown accustomed to having the dogs underfoot all the time without cringing." She shook her head so hard her ears rang. "No, Doctor, we'll need to schedule this for another time. Maybe in September, after Margaret Diane and Meghan have returned to Little Rock." Tears blurred her vision, and her throat went tight. She gripped the scratchy fabric sagging at her throat and battled against dissolving into wails of frustration and anguish.

Dr. Nobbs stepped close and took hold of her shoulders. "Mrs. DeFord, take a few deep breaths and bring yourself under control."

He spoke so calmly, so kindly, she automatically followed his direction. Her first breaths were carried on shuddering gasps, but eventually they smoothed. Her vision cleared, and she gazed into the doctor's sympathetic eyes.

"Are you calmer now?"

She nodded.

"Good. Please listen to me. It's imperative that you stay calm and as stress free as possible until this surgery is over. Undue stress causes your blood pressure to rise, and the increased blood flow can't make it through the constricted artery. You don't want to give yourself a stroke, do you?"

Miserably, Hazel whispered, "No."

He gently squeezed her shoulders, then stepped back and pinned her with a repentant look. "I wish I could send you on that vacation, Mrs. DeFord. It's very clear that you were looking forward to it. But I think you should be grateful that you came in for a checkup before you drove so far from home."

Hazel swallowed a sob. "I was going home."

He nodded as if her comment made perfect sense. "Let me step out and I'll have a nurse come in to help you get dressed. You're still a little shaky."

Such an understatement. Her entire body quivered as if an earthquake rattled the table beneath her.

"When you're ready, we'll go schedule that surgery, hmm?"

Would she ever be ready? He was waiting for a reply. She sighed. "All right." He moved into the hallway and pushed the door closed with a solid *click*. Hazel hung her head. A moan strained for release. Why, when she finally had a chance to find Maggie, had this happened?

A few self-pitying squeaks escaped her throat, and then she straightened her shoulders and sniffed hard. She would be strong. For Meghan, and for Margaret Diane, she would be strong.

Meghan

She couldn't remember the last time she'd been so frustrated. And scared. Somewhere in this building, her grandmother was being subjected to tests that made no sense, and no one would tell her anything. Who cared about Hippa? She wanted answers. She wanted her grandmother.

She'd been instructed to wait in a small room containing two couches, a television without a remote, and an empty coffeepot on a table. She wanted to pace, but her crutches prevented her from expelling the pent-up energy. So she flopped into the center of one couch and pulled out her phone. She intended to call Mom, but somehow her finger hit Sean's number instead.

"Hey, I wondered when you'd call. How'd your grandma's appointment go?"

A huge knot tangled her tonsils and she couldn't force words past it. Only a whimper emerged.

"Meghan? Is that you?"

She had to pull herself together. If she didn't control herself, he'd wonder if she was competent enough to hold down a job. She cleared her throat. Then again. "Yeah." She didn't sound like herself, but at least she was talking. "It's me."

"What's wrong?"

"I don't really know." She explained waiting for nearly two hours, then being sent to another building, then not being able to locate her grandmother. "All I know is they're doing a sonogram. But why? What are they looking for?"

"They haven't given you any indication at all?"

"No!" She ran her fingers through her hair and closed her eyes against the sting of tears. "Nobody will tell me anything."

"I don't blame you for being scared. If I were in your shoes, I'd be a little worked up, too."

She popped her eyes open. "You would?"

"Of course I would."

"But you believe in God."

"And you think that keeps me from being human?"

She processed his question. Embarrassment struck hard. "That was a stupid thing to say."

"No, Meghan, it wasn't." He spoke so reassuringly her tense shoulders automatically began to relax. "Believing in God helps. It helps a lot, especially in times when I can't understand. Fear and worry are very human reactions to the unknown. So when those emotions strike—and believe me, they strike me, too—I have to remind myself that He knows. And I have to trust Him to hold the people I care about even when I can't."

Had he trusted God to hold her when she was pinned in her car for hours waiting for the Jaws of Life to free her? She leaned forward, propped her elbow on her knee, and covered her eyes with one hand. She hugged the phone to her cheek and whispered, "I'm really upset right now. I came in here expecting the doctor to tell Grandma everything's good to go, and now I don't know if anything's good. What will I do if—"

"Don't." Although the word was sharp, his voice was gentle. Soothing. "I know it's natural to start expecting the worst, but it's too soon for that. You need to hold on to hope, Meghan."

"Hold on to hope . . ." "How?"

"By trusting that your grandmother is in good hands with the doctor. By trusting she's receiving the best care available. By trusting that God is with her and keeping her strong. She believes in Him, doesn't she?"

"Yeah. Yeah, she does." Grandma and Sean were the only two people in her world who believed in God. They were the two most stable, reliable, trustworthy people in her world, too. She needed them. Both of them. "That means He won't let anything happen to her, right?"

"Oh, Meghan . . ." She envisioned him doing a slow head shake, a tender smile lighting his dark eyes. "No one lives forever. Eventually her body will wear out and her soul will fly to Jesus."

She swallowed against the knot in her throat. "I'm not ready for her to go."

"Of course you aren't. We never are. But when the time comes, she'll be the happiest she's ever been, and she'll be happy forever. That's a whole lot better than anything we're offered down here."

"Miss DeFord?"

The intrusion of a female voice startled Meghan so badly her elbow slipped off her knee. She grabbed the couch cushion and righted herself. A different nurse, this one with ebony skin and a sweet smile, stood in the doorway. "Are you Miss DeFord?"

"Yes, I'm Meghan DeFord."

"I'm sorry we left you in here so long, honey. It took me a while to track you down. We have too many little waiting rooms in this building." Her deep chuckle erased a bit of Meghan's anxiety. She wouldn't be chuckling if something horrible had happened to Grandma. "Your grandmother's waiting to see you. I can take you to her."

Meghan held up one finger to the woman and rasped into the phone, "The nurse is here. She said I can go see Grandma now."

"All right. Let me know how she's doing."

"I will." She started to disconnect, then slapped the phone against her ear again. "Sean?"

"Yeah?"

She gulped. "Thank you." Such simple words, but what deep meaning they held.

"You're welcome. I'll be praying for you both. Bye."

Meghan dropped the phone in her pocket, grabbed up her crutches, and followed the nurse up a narrow hallway to an open door. The nurse gestured her inside, and Meghan nearly collapsed with relief when she found Grandma sitting in a plastic chair shaped like a scoop in front of a long, cluttered metal desk. Grandma held out her hand, and Meghan stumped over to her as fast as the crutches would allow.

She grabbed Grandma's hand—her warm, soft, familiar hand—and clung. "I was worried sick. Why did they take you for a sonogram? What were they looking for? Are you all right?"

Grandma gave Meghan's hand a little squeeze. Her eyes were red and watery, but her smile was intact. "Sit down and let me explain."

Meghan sagged into the second scoop chair.

Grandma sandwiched Meghan's hand between hers. "It looks like I won't be able to go to Cumpton. At least not for a while. The doctor is arranging for a vascular surgeon to unclog one of my arteries." She laughed softly. "This is good news. It means those funny spells I've been having where I can't get ahold of a word or I feel light headed will go away when the surgery is done."

Meghan blinked hard. She wanted to be as brave as Grandma, but underneath she was scared spitless. "They're doing surgery? When?"

"Dr. Nobbs is arranging it right now. It will be sometime early next week."

Meghan's spine became a boiled noodle. She slid farther down the seat and gawked at her grandmother. "So soon?"

"Well, now"—Grandma raised one eyebrow and assumed a crisp tone—"these things can't wait. I need blood flow to my brain. The quicker we get it done, the better for me. Don't you agree?"

Maybe Meghan had a blocked artery, too. Her head was spinning. "I . . . I suppose."

"And there's something I need you to do for me while I'm in the hospital."

Meghan forced her frame to stiffen. "Anything."

"I want you to let me buy you a plane ticket to Little Rock—"

"Grandma, no!"

"—to meet up with Sean and help him with the investigation." Grandma scowled at her so fiercely all other protests died on Meghan's tongue. "Don't you see, Meghan? It's as if God prearranged all of this. You're a cold-case detective. I can entrust this search into the hands of my own granddaughter." Tears swam in Grandma's eyes, but her beautiful smile radiated. "If you find Maggie, I'll be all fixed up and healthy and ready to meet her without any worry about forgetting something important or . . . or fainting at her feet."

Despite herself, Meghan choked out a laugh. "Oh, Grandma . . ." She leaned forward and wrapped her arms around her grandmother's neck. With her cheek pressed to Grandma's warm, moist temple, Meghan whispered, "I love you so much."

Grandma hugged her so tight the breath wheezed from her lungs. "I love you, too, my precious girl." She pulled loose and cupped Meghan's cheeks in her hands. "You'll go? For me?"

She didn't want to leave. She wanted to stay at her grandmother's side and make sure everything went okay with the surgery and recovery. Grandma had given and given and given to Meghan, but she'd never asked anything of her before. Could Meghan deny her now?

Sean's voice echoed through her memory. *"I have to trust Him to hold the people I care about even when I can't."*

She drew in a fortifying breath and nodded, dislodging the tears wobbling on her eyelashes. "I'll go. For you, Grandma, I'll go."

Thirty

eghan slept soundly on the other side of the bed, stirring jealousy because Diane couldn't sleep. Her mother was facing a carotid endarterectomy. Unfamiliar with the term, she'd asked to see the packet of information the doctor had sent with Mother. She'd also explored at least three different medical sites on the Internet. Now she knew too much. They would slice Mother's artery open and clean the vessel. The thought made her shudder. The potential risks paraded in front of her mind's eye, each accompanied by pictures straight from her imagination.

Some were mild, such as allergic reactions to medicines or an infection at the incision site. Others—bleeding on the brain, brain damage, a heart attack or stroke, a seizure—made her stomach churn with anxiety. Mother had always been so healthy, so strong and active. What would they do if she suffered a stroke and became incapable of caring for herself? Or had a heart attack and died in the middle of the surgery?

The worries were ludicrous, considering how she'd wanted an excuse to place Mother in some sort of care facility so Meghan wouldn't feel obligated to visit her every year. The possibility now loomed in front of her, stronger than before, and all she could do was lie awake and quiver in fear. What on earth was the matter with her?

She slipped out of bed. The dachshunds had been sleeping as soundly as Meghan, but when Diane tiptoed toward the hallway, a soft whimper rose from one box. She didn't need to turn on a light to know which dog had made the sound. She bent down at the first crate and unlatched it.

"Come on, Ginger." The dog nosed Diane's hand and delivered a warm kiss. Diane scooped the animal into her arms and carried her to the living room, where she found Mother sitting in her wingback chair.

"What are you doing up?" They asked the question at the same time.

Mother chuckled. She reached for the 1930s-style floor lamp next to her chair and pulled the chain for the second bulb. "Does Ginger need to go out?"

"No." Diane sank onto the sofa and tucked her feet beside her. She placed Ginger on the cushion next to her, and the dog wriggled halfway into her lap, her tail wagging. "I woke her, and I was afraid she'd wake the others, so I brought her out with me." She frowned. "Shouldn't you be resting?"

"Probably." Mother didn't sound concerned, but the fact that she had been sitting in the room alone at nearly midnight offered mute evidence of inner turmoil. "You said you woke the dog. Why are you still awake?"

Diane hung her head. How hypocritical she'd sound if she admitted she was worried about the surgery. About losing her mother. The hateful words she'd flung at Mother before storming out of the house when Meghan was a newborn haunted her. Did Mother remember, too?

Early November 1985
Little Rock, Arkansas

Diane left the steam-filled bathroom wearing her fuzzy robe and a towel wrapped loosely around her head. She'd spent nearly twenty minutes in the shower, letting the pulsing hot water penetrate her sore muscles. Even though Meghan was a full six weeks old and the doctor said the soreness of childbirth should be gone, Diane still suffered a deep ache in her lower back. If she never had another baby it would be too soon.

She rubbed the towel over her wet hair as she tiptoed across the bedroom floor to the bassinet in the corner. Not a peep came from the oversized wicker basket. She peeked over the edge, then drew back with a grunt of irritation. "She did it again." Why couldn't Mother stop interfering? Diane hated looking into the bassinet and seeing a burrito where a baby should be. How would Meghan grow if she was always bound up tight?

Diane threw the damp towel aside and unwound the receiving blanket from Meghan's sleeping form. The baby stirred, scrunched up her face in an awful yet somehow adorable scowl, then let out a weak wail.

At once Mother appeared in the doorway. "Is she all right?"

Diane huffed. "No, she's not. Why didn't you leave her the way I had her?" She scooped Meghan from the bassinet, cradled her in one arm, and bounced. The baby's wails increased in volume. Diane bounced harder, rocking back and forth at the same time. Meghan flailed her arms and poked her little feet from the bottom of the gown. Her wails turned into screeches of fury.

Mother hurried over and held out her arms. "Let me take her while you brush your hair."

Diane jerked away from her mother. "Shhh . . . Shhh . . ." She forced the sound through gritted teeth, but Meghan's piercing cries drowned it out.

Mother wrung her hands and followed Diane. "She likes to be held on your shoulder. And she's probably cold with her feet sticking out. If you're not going to use a blanket, let me put little socks on her."

"No!" Diane scurried to the opposite side of her bed.

"Margaret Diane, you're getting yourself worked up, which won't help calm her at all." She held out her arms. "Let me take her for a few minutes. When you've calmed yourself—"

"I'm fine!" Diane screamed the statement. For one second Meghan stopped howling. Then she began again in earnest. Diane growled and placed the baby on the bed. She stood back and watched Meghan kick and flail in spasmodic jerks, her little face so red it looked ready to pop.

Mother scooped her up, cradling her in the curve of her neck with one hand and snapping up a receiving blanket from the stack on the corner of

Diane's dresser with the other. She draped Meghan while crooning and gently swaying to and fro. Within a few minutes, the baby had calmed and lay hiccuping on Mother's shoulder.

Mother sighed and sent a puzzled look across the bed to Diane. "I heard her fussing when you were in the bathroom, so I came in. Her little hands were cold, so I wrapped her and she went right back to sleep. Did she awaken again? I'm sorry if I didn't hear her."

Diane balled her hands into fists. Her baby shouldn't be so comfortable in Mother's arms. Meghan was her child, not her mother's. Meghan needed to learn who was in charge, and it wasn't Grandma Hazel. "I accidentally woke her up when I took the blanket off her. I've told you and told you I don't want you winding those blankets so tight she can't move. Why do you keep doing it?"

"Because the binding reminds her of being in your womb. It offers her security."

Diane broke out in a cold sweat. She yanked the tie on her robe loose. "I can't stand being all bound up."

Mother's eyebrows descended. "But it isn't binding you up to wrap the baby."

Somehow in that moment, the tight hold Mother had always kept on Diane became the wrappings around Meghan. She would smother if her baby couldn't breathe.

She darted around the bed and snatched the baby from Mother's arms. The blanket fell on the floor. Diane kicked it across the room and deliberately raised the hem on Meghan's little gown so her feet were free. Even when the baby began to wail again, she didn't cover her.

Anger ignited on Mother's face. She pointed at Diane. "Margaret Diane DeFord, stop behaving like a spoiled child and do what is best for your baby. You're a mother now. Start acting like it."

"You mean start acting like you, Miss Perfect?" Diane snarled the words.

Mother pursed her lips. She drew back and shook her head. "If your father were here you wouldn't speak to me in that tone of voice."

The pain of loss swooped in with force. She wanted her father. She wanted Meghan's father. Tears filled Diane's eyes—hot tears of anger and longing and loneliness. "If Daddy were here he wouldn't let you touch Meghan. He'd protect both of us from you."

Mother closed her eyes for a moment and drew in a slow breath. "Obviously your hormones are still running amok. When you can speak rationally, we'll talk. Until then, give me the baby and let me wrap her." She held out her arms.

Diane pressed her spine against the wall. "No."

"Margaret Diane, you are too distraught to make good decisions. So I must make them for you." She moved closer.

Bound up . . . Mother was binding her up again. Diane double-wrapped her arms around Meghan's tiny frame. "You think you're the only one who can ever make the right decisions, but you're wrong. I can't change how you messed up my life, but you're not going to do the same thing with Meghan. We're leaving."

Mother folded her arms over her chest. "And where do you think you're going?"

Her calm demeanor, her implication that Diane had no other options, increased the fire of fury. "It doesn't matter as long as it's away from you."

"You're behaving shamefully right now, but I'm willing to excuse it if you'll give me the baby and take some time to calm yourself."

Diane released a shrill laugh. "It's not going to work. You're not going to take her away from me."

"Fine. Then I'll leave the room. Is that better? If I leave the room will you put a blanket around her and then dress yourself?" Mother lowered her arms and retreated a few steps.

Diane glared at her. "Yes."

"All right." She turned and moved stiffly out of the room.

Diane darted after her, then closed and locked the door. She put Meghan back in the bassinet and draped a blanket over her. While the baby weakly sobbed, Diane yanked a sweatshirt over her head and rummaged through her drawers for clean underwear and a pair of jeans that didn't cut her post-pregnancy middle in two. Once dressed, she wadded up half of her dresser's contents into the big duffle Daddy used to take on the road with him. The zippered pouches on both ends held Meghan's blankets, sleeping gowns, socks, and diapers.

She tossed her toiletries on top of her clothes, then zipped the duffle closed. It probably weighed over thirty pounds—ten pounds more than she was sup-posed to carry—but she slung its strap over her shoulder and then reached for Meghan. The baby lay on her back with her little arms over her head, her fin-gers curled, blue-veined eyelids quivering, and rosy lips puckered in a pout. The swell of love she'd come to anticipate each time she gazed at the sleeping baby rose up and nearly sent her to her knees.

She touched Meghan's flushed cheek. "She won't bind us up, Meghan. I promise."

Gently, she transferred the baby to the center of her largest baby quilt—the one Mother had saved from Diane's infancy—and folded all four flaps loosely around her. Then she tucked the bundle in the curve of her arm and unlocked the door.

Mother was standing in the hallway. "What do you think you're doing, young lady?"

"I told you I was leaving."

Hurt glittered in Mother's eyes, but Diane steeled herself against it. She wouldn't be manipulated. Not anymore. "Move."

Mother didn't shift a muscle. "It's dark outside. And cold. Is taking Meghan out of a warm house into the cold night a responsible thing to do?"

It wasn't, which made Diane all the more determined to do it. "She's my baby, Mother, not yours, so get out of my way and let me go."

Mother still didn't move, so Diane elbowed past her. Her head ached from listening to Meghan's screams. Her back and stomach muscles ached from the weight of the duffle. Her heart ached from the weight of resentment. She wrenched open the door handle and slammed the door against the wall. A chill wind smacked her face and she hesitated.

"Are you sure this is what you want to do?"

The quietly uttered question hovered around Diane like a storm cloud. How many times had Mother asked that same question? *"Are you sure this is what you want to do?"* when Diane took off her shoes to go barefoot on a hot July day. She'd burned her soles. *"Are you sure this is what you want to do?"* when Diane chose an art-appreciation class over music theory. She'd hated it from beginning to end. *"Are you sure this is what you want to do?"* when Diane refused to tell Daddy goodbye because if she didn't tell him, he might not go. But then he hadn't come home.

So much hurt filled her it had to come out. And it released in the ugliest words she'd ever spewed at her mother. "I wish you'd been the one to die instead of Daddy!"

Mother pointed to the door. "Then leave my house."

Present Day
Kendrickson, Nevada

The vivid memory sat like a stone on Diane's chest, making it hard for her to breathe. She'd come back after only two days away. None of her friends would let her stay because they didn't want a crying baby keeping them awake. But even though she'd gone back, she hadn't apologized. Mother never mentioned their argument, but she let Diane in when she rang the doorbell, and she stopped wrapping Meghan up in a cocoon for naps. So, in a way, Mother had apologized.

If Mother had a heart attack on the operating table and died, would Diane wish she'd said she was sorry? She stroked Ginger's silky ears and gathered her courage.

"Margaret Diane, it's late. Why don't you go to bed?"

Diane met her mother's gaze. Searched her mother's brown eyes. The droopy lids and the deep crow's-feet showed her advanced years, yet somehow her velvety irises were still as vibrant and attentive as they'd been when Diane was a child. She swallowed. "Are you going, too?"

"Soon." A slow smile tipped up her lips. She placed her hands on the arm-rests of the chair and raised her chin slightly, as regal as a queen. "I want to listen to the clock chime twelve."

"At twelve the princess turns into a scullery maid." Diane cringed. Why would she say such a thing?

Mother chuckled. "And the coach turns into a pumpkin, which isn't so bad. Then we can have pie."

Neither of them was making any sense. They should go to bed. Diane scooped Ginger into her arms and rose. She padded across the carpet. As she stepped through the hallway opening, she heard her mother's quiet voice.

"Pleasant dreams, sweetheart."

Diane froze. Without turning around, she nodded. "Yes. Thank you. You, too."

Thirty-One

Little Rock, Arkansas
Meghan

When Meghan rounded the corner to baggage claim in the Little Rock airport, Sean was waiting. He broke into a trot, met her beside a motionless carousel, and wrapped her in a hug. She'd never been happier to receive an embrace.

She grabbed him around the torso, and her crutches hit the floor, but neither of them let loose. Not even when a passerby sniped, "Get a room, buddy," and others laughed. She didn't care what anyone thought. After the past few stress-filled days, she needed comfort, and she would accept every bit of it Sean was willing to offer.

When they finally broke apart, she realized someone had rested her crutches against the foot-high edge of the carousel. Sean picked them up and handed them to her, and she got them in position while smiling her thanks.

He smiled, too, but it didn't quite reach his eyes. "You've had a rough couple of days. You okay?"

"No." No need to fib. He knew her well enough to see the truth anyway. "I'd rather be with Mom and Grandma. But this is what Grandma wants me to do, and I won't let her down." The same determination that had carried her forward since the doctor's discovery filled her again. She would find out what happened to Maggie. She wouldn't disappoint her grandmother.

The carousel's warning buzzer sounded, and then the black belt groaned into motion.

He gave her shoulder a squeeze, then pointed to a bench between carousels.

"Wait for me over there. I'll get your luggage." He grinned. "I know what it looks like."

"Only the biggest one. I left my smaller suitcase and duffle at Grandma's."

"Gotcha."

She worked her way between others waiting for their luggage. Three women wearing matching Red Hat Society T-shirts and purple feather boas had already claimed the bench Sean indicated. They were jabbering and laughing and didn't even glance up as she approached, so she stood beside the bench, leaned on her crutches, and stared at the backs of passengers crowded around the carousel.

She lost sight of Sean in the throng, but she didn't need to see him to sense his presence. Her frame still tingled from the strength of his hug. How had he known how much she needed that hug? In all their years of working together, they'd never embraced. High-fived, fist-bumped, nudged each other with their shoulders, once even grabbed hands briefly—a silent bestowing of strength— before ringing the doorbell of a family who'd been waiting for ten years for word on their missing grandfather. But never something as personal as a hug. Would it change things between them?

A pair of men parted and Sean emerged through the gap, her large suitcase in hand. "You ready?"

She nodded, and they made their way out of the airport to the parking garage and his waiting '96 Bronco. He tossed her suitcase in back with as much ease as most people would throw a feather pillow and then took her crutches. She balanced on one foot while he laid them in the back and closed the hatch. Then he escorted her to the passenger door, letting her hang on his arm and hop on her good foot.

As he unlocked the truck, he grinned at her. "Need a boost?" He'd asked the same thing the morning he picked her up for the drive to the airport to catch her flight to Las Vegas, and she gave him the same wrinkled-nose grimace she'd offered then. His laughter rang.

She climbed in, grunting a bit with the effort, and settled into the seat. The familiar worn mustard-colored leather offered her the second embrace since her arrival. A sigh escaped without her even realizing it.

He nodded as if agreeing with something she'd said and slammed her door. He jogged around the front of the vehicle and slid behind the wheel. He eased out of the tight parking spot. "You hungry? Thirsty? Need to stop anywhere before I take you home?"

She leaned her head back and enjoyed the flow of cool air on her throat. "I don't need a thing, thanks."

"Then we'll just get you to your place so you can relax." He stopped at the exit's crossing arm and rolled down his window.

Meghan grabbed her purse. "Let me pay for the parking."

His wallet was already out, credit card in hand. "I've got it." He poked the card in the machine and pushed a few buttons, and the arm rose. As he pulled out of the garage, he shot a grin at her. "I'll let you buy the first soft drink when we hit the road."

"Deal." She wriggled in a little more comfortably and propped her arm on the window ledge. "What time do you want to leave tomorrow?"

He draped one wrist over the top of the steering wheel. "I was thinking two or two thirty. It's only about three and a half hours to Bentonville, so that would put us there around suppertime. Give us a few hours to get unpacked, relax, and be ready to hit the ground running Monday morning. Sound okay?"

And give him time to attend church service. "Yeah, that sounds fine. Where is your reservation?" The unit never sprang for five-star hotels. Not that Bentonville, Arkansas, had any five-star hotels. But she'd be satisfied with something clean. And available.

"Ratzlaff arranged a business suite at the new hotel north of Bentonville. All their suites have two bedrooms with a sitting and cooking area between them." He glanced at her out of the corner of his eye. "If Sanderson was going with me, I'd put him up in the second bedroom. But I took the liberty of reserving a single handicapped room for you."

She wouldn't have expected anything less. She knew he wouldn't try anything funny if they did share the double suite, but with her in a different room, there'd be fewer speculations by the others in the unit. Her reputation was always safe with Sean. She appreciated it, and she told him so.

"No problem. The nice thing is all the handicapped rooms are on the first floor, so you won't even have to fight with an elevator."

They crossed the river, and Meghan enjoyed the view of the wide blue-gray ribbon of water weaving toward the eastern horizon. "Ah . . . I've missed seeing the Arkansas River every day." She remembered something and shifted to face Sean. "Grandma said that when she hired workers to put the pond in her backyard, she told them she didn't want a round or oval or even kidney-shaped pond. She wanted one as crooked as a dog's hind leg to remind her of the Arkansas River."

Sean burst out laughing. "Crooked as a dog's hind leg?"

Meghan nodded, grinning. "They told her she was crazy, but guess what? They did it. She's got a mini–Arkansas River in her backyard in Kendrickson." Sadness fell over her with such force her lungs lost their ability to draw a breath. She swallowed hard. "We've got to find out what happened to Maggie for her, Sean. We have to."

He reached across the console and took her hand. "Let me tell you what my grandmother used to say. 'Do your best and trust God with the rest. That's the way to find peace.'" He squeezed her hand, the touch gentle and reassuring. "I've learned she was right."

"Grandmas often are."

He lobbed a smile at her and released her hand. He pulled into the parking area for her apartment building and found an open space near the courtyard. "I'll walk you in. You take it easy between now and heading for Bentonville tomorrow. Flying will wear a person out."

She pushed her lips into a wobbly grin. "The airplane did all the work. I didn't have to flap my arms or anything, you know."

She expected him to laugh, but instead he fixed her with a serious look. "Then if you aren't worn out, how about I pick you up earlier, say . . . nine fifteen, and you can go to Sunday school and church with me."

He'd invited her before. At least a dozen times. And each time she'd politely declined. She drew in a slow breath. "You know what, Sean? I think I'd like that. I'll be ready."

Kendrickson, Nevada
Hazel

The smell of frying bacon pulled Hazel from a sound sleep Sunday morning. She rolled over and squinted at the little clock on her nightstand. The dial showed six fifteen. Her alarm wouldn't ring for another fifteen minutes, but how could she sleep with that wonderful aroma beckoning?

She forced her stiff limbs to carry her out of bed and to the hallway. She sniffed as she moved up the dark corridor. Was she imagining things? Maybe someone's house had caught fire. Maybe some teenagers had decided to race on a nearby street and burned rubber. Maybe only wishful thinking made her identify the scent as bacon. But the closer she got to the kitchen, the stronger the aroma, and her ears detected the distinctive *crackle* of grease in a pan. Yes, someone was cooking bacon.

She stepped from the living room carpet to the kitchen ceramic tile and gawked in astonishment. "Margaret Diane, what on earth are you doing?"

Her daughter turned, spatula in hand, and gawked back. She'd donned one of Hazel's aprons over her jeans and T-shirt. Little grease dots spattered the bib. "Why are you up already?"

Hazel moved a few inches closer to the counter, where her electric skillet held no fewer than a dozen slices of bacon. "I smelled bacon cooking and I thought a burglar had broken in."

Margaret Diane arched one eyebrow. "A burglar ... fixing himself breakfast?"

It made more sense than finding her vegan daughter frying pork. Hazel frowned and pointed at the pan. "Is that real meat or something simulated from tofu?"

"It's real." Margaret Diane faced the skillet and began flipping the curling lengths of bacon. A resounding sizzle rose as she laid each piece back in the grease. "I couldn't sleep, so I went to the all-night grocer over on Market Street about an hour ago. Since you're up, would you want to start toasting the English muffins? As soon as the bacon is done, I'll fry some eggs and we can make our own breakfast sandwiches."

Hazel remained rooted in place. She must be dreaming. She shook her head. Hard. A shake guaranteed to wake someone. But the scene didn't dissipate. "Are you all right?"

Margaret Diane grabbed a plate from the cupboard and layered it with paper towels. "I'm fine. I was just hungry for bacon and decided to make enough for both of us."

She'd made enough for the two of them, the neighbors, and all four dogs. "But you're vegan."

Margaret Diane aimed a sour look over her shoulder. "Toast the muffins, Mother."

Hazel decided not to argue. She slipped an apron into place and put the toaster to work. Fifteen minutes later they sat across from each other at the breakfast table and put together sandwiches. Hazel applied butter to her English muffins, but Margaret Diane slathered hers with mayonnaise. She also poured herself a cup of coffee and added cream.

Hazel tried to hold her tongue, but when Margaret Diane scuffed to the refrigerator and retrieved the package of processed cheese slices, she couldn't stay silent. "What is the matter with you?"

Margaret Diane flopped into her chair and peeled the wrapper off a slice of cheese. "Why do you think there's something wrong with me?"

Hazel gestured mutely to the items on the table. She didn't mention the early hour, although it certainly rolled through the back of her mind.

She shrugged. "We ate things like this all the time when I was growing up. I've been subjecting you to my food since I got here. So I decided, just this once, I'd cater to your preferences."

Hazel considered mentioning the doctor's warning about eating saturated fats and processed foods. But why start an argument first thing on a Sunday morning? "That's very thoughtful of you."

Margaret Diane broke off the corner from a slice of cheese and poked it into her mouth. "Too bad Meghan isn't here to have one. She's nuts about the fast-food muffin-and-egg breakfast sandwiches."

Her daughter had given her a small hint. Hazel put her hand on Margaret Diane's arm. "It does seem lonely here without her, doesn't it?"

Margaret Diane pulled her arm free. She folded a piece of bacon to fit the bottom half of a muffin, meticulously adjusting it so it didn't stick out over the edge. "I hope she doesn't overdo. The surgeon who put her ankle back together said it was a bad break and she needed lots of rest."

"Is that why you came out—to make sure she rested?"

Margaret Diane met Hazel's gaze. "In part." She slapped the top on her sandwich and lifted it to her mouth, but she paused before she took a bite. "Did you want to say grace?"

Unexpectedly, Hazel battled a rush of emotion. It no longer mattered what had compelled Margaret Diane to visit the grocery store in the early morning hours and shop for foods she hadn't eaten in over a year. All that mattered was she and her daughter were sharing breakfast on Sunday morning and she'd been given permission to ask a blessing over the food.

She nodded.

Margaret Diane put the sandwich on her plate and stretched her hand toward Hazel. Bacon grease, bread crumbs, and a dot of mayonnaise decorated her fingers. But Hazel took hold and held tight. She offered a short prayer, pushing the words past a lump of happiness in the back of her throat, and nearly crowed with joy when Margaret Diane echoed, "Amen."

They both picked up their sandwiches. Before Hazel took her first bite, she sent a hopeful look across the table. "We're up in plenty of time. Would you want to . . . go with me . . . to church?"

Margaret Diane chewed, swallowed, licked mayonnaise from her thumb, and finally shrugged. "Sure. Why not?"

"Oh. Oh, my . . ." Hazel gulped, almost too overcome to speak. "Thank you."

Margaret Diane flicked an unsmiling glance at Hazel and then focused on her sandwich. "No problem."

Not even a smidgen of enthusiasm colored her tone, but Hazel didn't care a bit. More than twenty years had passed since she'd shared a pew with her daughter. She laughed, unable to hold her joy inside. "First bacon, and now this! And it isn't even my birthday yet."

A grin twitched on the corner of Margaret Diane's lips. "Well, don't give yourself a stroke. Eat."

Still laughing, Hazel cheerfully complied.

Thirty-Two

Cumpton, Arkansas
Sean

Sean pulled onto the dirt road that served as Cumpton's main street at nine thirty Monday morning. Meghan had sat silently the entire drive from Bentonville, examining the information he'd collected. As he slowed the truck to a crawl, she looked up from the printed pages and gave a start. "Is this Cumpton?"

"That's what the sign on the edge of town said." The letters on the old warped wood were faded, but he'd been able to read them anyway.

Meghan turned a baffled look on him. "This is . . . I don't know what to call it."

"I know. Not much left here." Sean scanned the time-worn structures on both sides of the street. The brick false fronts rose to varying heights, with the tallest front on Cumpton Bank & Trust. Nearly every business boasted the name of the town—Cumpton General Merchandise, Cumpton Pharmacy & Drugstore, Cumpton Ready-Mades Shop. Clearly, at one time, people had taken great pride in their little community.

Although abandoned now, none of the buildings had broken or boarded-up windows. The raised, warped plank sidewalks weren't littered with trash or overgrown with weeds, the way one would expect in a near–ghost town. So someone still took time to keep the street looking neat. Maybe the owner of Cumpton Full-Service Gas. Lights glowed behind the plate-glass window of the tiny red brick building on the corner. A rusting, old-fashioned gas pump topped with a disc sporting a red flying horse stood sentry next to a modern-day pump.

He released a low whistle. Several years back, he'd watched a late-night science-fiction movie—obviously a low-budget flick—about a town struck by a meteor that froze it in 1930-something. He got the eerie feeling they'd just stumbled onto the movie set. If he pulled into the station, would the owner bustle out and offer to wash his windshield?

Meghan sat forward with her hands on the dash, her gaze roving from right to left. "The town is nothing like Grandma described."

"When was she here last?"

"For my great-grandmother's funeral—in the late sixties."

"A lot can change in forty-five years, Meghan."

"Obviously."

A block east of the business area, they found a two-story brick school-house. A limestone rectangular block above the padlocked front door was carved with letters announcing Cumpton Public School. On the north side of the building, dilapidated playground equipment stood silently in the over-grown play yard. The remains of a basketball court, the goal's rusty post empty of a hoop, sat in the middle of weeds on the south side. Bent venetian blinds flopped outside a broken window, rattling in the wind.

Meghan pointed. "That was Grandma's school. All twelve grades went there."

"Nobody's gone there for a long time."

She nodded, her face sad.

He drove through residential streets, which proved more disheartening than the business area. At least all the buildings, even if the businesses were no longer in operation, still stood. But fewer than three houses in various states of upkeep remained on each block. The other lots held rock foundations, some still supporting partial walls and all surrounded by waist-high weeds and trees badly in need of trimming. An occasional crumbling chimney pointed at the sky. What had the town been like in its heyday? His imagination wasn't vivid enough to paint the picture, but he bet Hazel DeFord would have been able to fill in the blanks.

"I'm glad Grandma didn't come with me to see this."

He offered Meghan a smile of understanding. He pulled under a maple tree so big the boughs reached almost all the way across the street. He put the truck in park but left the engine running so they could enjoy the AC. "What do you want to do? Start knocking on doors of the houses that still look occupied?"

"I guess so." Meghan placed the sheet of paper she'd brought with the names of people her grandmother mentioned on the console, and they both leaned in to examine it. "Maybe somebody will remember some of these people and can—"

Tap-tap-tap!

They both raised their heads at the same time, and Meghan's startled gaze moved beyond his shoulder. She pointed silently. Sean turned to look in the direction of her finger, and he drew back in surprise. A woman with a scraggly gray topknot and a narrow face as wrinkled as crumpled parchment stood outside the truck and peered in through the window. She tapped on the glass again and then swirled her hand.

Sean rolled down his window and turned off the ignition. Warm, sticky air met his skin, and immediately perspiration prickled. "Hello."

"Howdy." She curled her gnarled fingers over the edge of the window casing and rose on tiptoe, her beady eyes shifting from Meghan to Sean and back again. Her flowered housedress slid low and revealed her sharp collarbones. "You two ain't druggies, are you?"

Sean coughed into his hand to keep from laughing. "No, ma'am."

"That's good, because my husband, Hud—that's him over yonder." She bobbed her whisker-dotted chin toward a bungalow with a full front porch. An old man sat on the porch in a wheelchair. His pant legs were folded under at the knee, and he held a rifle across his thighs. "He don't take to druggies. He might not look too fierce, but I can tell you, he's tough. Spent three years in Vietnam, an' he's still got a sure aim. It'd be hard to drive out o' town with your tires full o' holes."

Meghan leaned forward. "Ma'am, I promise you, we aren't druggies."

The woman narrowed her gaze and stared hard at Meghan. Finally her face relaxed. "I guess you don't got the look of druggies on you. But what're you doin' sittin' here under my sugar maple? I ain't never seen you before."

Sean pulled a business card from his shirt pocket and gave it to her. "I'm Sean Eagle, and this is Meghan DeFord. We're detectives with the Arkansas Cold Case Unit in Little Rock."

The woman fingered the card, her eyebrows high. "Cold case . . . like what's on the TV?"

Sean swallowed a chuckle. People would probably be surprised to know how much television differed from reality. But he nodded. "Yes, ma'am, something like that. We're investigating a missing-child case from 1943—a little girl named Maggie Blackwell."

"You don't say!" Delight broke over her features. "You probably ain't gonna believe this, but my brother, Luther—Luther Krunk—bought the Blackwell farm at auction in 1969."

The hair on the back of Sean's neck stood up. One of the names on Mrs. DeFord's list was Krunk.

"He'd been kind of sweet on the older Blackwell girl, Hazel Mae, when they was in school, but she never paid him no mind. My mama said that one was always too lost with her nose in a book to pay attention to the folks around her. Well, Luther now, he gave up his road construction job an' piddled at growin' corn out there until he passed on three years back. His boy's livin' in the old house now since they couldn't get nobody to buy it. An empty house is an invitation for druggies to set up shop." She made a clicking noise with her tongue.

How many drug problems had the little town encountered for the woman to be so concerned about it?

She beamed a smile, giving them a view of a wide gap between her front teeth. "So you're huntin' Maggie Blackwell. I wasn't much older'n Maggie herself when she wandered off an' got lost in them woods. My mama used to scare me into stayin' close to home by tellin' about how that little girl fell in the creek an' got swept far, far away."

Meghan wriggled, eagerness dancing in her dark eyes. "Would you mind if we asked you a few questions?"

"I reckon I don't, but would you two mind comin' out to our porch? Hud'll want to listen in. Don't get too many visitors around here, an' he gets lonely. Besides, my toes're hurtin' from standin' on 'em. This is a mighty tall truck."

The truck wasn't all that tall. She was just that short. Probably no bigger than the average ten-year-old. Sean smiled. "Yes, ma'am. That would be fine."

She scuttled backward, the heels of her slippers stirring dust. "You come right on up to the porch. I'll fetch a couple of foldin' chairs for you—that rockin' chair you see next to Hud is mine—an' I'll bring out a pitcher of Kool-Aid. Hud an' me generally have some Kool-Aid in the middle of the afternoon, when the shade's moved on away from the porch, but we can do that early today without it hurtin' anything." Still jabbering her plans on entertaining them, she hurried toward the porch.

Sean grinned at Meghan. "I think we just made her day."

Meghan nodded grimly. "Clearly she likes to talk. Let's hope she says something worth hearing."

Meghan

The sagging porch roof provided shade, but a muggy breeze coursed over them, rustling the paper in Meghan's lap and turning the soft tendrils around her face into frizz. She took another sip of the sickeningly sweet Kool-Aid. Edith Yarberry, wife of Hud Yarberry, whose daddy had been Cumpton's longtime banker, must have gotten confused and doubled the sugar. Her stomach whirled. But maybe it wasn't the sweet drink making her sick to her stomach—Mrs. Yarberry hadn't stopped talking since she and Sean stepped onto the porch an hour ago.

Mostly she'd bragged about how Hazel Mae Blackwell lost out by not marrying Luther. When Meghan informed her that Hazel was her grandmother, Mrs. Yarberry paused, stared open mouthed at Meghan for a few silent seconds, then said, "Well, then, you'll really enjoy hearin' about this."

By the end of the sixth long-winded tale, Meghan was greatly relieved Grandma had "gone off to the college in Little Rock an' busted Luther's heart." Family get-togethers with this talkative woman would have been torture. But then, maybe at least they'd have had family get-togethers.

Mr. Yarberry stared at his wife, his unibrow shaped in a V. When she paused to take a breath, he said, "Edith, let me talk now."

She immediately clamped her lips together, linked her hands in her lap, and stilled the rocking chair. She smiled complacently at him.

Meghan stifled a sigh. She wished he'd made the request about forty-five minutes ago.

He'd leaned his shotgun against a stack of cinder blocks shortly after she and Sean joined him. Now he placed his empty glass on the blocks and cleared his throat. "You've been holdin' a piece of paper the whole time Edith's been talkin'. Can I see it?"

Meghan glanced at Sean and he nodded, so she handed it to Mr. Yarberry. "Those are people my grandmother remembered from town. We're hoping some of their relatives are still in the area and might have heard something from their folks that would help us."

He ran his finger down the list of names, working his lips in and out like a child blowing bubbles. "Most everyone on here's from my folks' generation. All long gone. Even those of my generation are mostly gone these days, too, although you'll find quite a few of their names on headstones in Cumpton's cemetery. Most of our young folks left Cumpton, lookin' for jobs in Bentonville or some of the other bigger cities."

After Mrs. Yarberry's shrill, fast-paced yammer, his voice was like warm honey flowing over biscuits. "Now this'un, Beth Spann. She married a car salesman from Beaty and raised her kids over there. She's been gone a couple years now an' is buried in the Beaty cemetery alongside her husband's kin. The Crudgington boys, Jay an' Barry, stayed around until '80, '81, or so. Then they sold off their folks' farmstead an' the older one, Jay, moved up near Denver, Colorado. Not sure where Barry landed."

Meghan glanced at Sean, who sat with his elbows on his knees, holding his sweaty cup between his palms. His expression said what she was thinking—they were wasting their time here. No one would know anything that could help.

"But now Elaine Burton . . ." Mr. Yarberry gave a solemn nod and flicked the page with his fingertips. "She's still in town. She stayed out at the orphanage even after her ma passed on an' the state closed the asylum. She married a local boy, Nolan Durdan. He's been gone now for, oh, I don't recall how many years. Been a while, though. Something to do with his kidneys. Up until he died, she an' him kept foster kids in the added-on part her ma built on the side of the old orphans' home. Like I told you, he's gone, but Elaine's still livin' there."

He passed the sheet to Meghan. "I'm not sayin' Elaine'll know anything that'll help you, but her ma knew everything that went on across Benton County. Nora Burton drove all over the countryside in her automobile, pickin' up orphans from different bus stops or train stations an' cartin' them to the orphans' home."

Mrs. Yarberry cackled and increased the speed of the rocking chair's motion. "Oh, how the folks around town was jealous of Nora Burton an' her automobiles. More than half the folks in these parts used horses and wagons clear into the forties, but Mrs. Burton bought herself a different motor vehicle every year from 1935 on. My daddy used to complain, 'Why don't she wear the new off 'em before she goes tradin' 'em in?' Daddy bought a Chevy in '52 and drove it until it fell apart in the eighties. Then he—"

The woman's husband reached over and placed his hand over hers. The chair and the woman's jabber came to a halt. He kept his hold on her hand and continued. "Yep, Nora Burton got around, an' she knew what'n all was happenin' everywhere. If she blathered it all to Elaine, an' if Elaine recalls any of it, there might be a tidbit or two you could use."

Mrs. Yarberry nodded so hard her topknot bobbled. "Chances are Nora Burton did repeat everything to her girl, because my daddy used to complain how that woman dearly loved to hear herself talk. She liked talkin' even more'n my own mama liked talkin', an' lemme tell you, my mama—"

"Liked to talk." Mr. Yarberry smiled. "They've likely figured that out by now, sweet pea." He picked up his glass and held it out to her. "Could you fill this for me again? My mouth's some dry."

She took it and bustled inside.

Mr. Yarberry aimed an apologetic grimace at Meghan. "Don't hold all her talk about her brother an' your granny against her, Miss DeFord. She idolized Luther. There was just the two of them kids in the family, an' she misses him something terrible. Other than Luther's lazy son, who don't come around at all, Edith's whole family is gone now. Well, except for me, an' I ain't much to brag on. Not since that land mine in 'Nam stole my legs."

Sean rose and put his hand on the man's sloping shoulder. "We appreciate your help, Mr. Yarberry. Thank you for taking time to talk to us."

"Talkin' don't cost nothin'." His blue eyes twinkled. "If it did, I'd likely be bankrupt with all the words my wife spends."

Mrs. Yarberry returned with a full glass of red liquid. "Here you go." She gave her husband the glass, then planted a kiss on his balding head. She straightened and flashed a smile at Meghan and Sean. "You two young folks stop by anytime. Me an' Hud are always here."

Meghan shook Mr. Yarberry's thick, leathery hand, then reached for Mrs. Yarberry's slender one. "Thank you for your hospitality. I would like to ask one more thing before we go."

"What's that?"

"Since you're familiar with the entire town, could you give me some easy-to-follow directions to the orphanage, the farm your brother bought at auction"—she wanted to see the house where Grandma grew up—"and . . . the town cemetery?"

Mrs. Yarberry's face pinched into a sympathetic pout. "You wantin' to pay respects to your kin?"

Meghan nodded.

"I'll write it all down for you so you can find those places. Not that it's easy to get lost in Cumpton—goodness knows, even back when we was young, the town wasn't big enough to hardly warrant a dot on the state map—but there's a handful of folks who aren't as friendly to strangers as Hud an' me."

Sean coughed, his telltale cover-up for laughter, and Meghan knew he was thinking about the rifle leaning against the cinder-block stack.

"You go wanderin' on their property, even by accident, they might sic the dogs on you."

Meghan thanked her for the warning.

She smiled. "Got to look out for Hazel Mae Blackwell's granddaughter. Why, if things'd come out different, you might've been my great-niece. Wouldn't that've been a blessing?" She turned toward the house. "Stay right here until I fetch a pen an' paper so I can write everything down for you. I'll make sure you don't go wanderin' where you shouldn't." The screen door slapped into its frame behind her.

Meghan hoped Mrs. Yarberry was less talkative on paper than she was in person. Her pulse thrummed with eagerness to visit with Nora Burton's daughter and find out what secrets her mother might have shared that would help in their search for Maggie.

Thirty-Three

Sean

Mrs. Yarberry's directions proved amazingly accurate. Sean followed them to the edge of town, along a tree-lined lane, to a three-story clapboard building badly in need of paint. A weathered sign stating Benton County Orphans' Home hung from a crooked bracket attached near the pair of oversized front doors. He hadn't expected something so big. How many children would have lived in the facility?

A single-story addition on the north side of the large structure spread across the ground. This section had a fresh-looking coat of pale-yellow paint, dark-green shutters, and ruffled curtains behind the windows. The addition must be the wing where the former director's daughter still lived.

He parked under a tree near a detached garage painted the same color as the addition. Mrs. Yarberry had told them to knock on the back door of the wing, and from this angle, he spotted a concrete slab and solid door on the northwest corner of the boxy add-on.

He turned to Meghan, who sat forward, seeming to examine the grounds. "Why don't you stay here until I know if she's home? There's no sidewalk that I can see, and the ground looks a little rough."

"All right. But come get me before you ask any questions."

"Don't worry, I will." He left the engine idling and trotted to the concrete stoop. He knocked, waited, then knocked again a little harder. But no one came to the door. He leaned out a bit to catch Meghan's eye. She held up her hands in a silent query, and he shrugged in reply. She gestured for him to return to the truck. He jogged back over and climbed in.

Meghan pointed to the garage. "One of the doors is open and there's no car. She must have run some errands."

She'd have gone to another town, then. Sean put his hand on the gearshift. "So what do you want to do?"

A hint of apprehension colored her expression. "I know you're on company time, but I'm not. Would you mind taking me to the cemetery and then to Grandma's old farm? I'd like to explore. Then we can come back here later and try to catch Mrs. Durdan at home."

There wasn't much else they could do. Sean put the truck in gear. "Let's go."

Mrs. Yarberry had told them the cemetery was behind Cumpton's stone chapel—*"Only buildin' in town built all of limestone. If you look close, you'll find little fossils in the blocks."*

Sean located the quaint structure tucked well back from the road. He followed a winding driveway to a square gravel patch where the people who attended service probably parked. As the woman had said, headstones were scattered like children's toys over the expanse behind the church on sloping ground so full of trees the entire cemetery was shaded.

He frowned. "You won't be able to navigate with your crutches. It's too uneven." If she fell and reinjured her ankle, he'd never forgive himself.

"Let me at least try." She was already reaching for the door handle. "If I can't make it, I'll give you my cell phone and let you take pictures of my great-grandparents' headstones."

"All right." He helped her out, then moved alongside her. Their feet crunched on the gravel, a somehow intrusive sound. He was glad when they left it for the quiet grass.

Someone had recently mowed, but apparently they'd left their weed eater at home. Tall, scraggly tufts circled each stone, hiding some of the words from view. Sean scanned the stones, searching for the name Blackwell. In the corner of the graveyard, beneath a towering pine with cones the size of a man's foot weighing down the branches, he finally found it. He pointed. "Over there."

Meghan planted the tips of the crutches in the grass and swung herself in the direction of the stones. She moved amazingly well over the rough terrain, only wobbling once, but Sean caught her elbow and kept hold until she regained her balance. Then she pulled loose and kept going. He stopped several feet away from the headstones, tense, ready to leap forward if she needed his stabilizing hand but sensing she needed a few minutes of privacy.

She stopped directly in front of the pair of stones. For a few seconds she stood as still as one of the solid monuments itself, her gaze seemingly fixed on the wedges of gray sandstone dotted with lichen. Then she drew in a breath, leaned on the crutches, and let her air release in a *whoosh*. "Burl Thomas Blackwell." She tilted her head slightly to match the angle of the leaning slab. "Mae Clymer Blackwell." Her tone held reverence. She glanced over her shoulder and shot him a teary grin. "Come meet my great-grandparents."

Sean ambled up and stood beside her. Blades of grass and weeds climbed too high to see little more than the names, so he crouched and began tearing them away. When he'd cleared a section, he gave a start. "Look here, Meghan. These stones were joined at one time. You can see where the piece cracked and broke into two halves. I bet it was meant to look like an open book."

She frowned at the tree. "Do you think the roots did it?"

"Probably. There is a pretty good bump in the ground right here at the center of the stone." He flattened the tall grass to give a better view of the headstones and then rose. "Do you want some pictures? I'll take them for you."

She handed him her phone, and he snapped close-ups of each half, then the whole, and finally backed up so he could catch Meghan gazing at the gravestones. While he snapped the photograph, she spoke.

"'Yet a little while, and the world seeth me no more; but ye see me: because I live, ye shall live also.'"

It took a moment for him to realize she was reading. The verse from John 14 had gotten split when the stone divided, but now with the grass crushed down, he could see it. His heart sang at its meaning, and a smile of joy pulled at his lips.

Meghan's face didn't reflect joy, however. Tears winked in her eyes as she settled her gaze on him. "It's so sad."

Sean's smile faded. "What's sad?"

"What this says. 'Yet a little while . . . ' Life is too short. I only have two people in my family—Mom and Grandma. Grandma's almost eighty and she's sick. Who knows how long she'll be around? Then when Mom's gone, it'll just be me." She sniffed. "I don't like to think about the people I love not being here anymore."

He closed the gap between them and gave her the cell phone. "I think you're looking at the verse wrong. You can't stop there. You have to continue until the end." The way he'd read to the end of the Bible. Victory awaited all who believed.

He squatted and touched the final words with his fingertips. "Look— 'Because I live, ye shall live also.' If your grandparents chose that verse, then I would say they believed in the saving grace of Jesus. They knew that earthly death leads to eternal spiritual life. They're still living, Meghan. They're enjoying a life that will never end."

She gazed down at him. Sunlight sneaked between leaves to dot her perspiration-dampened face. "You're talking about heaven, right?"

"Right." He straightened and brushed grass from his trousers. "There's another verse, also in John 14, also Jesus talking. He says, 'If I go and prepare a place for you, I will come back and take you to be with me that you also may be where I am.' He's referring to when He returns, but any believer whose body dies before that day is also taken to Him."

Sean slipped his hands into his pockets and rocked on his heels. "I chose to believe that when I was eight years old because my granddad died and I wanted to be sure I would see him again. My motivation for accepting Jesus as my Savior was a little skewed and selfish, but over the years, as my parents guided me in growing in faith, I came to realize what a gift Jesus gave me by saving me. Not only for eternity, but for now."

Meghan tipped her head. A strand of hair, pulled loose from her usual ponytail, waved alongside her cheek. "What do you mean?"

He anchored the hair behind her ear before answering, his finger trailing across her cheek. Her moist skin was as soft as he'd imagined. He pushed his hand into his pocket to keep from repeating the action. "While I'm here on earth, I have a constant companion so I'm never alone. When I'm not sure what to do, He's my guide. When I'm weak, He strengthens me. When I'm frustrated, He calms me. I can't imagine living without Him, and I can't imagine eternity separated from Him."

The joy of salvation rolled through him again, and a smile broke on his face without effort. "My folks are gone now, too, like Granddad and Nana Eagle and my other grandparents, who died even before I was born, but I'll see them again someday. They believed, and they're already in their heavenly mansions. I like to think they're saving a place for me at the banquet table."

Meghan sighed and returned her attention to the stones. "It's a nice thought."

Sean put his hand on her shoulder. "It's more than a thought, Meghan. It's truth." He pointed to the carved letters on her grandparents' gravestone. "'Because I live, ye shall live also.' Jesus's death on Calvary gave us the chance for life eternal. You can live forever with Him. All you have to do is believe." His heart caught, and without conscious thought, a prayer lifted. *Let her believe, Father.*

Meghan

Something deep inside of her pulled, creating a sweet ache in the center of her chest. Sean's words, combined with Grandma's teachings from the past and some of the things she'd heard at Grandma's church, tickled her mind and tapped at her heart. *"All you have to do is believe."* Could it really be that simple?

"I want to do what you just said—believe."

He leaned forward slightly, his face innocent and eager. "What's stopping you?"

She searched for the right words. "If . . . if I chose to believe right now, it would be for the same reason you did when you were a child. But I'm not eight years old. I'm beyond the age of intentionally making a selfish choice. Faith is too important to Grandma"—*and to you*—"for me to play at it. When I believe, I need to make sure I'm doing it for the right reason, okay?"

His smile didn't indicate disappointment, but she sensed he'd been hoping she'd say something else. "Okay." He glanced at his wristwatch and frowned. "The morning's getting away from us. How about we find your grandmother's farmhouse, take a few pictures there, then head back to the orphanage? Hopefully Mrs. Durdan will be back."

For reasons she couldn't explain, her desire to see the farmhouse had diminished. "Let's go to the orphanage now. I'm eager to find out what the woman remembers."

Back in the truck, Sean drummed his fingers on the steering wheel. "You know, it's well past eleven—lunchtime. Probably not the best time of day to bother somebody. How about we drive to Bentonville and get some lunch? Then we'll come back and go to the orphanage."

"Do you mind making so many back-and-forth trips?"

He shrugged. "It's not that far. And I don't know what else we'll do about eating. There's only the little gas station here, and I doubt there's much more than candy bars and potato chips available." He grimaced. "I'd rather have something substantial."

Meghan couldn't argue with his reasoning.

"Besides, grabbing lunch in Bentonville will give Mrs. Durdan plenty of time to return from wherever she went and get settled before we swoop in on her."

A worry struck. "You don't think she's left for several days, do you?"

"With her garage door up?"

Meghan groaned. Why hadn't she thought of that? Some detective she'd turned out to be.

Sean chuckled. "You know what, I just got another idea. Let's go to the orphans' home. If the car is still gone, I'll leave a note on one of my cards and wedge it into the screen-door frame. Then we can get some lunch and relax at the hotel and wait for her to call. What do you think?"

"I think that makes a lot of sense."

He grinned. "Good." He started the engine and put the truck in drive. "An hour or so at the hotel'll also give you a chance to text those pictures to your grandma and maybe give her a call and talk to her a bit."

She liked that idea, too. "Sounds perfect."

"Good. Let's go."

She and Sean didn't talk as he drove back to Bentonville. She was weary, as tired as if she'd run a marathon, and his face wore a mask of internal contemplation. Whatever he was thinking—or praying—about, she didn't want to disturb him. So she remained silent.

He pulled into a drive-through and ordered chicken-finger baskets. Then, with the smell of the food tormenting them, they returned to the hotel. His suite was bigger, but Meghan's room was closer to the lobby, so they ate at the desk in her room. When they finished, he headed to his suite and left her alone to call Grandma. Mom answered.

"Hey, how come you've got Grandma's phone?"

"She's resting. And get this—Miney is in there with her."

Meghan pulled the phone from her ear, gaped at it for two seconds, then put it close again. "You're making that up."

"No, I'm not. Sunday after church she let Miney sit with her in her chair, and after that she patted her leg to encourage her to follow wherever she went. She told me this morning after breakfast she wouldn't mind keeping Miney after I go home."

"And you told her to forget it."

"You bet I did! Part with one of my babies? Not a chance." Mom snickered. "But after she's recovered from her surgery, maybe we'll take her to the local animal-rescue society and see what's available. I think she'd enjoy a little four-legged companion."

Meghan's chest tightened. "Have they set the official time for the surgery?"

"Yes. Nine thirty tomorrow morning. I'm to have her at the hospital by seven thirty."

She'd tell Sean. He'd pray for Grandma. Meghan hung her head and pressed her hand to her eyes. "You know, as much as I hate the reason for it, I think it's good our vacation got postponed. And we might want to cancel it altogether." She described the dilapidated appearance of Grandma's former town. "I'm going to send a couple of pics Sean took at the cemetery of her parents' headstone, but I'm not sure I want her to see the town the way it is. It's pretty much . . . gone." Like her great-grandparents were gone. Like Grandma might soon be gone.

She sat straight up and blurted, "Mom, do you ever think about heaven?"

A nervous-sounding laugh came through the phone. "What?"

"Heaven. Do you think about where you're going after you die?"

"I try not to think about dying. It's a depressing topic."

"I've always thought so, too. But Sean . . ." She sighed. "Never mind. It's too complicated to get into. I'm going to text Grandma the photos I took. Please make sure she sees them, okay? And I'll call again either tonight or tomorrow morning before you go to the hospital so I can give her my love."

"She knows you love her."

For the first time Mom didn't sound sarcastic or jealous when addressing Meghan's love for Grandma. Her words seemed warm, affirming, accepting.

"And she loves you, too, as you well know."

Meghan nodded. She knew. Her phone buzzed. She peeked at the screen. "Mom, Sean's beeping in—he must have heard from the lady in Cumpton we need to see. I better go."

"All right. Talk to you later."

She quickly switched calls. "Hi. Did Mrs. Durdan call?"

Sean's laughter rolled. "Yes, she did, and she wants us to come for dinner. Apparently the people in Cumpton are hungry for company."

"So did you accept?"

"You bet I did. Pass up a home-cooked meal? Not this guy." He laughed again. "Meet me in the lobby at four thirty. She's expecting us promptly at five fifteen for appetizers. This ought to be an evening to remember."

Thirty-Four

Kendrickson, Nevada
Hazel

Hazel padded into the living room, yawning. The long-haired dachshund named, of all the ridiculous things, Miney trotted alongside her, doggy smile with lolling tongue in place. She chuckled at the animal's bouncing steps. Her love for animals had lain dormant for so many years. Just as letting her memories stir to life brought joy, allowing her affection for furry creatures to rise to the surface was a relief and a pleasure.

Even so, a hint of guilt hovered around her. She'd made a pledge long ago to never put an animal's welfare ahead of a person's. But did that have to mean she couldn't enjoy the dog's company? She would have to spend some time contemplating that question. After her surgery. In the meantime, the dogs were here. She might as well give them some attention.

Margaret Diane was curled in Hazel's chair with an open book facedown on her leg. "Oh, you're awake."

Hazel glanced at the grandfather clock. Nearly three. She'd slept much of the afternoon away. "And high time, too. I thought you were going to wake me at two thirty so we could take the dachshunds out to John Wedman's place before dinner?" The man had graciously offered to keep the dogs during Hazel's hospital stay. How she appreciated her wonderful church friends.

A sheepish look crept across her daughter's face. "I intended to. But when I looked in and saw both you and Miney sound asleep, I didn't have the heart to bother you. So I catnapped out here. By the way, Meghan called."

"She did? And I missed it?" Disappointment struck hard. "What did she say?"

"That she and Sean went to Cumpton today and took some pictures. She texted them to you if you want to peek."

"Of course I want to peek!"

"Word of warning, Mother. Meghan said your folks' headstone has divided into two. Probably because of tree roots. So don't be shocked."

Hazel held the phone at arm's length and opened her text messages. Three photos waited for her. She examined each in turn. Little wonder tree roots had affected the sandstone marker—the tree had grown considerably in the years since her parents were laid in the earth. She sighed. "My, it's been so long since I visited my mama's and daddy's graves that I forgot what they looked like. If you hadn't reminded me about it all being one piece, I don't know if I would have noticed."

She sent a smile over the top of the phone to her daughter. "Most markers in the cemetery had a picture of some sort—angels or lambs or Bibles. Mama always wanted a dove carved on her headstone, but Daddy said doves were meant for potpie. That's why there's no image above their names."

Margaret Diane released a half laugh, half snort. "He died first. So he wouldn't have known if she put a dove on her half of the headstone."

Hazel shook her head. "Oh, no, Mama always honored Daddy . . . even when he was cantankerous. That was the way of wives in those days." She'd tried to follow her mother's example, too, with Albert. Of course, Albert hadn't tested her conviction the way Daddy had Mama's.

Hazel looked at the picture with Meghan in front of the stones. Her granddaughter's bowed head and slumped frame, even though the crutches were partially responsible, seemed reverent. Fitting for the setting. She might show it to Punk and Rachel's granddaughter, who painted backdrops for the community theater. She'd like to have this picture representing different generations turned into a wall painting.

Hazel laid the phone on the end table. "Only three pictures? Surely they went to more places than the cemetery."

Margaret Diane smiled and shrugged. "You'll have to ask her when she calls. She said she'd call again tonight or tomorrow morning before your surgery."

Hazel hoped it would be tonight. After her long nap, she'd probably have trouble falling asleep. Talking to Meghan would take her mind off tomorrow's surgery, too. For now, there was something else she needed to think about. She put her hands on her hips. "All right, let's get these dogs over to John's before he thinks we've changed our minds about letting him puppysit, and then we need to figure out supper. Vegan fare, or something that will actually taste good?"

Margaret Diane burst out laughing.

Cumpton, Arkansas
Meghan

A newer-model sedan filled the stall that had been empty earlier at the orphanage garage. Sean parked under the tree in the same place as before, but this time Meghan got out, too. He stayed next to her as they crossed the uneven ground and dodged small tree branches littering the yard.

Sean stopped next to the concrete slab that served as a porch. He scratched his chin. "This could be tricky."

Meghan agreed. The slab was at least twelve inches high. She'd gotten accustomed to navigating stairs, but most treads were eight inches in height, tops. She might need a boost from Sean this time. She balanced on her crutches and prepared to swing her foot onto the slab when the door opened, releasing a wonderful aroma. A woman, tall and willowy, paused on the threshold. If Meghan didn't already know her age, she'd guess her somewhere between sixty and seventy-five. Her white hair flowed away from her rosy cheeks like soft wings, and her blue eyes sparkled with vitality.

Her eyes went wide and her mouth formed an O when her gaze met Meghan's. "Goodness, honey, be careful now. I told Nolan—that was my husband, God rest his soul—when he poured our porch, he needed to make it not so high, but he wanted it to be harder for little critters to go nosin' at our door." Her voice, with its gentle southern twang, sounded almost musical. "Bless Nolan, being a city boy before he moved out here with me, he didn't know a thing about the tenacity of wild critters. We still had mice and possums and the occasional skunk come callin'. The only creature the high stoop's kept at a disadvantage is the human kind."

By the time the woman finished her drawling speech, Meghan had managed to pull herself onto the concrete, and Sean joined her with a lithe leap.

The woman pressed her hand to her chest and blew out a breath. "Well, now, you two come right on in. I'm Elaine Durdan, used to be Elaine Burton, but I suppose you already know that." Mrs. Durdan held the door open with one hand and gestured them into the house with the other. She guided them to a round table in front of a row of waist-high windows looking out on a thick patch of pines and maples. A wood plate with a glass dome was already in the middle of the table, as well as two sets of tongs, dessert-sized plates, and napkins.

"Detective DeFord, Detective Eagle, sit yourselves down there. Munch on the cheese, grapes, and crackers while I finish our dinner preparations. Now, it's nothing special—baked chicken with herb stuffing and some of my home-canned green beans. It might not be fancy, but there'll be plenty. I still can't seem to get used to cooking for one. I gave up fostering children eleven years ago when Nolan died, but before that there were always half a dozen or so youngsters crowded around the dining room table. These days I sit in here by myself, and my table seems so lonely. It's a real treat to have guests tonight."

Sean pulled out Meghan's chair, then took her crutches and leaned them in the corner. "Believe me, Mrs. Durdan, the treat is ours. When we're on an assignment, we mostly eat at fast-food restaurants. If dinner tastes half as good as it smells, we're going to leave here happy this evening."

She laughed and tugged oven mitts over her hands. "I hope you'll leave here happy for more reasons than a full belly. I'd like to give you as much help as possible with your investigation. I've never been involved in something so excitin'." She removed a beautifully browned chicken from the oven and set it on the butcher-block counter. "But I don't know why you think I can help."

Meghan rested her hands on the table. "Mr. and Mrs. Yarberry gave us your name. They said your mother traveled all over the county and may have seen something questionable. We're investigating the possible abduction of several children between 1937 and 1946, including a three-year-old named Maggie Blackwell from here in Cumpton in 1943."

Mrs. Durdan pursed her lips and shook her head. She transferred the chicken from the roasting pan to an oval platter. "Oh, yes, the Gypsy child snatchings. Mother talked about it so many times. I imagine every parent in town used Maggie Blackwell's story as a warning to their youngsters to run away if they ever saw a Gypsy wagon. So are you trying to find those Gypsies? I'm sure they're all dead and gone by now."

"Mrs. Durdan, we don't believe—"

"Let's save our investigation for after dinner, all right?" Sean gave Meghan a warning look, then turned a smile on their hostess. "Never mix business with pleasure."

The woman laughed. "You're a wise man, Detective Eagle, just like my Nolan."

During dinner, Mrs. Durdan kept up a steady stream of one-sided conversation. They learned more than they would have asked about the woman's personal life, including the fact that she and her husband weren't able to have children of their own.

"We never knew which of us was, shall we say, incapable since we never saw a doctor, the way folks do today. I suppose I feared I'd blame Nolan if it was his fault, and he feared he'd blame me if it was my fault, so we just took in foster children and satisfied ourselves with that. I was used to lots of children around since Mother ran the orphans' home and I helped as much as I could.

Then when you count the foster children . . . Well, I surely raised more children than I ever would have if I'd had some of my own."

Sean forked up a bite of stuffing and stabbed some chicken with it. "What
keeps you here now that all the children and your husband are gone?"

Her brow puckered as if she considered the question ludicrous. "Where
else would I go? I was born here. My mother and father and husband are buried
in Cumpton Cemetery. The foster children who never got adopted, and even
some who grew up here when Mother was still running the orphanage, come
back and visit me. They wouldn't know where to look if I moved away. Besides,
this land is mine, and the buildings. Mother bought it all from the state when
they closed the orphanage in 1959. Then she signed it over to me. She paid a
highfalutin lawyer from Bentonville to do the papers so it would be legal and
nobody could take it away from me."

Sean raised his eyebrows. "She must have had a lot of business savvy."

"I don't know about her being savvy. I do know she never wanted me to be
forced to take a lowly position like hers to keep bread on the table. So it makes
sense for me to stay. This is . . . home."

A funny tingle made its way up Meghan's spine, but she couldn't discern
its source. She chopped a green bean in half and carried it to her mouth. "You
don't think you'll ever move away from here?"

Mrs. Durdan smiled. A lovely, complacent, peaceful smile. "Honey, the
next place I move will be Cumpton Cemetery, in the plot right next to Nolan's.
And according to the papers Mother had drawn up at the lawyer's office, the
day after they lay me in the ground, officials are to set fire to this place and burn
it to the ground."

Sean and Meghan exchanged startled looks. Sean said, "Why?"

Mrs. Durdan drew back, surprise on her face, too. "You know, I'm not
altogether sure. But, knowing Mother, she had her reasons. Of course, I can't
ask her what they are anymore, since she isn't here. But although she was a very
outgoing person—always out and about, talking with folks and going here and

there—in some ways she was also a very private person. She didn't care for people poking their noses into her affairs."

She sat back and pointed at them in turn with her fork. "Why, I recall one September afternoon, shortly after school had started in '48—my last year of school here in Cumpton—a fellow came to the door to ask about buying her 1946 Plymouth. He said the dealer in Rogers had told him she intended to trade it in for a brand-new custom four-door Dodge sedan, and this fellow said he'd give her two hundred dollars more than trade-in if she'd sell it outright to him. My mother pitched a fit right there in the yard. She told that man to tell the gabby dealer in Rogers to never expect any business from her again. From then on, she bought all her cars in Centerton."

Shaking her head, she poked the last two green beans on her plate with her fork. "She didn't mind driving all over the county in her cars, and she didn't mind involving herself in sharing local gossip, but she didn't want people talking about her. She was peculiar like that. So when she made the arrangements for this place to be burned, she was probably thinking about strangers poking around out here."

Sean wiped his mouth and dropped his napkin onto his empty plate. "If she was able to purchase new cars every year, the state must have paid your mother fairly well as director of the orphans' home. Or did the state buy the vehicles for her since she had to transport children?"

Mrs. Durdan gave a little gasp. "Oh, I was never privy to Mother's financial arrangements with the state, Detective Eagle. She considered me a child, even if she did depend on me quite a lot. But I do know she was meticulous with her record keeping. She had three books—one to show how the state's money was spent and one with information about families who adopted a child from the home. A representative from the state came out every three months or so to check the books, and he never found one questionable thing. Mother was quite proud of that."

Meghan frowned. "What was the third book?"

"The third one?" Mrs. Durdan blinked twice, confusion registering. "You know, I'm not sure. She never brought it out for visits, yet I saw her writing in it quite often. It was different from the others because it had a large pocket at the back where she kept letters."

She shrugged and laid her napkin aside. "Maybe it was her personal accounting book. When the orphans' home closed, a gentleman from the state came and took the income-and-expense ledger and the adoption-records one. But Mother's other book is still safe in a locked cabinet in her office in the basement part of the orphanage. I suppose the book will go up in smoke the same as the building someday."

Thirty-Five

*M*eghan snapped her seat belt and then shot an eager grin at Sean. "Are you thinking what I'm thinking?"

"If you're thinking Mrs. Nora Burton had something to hide, then yes, I'm thinking what you're thinking." He started the engine, did a three-point turn, and aimed the truck for the road.

"Do you think it has anything to do with Maggie?"

"I have to admit, if Mrs. Burton wanted to sneak off with children without anyone suspecting her, she had the perfect setup. She was known for transporting kids, and with an automobile, she could get from place to place fairly quickly. And by changing automobiles frequently, even if someone saw a child whisked away in a blue Ford, it wouldn't be long before she'd be driving a green Plymouth. Perfect cover."

Meghan held her hands wide. "But why would she take children? Gracious sakes, she had a whole orphanage full of kids to take care of. Why take more?"

"I don't want to venture a guess at this point, but there are some things I want to explore. Something isn't adding up." Sean nodded toward his leather briefcase, which was wedged in by Meghan's feet. "Take out my tablet, please, and let's make some notes before we forget everything Mrs. Durdan told us."

Meghan retrieved the tablet, placed it on her lap, and opened the memo app. They should've taken notes during the conversation. What if they didn't recall everything of importance? They'd spent more than two hours with Mrs. Durdan, and she'd shared nonstop. Urgency made her hands tremble.

"Okay, chime in with anything you don't hear me say." She began tapping on the tablet's touch keyboard, reading aloud as she went. "Mrs. Burton traveled to every city in Benton County and occasionally crossed into Oklahoma when picking up or delivering children. She had enough money to purchase new vehicles nearly every year—even during the Depression!—and bought outright the orphanage property when the state closed the facility."

She paused and crinkled her brow. "How much do you think she paid for the orphans' home? I mean, it seems as though it should be pretty pricey to buy a property of that size, but maybe since the building wouldn't be of much use anymore, the state let it go for next to nothing."

"It should be part of the public records. I'll explore that on my computer tonight." He reached over and pointed to the list she'd started. "Put on there what Mrs. Durdan said about her mother keeping careful financial records. I want to know what salary she received every month for running the orphanage. I'm sure room and board were part of the package, so I'm mostly interested in what she got in actual cash payment so I can balance that against her purchases."

Meghan added his thoughts and then sat, fingers idle, her brain racing. "Isn't it interesting how Mrs. Durdan talked about the Gypsies? At least three times she mentioned Gypsies and how they would steal children. Obviously her mother drilled that into her, and the poor lady still believes it. Why didn't you tell her there's no real proof Gypsies have ever been responsible for stealing children?"

Sean shrugged. "What would it have accomplished? No one wants to find out they were lied to by someone they loved."

"True." Meghan cupped her chin and gazed out the window at the countryside. They'd reached the paved road and the ride was much smoother, but thick trees on both sides of the road threw heavy shadows across the blacktop and hid all but brief glimpses of the evening sky. Anything could lurk in the gray woods, and they wouldn't know until it leaped out at them.

She shivered.

"You cold?" Sean reached for the AC buttons.

"No. I'm . . ." What? She licked her lips and tried to turn her thoughts into words. "Edgy. And I'm not sure why."

"Me, too." His grim statement surprised her. Sean generally didn't let a case affect him. At least not outwardly. He gripped the steering wheel with both hands and sent an unsmiling glance in her direction. "Let's spend tomorrow at the hotel on the computer. We might need to call Sanderson and have him explore a few things not available through public records. Either way, I'm going to have him overnight a DNA kit to your grandmother."

Meghan jolted. "Her DNA?"

"We could use yours since you're a blood relative, but hers would be better." His tone was musing, as if he'd forgotten she sat next to him.

"Sean, why do you want Grandma's DNA?"

He glared at the dark road ahead, his gaze darting from one side to the other, the muscles in his jaw twitching.

"Sean?"

He glanced at her, his brows low. "I want it as a comparison. Just in case."

His comment increased the unsettledness under her skin.

"And, Meghan, I think we need to concentrate our investigation on Nora Burton."

Las Vegas, Nevada
Diane

Diane held the bag with Mother's extra clothing, toiletries, and Bible on her lap, hugging it in lieu of hugging her mother. Her stomach cramped from hunger—Mother hadn't been allowed any food or liquid that morning, so Diane hadn't partaken either—and also from worry. Mother seemed nonplussed, however. She flipped pages in a magazine, pointing out pictures or headlines that caught her attention, so serene it set Diane's teeth on edge.

A middle-aged, smiley woman in light-blue scrubs, what Diane recognized as surgical gear, entered the room from a hallway and moved directly to them. "Good morning, Mrs. DeFord. Or do you prefer to be called Hazel?"

"Mrs. DeFord is fine."

"Very well. I'm Liz, and I'll be helping to take care of you today. Are you ready to go back?"

"I suppose it's too late to object now."

Liz laughed. "Yes, you're probably right. And who is this with you?"

"My daughter, Margaret Diane. She prefers to be called Diane."

To Diane's memory, it was the first time her mother had ever acknowledged her life-long preference for the shortened name. She swallowed the lump that filled her throat. Mother set the magazine aside, and Diane rose with her.

Liz's lips puckered into a sympathetic pout. "Actually, Diane, I need to take your mother by herself right now. We're going to a pre-op room. We'll do a few tests and put in her IVs. When that's done, I'll come get you so you can sit with her before she goes to the operating room."

Diane offered her mother the bag.

"Go ahead and keep that with you for now, if you don't mind." Liz aimed her smile at Mother. "Are you ready, Mrs. DeFord?"

Mother went with the woman, smiling and chatting as if they were heading to a social event. Diane sank into the chair and gripped the bag to her spinning stomach. A vending machine with a variety of snacks from sweet to salty stood in the corner next to a counter with a monstrous three-burner coffee maker. Half-full pots of dark coffee rested on two burners, and the third held water. On the corner of the counter, cups, wooden stir sticks, and several clear plastic buckets containing packets of sugar, powdered creamer, and tea bags were arranged on a wooden tray. Maybe if she ate and drank something she'd feel better.

A half hour later her stomach was still pinching. The granola bar and hot tea hadn't settled her at all. In fact, she feared she might throw up. She grabbed Mother's bag and headed for the receptionist's desk, intending to ask where she could find a bathroom. Before she had a chance to ask, Liz bustled toward her.

"Diane, your mother is all settled. Would you like to come back and sit with her until the surgery?"

Diane battled a wave of nausea. She grimaced.

"Most patients find it comforting to have someone familiar close by while they're waiting."

The woman had misinterpreted Diane's reluctance, but Diane didn't want to explain. Maybe her stomach would settle down once she'd seen Mother and talked with her a little bit. "Yes, thank you, I'd like to go back."

Liz led her up a long hallway and around a corner into a large rectangular area. A long counter filled the middle of the floor, and sliding glass doors with curtains hanging behind them lined both sides. The nurse guided Diane to the middle room on the right-hand side. She took Mother's bag and instructed Diane to use some of the antiseptic foam from a bottle mounted on the wall. Then she gestured to a gap in the curtains.

"We gave her a mild sedative to help her relax. Her blood pressure was elevated—typical for someone who's about to undergo a serious procedure. So she might be a little groggy."

"All right."

The nurse returned the bag to Diane. "I'll be right out here finishing some paperwork if you need me." She patted Diane's arm and then stepped behind the counter.

Diane slipped through the opening and crossed the tile floor of the small room, keeping step with the steady *beep-beep* of one of the machines. She placed Mother's bag on a plastic chair against the wall, then turned and curled her hands over the bed railing. She swallowed. Mother looked so frail, so helpless in the hospital gown. A blue paper cap covered her snow-white hair, and lines trailed from her hand—one to a fat plastic bag of clear liquid mounted on a pole and the other to a black box that flashed numbers on a digital screen. If she appeared so weak and weary before the surgery, how would she look afterward?

Mother's eyes opened. Her gaze latched on to Diane's so quickly it made Diane wonder if she could see through her eyelids. "Hi, honey."

Diane took Mother's hand—the one without the IV and pulse clip on her finger—and smiled. "I didn't mean to disturb you. Just wanted to peek at you again before you go back. To help me remember you pre-Frankenstein scar."

Mother laughed softly. "The doctor assures me the scar will disappear into my neck wrinkles by Christmastime. I suppose that's one good thing about being as old as Methuselah—I have neck wrinkles to hide my scars."

Diane offered the expected chuckle. "Wrinkles or not, you're still beautiful, Mother." She gave a little jolt of surprise. She wouldn't have expected to say such a thing. She cleared her throat. "You probably need to rest. I'll go to the—"

Mother's fingers curled tight around Diane's. "I'll have plenty of time to sleep afterward. Stay with me."

Diane read a flicker of fear in her mother's eyes. She nodded. "All right."

Mother sighed. "It's good to see someone who isn't wearing scrubs, but you still smell like alcohol." She wrinkled her nose. "I'd prefer the smell of your awful tea to the antiseptic aroma everyone carries around here."

Diane choked back a laugh. "My tea isn't awful."

"You've grown immune to it. Trust me, Margaret Diane, it's awful."

Diane let the laugh escape. "You're impossible."

Mother gave a slow-motion wink. She yawned. Her eyelids slid closed.

Diane hung her head and bit her lower lip. Her stomach began to roll again. She should go, but she needed to say something first. She glanced over her shoulder and past the two-foot-wide opening in the curtains. Hospital personnel were engaged in various acts of busyness, but no one seemed to be approaching. Heart pounding, she leaned close to Mother and lowered her voice to a whisper so soft it was almost silent. "Don't die."

Mother's eyes opened again. Such empathy glowed in her brown irises, tears immediately formed in Diane's eyes.

Mother lifted her hand and cupped Diane's cheek. "There's little risk of that happening today, Margaret Diane."

Diane pressed her hand over Mother's, holding it in place. She wasn't just talking about today. She didn't want her mother to die. She didn't want to be both fatherless and motherless. The deep fear surprised her and left her weak and quivering. She licked her lips, and she tasted salty tears. Another surprise.

"I'll be all right. Dr. Nobbs said Dr. Bashad is the best in the state, so don't worry."

Mother, the one facing major surgery, was reassuring Diane. How could Mother be so calm? "Aren't you scared at all?"

"Of course I am. That's why they put the calming juice in my IV. My blood pressure showed higher numbers than our Razorbacks have ever scored."

Diane guided Mother's hand to the bed but continued holding it. "Maybe I need some calming juice."

"No, sweetheart, what you need is faith."

Diane's spine sagged. "You're going to talk to me about faith . . . now? Here?"

"There's never a time or place where the topic of faith isn't appropriate. Listen to me, Margaret Diane . . ."

How could she say no, given the circumstances? "I'm listening."

"There's no reason for you to fear my dying. I know where I'm going, and I'll see my parents, my grandparents, your father, and so many others who have gone on before me. Best of all, I'll see my Jesus. Of course, I'd rather it didn't happen today. I've still got a few things I want to get done down here."

Diane nodded. Like finding Maggie.

"But either way, it's in God's hands. I trust Him."

Longing swelled in Diane's chest, a longing that both frustrated and flustered her. "How can you be so sure?"

"Why, how can I not?" Mother gazed tenderly at Diane's face. "God is strong enough and wise enough to craft this world. He put the universe in order. The sun, the moon, the planets, the seas—they all work together at His command. If He can accomplish all that, it stands to reason He can handle something as insignificant as this moment."

Sadness colored her expression briefly. "And I'm very sorry it's taken me so long to fully understand the truth of what I just told you. If I'd accepted it earlier, I would have been a much better mother to you. Please forgive me, Margaret Diane."

Acid stung the back of her throat. Diane gulped. "Mother, I—"

Someone whisked the curtains aside. "All right, Mrs. DeFord, the surgeon is ready for you." Liz approached the bed, her face and voice obnoxiously cheerful. Two others in blue scrubs followed her. They surrounded Mother. One began unhooking things and the other frowned at the numbers blinking on the screen.

Liz touched Diane's arm and guided her out of the way. "There's a nice waiting room to the right of the elevators on the second floor. When your mother's surgery is finished, that's where the doctor will look for you to tell you how things went."

"And then I'll get to see her?" Words pressed for release. Diane needed to say them.

"Not right away. She'll need an hour or so of recovery before we move her to a regular room. Once she's settled, someone will come for you. So please go on up and make yourself comfortable, all right?"

The two hospital workers wheeled Mother's bed past them. Liz scurried after them. She sent a smile over her shoulder.

"Don't worry, Diane. We'll take good care of your mother."

Diane marched over and stepped outside the curtains. "You'd better!"

Thirty-Six

Bentonville, Arkansas
Sean

His partner was in the room with him, but Sean worked alone. And he didn't mind. Meghan slumped in the corner of the sofa with his files of information spread on the arm and across the cushion beside her, presumably examining the documents, but she never released her grip on her cell phone. With her grandmother undergoing surgery, Meghan's focus was miles away. Between searches on the Internet and calls to government agencies, he paused to offer prayers for Mrs. DeFord, the surgeon, Meghan, and her mother.

He glanced at the notes he'd scribbled over the course of the morning. Thanks to online census records, he'd discovered that Nora Burton was paid a yearly salary of $400 in 1940. Not an insignificant amount of money for that time, but not elaborate either. She didn't have any expenses to speak of—the helpful clerk at the Bentonville courthouse confirmed the state paid all expenses, including electricity, food, clothing, and medical care for everyone at the orphans' home—but $400 hardly accounted for extravagance.

Even if Mrs. Burton received a yearly raise, how had she bought a new car every year plus saved enough to put her daughter through college, buy the property—according to the clerk, the state had received $12,400 for the three-acre plot and all buildings—and fund the addition on the side of the orphanage? Maybe she'd inherited money from someone. Or maybe she'd found another way to pad her bank account.

Suddenly Meghan let her head drop back, and she groaned.

Sean set his work aside and crossed to the sofa. He perched on the opposite end. "You know what they say—a watched phone never rings."

She grimaced. "That's a watched pot never boils. And it isn't true, by the way. It will boil. It just feels like forever if you're sitting there watching."

"Spoken from experience?"

"Sadly, yes. I disproved the theory for my second-grade science-fair experiment." She slapped her hand on the armrest, sending papers flying. "Why doesn't Mom call? Grandma's surgery was supposed to start at nine thirty. Grandma told me this morning the surgery would take an hour and a half to two hours. Well, it's been two hours and forty-five minutes. So why doesn't somebody call?"

Sean didn't know. "There's another saying—no news is good news."

She ran her hands through her tousled brown hair and groaned again.

He needed to get her mind off her worries, so he shared the information he'd uncovered. She listened, but not with the attentiveness he'd come to expect from her. She was still worried. He sighed and rested his elbows on his knees.

"Meghan, close your eyes."

She narrowed her gaze but she didn't close them.

"C'mon. I'm gonna pray."

Now she snapped them closed, leaned forward, and folded her hands.

Sean closed his eyes, too, and addressed his Father. He prayed the same things he'd offered during the course of the morning—for wisdom and steady hands for the doctors, strength and healing for Mrs. DeFord, comfort and peace for Meghan and her mother—but he said it all out loud so Meghan could hear. Maybe he should have done that earlier, because when he said "amen" and opened his eyes, she seemed more relaxed than she had since she knocked on his door at eight fifteen that morning.

He pushed himself to his feet and stretched. "It's way past noon. I'm hungry. Let's go get a pizza." Standard on-the-road fare.

"Not until I hear from Mom."

"Well, then, how about you stay here and keep working? I'll go get a pizza and bring it back, and we'll eat in the room." They might as well make use of the table and chairs in his kitchenette.

She shook her head and gripped her stomach. "I don't think I can eat."

"Not eating won't make the phone ring."

"I know, it's just . . ."

He settled his weight on one leg and gave her a firm look. "What would your grandmother say if she knew you were skipping a meal?"

Sheepishness crept over her features. "She'd tell me to eat."

"And you should always do what your grandmother tells you." He grinned and headed for the door. "Pepperoni with extra cheese?"

"And mushrooms."

"On your half."

"And green peppers on yours?"

Now she sounded more like herself. He gave a mock salute. "I'll be back soon. Keep working. And don't worry. Your grandma's in good hands."

Las Vegas, Nevada
Diane

Dr. Bashad took Diane's hand between his. "In all likelihood, she is experiencing a metabolic reaction to the anesthesia. Since she has never had surgery before, there was no way to know how her body would respond to it."

"But a coma?" Diane frowned at the kindly Middle Eastern man. First he'd told her the surgery was a success, and now he explained that Mother's body had closed down and she was unresponsive to stimuli. The two halves of the verbal report didn't seem to match. "I read the paperwork she brought home about carotid endarterectomy, including the risks. It said she might have a stroke or a heart attack. But there wasn't anything in there about a coma." Anger born of fear sharpened her tone. "If it's a possibility, you need to warn people about it."

Sympathy glimmered in his dark eyes. "I know this is a shock to you. I'm sorry it has happened. It's not common for someone to slip into a coma after surgery, but it isn't completely unheard of either. The very old and the very young seem to be most susceptible to a physiological shutdown when they've been subjected to the stress of an operation and the accompanying combination of medicines."

She'd never been one to let someone she didn't know hold her hand, especially someone who'd dealt an emotional blow, but at that moment Diane could only be grateful for the compassionate contact. Without it, she'd collapse in a puddle on the floor. She swallowed tears and forced a question. "Do you have any idea how . . . how long she'll be . . . shut down?"

"Unfortunately, no. Some people revive within a day or two, and others remain unresponsive for weeks or even months." He sighed, patting her hand. "We will simply have to wait and see."

"That doesn't help much."

"No. No, I realize it doesn't, but it is the best I can tell you right now." He withdrew his hands, and Diane hugged herself. "We are transferring your mother to the intensive-care unit. They generally do not like to have visitors there, but I will let them know they're to allow you to sit in the room. Would that be helpful?"

A hysterical laugh built in her throat. Did he really think it would make her feel better to sit and observe her mother lying in bed like a corpse in a coffin? She jolted to her feet. "I need to call my daughter."

"All right. Call her. Take as much time as you need. Then, when you're ready, go to the receptionist's desk downstairs. I'll leave a message for you there with your mother's room number."

Before he reached the door to the hallway, Diane was punching in Meghan's number.

Bentonville, Arkansas
Sean

Sean balanced the pizza box on one hand and aimed his room card for the slot. As he popped the card in the scanner, the sound of weeping met his ears. He froze in place, looking up and down the hallway for the source of the sound. At the far end of the hall, a maid retrieved a stack of towels from her cart, but she didn't appear distressed.

The keening came again. He tipped his head toward his door. His heart fired into his throat. Yes, it was coming from his room. He plopped the pizza on the floor and wrenched the doorknob. He burst into the room, calling Meghan's name as he crossed the threshold. She was huddled in a ball at the end of the sofa, where he'd left her a little more than a half hour ago. He sank onto the sofa, crushing several papers, and took hold of her shoulders. "Meghan, what happened?"

"Grandma . . ."

He braced himself for the news that Hazel DeFord had died on the operating table.

She choked on a sob and swiped her nose with her fingers. "She's in a coma."

He rubbed his hand back and forth across her shoulder blades. Her muscles were taut, tense, and quivering. "Did she get a blood clot or something during the surgery?" He didn't know much about operations, but he'd never heard of anyone lapsing into a coma because of one.

"No." Her voice shook as if she were running a high fever. "The doctor thinks it's a . . . a metabolic reaction to anesthesia."

"Well, then, will she come out of it when the anesthesia wears off?"

She shrugged. "Mom said they have no way of knowing when or if she'll come out of it, because it's a rare thing to happen. And because of her age." Her chin crumpled. "I shouldn't have come here. I should have stayed with her."

Meghan's being at the hospital wouldn't have changed the outcome, but she already knew that, so he didn't need to say it. Instead he followed his instincts and wrapped his arms around her. She clung even harder than she had at the airport when he'd pulled her into his embrace. He held her, rubbed her back, let her cry. And he prayed for God to provide the comfort she needed. He'd pray for Mrs. DeFord later. Right now Meghan needed God's peace.

A knock at the door interrupted. Meghan pulled loose and turned her face away. Sean grabbed a box of tissues from the desk and dropped it next to her before crossing to the door.

The maid he'd seen earlier stood on the other side with his pizza box. "Did you want this thrown away?"

He took it. "No. I forgot it was out there."

She gave him an odd look. "All right. You have a good day, sir."

"Thank you." He closed the door and hurried back to Meghan. He slid the pizza on the table along the way and sat on the edge of the cushion. She'd used half a dozen tissues, and she held them in a wad. He'd known her for six years, and not once in all that time had he seen her succumb to tears. Her red-rimmed eyes, blotchy face, and tear-stained cheeks made him ache.

He snagged the little waste can from the end of the sofa and held it out to her. She dropped the soggy tissues and leaned forward, head down, her pose dejected. He brushed her arm with his fingertips. "You gonna be okay?"

"I don't think so."

"Do you want me to pray again?"

She shook her head.

The refusal stung. "Why not?"

"Because I want to pray."

Hope exploded through Sean's chest.

She raised her face and met his gaze. Tears deepened her velvety eyes. "I've been thinking . . . about Grandma. And my great-grandparents. And you."

He tipped his head to the side. "Me?"

"Yes. You're so certain. Of where you'll go if you die. How you'll see the people you love again. Maybe I'm scared, maybe even a little selfish, but I want your certainty. And I want even more than certainty about heaven." She reached out and he caught her hands. "The people at Grandma's church sang this hymn—something like, 'I'm so glad I'm a part of the family of God . . . '"

She didn't get the tune quite right, but Sean recognized it. He sang his favorite part—" 'Joint heirs with Jesus as we travel this sod . . . '"

"Yes. Joint heirs. Jesus is God's Son, and if I'm His joint heir, then I'll be God's daughter, right?"

His pulse doubled its tempo. "That's right. Galatians 3:26 says, 'So in Christ Jesus you are all children of God through faith.' And Acts 16:31 tells us how to make it happen—we believe that Jesus is who He says He is. That's what's called faith, Meghan. Once you're a joint heir with Jesus, you'll have the same source of peace, strength, and wisdom I was talking about at the cemetery." He held his breath for a moment, not wanting to push her but so eager for this woman who'd stolen a piece of his heart to find her way Home. "Is . . . that what you want?"

She nodded, and fresh tears spilled down her cheeks. "I've never had a real family. I've never had a father. I want that. More than anything."

"Then tell Him."

She lowered her head and scrunched her eyes tight. Her fingers clenched his hand like a vise, and he squeezed back as he closed his eyes. "Dear God, I want You. I want Your Son. I want to live better, braver, like Grandma and Sean. I've seen You in them. Please be in me, too. Let me be . . . Yours. For now and forever." Her voice broke, and warm tears dripped on the backs of Sean's hands. "Thank You, God. Thank You, Father. Amen."

They opened their eyes at the same time and their gazes collided. Her brown irises still swam with tears, but peace, joy, and wonder bloomed in her expression. Although she'd said nothing remotely close to the sinner's prayer he'd seen printed on prompt cards or in the back of witnessing booklets, he knew without a doubt the sincerity of her request had gone directly to Father-God's ears. Meghan DeFord had just been born into the family of God.

So many things ran through his mind. He wanted to tell her about faith, about growing in grace, about the way his heart was trying to beat right out of his chest with love for her. But he couldn't. Not with her grandmother lying in a coma in a Las Vegas hospital. He gave her hands a final squeeze.

"So what're you going to do? Catch a flight back to Vegas?"

She shook her head.

"Then what?"

"Finish the investigation. As fast as we can. Find Maggie. Take her to Grandma." With each short sentence, her spine straightened, her chin rose, and her shoulders squared. The most beautiful smile burst across her face. "Let's bring Maggie home."

Las Vegas, Nevada
Diane

"Ms. DeFord? Ms. DeFord . . ."

Someone shook Diane's shoulder. She jerked away from the hand, and a cramp caught her neck. She grimaced, opened her eyes, and gripped the cramping muscle. An unfamiliar woman with her blond hair pulled up in a messy bun stood only a few inches away. Diane scowled at her. "What do you want?"

"I'm sorry to bother you, ma'am, but it's time to clean the room."

Diane looked around in confusion. Gray walls. Blue curtains. A black box flashing numbers. And a steady *buh-beep, buh-beep, buh-beep* measuring her mother's heartbeat. Reality eased through her brain. The hospital room.

She forced her stiff body to sit up in the chair where she'd spent the night. "Go ahead and clean. You won't bother me."

The woman grimaced. "I'm very sorry, Ms. DeFord, but you'll have to leave the room while it's being cleaned. Hospital policy."

Diane rose and moved to her mother's bed. She gazed down at Mother's quiet face. Eyes closed, mouth slightly open, clear tube feeding oxygen into her nostrils. Exactly the way she'd been last night before Diane fell asleep. She sighed and faced the woman. "How long will it take to clean the room?"

"Around forty minutes. Then an aide will give Mrs. DeFord a sponge bath, switch out the dressing on her wound, and change her diaper."

Diane cringed. Her regal mother in a diaper. She hoped when Mother awakened she would have no memory of the indignity. "So . . . an hour then?"

The woman moved close to Diane. "Are you sure you wouldn't like to go home for a few hours?"

Since John Wedman had the dogs and Meghan was in Arkansas, there was no reason for her to go to the house. Except to shower. She could smell herself. A shower would probably make everybody she encountered happy. But she didn't want to leave Mother. She shook her head.

"Ms. DeFord, may I be frank?"

Diane offered a stiff nod.

"I know it's difficult to leave the bedside of a loved one, but if you don't take care of yourself, you won't be any good to your mother. Go home. Eat a good meal. Take a long shower or soak in a bathtub. Pamper yourself a little bit. Then come back. I promise we'll take good care of her while you're gone."

Diane pulled in a shuddering breath. "May I be frank with you?"

"Of course."

"When she opens her eyes, I want her to see that I'm here. It is very important that she sees me when she wakes up." Tears distorted her vision. She whisked the moisture away with her fingers and lifted her chin. "She was always there for me. I need to be here now. For her."

The woman glanced at the black box mounted above Mother's bed, then at a small computer screen. She frowned at the screen for several seconds, sighed, and faced Diane again. "To be perfectly honest, I think you'll be safe to leave. Her vitals show no indication of change. She isn't likely to rouse in the next few hours." A sad smile played on her lips. "It's all right if you go. The poor woman won't know the difference."

Thirty-Seven

Cumpton, Arkansas
Meghan

The drive to Cumpton seemed shorter with the morning sun sending fingerlike beams of silver above the clouds and making the tree leaves glow like emeralds. The eerie feeling she'd experienced during Monday evening's return to Bentonville had fled, and even the heaviest burden of worry had lifted. During her morning phone call, she'd tried to convince Mom to entrust Grandma into God's hands, but she wasn't sure she'd succeeded. Mom promised to give Grandma a kiss and an "I love you" from Meghan. She prayed the words would penetrate and settle deep in her grandmother's subconscious.

Sean had made a morning phone call, too, to Mrs. Durdan, so she was expecting them. She probably wasn't expecting what they intended to ask, though. And she would probably deny them. Meghan wouldn't get testy if she did—she understood wanting to protect someone she loved. But they needed to see Nora Burton's financial records. If they were chasing the wrong lead, they needed to figure it out now rather than waste time.

Meghan suspected they weren't on the wrong track. "But what if we're too late?"

"What?"

She hadn't realized she spoke aloud until Sean shifted to grin at her. She snorted a short laugh. "Sorry. I was thinking. About Mrs. Durdan and the unlikelihood that she'll willingly let us see her mother's record book." Her chest constricted. "And even if she does and we find out that Nora Burton was somehow involved in Maggie's disappearance, Maggie would be seventy-three years old by now. A lot of people don't live into their seventies. We could find out that, yes, Mrs. Burton did something with her but still be too late to reunite her with Grandma."

"And if that's the case, at least your grandmother will have closure. Closure's worth a lot." Sean reached across the console and squeezed her hand. He'd touched her a lot in the past two days—comforting touches, reassuring touches, friendly touches. She'd come to expect and appreciate it. More than she probably should. "But don't jump ahead, okay? One step at a time. All we're trying to find out right now is how Mrs. Burton came up with the money for the extra things she bought. Mrs. Durdan might have a logical explanation— such as an inheritance."

"But the money and Mrs. Burton's secretiveness about her financial dealings seem so fishy to me."

"It seems fishy to me, too, but there are lots of ways to bring in extra money, and not all of them are illegal. So let's get the facts before we form conclusions."

They reached Cumpton, and Meghan pulled out her cell phone to snap photographs as Sean drove along the street. She might not end up showing them to Grandma, but she wanted to have them just in case. They followed the tree-lined drive to the orphans' home. Mrs. Durdan was in the yard, wearing a big floppy hat and gloves and picking up sticks. She dropped her armload beneath a tree and waved when they pulled up close to the garage.

She smiled as they crossed the yard, Sean tempering his stride to match Meghan's crutches-limited progress. "Good morning, Detective Eagle and Detective DeFord. Have you had your breakfast? I baked muffins this morning, chock-full of apples and pecans from trees right here on my property."

"We did have breakfast, but I won't turn down a muffin." Sean offered Mrs. Durdan his elbow.

"Now, aren't you the gentleman." With a girlish giggle, she pulled off her glove and took hold. They moved together toward the house. "I was certainly surprised to hear from you again. Did something I say help you in your investigation?"

Sean stepped up on the stoop, gave Mrs. Durdan a little pull up beside him, then seemed to hold his breath while Meghan heaved herself up, too. "There are a few things we'd like to clarify, if you don't mind."

"Not at all." She gestured them inside, and they followed her to the clean, good-smelling kitchen and the same little table they'd sat around for supper. She poured steaming coffee into thick mugs and served muffins, talking all the while. "I hope you know you've got the whole town of Cumpton—well, what's left of it—abuzz. Edith Yarberry's spread the word about cold-case detectives digging up graves. Half the people want to stand and watch, and the other half are readying to run the two of you out of the county if you bother any of their kin."

She sank into her chair and removed her hat, chuckling. "There hasn't been this much excitement since Timmy Rodgers dumped a pint of green food coloring in the Palmers' backyard well. And that was clear back in '63. So you can tell we've been needin' a little something to rile us up." She took a breath and smiled. "Now, what can I do for you two today?"

Sean took a muffin and broke off a small piece. "We're hoping you can satisfy our curiosity."

"About what?"

"You've carved a fairly comfortable life here for yourself. You told us on our last visit that you attended the University of Arkansas. Your mother made that possible for you?"

"Oh, yes. She'd been puttin' money aside since I was a little girl. When the time came, I had all I needed to cover my tuition, room and board, and books. Since Mother always had to work so hard, she wanted me to have an education so I could get a better job. Would you believe I got my degree in accounting? Not something many women pursued, but it sounded so excitin' at the time."

Mrs. Durdan ducked her head and released a rueful chuckle. "I certainly disappointed Mother when I ended up working for the state as a foster parent.

But I didn't see the need to secure a better-payin' job since Nolan earned a fair wage as a mechanic and we had this nice house ready for us."

Meghan stayed quiet and let Sean do the talking, but she observed Mrs. Durdan's face. She'd learned to discern whether a person was being completely honest or hiding something. So far not even a hint of guile had made itself known.

Sean finished one muffin and reached for a second, his stance relaxed. "I'm impressed how your mother was able to provide so well for you. As you've pointed out, she was 'only' a state worker and she had a lot of concerns about finances. Yet you didn't seem to lack for what her generation would call the creature comforts. Did she inherit some money from her family that allowed for extras?"

"Oh, no, Mother came from a very poor family. Twelve children in all, and a father who gambled away what little money he earned. If it wasn't for the benevolence offerings given at the church her mother attended, she'd have gone barefoot even in the winter because there wasn't money for shoes. She knew hardship, Detective Eagle. I suppose that's why she had such compassion for destitute children."

"Very commendable." Sean paused long enough to chase a bite of muffin with a slurp of coffee. He settled the cup on the table. "She must have had some secondary means of income, then."

"Well, only one, as I recall."

"What was that?"

Mrs. Durdan turned her gaze to the window. Meghan read both worry and uncertainty in the crinkle of her brow.

"Mrs. Durdan?" Sean spoke gently yet with a note of authority. "How else did your mother earn money?"

Slowly the woman shifted to look at the two of them again. "Mother never wanted me to talk about what she called her Christian dealings. She said the Bible speaks clearly that a person never lets the right hand know what the left hand is doing. She feared reprisal from the Lord if we talked about it."

Meghan leaned forward slightly. "Since she's gone now, do you think she'd mind?"

Mrs. Durdan fixed a stern look on Meghan. "My mother might be gone, but there are people here in Cumpton who still remember her. I don't believe she'd approve of me sharing the way she helped the unfortunate. I already told you, she was a private person."

Sean linked his hands around the coffee cup. "Ma'am, it would help our investigation if we knew what she was doing. We need to close doors that lead us astray in order to find the door that leads to answers. Does that make sense?"

"I suppose it does." She bounced an uncertain glance from Sean to Meghan. "If I tell you about Mother's Christian dealings, you won't brag on it to folks around Cumpton?"

"No bragging. I promise." Sean said it first. Then he turned to Meghan and she recited the pledge, too, although she wondered how they would keep things quiet if Mrs. Burton had stolen children.

"All right, then." Mrs. Durdan took in a big breath, held it for several seconds, and then let it whoosh out. "My mother helped childless couples who longed for children and who would love and provide well for them."

Sean tilted his head. "She handled private adoptions?"

"That's right."

Meghan shook her head. "Why should that be kept secret?"

"Well . . ." Mrs. Durdan picked at a snag in the linen tablecloth. "Because some of the children didn't come from here at the orphanage. She rescued the children from hurtful situations. It always bothered her how folks who didn't seem to know one thing about lovin' and carin' for their youngsters had whole housefuls, while others who had the means to provide well had none. So she tried to . . . balance the scale."

Sean flicked a meaningful look at Meghan. "How did she know the children were in need of rescue?"

Sadness glimmered in the woman's blue eyes. "Mother had a real sensitivity to children in need. With all the traveling she did, she saw lots of things.

Things that made her heart hurt. And she wanted to make a difference. So she decided to be a kind of Robin Hood—you know the story about the man who stole from the rich to give to the poor? Mother loved that story. But she gave it her own twist. She rescued little children born to poor or unfit parents and sent them to families better equipped to care for them."

Meghan's great-grandfather had been a drunkard. Had that been reason enough for Mrs. Burton to steal little Maggie away? Her mouth was dry, and she took a quick sip of her coffee. "It sounds as if your mother had a great deal of . . . empathy."

Mrs. Durdan nodded. "Yes, ma'am, she surely did."

"But I wonder how she knew she was sending these children to better families than the ones they were born into."

"Oh, she made sure the adoptive families were wealthy by asking for a placement fee. If the family could afford the fee, then she knew they could afford to raise the child."

Meghan's flesh prickled. She squirmed in the chair, eagerness sending a rush of adrenaline through her. "Did she keep in touch with the families afterward? Do you know where the children were sent?"

"She never communicated with the families afterward—at least not to my knowledge. But most of the children went to California." She sighed, and a satisfied smile lifted the corners of her lips. "Mother said they'd live with sunshine the rest of their days. She was always very proud of sending them to such a happy place."

"So you mean—"

Sean shot Meghan a silencing look. He rose. "Thank you very much for the information, Mrs. Durdan. You've been very helpful." He stuck out his hand, and Mrs. Durdan took hold. Meghan recognized a hint of sympathy lurking behind his smile. "We'll scoot out now."

He cupped his hand around Meghan's elbow and escorted her to the truck. Meghan glanced toward the house, where Mrs. Durdan watched them from the kitchen window while Sean opened the door for her. She grunted as she climbed into the seat, then clamped and unclamped her hands as she waited for Sean to slide in behind the wheel.

The moment Sean slammed his door behind him, Meghan exploded. "The woman is delusional. She can't honestly believe her mother was some kind of avenging angel bent on saving the world's children, can she?"

Sean twisted the key in the ignition, and the truck's engine roared to life. "Whatever she believes, she's given us probable cause for a search warrant." He drove up the lane, scowling through the windshield—what Meghan had come to call his deep-thought scowl. "Call Captain Ratzlaff and tell him what she said. He'll need to make the call to the Bentonville courthouse and get a judge to sign off for us to search the orphanage. Tell him we need access to Mrs. Burton's office and her personal accounting book."

Meghan pulled out her cell phone and brought up the captain's number. "Should we put a rush on it?" Trying to get things accomplished across counties could take several days. "If we have to wait, do you think the book will still be there when we get back with a warrant? Mrs. Durdan might hide it."

His expression faded to sadness. "I doubt it, Meghan. She's so sure her mother's motivations were pure and honorable. You heard what she said about right hands and left hands—she's stayed quiet all these years so her mother's good deeds would be honored by God. Maybe her mother was the delusional one who really believed she was doing the right thing delivering those kids to wealthy parents. Who knows? But the birth families deserve the truth about what happened to their children. So let's get that search warrant and pray Mrs. Burton didn't throw away the addresses of the adoptive families in California."

Meghan grimaced. "The happy place of sunshine."

Thirty-Eight

Las Vegas, Nevada
Diane

Was it happy wherever Mother was? Diane smoothed Mother's hair. The nurse had given her a dry shampoo early that morning, but the snow-white strands seemed lank. Lifeless. As lifeless as Mother.

Diane pulled the chair close to Mother's bed and stacked her arms on the cold iron bed rail. For two days now Mother had lain quiet and unmoving. Diane rested her chin on her arms and gazed at her mother's face. Mother didn't seem to be in any pain. It appeared a deep, restful sleep had claimed her. Her chest rose and fell in slow, steady breaths, but other than that small movement, she might have been carved of stone.

Music played softly on a portable CD player delivered by some of Mother's church friends the previous evening. They'd come with the player and a stack of CDs, all of hymns played on the piano, which they said Mother would enjoy. While they were there, they circled the bed, held hands, and prayed. Diane had joined the circle and, during the prayer, kept her eyes open and fixed on Mother's unresponsive face. She'd added her prayers that somehow the words being lifted to the God whom Mother loved and faithfully served would be heard and He'd answer their pleas for her to awaken. But surgery was now forty-eight hours past, and so far there'd been no change. Diane wasn't sure if she was more disappointed or angry at God's seeming inattention.

Two hospital workers, this time both men, strode into the room. She'd seen an endless parade of people coming and going. All of them seemed capable. To the letter, they performed their tasks without hesitation. But some were more compassionate than others, pausing to touch Mother's hand or give Diane a smile of encouragement. The two latest ones seemed more focused on their job than the patient lying on the bed.

Diane remained seated while one of the men replaced the flattened, empty plastic bag dripping fluids into Mother's IV with a fat, full one. The other man stopped at the end of the bed. He flopped a clipboard with some sort of chart caught in the metal clip onto the bed near Mother's thigh and lifted the sheets, exposing Mother's feet. Curious, Diane shifted her gaze to him. He flicked the sole of Mother's right foot. So hard it snapped like someone snapping their fingers.

Diane launched upright. The chair skidded backward on the tile floor, screeching like an angry cat. "What are you doing?"

"Checking for a response." He positioned his hand to flick the other foot.

"Stop that!" Diane grabbed his wrist and glared at the man. "You're going to hurt her."

He angled a stern look at her. "Ma'am, I need to chart her responsiveness."

"Well, you don't need to be so rough." She flipped the sheets back in place. Yanking up the clipboard, she blinked hard against tears. "If you left a bruise on Mother's foot, I'll file a complaint with the hospital."

He held out his hand. "May I have my clipboard, please?"

Temptation to slam it against the side of his head teased, but she slapped it onto his palm.

He scribbled something on the paper and then tucked the clipboard under his arm. "I understand that you're upset. It's to be expected, given the circumstances. But being overprotective won't help us. Or her." He tossed the curtains aside and left, and the second man followed without a word.

Diane sagged into the chair. *"Overprotective . . ."* The word reverberated through her mind. That's what she'd called her mother. Over and over again, she'd railed against Mother's overprotectiveness. And for the first time, she fully understood Mother's motivation. Mother loved her. Loved her so deeply and expansively that she tried to weave a cocoon of protection around her. Not a cocoon to stifle her, but a cocoon to keep her safe. Why hadn't she been able to understand before now?

She rose on shaking legs and returned to the bed. She took Mother's hand between hers and squeezed, hoping against hope that she would squeeze back. "Mother?" She whispered first, then repeated it half a dozen times, a little louder each time, giving her hand squeezes with each utterance.

Diane's nose stung with the effort of holding back tears. Prayer and her mother's favorite songs hadn't wakened her. The flick on the foot hadn't wakened her. Holding her hand and speaking to her got no response. Would anything break through the wall and bring Mother back again?

At noon, the cleaning crew shooed Diane out of the room so they could change Mother's sheets and whatever else they did to tidy the place. She grabbed her digital notebook and headed for the hospital cafeteria, where she'd already picked at several meals. Not that the food wasn't good. They even had vegetarian options that fit her vegan lifestyle. She couldn't complain about the few bites she'd taken. But swallowing proved difficult with the huge amount of worry filling her.

If she couldn't eat, she'd connect to the hospital Wi-Fi and do more research on comas. She'd already made a short list of suggestions for reaching Mother, but there had to be more. She'd uncover them all, practice them all. She wouldn't quit until Mother opened her eyes and fussed at her again. She blinked back tears. She couldn't believe she missed hearing her mother's chiding *"Margaret Diane,"* but she did.

She fixed a salad from the bar of fresh vegetables, grabbed a wedge of lemon from the drinks counter to use as dressing, and selected a bottle of coconut-infused sparkling water from the refrigerator. As she stepped up to the cash register, someone pushed in close behind her and stuck out a debit card.

"Let me get that."

The cashier took the man's card and swiped it before Diane had a chance to protest. She stepped away from her tray and turned her full attention on the man—tall, with thick steel-gray hair combed straight back from his forehead and eyes almost the same color as his hair. Dressed in navy trousers and a white button-up shirt and striped tie, he stood out from every other person in the cafeteria, and he didn't appear threatening. But she wasn't in the habit of letting strangers pay for her meals, and she told him so.

He smiled and little fans expanded at the corners of his eyes. "But I'm not a stranger."

She frowned. "Do I know you?"

He picked up her tray and gestured with his chin toward the eating area. "Let's get out of the way of those behind us."

A glance confirmed several impatient people with loaded trays. Diane followed him to a booth and slid in. The cafeteria was crowded, half the people in hospital scrubs, the other half not. She even spotted a security guard. If this man proved dangerous in any way, she'd be able to scream for help.

He placed her tray in front of her and sat across from her, his gentle smile still intact. "Please forgive my unexpected intrusion, Ms. DeFord. I stopped by your mother's room, and the orderly told me you'd gone to the cafeteria." He stuck his hand across the table. "I saw you in the congregation with your mother last Sunday, but I didn't get a chance to talk to you before you left. I'm D. A. Raber, your mother's pastor."

Now she remembered. Since he didn't have his suit and Bible, she hadn't recognized him. Diane shook his hand. "It's nice to meet you."

He linked his hands and laid them on the table. "May I bless your meal for you?"

"You already paid for it. But if you want to pray over it, too, I won't stop you." The snide comment emerged so easily. Too easily. She experienced an immediate burn of shame, but he didn't seem affected. He smiled and bowed his head.

"Dear Father, thank You for this food and for the nourishment it provides. Bless it now, and may You also bless both the preparer and the receiver. Amen."

Diane picked up the salt and pepper shakers and applied them liberally to the salad. "I'm sorry you came when they were cleaning Mother's room. They chased you out, didn't they? They're real sticklers about no one being in there during the cleaning routine. But if you don't mind staying for a half hour or so, you'll be able to go in and see Mother when they're finished."

"Actually, I came to see you."

She raised her eyebrows. "Me? I'm all right."

His gentle smile and the warmth in his eyes voiced a silent argument.

She frowned. She squirted lemon juice and then jammed her fork into the mound of mixed greens. "Really, I'm fine."

"Then you must have a very strong spirit. Most people who sit beside the bed of a relative in ICU are distraught and full of 'why' questions."

Diane wished she could refute his statement, but his words were too true to deny. She set her fork aside. "Actually, I do have a major 'why' question. You're a minister, someone who's close to God, right?"

"We speak frequently."

The matter-of-fact statement could have held arrogance or even humor, but she didn't see either on his square, honest face. She sensed she could trust him—not a feeling she experienced very often when it came to men.

"What's your question, Ms. DeFord?"

"Why isn't He answering?" The words exploded, harsh and accusing. She grabbed up her water bottle, twisted off the cap, and took a long drink. The cool liquid soothed her dry throat and eased a bit of the fire that had risen in her chest.

"I believe He is."

She snorted in disbelief. "What?" She waved her hand, envisioning Mother's still, seemingly lifeless frame on the white sheets upstairs. "Did you peek at Mother when you were in her room? Are her eyes opening? Is she moving her hands or legs? Is she saying anything? No. She's just lying there, unaware. So the prayers those people from your church came and said have been ignored. He's not answering."

He leaned forward until his elbows rested on the tabletop. Earnestness brightened his eyes. "First of all, God never ignores the prayers of His children. It tells us in 1 John 5:14 we can confidently approach God, knowing that whatever we ask in His name will be heard. Please believe me. God heard every word lifted to Him. His silence doesn't mean He's ignoring us."

She pushed the salad aside, her appetite gone. "That's what it feels like."

He sat for several seconds, quiet, seeming to examine her. Just when she was ready to storm out of the booth and march upstairs, he said, "Are you familiar with the biblical account of Job?"

Many years had passed since her church days, but she remembered the minister preaching about Job. She'd thought then that God was pretty unfair to place so much hardship on one person, and she wasn't eager to review the story. But she should be honest with a preacher. She nodded.

"Then you know he faced some of the worst things that can befall a man—the loss of his property, friends, children, and even his health. His own wife advised him to curse God and die. He prayed repeatedly for relief, and God heard those prayers, but His answer wasn't what Job wanted to hear. Not at first. Do you know why?"

She couldn't remember the end of the story. She shrugged.

"Because those watching Job's battle needed to see the depth of his trust in his God. If Job had only suffered a stubbed toe and continued to trust the Lord, what example would that have set? But his suffering was severe. At one point he bemoaned that his lyre was tuned to mourning."

Diane's mind's eye flooded with an image of her mother. Her heart ached. "I can kind of relate to that right now."

"I'm sure you can." His tender expression let her know he empathized with her pain. "Job was trapped in a miserable, undeserved, pitiful place. And yet do you know what He said to God?"

She shook her head.

"He said, 'I know that you can do all things; no purpose of yours can be thwarted.'" He paused for a moment, his brows low and intensity glimmering in his gray eyes. "You see, even in the ash pile of despair, Job trusted that God hadn't abandoned him. In another Scripture passage, he questioned why God allowed the heartaches to come. But in spite of all the pain and suffering, he held to his faith. He set an example for others to follow. He believed there was a purpose for his suffering. He didn't know what it was, but He trusted God to reveal it in His time." A soft smile broke over his face. "And God did. But not on Job's timetable. On His own."

Diane tipped her head, frowning. "So you're saying God heard the prayers and He'll answer them, but only when He's good and ready?"

"That's one way of putting it. Another is that God knows the best answer, and He will reveal it at the right time." He chuckled. "My wife likes to say God doesn't operate on our schedule. Yet He's never late—He's always on time."

Hope flickered to life in the center of Diane's heart. "So when the time is right, my mother will wake up."

He placed his hand over her wrist, sympathy glowing in his eyes. "Ms. DeFord, only God knows if your mother will wake or not. But whether she does or she doesn't, I can assure you that whatever happens will be what's best for her and what will best bring glory to Him."

Hope's tiny flame died beneath a wave of icy anger. "And what about me? Or my daughter? Is it best for us for someone we b-both love to be taken from us before we're ready?"

"All I can say for sure is that God often works His will in the least expected ways." He withdrew his hand. "Every challenge is an opportunity for us to grow in our faith and dependence on Him. However He chooses to answer our prayers for your mother to open her eyes and return to us strong and bubbling with life, I have to believe, like Job, that there is a purpose for the answer."

"Even if it's no?" The question grated past her dry throat.

"Even then."

She took another drink, but it did nothing to wash away the acidic flavor of fear lingering on her tongue. "I need to get upstairs. They're probably done cleaning by now, and I don't want Mother to be alone."

"Ms. DeFord, your mother is a temple for the Holy Spirit. She is never alone."

She slid out of the booth and rose. He stood, too, and held out his hand. She took it, expecting a quick handshake, but his fingers wrapped around her hand in a firm grip and held tight.

He smiled. "If you don't mind, I'd like to go up with you and spend a little time with Hazel. While I'm there, I'll pray for her, and for you and your daughter."

"Just pray for Mother." Diane slipped her hand from his grasp, grabbed up her notebook, and headed across the floor. "Meghan and I are fine."

Cumpton, Arkansas
Meghan

Meghan waited at the top of the narrow concrete staircase leading to the basement of the orphans' home, her entire body twitching with eager excitement. After two full days of hanging out at the hotel and waiting for a judge to approve the search warrant, they had it in hand. And now, a day past the expected stay in Cumpton, Sean and three officers from the Bentonville police department were finally going through Mrs. Burton's office. Her crutches prevented her from joining the search, but she trusted them to locate what they needed in order to prove or disprove their theory about Mrs. Burton's activities. Better still, she trusted God to guide them.

Mrs. Durdan's shocked, betrayed expression remained etched in Meghan's memory. Soft sobs drifted through the open doorway between the orphanage and the woman's private quarters. Guilt pricked hard. Mrs. Durdan had been so kind and hospitable. Meghan took no pleasure in shattering her world, yet the truth needed to be uncovered. While she waited for the men to finish their search, she prayed the woman would eventually be able to forgive them.

Muted voices followed by the *thud* of footsteps rose from the bottom of the stairs. Meghan stepped aside as Sean, followed by the officers, ascended. Each of them carried stacks of papers or files. Two of the officers went directly into the attached apartment, and the third remained with Sean, who held up a leather-bound journal, his grin triumphant.

"This is it. A list of every child Mrs. Burton sent to California to be privately adopted."

Meghan's heart fired into her throat. She clamped the crutches with her elbows and held out both hands. "May I see it? Is Maggie's name on the list?"

The remaining officer stood with his chest puffed importantly. "The children's names aren't listed. Just a date and their descriptions. But there are thirty-one in all." He blew out a breath. "That Nora Burton was one busy lady. You two have opened a Pandora's box. The media will have a field day with this." He aimed a frown at Sean. "I'll give you some time to go over the notes with your partner. Then we'll bag the journal and get it entered with the other evidence." He strode through the doorway.

Meghan gazed in shock at the open book. Someone—presumably Mrs. Burton—had divided the pages into four columns. She glanced across the headings. *Description Wanted, Child's Age, Date of Delivery,* and *Adopting Family.* Six pages were filled with information. "I can't believe there are so many . . ." She lifted her gaze to Sean's grim face. "Why did only ten come up in the database as missing?"

"It'll take some more digging to sort it all out, but from notations she made in a separate journal, we suspect she started out with honest intentions—truly offering indigent parents the chance to let their infants or small children be sent to families who would give them a better life. If parents signed away their rights, they wouldn't turn around and report their children as missing, so the names wouldn't show up in any database."

Indignation struck as thoughts of the man who'd never bothered to be part of her life tickled the corner of her mind. "It's hard to believe parents would give away their children."

Sean offered a sad smile. "Think about the time, Meghan. It was the Depression. A war was raging in Europe. A lot of people were hurting. If they couldn't feed and clothe their kids, the kindest thing would be to give them to families who could take care of them."

"The kindest thing . . ." She'd have to think on that later. She nodded, pushing aside her personal reflections. "All right. Desperation probably would lead some to make painful choices. But if people were willing to sign over their children, why would she need to take some without their parents' permission?"

"It's hard to say. Maybe she asked and the parents refused and she really believed she was rescuing them. Maybe she got greedy and wanted more placement fees, as she called the payments in her records. Maybe the adoptive parents wanted a certain look or a certain gender and she took children who fit the description so she wouldn't disappoint a client. The fact that every child taken from Benton County had blond hair and blue eyes makes me suspect the latter reason." He shrugged. "But we'll probably never know for sure."

Meghan scanned the entries, reeling. "The whole thing is unbelievable." She gasped and almost dropped the journal. Sean steadied it and she pointed to one entry. "Look here. 'Girl: blond-haired, blue-eyed, sunny disposition; age approximately three; July 17, 1943; Waldo and Rosemary Plum, San Francisco, California . . . '" Excitement coursed through her. Her entire body began to quake. "The age, the description, the date—this all fits what Grandma said about Maggie. This has to be her."

Sean grinned. "I think so, too."

"Oh, Sean . . ." She closed her eyes for a moment, trying to imagine Grandma's face when they told her they knew what had happened to Maggie. Then sorrow struck with such force her knees went weak. She'd talked to Mom twice a day since Grandma's surgery, and so far there was no sign of Grandma awakening. She opened her eyes and gazed at Sean through a sheen of tears. "Do you think Grandma will wake up so we can tell her?"

He cupped her face, his touch gentle and comforting. "You know what? If we don't get to tell her, she'll still find out. When she reaches heaven, all her questions will be answered. She'll know. I really believe . . . she'll know."

Thirty-Nine

Las Vegas, Nevada
Diane

*D*iane slid her cell phone into her purse, then leaned her forehead against the cool windowpane. She wasn't allowed to talk on the cell in Mother's room, so when Meghan's call came in, she'd hurried to a little alcove that looked out over the parking lot. Terrible view but a private spot. Perfect for such an important conversation—absolutely no distractions.

By Monday morning, Meghan would be back in Nevada. She and her partner had gathered all they needed in Cumpton and won the battle with the local precinct for jurisdiction over the evidence from the old orphanage. When Sean reached Little Rock, he intended to turn his full attention to tracking down the family who apparently adopted Mother's little sister. Hearing Meghan's excitement, even though her croaky voice gave evidence of her weariness, gave Diane a much-needed lift. But then Meghan had asked about Mother, and Diane had to tell the truth.

"There's still no change. The doctors did a brain scan yesterday afternoon, and they didn't see signs of damage. Her neurons are intact and her brain responds to stimuli, but for some reason we don't understand, her body's responses have shut down. Which means she's . . . lost inside of herself somehow."

When Diane shared the doctor's intention to move Mother from ICU to a room in the hospice section of the hospital, Meghan broke down. And Diane cried with her, something she had determined she would not do. But now in the aftermath of the release, she couldn't deny its benefit. The fierce ache in the center of her chest had eased, and her stomach didn't hurt as much. Maybe letting the emotions out was better than holding them all in.

She pushed off from the window and sighed. She should return to the room. The nurses, nurses' aides, orderlies, even the Spanish-speaking woman who emptied the rubbish bins twice a day had gotten accustomed to her presence. They worried if she spent too much time away from her chair. She found their concern touching and hated to worry them.

Yet she'd never minded worrying her mother.

The thought brought her feet to a halt. Guilt swooped in, dark and nagging. She sagged against the wall. What if Mother never came out of the coma? What if Diane didn't get the chance to apologize, to ask forgiveness, to tell her mother she loved her? If she'd lost her chance to make things right with Mother, she might wither away and die, too.

Why had it taken something so awful to make her realize how much Mother meant to her?

But at least the surgery and subsequent coma had given her a chance to view their relationship from another angle. At least she'd gained an understanding of Mother's obsessive worry over her. Maybe that's what Reverend Raber meant when he said God had a purpose in suffering.

She entered the room and crossed to her chair. As usual, music flowed from the CD player. Soft. Soothing. Not quite loud enough to drown out the *beeps* and *tweets* from the equipment in the room, but loud enough to distract from it. Diane recognized the melody, and words began singing in the back of her mind.

"Amazing grace, how sweet the sound, that saved a wretch like me . . ."

June 1974
Little Rock, Arkansas

Diane gripped her pink Bible with both hands and gathered her courage. The preacher stood down there in front, waiting. He said if anyone wanted to be saved, they should walk to the front of the church and tell him. All around her, people were singing what the preacher'd called the hymn of invitation. That's

how it felt—like it was inviting her to step out of the pew and go to the front
and tell the preacher she wanted Jesus to take all her sins away.

She had lots of sins. She'd stolen a dollar from her friend Cindy Regier's
piggy bank when Cindy wasn't looking. She'd copied some spelling words
from John Esslack's paper last Friday in school because he always got one hun-
dreds. She'd told some fibs, too. All those sins sat so heavy on her. She wanted
them gone, and there was only one way to do it.

"... *And grace shall lead me home . . .*"

Diane stepped into the aisle. Mother gasped and grabbed Daddy's arm.
They both looked at her, joy on their faces. Would they come, too? Then
Mother flicked her fingers at her. Daddy mouthed, "Go on, honey." And she
went. Straight to the preacher. And she knelt next to him beside a padded
bench and told Jesus she wanted Him to save her from her sins. All those bad
feelings tumbled right off her, and when she stood she knew she was all clean
and shiny, like she'd had a bath on the inside.

She raced back up the aisle to Mother and Daddy, and they hugged her
and told her how proud they were of her. She told them, "I'm so happy. I'm
more happy than I've ever been!"

Mother cupped her face and smiled through her tears. "That's the joy of
the Lord, honey, and it's better than happiness. Happiness is fleeting, but the
joy of salvation is forever. You walk with Him now, and you'll never lose that
joy no matter what comes."

Present Day
Las Vegas, Nevada

Sometime after Daddy died and Mother's hold became so fierce it threatened
to choke her, Diane had buried her joy under a blanket of resentment. She'd let
her hurt over Daddy's dying, her anger at Mother's obsessive protectiveness,
Kevin's abandonment, even her frustration with church people who'd turned

up their noses at her steal away the joy her mother said would be hers forever. Was it still available to her? Or had God given up on her? There was only one way to find out.

She bent forward, folded her hands, and closed her eyes. *God, I'm sorry for pushing You away. Please forgive my selfishness and my foolish pride. Please restore my joy in You. And if . . . if Mother goes to You instead of coming back to us, please tell her how much I love her, and tell her I'll see her again soon.*

"He will my shield and portion be, as long as life endures . . ."

The words crept through her memory and brought a fresh sting of tears. Tears not of loss but of renewal. She'd wasted so much time in anger and childish resentment, but with her confession to her heavenly Father came a wave of peace so real it effused from every pore of her body. A sweet essence filled her nostrils and she inhaled deeply, allowing the aroma to cleanse every foul stench of bitterness, regret, and displaced anger. In its stead came joy. A joy only the Lord could provide.

She might still be stuck in her ash pile, but she wasn't alone. And she would trust God to lift her from it when He deemed the time right.

Meghan

Grandma's friends Punk and Rachel picked up Meghan from the airport when she arrived in Las Vegas at eleven o'clock in the morning on July twenty-ninth. The kind couple embraced her as if they'd known her forever, and hugging them was almost as good as hugging Grandma. Not quite, but almost.

Rachel rubbed Meghan's tense shoulders while Punk retrieved her suitcase. "We'll get you to Hazel's so you can rest up a bit, and when you're ready, we'll grab lunch somewhere and then take you to the hospital."

"Honestly, I'm not tired, and I'm really not all that hungry, either. If it's all right with you, I'd like to go straight to the hospital instead." Desire to see Grandma, even if Grandma couldn't see her, made Meghan's insides hum. She had something important to tell her, and she wouldn't be able to rest until she'd said the words directly into her grandmother's ear.

Punk strode up pulling Meghan's suitcase, and Rachel repeated what Meghan had told her.

Punk smiled. "All right, then. Straight to the hospital it is." He set off, and Rachel and Meghan followed him.

Rachel lightly held Meghan's elbow. "We've been watering Hazel's plants and taking in her mail since your mama's been reluctant to leave your grandma's side. Now that you're here, maybe you can convince Diane to spend a night in a bed instead of one of those hard chairs."

"I'll do my best." Meghan forced a light tone, but underneath emotion tightened her chest. She would never have imagined her mother camping at Grandma's bedside. The image filled her with the desire to cry tears of both joy and anguish.

She settled into the back seat of their sedan behind Rachel. The seat belt held a lunch-sized cooler in place behind the driver's seat. She chuckled at the sight. "You all take safety to a totally different level than anyone else I know."

Punk bounced a grin at her. "We didn't want that rolling around and upsetting the contents."

Rachel peeked over the back of the seat, her eyes sparkling. "The airplanes don't feed you like they used to. Pop the lid on that thing and help yourself."

Meghan unsnapped the lid and peeked inside. Two cans of Dr Pepper and a box of Junior Mints rested on a bed of ice. Tears blurred her vision. She'd said she wasn't hungry, and she'd been truthful, but she couldn't leave those Junior Mints in there. She sent a wobbly smile at the gregarious pair. "Thanks so much."

She opened the box and popped one in her mouth as Punk pulled the vehicle into the flow of taxis, limos, and other cars. Riding in the back seat with the strong mint flavor on her tongue reminded her of the limo ride to Grandma's. Was it possible she'd arrived in Las Vegas just over two weeks ago? She felt as though she'd lived years' worth of emotions in the span of seventeen days.

When they arrived at the three-story red brick building shaped like a giant L, Punk dropped her and Rachel off at the front doors, then went to park. Rachel had visited the hospital before, so she guided Meghan to the second-floor hall reserved for hospice patients. When Mom told her that Grandma was going into hospice, Meghan's heart had nearly shattered. Hospice had always meant the last stop before death. But according to the sign near the double doors separating the hall from the activity of the elevators, the area was for long-term palliative care. The definition gave her hope.

They waited outside the doors until Punk arrived, and then the three of them went together to Grandma's room. Mom was there, sitting in a vinyl-covered chair next to Grandma's bed. She rose when they entered, held out her hand to Meghan, and beckoned her forward.

Meghan froze six feet from the bed. She stared at Grandma, her pulse thudding and gooseflesh breaking out all over her body. How could someone change so much in such a short period of time? Grandma looked like a skeleton with skin draped over it. How much weight had she lost? A puckering line marred her neck, the pink scar almost neon against the pallor of her skin. She'd wanted to tell Grandma something important, but now that she'd seen her, fear gripped Meghan. She couldn't approach the bed holding what seemed to be only the shell of her dear grandmother.

"Meghan?" Mom's voice barely carried over the piano music playing from somewhere in the room. "Aren't you going to give your grandmother a hello?"

Rachel gave her a nudge on the spine. "Go on, honey. Greet your grandma. She needs to hear your voice."

Meghan shot a panicked look at Rachel. "Will she hear me? She looks . . . She looks . . ."

Rachel's eyes glowed with sympathy. "I know she looks grim, but she's still in there."

Punk stepped behind Rachel and put his arm around her waist. "Rachel's right. While Hazel's heart beats, there's still hope. Don't stay back now. You'll only regret it later."

Mom's hand waited for Meghan to take hold. Meghan drew in a breath, sent up a silent plea to the heavens for help, and moved forward. Mom curled her hand through Meghan's elbow and leaned in, bumping shoulders with her. She whispered, "Talk to her. Trust me, you'll be glad you did."

Puzzled, Meghan gazed into Mom's face. The stern V between her eyebrows was relaxed, and her eyes seemed clearer and less strained than they had in years. Meghan gave a little start as she recognized the expression in her mother's face. Peace. Mom looked peaceful. Exactly what Sean had prayed for. Exactly what she had found during her week in Cumpton, thanks to Sean's gentle guidance.

Meghan's heart fluttered. "Mom, have you—"

"Shhh." Mom turned her toward the bed. "Talk to me later. Right now, talk to Grandma. Tell her everything you want her to know."

Meghan understood the part Mom didn't say out loud—*in case you don't get another chance.*

Meghan nodded. She blinked back tears, leaned as far over the bed as she could, and whispered into her grandmother's ear. "Grandma? It's Meghan. I need to tell you something important."

Forty

Hazel

igh, Hayzoo Mae! Push me high!" Maggie's squeal carried all the way across the school's play yard. They had it all to themselves, unusual for such a beautiful Saturday afternoon. Hazel had given Maggie rides on the merry-go-round, the teeter-totter, and now the swings.

Hazel caught the squeaky chains, pulled back, and let go. Maggie swung forward, her bare feet pumping the air. Her giggles rang. Hazel couldn't help smiling. She'd fussed when Mama told her to keep Maggie occupied so she could finish canning beets, but Hazel was glad they'd come. Maggie's joy was contagious.

The swing slowed and Maggie kicked, her little feet flailing. "Again, Hayzoo Mae! Way up high!"

Hazel caught the chains and pulled back. "Okay, way up high. Ready?" She stretched on tiptoe and released the swing with a push that sent Maggie sailing.

"Wheeeee!" The wooden seat detached from the chains, and Maggie turned circles in the air.

Hazel gasped in horror and darted forward, hands reaching. The chains slapped her as she ran under the swing frame, but she didn't care. "Maggie! Maggie!" Her sister continued to somersault against the background of blue sky, becoming smaller with every turn until Hazel couldn't see her anymore.

Hazel stared for long minutes at the sky, her heart pounding, her eyes desperately seeking. Then her knees gave out. She dropped into the grass, a grass so thick and green it could swallow her up, and sobbed. She'd lost Maggie. What would Mama and Daddy say?

Someone tapped her on the shoulder. Margaret Diane stood over her, puzzlement creasing her youthful face. "Mother, what are you doing? Dinner's going to burn."

Hazel looked around in confusion. Pots and pans, two and three high, covered every burner on the stove. Steam rose from the pots, and belching bubbles flowed over the edges and onto the stove's enamel top. She pushed herself to her feet and scurried across green speckled linoleum to the stove. There were too many pots, too many things cooking. She should take some off. She should stir the burbling brews. Where were her hot pads? Where were her spoons? Panic built in her chest. Her hands flew around helplessly.

"Grandma, guess what?" A little pigtailed girl appeared next to the stove. The freckles dotting her nose glowed like new pennies, and her dark-brown eyes sparkled as if diamonds were imbedded in the irises.

The smell of mint surrounded her, a delightful scent. A calming scent. It emanated from the child. Hazel leaned toward her, eyes closed, senses seeking.

"I found Him. In Cumpton, at the cemetery, I found Him. Now He's mine, and I'm His. Are you happy, Grandma?"

Joy exploded in Hazel's chest. The stove, the pans, her worry about Maggie . . . Everything slipped away and only joy remained. She pulled in deep breaths of the wonderful aroma. Peace fell around her, as comforting as a warm quilt on a winter night. She sighed. "Mint . . ."

Startled gasps exploded.

Hazel frowned, confused. Had she said something inappropriate? What had she said? Oh, she remembered. The spicy scent still lingered in her nostrils. She sampled the word again. "Mmmminnnt."

Diane

Diane gently pushed Meghan aside and leaned in, searching her mother's face. "Mother, say it again. Say 'mint.'"

Behind her, Meghan and Rachel crowded close. Punk hurried to the door and called, "We need a nurse in here! Hurry!"

Diane gave her mother's shoulder a gentle shake. "Go ahead. Say 'mint.' Say 'mint.'"

Mother scrunched her face like a child being forced to swallow medicine. "Mmmmm . . ."

The day nurse, Charlotte, clattered to the opposite side of the bed. "What's wrong?"

"Nothing's wrong!" Joy laced Meghan's voice. "Everything's wonderful. Grandma is talking!"

Charlotte's face lit. "She's talking?"

"She said 'mint'!" Meghan laughed, and the scent of peppermint and chocolate from her breath reached Diane's nose.

Diane laughed—a flow of happiness. "And I think I know why." She turned her hopeful gaze on Charlotte. "One word can hardly be called having a conversation, but it's a start, isn't it?"

"Yes, ma'am, it certainly is." Her smile bright, Charlotte backed toward the door. "I'm going to go let the doctor know she's showing signs of waking."

Diane threw her arms around Meghan. Rachel and Punk joined the embrace. While "Victory in Jesus" played on the CD, Punk led them in a prayer of gratitude.

Less than an hour later, the doctor confirmed that Mother showed small signs of responsiveness. He gently cautioned them not to expect miracles— "Mrs. DeFord has been in a state of unconsciousness for seven days. There could be cognitive or physical impairment even after she fully wakes." But Diane clung to hope. Mother had been aware of the mint on Meghan's breath and reacted to it. She hadn't slipped completely away. She would come back to them.

Of course, Diane wanted a quick and dramatic return, as immediate as the departure had been. But instead of leaping, Mother crept back. By the end of the day, she'd opened her eyes briefly. The next morning, she kept her eyes open for several minutes and seemed to track Diane pacing at the end of the bed. Two different times she spontaneously squeezed Meghan's hand. On the first day of August, because her breathing had regulated, they removed the oxygen tube, and she wriggled her nose so exuberantly Diane and Meghan laughed until they cried.

On August third, Meghan took Mother's hand. "Grandma, I'm going to ask you a question. If the answer is yes, squeeze my hand once. If it's no, squeeze my hand twice." She licked her lips. "Do you have a daughter named Margaret Diane?" Diane and Meghan held their breath, and after a pause of three seconds Mother's fingers closed around Meghan's hand. They cried in joy, and over the day they played the question game with Mother once every hour. She rewarded them each time with the appropriate answer.

Midmorning August sixth, a full two weeks after Mother's surgery, Charlotte came in with a cup of broth and a spoon. She raised the head of the bed and put a very small amount—perhaps a fourth of a teaspoon—of broth into Mother's mouth. Mother's eyes flew open. She swallowed and opened her mouth for more. For half an hour, the nurse sat by the bed and slowly spoon-fed Mother the broth before she grew weary and drifted off to sleep. The nurse rose, triumphant. "If she can keep that up, we'll be able to wean her from the IV feedings. Then she'll be able to put some weight back on."

For the rest of the week, they kept track of Mother's awake minutes—when she kept her eyes open and watched them as if memorizing their every move. To Diane's delight, the awake and the sleep hours nearly matched, minute for minute during the daytime hours. Doctors, nurses, aides, even medical students stopped by the room at various times during the day to check Mother's reflexes, ask her questions, and quiz Diane and Meghan on their observations. It thrilled Diane to witness their excitement at her mother's progress.

Sunday, while Mother's congregation gathered for worship and Meghan and Diane sang to the CD player's music, Mother opened her eyes and made soft noises along with them. Diane took her hand. "Mother, are you singing?" Mother squeezed. The hardest squeeze yet. And she wheezed, "Siiiiiiing."

Three weeks after her surgery, hospital orderlies transferred Mother from the hospice unit to the regular-care section. Nurses clapped and cheered as the bed wheeled past, and tears stung Diane's eyes. When Mother was on her feet again, the three of them would come back with flowers and chocolate to thank the kind souls who'd given her such wonderful care.

They settled Mother in the new room, which looked out over a flowering courtyard. As the orderlies turned to leave, Meghan's cell phone beeped its text announcement. She pulled it from her pocket, and a smile broke across her face. "It's Sean."

Diane adjusted the covers and laid Mother's arms on top of the blanket. Mother's dark eyes never wavered from her face. "Is he just checking in?"

Meghan squirmed on the chair, as bouncy as a child at her birthday party. "No, listen to this." She held up the phone and read. " 'After hitting several dead ends, I found a man named Eric Plum from the Bay area whose great-uncle Waldo and great-aunt Rosemary adopted a girl during the forties. They named her Emily. She's widowed now, the mother of three—two girls and a boy.' "

Diane's heart lurched. If this woman and Mother were sisters, then Mother had nieces and a nephew.

" 'He agreed to pass along my message about possibly meeting her biological sister. Now we wait for her call.' "

Diane crossed to the chair and peered over Meghan's shoulder at the message. "Ask him how we'll know for sure if this woman is Maggie." She didn't want to get Mother's hopes up unnecessarily.

Meghan tapped the tiny keyboard, then waited. A few seconds later, the cell beeped. Meghan read, " 'DNA will either prove or disprove their relationship. But first Emily Plum Weaver has to agree to be tested. Pray!' " Meghan tapped a quick agreement, and then she angled a frown at her mother. "Did you send Grandma's cheek swab to the lab?"

"Of course. The same day the kit arrived. Do you think Sean has the results by now?"

"If not, he'll contact the lab techs and get them on it. He told me last night when we were talking that news reporters have been hounding him and his temporary partner about this case. Word's getting out about the orphanage director who shuttled children out of state." Her face fell. "I feel so bad for Mrs. Durdan. She didn't want anyone to know what her mother had done, and now everyone will know. She'll be devastated."

Diane put her hand on Meghan's shoulder. "It will be hard for her, I'm sure, but she isn't responsible for her mother's choices. She shouldn't feel guilty about it."

"Still, there will probably be some people in Cumpton who blame Mrs. Durdan for the things her mother did. And she'll probably blame herself. I'd feel pretty bad if I found out the reason I had an education and place to live was because you'd been kidnapping children from their families for money."

Diane smoothed her daughter's hair. "I tell you what. When Mother and Maggie—or Emily, if she's the one—have met, we'll take lots of pictures of them together. Then we'll send a letter to Mrs. Durdan along with a photo and thank her for making it possible for the sisters to be reunited. Maybe it will take away some of the sting."

A weak smile played on Meghan's lips. "Thanks, Mom. That's a good idea." She glanced toward the bed. Mother's eyes had slipped closed, but her fingers were twitching as if she played a flute in her sleep. "I hope by the time we figure out whether or not this Emily really is Maggie, Grandma will be fully aware and able to meet her. It'd be pretty sad to go to all this trouble only to fail."

Diane pulled up the second chair and sat near Meghan so their knees bumped. She took her daughter's hand and peered intently into her brown eyes. "There's no failure anywhere in this venture. The whole thing feels . . . orchestrated."

Meghan tilted her head. "What do you mean?"

"Well, first of all, your accident. If you hadn't been in that three-car pileup, you wouldn't have come to spend time with Mother, which prompted me to come, too. We wouldn't have planned the trip to Cumpton, which led us to send Mother for a checkup, and we wouldn't have known her artery was blocked. Do you see?"

Meghan nodded. "I do. I hadn't quite put it together like that, though. Maybe it was all orchestrated by God."

"I'm convinced of it." Diane drew a slow breath, gathering courage. "And there's more. I've come to love my mother again. I've reconnected with the faith I had as a child. I still need to ask forgiveness for the hateful way I've treated her for so many years, but I know without a doubt she will grant it."

Meghan angled a soft smile toward the bed where Mother slept peacefully. "Yes. She will."

"And I need to ask your forgiveness, too."

Meghan's eyebrows rose. "Me? What for?"

"For not letting you know how much I love you." Tears flooded Diane's eyes, making Meghan's image waver. "I was so determined to not be my mother that I went to the opposite extreme. I didn't show enough affection. I didn't protect you enough. And I didn't give you the most important thing of all— faith. That's my biggest regret. I'm very sorry, Meghan. I do love you, more than I can say, and I hope you'll forgive me."

Meghan threw her arms around Diane. "Mom, nobody's perfect. I don't expect you to be. You did your best. I know you love me, and I love you. There's nothing to forgive."

Diane pulled free. She took hold of Meghan's hands. "One more thing." Although she'd prayed long and hard and knew what she had to do, this wouldn't be easy. "About your father . . ."

Meghan's eyes widened. She sucked in a breath and seemed to freeze.

"You deserve to know his name. Seek him out if you want to." Her chest ached. Would he reject her precious daughter again? She held tight to Meghan's hands and winged a prayer heavenward for God's will. "If you want me to tell you who he is, I won't refuse."

Meghan sat for several silent seconds, chewing her lower lip, her eyes un- blinking. She released her held breath. "Thank you, Mom. I want to know. But not . . . yet." A tender smile grew on her face. "Right now, I want to spend time getting fully acquainted with my heavenly Father. He'll let me know when the time is right to find my earthly one."

They hugged long and hard, and when they parted they realized they were being watched. Mother's dark eyes glistened. Her chin quivered.

Diane rose and hurried to the bed. She slipped her hand beneath her mother's. "Are you in pain?"

Two deliberate squeezes gave the answer.

"Are you sure?" Her tears concerned Diane.

Squeeze.

"Then . . . may I ask you a question?"

Mother never broke eye contact. Another single squeeze granted permission.

Diane leaned close. "I am so sorry for interpreting your love as interference. I've treated you badly for years. I tried to keep Meghan from you. I was wrong and I know I hurt you. Can you ever forgive me?"

At once Mother's fingers closed on Diane's hand. Firmly. Emphatically. The tears escaped the corners of her eyes and rolled toward her smile. Her lips parted. "All"—her voice was raspy, like the grate of rusty gears—"is forgiven. And forgotten."

Diane bent low and touched her forehead to her mother's. "Thank you."

Mother's arm lifted and curled over Diane's shoulders. "Thank you for coming home."

Epilogue

W hen is their flight arriving?" Hazel fingered her pearl necklace and stared at the wide opening to baggage claim. In her purse, she carried a recent photograph of Emily Plum Weaver, who bore a striking resemblance to Mae Clymer Blackwell. Even without the DNA proof, Hazel would have known the woman was her long-lost little sister all grown up.

Meghan urged her toward a row of chairs where Margaret Diane sat, keeping watch over a pile of gift bags—the biggest one for Emily and smaller ones for each of her children and the grandchildren who were traveling with them. "Not for another ten minutes, Grandma. Come. Sit. Relax."

"Relax . . ." Hazel sat but she *tsk-tsk*ed. "How can I relax with those television people swooping in like a horde of locusts? I never dreamed I'd be on national television. It's more than a little unnerving." She flapped her hand at the cluster of cameramen and reporters currently interviewing Sean. She leaned close to Meghan and lowered her voice to a whisper. "But Sean seems to be handling it well."

A becoming blush stole across her granddaughter's cheeks. "Sean handles just about anything people throw at him, including the publicity from this case. None of us expected it to snowball like it did. The reunions will likely go on for months as families come together. But it's only fitting that yours is first, Grandma, since trying to find Maggie started it all."

Margaret Diane poked her thumb toward Sean. "I hope he doesn't get big headed over the attention. There's nothing less attractive than a big-headed fiancé."

"Mom . . ." Meghan rolled her eyes and Margaret Diane chortled.

At first Hazel had wondered how Meghan and Sean would balance working together as husband and wife, but she'd come to the conclusion that if anyone could do it and do it well, it would be those two. They'd started out as very good friends and they respected each other. Those were the foundations of a lasting relationship. And, of course, they were building on their common faith in Jesus Christ, the best foundational rock of all.

Gratitude filled her that her granddaughter had a trustworthy, God-honoring man on whom she could depend. Especially since Margaret Diane would be moving from Little Rock to Kendrickson over the Christmas break and taking a teaching position in Las Vegas. Nevada was lucky to get someone with her drive and passion for education. Initially Hazel had been apprehensive about her daughter moving closer. Margaret Diane always complained about the Nevada heat. But her sweet statement—*"I can put up with the heat if it means having more time with you, Mother"*—chased every bit of concern away. After all their years with states separating them, she would enjoy having her close by.

Hazel gave Meghan's hand a pat. "There's one way to cure a man of a big head."

Meghan's face lit with interest. "How?"

Hazel flicked a secretive look left and right. "Go up behind him in a public place, give him a little pinch on the bottom, then back away and pretend to be shocked. Say loud enough for everyone to hear, 'I'm so sorry—I thought you were my husband!' Then hurry away. It's sure to deflate any man's puffed-up ego."

"Mother!" Margaret Diane burst out laughing. "You wouldn't do something like that."

Hazel pressed her palm to her chest and feigned innocence. "Of course I wouldn't. I was talking about Meghan."

The three of them were still laughing when Sean strolled over and flopped into the chair next to Meghan. He linked fingers with her and grinned at them. "What's so funny?"

"Never mind." Margaret Diane cleared her throat and wiped the smirk from her face. "Were you able to convince the reporters to give Mother and her sister a little privacy before pushing in for an interview?"

He nodded. "It took some doing. They want to capture the emotion. But I assured them there will be more than enough emotion to last for several minutes. They'll be rolling, but they'll keep their distance until I give the signal." He glanced at a newspaper lying on the chair beside him and gave a little jolt. He yanked it up and held it out for them to see. "Hey! Look at this—we even made the Vegas paper." The headline read "Arkansas Cold Case Detective Uncovers Child-Stealing Operation 7 Decades Old." A color photo of him holding black-and-white pictures of children, including the one of Maggie with her doll, was placed prominently beside the article. He grinned. "I don't look too bad in newsprint, do I?"

Hazel bumped Meghan with her elbow. "Better get your pinching fingers ready."

Meghan hunched her shoulders and giggled.

A flow of people came around the corner. Sean set the paper aside and bolted from his chair. "That's probably their flight. Come with me, Grandma Hazel."

He helped her from the chair and then escorted her to an open space marked off with yellow tape between a row of three slot machines and the glass wall of a gift shop. He held up the poster they'd made the evening before with a simple message—WELCOME TO VEGAS, EMILY & FAMILY. Hazel had wanted to put *Maggie* instead of *Emily*, but both Margaret Diane and Meghan encouraged her to use the name Maggie's adoptive parents had given her.

It pierced Hazel's heart, but she understood the wisdom. Emily probably didn't even remember being Maggie. Hazel would be satisfied with having her sister in her life again, no matter what name she used now.

The cameramen aimed their lenses, and the reporters stood tense and ready. Hazel glanced over the sea of faces, searching for the one she'd longed to see for seventy years. And finally a sweet-faced woman with sky-blue eyes, wavy snow-white hair, and a petite figure rounded the corner. Three couples in their mid- to late forties and three teenagers surrounded her. Hazel recognized all of them from the photographs sent from California. Her heart exulted, *Maggie!* Hazel covered her mouth with trembling fingers, but a gasp still escaped.

With the noise of slot machines and people talking, Maggie couldn't have heard the gasp, but the moment it released, she angled her face, and her gaze met Hazel's. Her attention flicked to the poster and then back. A smile grew on her face. The smile whisked Hazel backward in time so rapidly that dizziness briefly struck. She caught Sean's arm for a moment to steady herself, and then she left Sean behind and took stumbling steps toward her sister.

Oh, how she wished she could run the way Maggie used to run to greet her when Hazel returned home from school. But age and the crepe rubber soles of her shoes catching on the carpet hindered her. Maggie moved away from her family, too, and held her arms wide as she came. They met on a patch of carpet splashed with bright lights from one of the slot machines, the same way the sun had dappled the grass on their last day together. Hazel released a little cry of elation and wrapped her sister in her arms. They clung, both laughing, both crying, soft cheeks pressed against each other and snowy hair tickling.

"I've missed you so much." Hazel whispered the admission into Maggie's ear.

"And I you."

Hazel pulled back, startled. "You remember me?"

Tears slid down her sister's gently lined cheeks, but they didn't wash away her smile. "You are the Hayzoo Mae who visited my dreams. I never forgot."

The childish name sounded so natural, was so welcome, Hazel experienced another rush of warm tears. They embraced again, rocking gently. She could have held Maggie forever, but someone touched her shoulder. With reluctance she released her hold and found Margaret Diane standing near with Meghan. They'd brought the gift bags.

"Mother, wouldn't you like to meet your nieces and nephew?" Margaret

Diane handed the largest bag to Hazel. "You'd probably like to give this to Emily, too."

"Yes, I would."

Maggie gestured for her family to come close, and Hazel introduced her daughter and granddaughter to them. Maggie in turn introduced her son, daughters, in-laws, and grandchildren. And then Hazel couldn't wait any longer. She handed the bag to Maggie. "This is for you."

Maggie placed the bag on the floor and pushed the tissue aside. She lifted out the doll Hazel had purchased in the antique store, and her eyes grew round. "Is this . . . ?" She turned to her son, who pulled the newspaper article from his pocket. She pointed to the doll in the newspaper photo.

"It's exactly like the one Daddy bought you for your third birthday. You never let it out of your sight until the day you went away." Hazel gripped her sister's hands, holding both her and the doll. "Now you have one again."

While Margaret Diane and Meghan gave the framed reprints of Maggie with her birthday doll to Maggie's son and daughters, the reporters crowded in for questions and photographs. And Hazel discovered it wasn't so hard to be filmed after all. Joy and thanksgiving erased all discomfort. She kept her arm around her sister's waist and smiled into the camera as she answered their questions.

After several minutes, though, she grew weary of their intrusion. She wanted Maggie and her family to herself. She held up her hand. "Thank you, but that's all."

One reporter leaped forward and poked the microphone in her face. "One last question, Mrs. DeFord. Who do you hold responsible for having been robbed of the last seventy years with your sister?"

Hazel frowned at the young man and shook her finger. "All of that is over and done. Holding a grudge doesn't hurt anyone except the one who chooses bitterness." A sheepish look flitted across his face. She smiled and added, "I'd rather give praise to the ones who brought us together again—my daughter, my granddaughter, and Detective Eagle." She gestured as she spoke, inviting them to come close. "And, most importantly, God. I've hoped for this day for seventy years, and He not only opened the doors for me to find my sister, He brought all of us together." She held her arms to indicate both her and Maggie's families. "So He's the One who receives the glory today."

The reporters departed, and Sean leaned in and delivered a kiss on Hazel's temple. He straightened and grinned. "That last part will probably end up on the cutting-room floor, you know."

She shrugged. "It can't be cut from my heart, and that's what matters." She aimed her smile at the cluster of people. "There's a turkey and roasted tofu"—she winked at Margaret Diane—"in the oven at my house. Shall we go celebrate Thanksgiving?" Tears flooded her eyes, and she folded Maggie in another hug. "Our families' first Thanksgiving together . . ."

Maggie squeezed hard. "But not our last, Hazel." They pulled apart and smiled into each other's eyes. "God willing, it won't be our last."

Readers Guide

1. Hazel allowed her fear of losing someone she loved to make her overly protective of her daughter, which damaged their relationship. How do we learn to set aside fear and choose to trust God even when bad things befall us or our loved ones?

2. Hazel's overprotectiveness drove Diane to be a much less affectionate mother to her daughter, which in turn left Meghan wondering if her mother truly loved her. Why do past events affect present situations? How can we be certain we aren't allowing the past to negatively influence our present?

3. After Maggie disappeared, Hazel's father turned to alcohol for comfort. What other hurtful things do people use to numb their pain or escape their problems? Why aren't these long lasting? As Christians, what should we do when life feels overwhelming?

4. Diane made the decision to accept Jesus as Savior when she was a child, but then resentment toward her mother and some judgmental people at church led her to run from God. Have you ever been tempted to judge people for choices they made that offended you? Is this what we are called to do as Christians? How can we love the sinner while abhorring the sin?

5. Meghan viewed Hazel and Sean as the two most stable, dependable people in her world. What made them different from everyone else?

6. Diane believed that God orchestrated events to bring Meghan, Diane, and Hazel together. Do you believe God plans our pathways or merely uses our pathways to bring us to His will? Explain.

7. Hazel told Meghan, "There is no one so damaged that grace can't redeem him. . . . [God] never sees us as too far gone." Do you believe this? Why or why not?

8. Sean had a strong faith, which he shared with Meghan in both word and action. He told her "God's got this" when referring to her grandmother's surgery and the search for Maggie. How can we trust that "God's got this" when we encounter challenges in our lives?

Acknowledgments

As always, great appreciation goes out to my family—my wonderful parents, who taught me to love Jesus and to always chase my dreams; my husband, who handles the mundane so I can escape into my make-believe worlds; and my children and grandchildren, who give my heart a reason to sing.

Special thanks to my daughters—Kristian, Kaitlyn, and Kamryn—for putting up with my many failings. As Diane told Meghan, "Everything I did was out of love." Now that you are all mommies, too, I hope you understand.

A special shout-out to my Lit and Latte ladies for your prayers—I finished this manuscript on time, so God certainly answered.

Another special thank-you to my dear soul sister, Kathy—all those trips to Las Vegas gave me a base on which to build. Your friendship is so precious to me. I love you muchly!

Thanks to my agent, Tamela, who works behind the scenes to make my dreams of writing possible.

Appreciation must be offered to Tanya Emery, my church friend whose Arkansas accent let me hear the characters clearly in my head.

Huge thanks to Shannon, Julee, Jamie, Jessica, and the entire fiction team at WaterBrook—your advice and expertise is invaluable as I grow in this craft.

Finally, and most importantly, praise be to God, who guides me, molds me, upholds me, and forgives me. You are my Strength and my Joy forever. May any praise and glory be reflected directly back to You.

Visit the Old Order Mennoni community in the Zimmerman Restoration Trilogy.

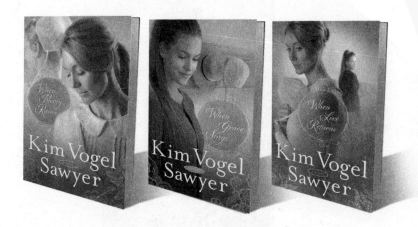

Revisit history in another Kim Vogel Sawyer novel...

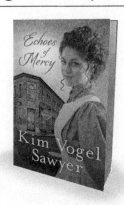

Read an excerpt from these books and more at WaterBrookMultnomah.com

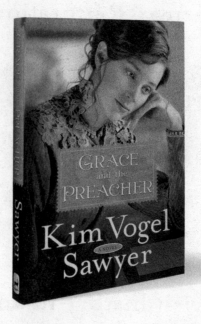

It's 1882 and twenty-four-year-old Grace Cristler dreams of having a godly husband and a home she can call her own. It finally seems possible when a new minister arrives in her small Kansas town. But when she discovers Theophil Garrison's true identity, will she be willing to accept the real Theo and God's new plan for her life?

Read an excerpt from this book and more at WaterBrookMultnomah.com

WATERBROOK